STANTON apparentl was sadd mount an startled Penelope.

"Now," said Horseley, a Colt in his hand, "I reckon I'm in a position to bargain for a horse."

"You're in a position to get yourself shot dead," McCaleb said. "Let her go, and maybe we'll forget this ever happened."

Horseley laughed. "It doesn't pay to be too trusting, McCaleb. This little filly's goin' to ride with me a ways. Maybe a long ways, if any of you follow."

But Penelope had other ideas. While Horseley had a brawny arm about her waist, the girl had full control of her feet. She stomped on her captor's toes, and involuntarily his grip loosened just enough. Penelope went limp and slipped to the ground. It was just the break McCaleb was waiting for. His Colt roared an instant ahead of Horseley's . . .

THE DEADWOOD TRAIL

RALPH COMPTON

St. Martin's Paperbacks

This is a work of fiction, based on actual trail drives of the Old West.
Many of the characters appearing in the Trail Drive Series were very
real, and some of the trail drives actually took place. But the reader
should be aware that, in the developing of characters and events, some
fictional literary license has been employed. While some of the characters and events herein are purely the creation of the author, every
effort has been made to portray them with accuracy. However, the
inherent dangers of the trail are real, sufficient unto themselves, and
seldom has it been necessary to enhance their reality.

THE DEADWOOD TRAIL

Copyright © 1999 by Ralph Compton.

Trail map design by L. A. Hensley.

ISBN: 0-312-96816-7

Printed in the United States of America

St. Martin's Paperbacks edition / January 1999

10 9 8 7 6 5 4 3 2 1

AUTHOR'S FOREWORD

Upon completion of the Union Pacific Railroad, the United States government closed all the forts along the Bozeman Trail in a vain effort to keep peace with the Sioux. But there would be no peace with the Sioux. In 1874, Lieutenant-General Philip Sheridan ordered a reconnaissance and survey of the Black Hills. While Sheridan intended to send George A. Custer and ten troops from the Seventh Cavalry for a quick scout, official Washington had other ideas. When the expedition got under way, it moved slowly, clumsily, for there was a large number of covered wagons. On August 13, 1874, a New York newspaper printed a story that rocked the nation. Gold had been discovered in the Black Hills!

Despite the treaty with Red Cloud's Sioux, miners came from near and far. Attempting to preserve the peace with the Sioux, General Sheridan ordered Custer and his men to force the miners out of the hills and back to the settlements. Violators would be arrested, their wagons and outfits burned. But all Sheridan's efforts were for naught, for lobbyists in Washington were demanding that the Black Hills be settled and developed.

Would-be miners arrived by the hundreds, and early settlements—such as Custer City and Deadwood—sprang up overnight. Custer City's population had grown to eleven thousand by the end of the year. A second government expedition confirmed Custer's report of the discovery of gold a year previous. In the summer of 1875, Senator William Allison of Iowa was put in charge of a thirteen-man commission that would attempt to purchase the Black Hills from the Sioux. But the Allison commission failed and their offer of six million dollars was rejected. Tough old Sitting Bull sent them word, "I have no land to sell."

After a terrifying confrontation with the angry, armed Sioux, the Allison Commission recommended that the government offer a fair price for the Black Hills and then force the Sioux to accept. November 9, 1875, E. T. Watkins, special investigator for the Department of the Interior, agreed with the Allison Commission. Going a step further, Watkins urged that soldiers be sent. Indian Commissioner E. P. Smith agreed.

The Bureau of Indian Affairs made one final effort to keep the peace. Nonagency Sioux must return to the reservation on or before January 31, 1876. All failing to do so would be considered "hostiles," subject to discipline by soldiers. Although it was the dead of winter, some of the Sioux registered at the Red Cloud Agency, only to learn that the Bureau of Indian Affairs had no accommodations or food for them. Nothing could be done without approval from Congress, and official Washington had recessed until after Christmas. General John Gibbon charged the Bureau of Indian Affairs with criminal negligence, but the Bureau of Indian Affairs would not back down. General Phil Sheridan was ordered to proceed against the "hostile" Sioux as quickly as possible after the expiration of the deadline. But while the soldiers were in the field—March 1876—a New York newspaper broke a scandal that shocked the nation and shook the Bureau of Indian Affairs to its foundation. It was a kickback scheme in which sutlers and post traders were given government licenses. In return, they kicked back a percentage of their income. The leader of what became known as the "Indian Ring Scandal" turned out to be General William Belknap, President Grant's Secretary of War. As the scheme unfolded, Orvil, the President's brother, was found to be one of the middlemen.

On July 22, 1876, Congress reacted to the panic that followed Custer's defeat at Little Big Horn. A bill was passed forcing the Sioux to surrender their rights to the Black Hills and the Powder River country. The thievery was justified by claiming the Sioux were guilty of violating the Treaty of 1868. The chiefs were forced to sign the agreement, and it was over. Chief Red Cloud—who would live another thirty years—summed it up:

"The white man made us many promises, more than I can remember. But they never kept but one. They promised to take our land, and they took it."

Judged by the passing of time and a recording of their deeds in the pages of American history, these high-level thieves and scoundrels of more than a century ago are not looked upon with high regard. Nor should they be.

CAST OF CHARACTERS

THE LONE STAR OUTFIT FROM WYOMING

Benton McCaleb, trail boss, and his wife, Rebecca.

Monte Nance, Rebecca's brother. A two-gun ladies' man.

Brazos Gifford and his wife, Rosalie. . Penelope, their headstrong daughter, had all it took to get herself in big trouble.

Will Elliot and his wife, Susannah.

Goose, a semi-civilized Lipan Apache who is not opposed to scalping his enemies.

Pendleton "Pen" Rhodes, Jed and Stoney Vandiver. Texas cowboys who brought a herd of Texas longhorns to the High Plains and remained there.

THE NELSON STORY OUTFIT FROM VIRGINIA CITY, MONTANA

Calvin Snider, trail boss, and his wife Lorna.

Tom Allen and his wife, Jasmine.

Bud McDaniels, Jasmine's troublesome brother. He made one mistake too many.

Curley, Bud's long-suffering wife.

Quickenpaugh, an east Texas Comanche who once rode with John Wesley Hardin. The Indian's interest in Curley is returned, and Bud intends to kill Quickenpaugh.

Arch Rainey, Hitch Gould, Mac Withers and Smokey Ellison are former Texans.

Oscar Fentress is a black man from Texas, and he has many talents. He can patch up gunshot and knife wounds, punch cows, and pull a gun.

Bill Petty is a Montana cowboy who's more than earned his spurs.

Quanah Taylor is a young Texan with a ready smile and a fast gun. When he found the girl he wanted, he'd kill for her, if he had to.

DEADWOOD TRAIL

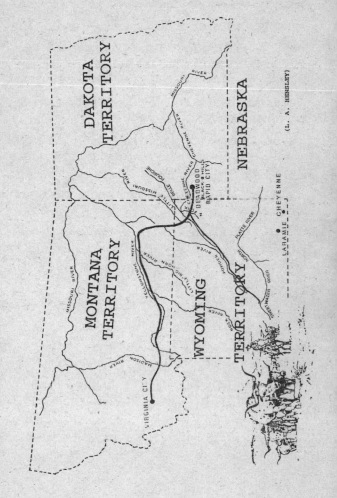

(L. A. HENSLEY)

PROLOGUE

NELSON STORY, A TWO-GUN giant of a man, had defied all odds, driving a massive herd of longhorn cattle from Texas to Virginia City in 1866. Now Story was a wealthy man, with hundreds of acres of land on which fed a prosperous new breed of cattle and large herds of horses. Reaching the cabin where his *segundo*—Cal Snider—lived with his wife Lorna, Story knocked on the door. He was genuinely fond of all the Texans who had come north and had remained with him.*

"Come on in," Cal invited.

"Something smells almighty good," said Story. "Cal, I knew you were doing the right thing when you stole this young lady from Texas. Lorna, you're prettier than ever."

"Men are all alike," Lorna said, in a pretended huff. "One whiff of a fresh-baked pie, and they'll tell you anything."

Cal and Story laughed, for it was a ritual they had enjoyed many times. Lorna cut one of the apple pies in quarters. Both men were served a huge slice of pie and a steaming cup of hot coffee. Not until they had finished their pie and were sipping their coffee did Story get to the purpose of his visit.

The Virginia City Trail (Trail Drive #7)

"You're aware that we've promised delivery of two hundred horses to the army outpost in Dakota Territory by mid-June?"

"I am," said Cal, "and I'm also aware that the Sioux have been pushed just about as far as they intend to go. When they bust loose, it'll be hell with all the fires lit."

"Don't think I haven't given it some thought," Story said. "We won't need many riders for the horses, but we'll likely need as many as we can get, to fight the Sioux."

"You talk like you aim to ramrod this drive yourself," said Cal.

"I do," Story said, "unless something or somebody changes my mind. It's a dangerous undertaking, the Sioux on the prod. I'll ask no man to take a risk that I won't."

"I know that, Mr. Story," said Cal, "and so does the rest of the outfit. I bossed the drive into Nebraska two years ago. Let me choose my riders, and I can handle this one."

From the corner of his eye, Cal caught a glimpse of Lorna. Her face was pale, her lips tight, and there was a gathering storm in her eyes. Story spoke quickly.

"While the Sioux threat is bad news, there's good news too. The discovery of gold in the Black Hills has brought literally thousands of miners into the area, and there's a need for beef. Through the army, I've been sent word there's a speculator who will buy all the beef he can get, at boomtown prices. Milo Reems has quoted me fifty dollars a head."

"Driving horses *and* cows, we'll need a bigger outfit," said Cal. "That might counter the Sioux threat. How many cows you got in mind?"

"Five thousand, maybe fifty-five hundred," Story said, his eyes on Lorna.

"Cal Snider," said Lorna, "I have something to say."

"You can have your say," Story said, "but let me finish. All of you know of my holdings in Montana. If I never sell another horse or drive another steer to market, I won't be hurting. As you know, most of you Texans who stayed with me have been taking your pay in cattle. According to my figures, you, Tom Allen, Arch Rainey, Hitch Gould, Mac Withers, Oscar Fentress, Smokey Ellison, Quanah Taylor, Bill Petty and Bud McDaniels own enough cattle that you'll each be able to sell off five hundred head without touching your breeding stock.''

"You'd let us drive *our* cows to market?'' Cal asked unbelievingly.

"As long as you deliver my two hundred horses to the army outpost,'' said Story.

"You're a white man, Mr. Story,'' Cal said. "Have you talked to the others?''

"No,'' said Story. "I felt I should talk to you first. It'll be a hard trail, and I believe the others will base their decisions on yours.''

"I'll do it, and bless you for the opportunity,'' Cal said.

"Then I'll supply a chuck wagon and grub,'' said Story, "but that's the best I can do. I spoke to Sandy Bill, and he says he's rode his last trail as a biscuit-shooter. I reckon all of you will have to take turns doing your own cooking.''

"I don't think so,'' Lorna said. "I can cook, and I'm going.''

"No, you're not,'' said Cal. "I forbid it.''

"Just wait until Mr. Story talks to the others,'' Lorna said. "Then we'll see.''

When Story had gone, Cal wasted no time in renewing the argument.

"Damn it, Lorna, I won't put you in danger of being scalped by the Sioux, drowned in a river crossing or subjected to naked cowboys.''*

Lorna laughed. "I've been subjected to all that, and before you try changing my mind, you'd better wait until Story's talked to the others. I can tell you right off, Jasmine won't stay behind while Tom Allen goes off to be shot and

The Virginia City Trail (Trail Drive #7)

scalped, and I doubt that Curley will feel any different
when it comes to Bud going."

VIRGINIA CITY, MONTANA TERRITORY.
DECEMBER 31, 1875

"If Cal's trail-bossing, count me in, Mr. Story," Tom Allen
said.

"If my brother Bud's going," said Jasmine, "count me
in. I have more at stake than he does."

"You can't do anything that Bud can't do," Tom argued.

Jasmine laughed. "When you're not shooting or being
shot at, I can strip down and see that your blankets are
warm."

Refusing to look at her, Tom Allen turned a brilliant red.
Nelson Story laughed, and it came as no surprise when,
having laid out the proposal before Bud and Curley
McDaniels, Curley announced her decision to accompany
the drive.

"No," Bud said, "you can't go."

"Bud McDaniels," said Curley, "the first time you saw
me, and for a long time after, I rode, fought and swore like
a man. I can still out-cowboy any damn rider in this outfit."

"I ain't arguin' that," Bud said. "I just don't want you
riskin' your neck when you don't have to."

"Mr. Story," said Curley, "have Lorna and Jasmine
agreed to stay behind?"

Story laughed. "I wish you hadn't asked me that.
They've both vowed they're going all the way. Sandy Bill
claims he's too stove-up to cook for another trail drive, and
Lorna has vowed she'll be the cook."

"Then she'll need help," Curley said. "Besides, I can
rope, ride and shoot, if I have to."

"If Jasmine's goin', then I ain't," said Bud. "I've spent
half my life in her shadow, and she can do everything better
than I can."

"From what I've heard, she can't drink rotgut whiskey nearly as good as you used to," Curley said. "She's your sister, and she could have left you in Texas to drink yourself to death. Don't you think it's time you considered somebody other than yourself?"

"Listen," said Story, "as far as I'm concerned, both of you proved yourselves on the drive from Texas nine years ago. I must talk to the others, and if you're not going, Bud, then speak up. We'll have to work around you. Jasmine can be responsible for your herd."

It had the desired effect. Curley's eyes twinkled as Bud McDaniels stormed to his feet.

"I'll be responsible for my own herd. I don't need some female lookin' out for me."

"You'll go with the drive, then," said Story.

"I'll go, if we have to fight every damn Indian in the Sioux nation," Bud gritted.

When Story had gone, Bud McDaniels went to a cabinet, taking from it a full bottle of whiskey and a shot glass. He sat down cross-legged before the fire, uncorked the bottle and poured the shot glass full. He sat there a long time, aware that Curley was watching him. But the girl said nothing. Finally, without touching the whiskey, Bud got to his feet and emptied the shot glass into the fire. He followed it with what remained in the bottle.

"Quickenpaugh," said Story to the Comanche horse wrangler, "I want you to take the responsibility for getting two hundred head of horses to the army, in Dakota Territory. Will you do it?"

"*Si,*" Quickenpaugh said.

"Good," said Story. "All the others have agreed, and there'll be fourteen of you going. You've been around these *hombres* for a good ten years. Choose the men you'll need as horse wranglers."

"Arch Rainey, Hitch Gould and Mac Withers," Quickenpaugh said.

Nelson Story nodded. Quickenpaugh was as good as any man in the outfit when it came to riding and roping, and few were his equal with a Bowie or Colt. It was to his credit he had made a place for himself—a hated Comanche—among hard-riding Texans.

With considerable satisfaction, Story again called on Cal Snider.

"It's all settled," said Story. "Quickenpaugh will take responsibility for the horses, and Arch, Hitch and Mac will be his wranglers. That will leave ten of you to handle the herd, if we include Lorna, Jasmine and Curley. Will that be enough, or should I round up a few more?"

"We'll manage," Cal said. "Everybody on this drive will have a stake in the herd, and I'd like to keep it that way. Once the herd and the horses are trail wise, Quickenpaugh and his riders can help keep them moving."

"I'm glad you've included Jasmine, Curley and me," said Lorna, "but are we to become cowboys or cooks?"

"Maybe both," Cal said. "One of you will have to drive the chuck wagon. You can take turns doing that, and whoever's in charge of the wagon for the day will become the cook."

"Fair enough," said Lorna. "Now who's going to look after our spreads and remaining cattle while we're away?"

"I'm hiring a dozen extra riders," Story said. "We'll need them here on the ranches. Especially during the hard winter months."

"Mr. Story," said Cal, "there's just one thing that bothers me about this drive, and it's not the danger from the Sioux. I don't like speculators. If somebody gets there ahead of us with a herd, we could end up without a buyer."

"I don't expect that to be a problem," Story said. "Thanks to barbed wire, the days of Texas cattle drives are about over. You'll be trail boss, and except for Quickenpaugh, all your riders will own a piece of the herd, so do what you must. It's a boomtown, and if you get the herd there, I can't imagine anything going wrong."

But Cal Snider's suspicions were justified. Something *could* go wrong, and it did. At the end of the Deadwood Trail.

SWEETWATER VALLEY, WYOMING TERRITORY.
JANUARY 2, 1876

Former Texas Rangers Benton McCaleb, Brazos Gifford and Will Elliot had first trailed a herd north to Colorado, with Charles Goodnight. Seeking to escape the reconstruction in postwar Texas, they had brought a herd north, with intentions of staying. The rest of the outfit had consisted of Rebecca Nance, her young brother, Monte, and a Lipan Apache who was known only as Goose. While in a Denver jail, Benton McCaleb had hired three more able riders. Pen Rhodes, along with Jed and Stoney Vandiver, went with the drive north to Wyoming, and remained with the outfit. McCaleb eventually married Rebecca Nance in Cheyenne. Rosalie, the girl Brazos Gifford married, had a young daughter, Penelope. Will Elliot fought for and won the hand of Susannah, a local schoolmarm. Calling themselves the "Lone Star" outfit, they settled in Wyoming's Sweetwater Valley in June 1868.* Now, on their Lone Star range in Sweetwater Valley, Benton McCaleb had called together his friends and partners, Brazos Gifford and Will Elliot.

"We've done well, driving cattle to Cheyenne, to the Union Pacific loading pens," said McCaleb, "but Deadwood may be the last boomtown. There may never again be such an opportunity to trail a herd to a camp where the sky's the limit."

"If you're favoring it," Brazos Gifford said, "you don't have to convince me. I'll go."

"So will I," said Will Elliot, "but with the Sioux gettin' ready to fight, we may need more riders than we have."

"We're fortunate to have fourteen Lipan Apache riders,

The Western Trail (Trail Drive #2)

thanks to Goose leading them here from their village in south Texas," McCaleb said. "Including the horse outfit belonging to Goose, we have six ranches here, all under the Lone Star brand. I think we can safely leave our holdings in their care, while we trail a herd to the gold fields, near Deadwood."

"Besides the three of us," said Will, "there's Monte Nance, Pen Rhodes, Jed and Stoney Vandiver and Goose, if you're aimin' for him to go."

"The Sioux threat being what it is, we'll need Goose," McCaleb said.

"Eight riders," said Brazos. "Maybe enough for three thousand head."

"No more than that," McCaleb said, "and there's no way we can take a chuck wagon. We can't spare anybody to drive it."

"I reckon you won't like this idea too much," said Brazos, "but Rebecca, Rosalie or Susannah can handle up to a four-horse hitch. So can Penelope."

"You're right," McCaleb said. "I don't like it. Not when it seems there's a chance the Sioux are about to take the warpath."

"We could do worse than take our womenfolks with us," said Will. "Don't forget, all this Powder River basin was once Sioux hunting grounds. They might just decide to take it back, while we're away."

"It's possible," McCaleb said. "I'll see how Rebecca feels. It'll be up to you *hombres* to talk to Susannah and Rosalie. Brazos, if Penelope goes, that's up to you."

Rebecca had been with Rosalie, at Brazos Gifford's place, allowing the three men the privacy of the McCaleb cabin. When Brazos returned home, Rebecca left immediately. She found McCaleb waiting for her. He quickly told her of the decision he, Brazos and Will had made.

"Of course I can go," said Rebecca. "God knows, the only event that might keep me here will never happen."

"For God's sake, let's not go through that again," McCaleb said wearily. "Brazos and Will have been in double harness with Rosalie and Susannah near as long as you and me, and they don't have any younguns. Hell, it must be somethin' in this High Plains air."

"At least Rosalie has Penelope," said Rebecca folornly.

"Let her and Brazos worry about that," McCaleb said. "The girl's barely eighteen, and wild as a ring-tailed cat-amount. She'll mount a horse that just purely scares the hell out of me. Brazos ought to take her along, to keep the Sioux off the rest of us."

"You're unfair, Benton McCaleb," said Rebecca. "What do you expect of the girl, when she's never around anybody except Indians and gunfighters?"

"The Indians are more civilized than the bastards we run out of here," McCaleb replied, "and if the gunfighters you're referrin' to are Will, Brazos and me, we never shot any varmint that wasn't deserving of it."

"I know that," said Rebecca. "I'm sorry."

Brazos Gifford encountered more enthusiasm than he had expected. Especially from his daughter, Penelope.

"It's a perfectly glorious journey," Penelope cried. "I'll be the best damn cowboy in the outfit."

"Young lady," Rosalie scolded, "don't you ever let me hear you swearing again."

"I'll be careful, Ma," said Penelope. "You won't hear me."

Brazos laughed. Rosalie glared at him, then turned her attention back to Penelope.

"I mean it," Rosalie said. "I'll skin you out of those cowboy duds and you'll be wearing frilly dresses and pantaloons."

"Do that," said Penelope, "and there'll be men coming from all over Wyoming just to watch me mount and dismount."

Brazos managed to contain his laughter until she had stomped out of the house.

"You're no help," Rosalie complained. "She's trying her best to be like you. I won't be a bit surprised when she sets up a howl for a pistol of her own."

"She has one," said Brazos calmly. "I gave it to her for Christmas."

"You knew I wouldn't approve," Rosalie said. "She'll become an old woman, wandering about in breeches and carrying a gun, never knowing how to be a lady."

"She's got everything in the right places," said Brazos, "and when the time comes, you can bet she'll be every bit the lady. Now how do you feel about making the drive from here to Deadwood?"

"You know I'll go," Rosalie said. "I never go anywhere, except maybe to Cheyenne once a year. What about Rebecca and Susannah?"

"McCaleb and Will are talkin' to them, I reckon," said Brazos. "The three of you can be a real help to us, if you'll take care of the cooking. You can take turns handling the wagon. Penelope too, if she wants."

"Penelope doesn't want," a voice said, just outside the door. "I want to ride hard, to swim rivers and shoot Indians. Just like the cowboys."

"Oh, my soul and body," Rosalie groaned.

Brazos laughed. "Don't give up on her yet. I'll see that she gets a bellyful of real cowboying before we reach Deadwood, and I promise she won't swim the rivers naked."

Susannah listened patiently as Will Elliot explained the planned trail drive to her.

"I'll go," said Susannah. "I don't know if you've noticed or not, but there are times when all I have to do is look out the door at cows grazing along the river. I'd welcome a chance to cook on a cattle drive, or even to ride drag. Sometimes I envy Penelope. She's wild as a hare, as unrefined as a cowboy, but she fits her environment."

Will said nothing, for there was nothing he could say. Susannah, once a teacher, had a longing for children of her own, but for seven long years she had been barren . . .

Once McCaleb learned that Rebecca, Rosalie, Susannah and Penelope would make the drive to Deadwood, he sought out Goose, the Lipan Apache, and Belleza, his Crow woman. It was only fair that she be asked to accompany the drive, if she desired. While Belleza had learned little English, Goose had learned much. It was he who related Belleza's words to McCaleb.

"Belleza no like towns," said Goose. "She stay with cows and horses while we go."

McCaleb grinned at Belleza, letting her know that her choice was acceptable. But the Crow woman had knowledge that even Goose lacked. Before the snows came again, Goose would become a father . . .

There was snow throughout January. Not until the first week in February did the cold and the snow loose its grip on the High Plains.

"I must get to Cheyenne with the wagon," McCaleb said. "We'll be needing supplies for the drive, and soon as the worst of winter's behind us, we're gonna be starting those cows on the trail to Deadwood."

"If this winter's like all the others, we'll be lucky to be on our way by mid-April," said Will.

"I think we'll have to do better than that," McCaleb said. "We'll likely hear news of the gold strike in Cheyenne, and if we hear it, so can everybody else. Tomorrow, Rebecca and me will take the wagon and head for town."

"Some of us had better ride with you," said Brazos. "While the Sioux are raisin' hell in Dakota Territory, we don't know they're all there. Might be some hostiles between here and Cheyenne."

"Brazos is right," Will said. "This is no time for you to be shot full of arrows and scalped, McCaleb. If it wasn't for you, one of us would have to boss that trail drive to Deadwood.''

"Your concern for my carcass is touching," said McCaleb. "We'll do it like we did in the old days. Will, you and Brazos bring Susannah and Rosalie, and go with us."

"Rosalie and me can't, unless Penelope goes too," Brazos said.

"Then bring her," said McCaleb.

CHEYENNE, WYOMING TERRITORY.
FEBRUARY 15, 1876

The women had remained at the hotel while McCaleb, Brazos and Will had taken the wagon to the mercantile to be loaded. McCaleb had bought a copy of the local newspaper and had found something of immediate interest.

"There's a speculator in Deadwood, and he's buying all the beef he can," McCaleb said. "His name is Milo Reems. He's asking owners of herds to telegraph him commitments."

"That's gettin' a mite previous," said Will, "committin' ourselves to a gent we've never heard of, not knowin' what he aims to pay."

"I'm thinkin' the same way," Brazos said. "I don't trust speculators. Matter of fact, I don't trust any man, when it comes to women or money."

"There's no trust involved," said McCaleb. "If his deal don't measure up, we don't sell to him. Let's telegraph him and ask for a reply, telling us his best price."

McCaleb sent the telegram, and within two hours, had an answer. It read: *Purchase of three thousand head confirmed* STOP *Fifty dollars a head* STOP

"Tarnation," Brazos said, "if we can believe that, we're looking at a hundred and fifty thousand dollars for three thousand cows."

"Seein' as how we don't surrender the herd until we're paid," said Will, "how can we lose?"

"I don't know," McCaleb said, "but there's somethin' about all this that just seems too good to be real."

"We have his telegram, with his quote and his name signed to it," said Brazos. "That ought to be worth something. All he has from us is a promise to deliver the herd. If he falls down on paying, then we don't deliver."

VIRGINIA CITY, MONTANA TERRITORY.
FEBRUARY 20, 1876

"The chuck wagon's loaded and ready, Mr. Story," said Cal Snider. "Come March first, unless the weather's turned bad, I'm thinking we'll take the trail to Deadwood."

"That might be wise," Nelson Story said. "The Sioux may be holed up, awaiting spring. Once you reach the Bozeman, there'll be danger every mile of the way."

"We're keepin' that in mind," said Cal. "We figure we'll come out better fightin' snow than fightin' Sioux."

"*Bueno,*" Story said. "Do you have enough horses in your remuda?"

"Every man has three," said Cal. "That should be enough."

"Remember, you're delivering two hundred head to the military," Story said. "You're welcome to the use of some of them, if you need them."

"Thanks," said Cal.

The weather continued mild, and on March 1, 1876, Cal Snider and his riders headed their herd—more than five thousand strong—eastward. Just a day later—in Wyoming—Benton McCaleb and his outfit moved their herd of three thousand head along toward the south fork of the Powder River, toward the northeast. Thus the two herds moved toward the same destination, two outfits destined to join together against a swindle unlike any that had ever hit Dakota Territory.

1

Snow glistened on mountain peaks to the west, and there were patches of it on the lee side of hills, where the sun shone briefly. More than five thousand head of unruly cattle were strung out, plodding eastward. The drag riders left no slack, for right on their heels were the two hundred horses intended for the army, as well as the outfit's remuda. Mac, Arch, Hitch and Quickenpaugh kept the horses in line. Directly behind the horse herd came the chuck wagon, Jasmine at the reins. Lorna and Curley rode drag, in the company of Oscar Fentress and Smokey Ellison.

"I know Mr. Story's been breedin' these varmints for nine years," Curley said, "but I can't see they're a damn bit smarter than those jugheaded longhorns we brought here from Texas."

"I think there are some things that can't be bred out of them," said Lorna. "Have you ever noticed that when you want a cow or a group of cows to go one certain way, they'll run themselves ragged going some other way?"

"I've noticed that," Curley said, "but I'm not near as concerned with the ignorance of the cows as I am the condition of my backside. I'd have been spending more time in the saddle, if I'd known this drive was coming."

"So would I," said Lorna. "That's why I offered to do the cooking. The seat on the wagon box is hard enough, but it won't leave you with saddle sores. Tomorrow will be your turn with the chuck wagon.''

"No," Curley said. "You take it tomorrow, and I'll take it the third day. That's the way Cal set it up. You don't want him thinkin' we can't cut the mustard, do you?''

"My God, no," said Lorna. "I brought three tins of sulfur salve. Until we toughen our hides, we can doctor our saddle sores at night.''

At that moment, three drag cows wheeled and, evading the drag riders, ran headlong toward the oncoming horse herd. Only the swiftness of Quickenpaugh prevented the horses from stampeding. The Comanche managed to get between the lead horses and the oncoming errant cows. Using his doubled lariat, he swatted the cows on their tender muzzles, and with the help of the drag riders, the troublesome trio again took their places within the herd.

"Lawd God," said Oscar Fentress, wiping his ebony brow, "that be close. Cal think we all be sleeping.''

But Cal and his companions were having their own problems. Cal rode point, while Bill Petty, Tom Allen, Quanah Taylor and Bud McDaniels were the flank riders. Much of the longhorn temperament had been bred out of the cows, but they seemed to have retained all or most of the cussedness of their longhorn ancestors. Sundown only minutes away, they gave it up, bedding down the herd for the night. The wind, out of the northwest, had a frosty bite to it.

"I'm thinkin' we should have delayed this drive at least until April first," Tom Allen said. "If I'm any judge, there's more snow on the way.''

"Nobody objected when I set the starting day," said Cal with some irritation.

"Like it or not," Bill Petty said, "we're neck-deep in a trail drive. Whatever happens, I reckon we'll have to make the best of it.''

"There be water," said Oscar. "Was there shelter, this wouldn't be so bad.''

"If we had ham, we could have ham and eggs, if we had

some eggs," Smokey Ellison said. "We better get these varmints on the trail at daylight, and start lookin' for an arroyo deep enough to keep the snow off of us."

"The tents Mr. Story insisted we bring may be a great help," said Lorna.

Supper was a mostly silent affair, each of them aware that if fate was unkind to them, they might be plagued by snow until April and beyond.

"We'll go with two watches," said Cal. "The first to midnight, and the second until first light. Arch, Hitch, Mac and Quickenpaugh, I want you on the first watch. The rest of us will relieve you at midnight."

"You're forgetting Curley, Jasmine and me," said Lorna.

"Yes," Curley said, "we have as much at stake as any of you."

To the surprise of them all, Cal Snider didn't lose his temper.

"Sorry," said Cal, "it's been a long day. Curley, you and Jasmine take the first watch with Arch, Hitch, Mac and Quickenpaugh. Lorna, you'll take the second watch with me."

"I ain't sure I want my woman standin' watch with a bunch of *hombres*," Bud said.

"Bud," said Curley, "these are the same *hombres* that came up the trail from Texas with us near ten years ago."

"She's right, Bud," Jasmine said. "Now shut up."

"When this herd's sold," said Bud, "I might just take my share and ride *back* to Texas, or at least far enough so's my big sister can't tell me to shut up."

"You do," Curley said, "and you'll go by yourself. It's not home to me anymore."

"The order stands, then." said Cal. "Jasmine and Curley, you'll take the first watch, and Lorna, you'll be part of the second."

The three women worked together getting the supper ready and cleaning up afterward. When it was time for the first watch to begin circling the herd, Jasmine and Curley saddled their horses. Bud McDaniels said nothing.

Jasmine and Curley rode out together, and when they were far enough away, Curley had something to say.

"Bud and his damn pride. He'll never outgrow it, will he?"

"I don't know," said Jasmine. "I have my doubts. But the last thing Cal needs on this drive is females that need or expect to be coddled."

Curley laughed. "If anybody has a right to whine, it's me. I have saddle sores as big as silver dollars on my behind, and here I am in the saddle for seven more hours."

"I'm glad you didn't say anything around Bud," Jasmine said. "Once this watch is done, I'll get some of Lorna's sulfur salve and ease your pain. You may have to do the same for me."

SOUTH-CENTRAL WYOMING TERRITORY.
MARCH 3, 1876

With Benton McCaleb as trail boss, the Lone Star herd moved north, along the Powder River. Brazos Gifford, Will Elliot, Monte Nance and Pen Rhodes were the flankers, while Jed and Stoney Vandiver—assisted by Penelope and Rebecca—rode drag. Goose, the Lipan Apache, was far ahead of the herd, scouting for possible Indian sign. It was Rosalie's turn on the high box of the chuck wagon, and it trailed along behind the drag riders. The herd had been bedded down along the Powder when Goose rode in. McCaleb and his riders all gathered around to hear what the Indian had to report.

"No sign," said Goose. "Snow come."

"That's what I been sayin' all day," Monte Nance said.

"We know," said Brazos wearily. "We know."

"It's a risk we had to take," McCaleb said. "We have no choice, unless we turn back to our home range. Does anybody favor that?"

"Hell, no," said Will Elliot. "We're Texans, and we don't start anything we can't finish."

"Well, I favor goin' back," Monte Nance said. "We ain't more than thirty miles out."

"Little brother," said Rebecca angrily, "if you don't have the sand for this drive, saddle up and head for home. The rest of us are going to Deadwood."

There were shouts of agreement from the rest of the outfit. Monte Nance curbed his angry response, bit his tongue and said nothing. Before it was time for the start of the first watch, the wind turned colder and changed direction, coming out of the northwest.

"It'll be blowin' like hell wouldn't have it by morning," Brazos predicted.

"I'm afraid you're right," said McCaleb. "We won't have time to find shelter any better than we have right here, which is practically none. The best we can do is break out all the extra canvas and set up some windbreaks while it's still light enough to see."

"We'll be needin' firewood, and lots of it," said Brazos. "Suppose I take Jed, Stoney and Will, and drag in some wood, while the rest of you put up the windbreaks?"

"Do that," McCaleb said. "It's gettin' colder by the minute, and we'll be needing a fire tonight."

Instead of taking turns cooking, Rebecca, Rosalie and Susannah joined forces each day, making the cooking and the cleanup far easier than it might have been. Not to be outdone, Penelope had taken to helping them. Monte Nance eyed Penelope, and while she paid him no attention, Rosalie watched him warily. Monte was more than ten years older than Penelope, and while she showed no interest in him, Rosalie knew just how unpredictable her daughter was. Not until the first watch did she have a chance to talk to Brazos. The snow had not begun, and Brazos dismounted.

"This is the only time I can talk to you without the others hearing," said Rosalie. "I'm worried about Penelope. Monte's looking at her all the time, and I have a good idea as to what's on his mind.''

"Penelope's just as beautiful as her mama," Brazos said, "and there's no law against a man looking. I doubt she's ever spoken a word to him. He's Rebecca's brother. Have you said anything to her?''

"No," said Rosalie. "What can I say? Monte's a man, if size means anything, and he's forever on the outs with Rebecca as it is. Anything she might say will just go in one ear and out the other. Besides, I'm afraid Penelope will find out. Nothing makes a good-for-nothing man look better to a girl than having someone warn her to leave him alone.''

"Then I reckon we'll have to trust Penelope's judgment," Brazos said. "Just don't fret any more about it, until you're sure there's cause. Monte still has some growing up to do. Some hard months on the trail might be a start.''

Rosalie sighed. "I just don't want him learning at Penelope's expense.''

The dawn broke gray and dismal. There was no sun, for the mass of clouds that had blown in from the northwest seemed to rest on the very tops of the trees. The outfit was in the midst of breakfast when the sleet began. They sought cover behind their canvas windbreaks, but the wind's icy fingers found them, rattling sleet off the brims of their hats and stinging their faces.

"The herd's startin' to drift with the storm," Will shouted.

"Take Pen, Jed and Stoney and head them," said McCaleb. "When you get 'em bunched, all of you circle them, just as we do at night.''

"We'll have to watch them all the time," Brazos said. "When cows get slapped in the face with sleet or snow, all they know is to turn their behinds to it and drift.''

The sleet soon diminished and the snow began in earnest. In the early afternoon, Bent McCaleb, Brazos, Monte and

Goose took the second watch. Not to be outdone, Penelope saddled her horse and rode with them.

"Don't forget Rosalie and me," said Rebecca. "We've stood watch before."

"You'll likely have a turn at it, if this snow don't let up," Will said. "With no cover for the herd, we'll have to circle them day and night or they'll drift away."

As the storm worsened, thunder rumbled, and the cattle bawled uneasily. The icy wind whipped out of the northwest, like a thing alive, and the thunder came closer. Most of the cattle had turned their backs to the storm, and they became more spooked with each clap of thunder.

"Watch them," shouted McCaleb over the roar of the storm. "They're gettin' ready to run."

The next clap of thunder seemed to shake the very earth, and the herd lit out eastward in a spooked, bawling frenzy. From his position, Monte Nance had the best opportunity to get ahead of the rampaging herd, and he did so. But his horse slipped in the deepening snow, throwing Monte to the ground. Before he could recover the reins, the animal had galloped away. On came the herd, more than twelve thousand thundering hooves. Frozen in his tracks, Monte Nance stood there, his arms flung toward the heavens as though pleading for salvation. Suddenly, darting in ahead of the lead steers came a horse and rider.

"No," Brazos Gifford shouted. "Penelope, no!"

But with the roar of the storm, Penelope might not have heard. Leaning far out of the saddle, she extended her left hand. Desperately, Monte caught it and swung onto the horse behind her. Monte could hear the rumble of hooves over the roar of the storm, as the stampeding herd drew ever closer. Penelope's horse stumbled once, and it seemed all was lost, but the animal recovered and ran on. Finally out of danger, Penelope reined up and slipped out of the saddle. When McCaleb, Brazos and Goose arrived, the girl had her arms around the neck of her faithful horse. Monte Nance stood beside the horse as though he needed support.

"Girl," said McCaleb, throwing his arms around Penelope, "that's the bravest thing I've ever seen. Without you, he'd have been trampled to a pulp."

Even in the swirling snow, they could see the grin on the Indian's face. Goose seldom showed any emotion, but he knew courage when he had witnessed it. Brazos dismounted, and Penelope turned to him.

"You brave, foolish girl," Brazos said. "If your horse had fallen—if you hadn't made it—how in tarnation would I have told your mama?"

Penelope laughed. "Don't tell Mama *anything*. I told you I was going to be the best damn cowboy in the outfit. I only did what any one of the rest of you would have done, if you'd been close enough."

"Far as I'm concerned, you're a top hand," said McCaleb. "There's not a man among us who could have reacted more swiftly or done as well. Monte, you owe her."

But Monte Nance said nothing. It seemed the praise heaped on Penelope only increased his humiliation. As though in search of his horse, he stumbled off into the snowy darkness.

"Damn him," said McCaleb. "The ungrateful varmint."

"Let it go," Brazos said. "I can't risk Rosalie hearing of it."

"We might as well get back to camp and get some sleep," said McCaleb. "We can't do a damn thing toward gathering the herd until first light. I just hope the rest of the outfit managed to grab a horse from the remuda before it lit out after the herd."

SOUTH-CENTRAL MONTANA TERRITORY.
MARCH 3, 1876

Lacking anything better, Cal Snider and his outfit had bedded down their herd along a river, leaving a tree-studded ridge between their camp and the oncoming storm. Story had supplied them with three tents, and the wild wind played havoc with them, ripping the tent pegs out of the half-frozen ground repeatedly.

"Let's spread them out and use the canvas as wind-breaks," Cal Snider said. "They'll do to keep the worst of the wind and snow off us and our cook fires."

It was a workable idea, for the lee side of the ridge blunted the impact of the roaring storm. Before the storm had struck, they had dragged in all the windblown and lightning-struck trees they could find, knowing they'd need the wood.

"This may not turn out as bad as we expected," said Bill Petty. "Maybe it's just me, but it don't seem like the wind's as fierce as it was."

"I hope you're right," Cal said. "I can't tell that it's let up at all."

Arch Rainey, Hitch Gould, Mac Withers, Oscar Fentress and Quickenpaugh rode in to one of the fires. Dismounting, they moved as close to the fire as they could.

"Man and hoss can't stand more than four hours in that," said Mac, through chattering teeth. "Some of you take over the watch for a while, so's we can get warm."

"It be the God's truth," Oscar said. "I look down to be sure I still got feet."

"Tom, Bill, Smokey, Quanah and Bud," said Cal. "I'll be joining you. Let's saddle up and get started, before the herd decides to drift."

The riders who had just returned to the fire hunkered around it, sipping from tin cups of scalding coffee. Quickenpaugh still wore buckskin leggings and moccasins, but he had adopted some of the more sensible ways of the white man. The Comanche wore a heavy, sheepskin-lined coat that reached almost to his knees. A similarly lined hood protected his ears, while on his hands were wool-lined leather gloves. The rest of the outfit was dressed in much the same manner, wearing their holstered guns beneath their heavy coats. But the Comanche's Colt was on the outside of his coat, with his Bowie knife slipped in beneath the pistol belt.

"These brutes ain't gonna stand here much longer, with no graze," Tom Allen said.

"I know," said Cal. "The horses, and even the chuck wagon mules, are pawing away the snow to get at the grass underneath. Why in thunder couldn't cows have had the good sense to do that?"

Tom Allen laughed. "Maybe it's the Almighty's idea of a joke. It might be funny to us, if we wasn't so close to it."

Conversation ceased when Bud McDaniels joined them.

"Don't make no sense, us out here freezin' our bohunkers off," said McDaniels. "If all these varmints decide to run, there ain't no way we or a hundred like us can stop 'em."

"Damn it," Cal said, "we're here to change their minds *before* they start to run. If you ain't up to it, then get on back to camp and tell Lorna she's taking your place."

Cal's acid-tongued response had the desired effect.

"Ain't no damn woman taking my place," shouted Bud.

He turned away and was soon lost in the swirling snow. Tom Allen laughed. "It's just as well Jasmine can't hear you," Cal said. "I know he's an embarrassment to her, and there's not a thing any of us can do about it."

"I know," said Tom soberly. "Jasmine had hoped gettin' him out of Texas and having him marry Curley would settle him down, but I doubt it. I hate to say it, for Jasmine's sake, but Bud McDaniels won't change until he takes up playin' the harp. That is, if the Almighty aims for him to have one."

"Maybe things will be different when him and Curley has a youngun," said Cal.

"I doubt that will happen," Tom said. "From what Jasmine's learned from Curley, she's had Bud bunkin' alone, hopin' he'll have enough pride to mend his ways."

"It's not working," said Cal. "He's getting worse. He's

taken to baiting Quickenpaugh for no good reason. I've warned him, and if he continues, I aim to let Quickenpaugh teach him a lesson.''

The storm continued, and after four hours, Cal and his companions were relieved by the rest of the outfit, with the exception of the women. Lorna, Jasmine and Curley were busily preparing supper.

''Supper's smellin' mighty good,'' Arch Rainey said. ''Don't forget we're out there.''

''We'll relieve all of you so you can eat,'' said Cal.

The storm continued through the night, but come the dawn, the snow had lessened. An hour later, it had stopped altogether. The wind eased up, and even without the sun, there was a marked difference. It seemed almost warm.

''Yeeehaaa,'' Quanah Taylor shouted. ''We made it.''

''Not yet,'' said Cal. ''We can't move on with the chuck wagon hub-deep in mud. We'll be here until the sun melts most of the snow and dries up some of the mud.''

Not until the eighth of March did Cal resume the trail drive. Even then, the women had trouble finding high ground. More than once, the chuck wagon became so bogged down that the mules couldn't free it, and teams of horses had to be harnessed along with the mules.

''I'm sorry,'' said Lorna, who had been driving the chuck wagon. ''It just started sliding and a rear wheel dropped into a hole. There was nothing I could do.''

''That's what comes of havin' a female trying to do a man's job,'' Bud McDaniels said.

''Then *you* take over the chuck wagon,'' said Jasmine angrily. ''God knows, you're not worth a damn at anything else.''

''Bud's ridin' drag, and he'll stay there until I say otherwise,'' Cal said. ''I'd take it kindly if all of you will keep your opinions to yourselves. Once we get this horse herd and the cattle to Deadwood, those of you wantin' to fight are welcome to have at it. Remember that until then, I'm trail boss, and anybody raisin' any unnecessary hell will answer to me."

The chuck wagon was again freed, and the drive continued. Not until they had bedded down the herd and the first watch had taken to their saddles did Lorna have a chance to talk to Cal.

"I hate Bud McDaniels," said Lorna vehemently. "I'm not surprised Curley won't let him into her bed. He can't do anything right. If it wasn't for Jasmine, I'd drive the toe of my boot into his carcass where it'd do the most good."

"I think Jasmine may do that herself," Cal said, "and I want you to stay out of it. If he bullyrags Quickenpaugh again, I'll let the Indian make a believer of him."

"Quickenpaugh will kill him."

"I'll see that he stops short of that," said Cal. "By God, a man with a wife like Curley and a spread of his own has got to grow up."

Jasmine had just had a bitter conversation along the same line with Tom Allen.

"Damn him," Jasmine said, "Curley making him sleep alone is not enough. She ought to put him in the barn with the rest of the animals. After what he said today, Lorna should have clawed his eyes out."

"I have an idea this drive will make or break him," said Tom.

"I hope it does," Jasmine said. "I'd as soon see him dead as have him drift on like he is, a disgrace to me and the outfit."

Their first day on the trail after the storm was the most difficult, for the uneven land over which they traveled was deceptive. Four times the chuck wagon needed extra teams to free it from unseen mud.

"Tomorrow will be better," Cal predicted. "The sun's sucked up just enough water that you can't really tell what's solid ground and what's mud."

"We could have left the wagon behind and used pack mules," said Bill Petty.

"Yeah," Quanah Taylor said, "and we'd be half starved by now. The good grub's worth wrasslin' the wagon out of bog holes."

With the exception of Bud McDaniels, the others quickly agreed. The passing of the storm had done much to restore their good humor. But during the night, when McDaniels was on watch, he got himself in trouble with the outfit in general, and Quickenpaugh in particular. It began with an angry shout from Curley.

"Leave me alone," the girl cried.

Cal and Quickenpaugh reached her first. Her Levi's were down around her ankles, and she tried vainly to hold her shirt together, for the buttons had been ripped off. McDaniels was crouched in the moonlight, looking for all the world like an animal at bay.

"I'm just takin' what's mine," McDaniels snarled.

"I told you I don't want you," said Curley. "Not now, not ever."

Before Cal could respond, Jasmine was there. She slapped Bud so hard, he rocked back on his heels. He responded with a vicious right that might have broken the girl's neck, but it never landed, for Quickenpaugh was there. He caught McDaniels's arm and flung him half a dozen feet into a patch of thorn bushes.

"You heathen bastard," McDaniels said, "you'll never get to Deadwood alive."

"You fool," said Jasmine. "Quickenpaugh's more civilized than you'll ever be. He'll be there when we reach Deadwood, but I doubt you will be."

With that, she turned away, Tom going with her. Realizing that Cal still had something to say, the rest of the outfit quickly left him alone with Bud McDaniels.

"McDaniels, you've done a lot of things that turned my stomach, but this ranks among the worst."

"Don't you go talkin' down to me," said McDaniels. "You wouldn't be so damned high and mighty, if you was in double-harness with a female that won't let you get close.''

"It's a woman's right to choose," Cal said, "and I think she'd prefer no man at all to the hairy-legged coyote you've turned out to be. You were on first watch, and that don't include romancin' Curley, even if she'll have you. Go after her again, and you'll answer to me. Taunt Quickenpaugh into a fight, and I'll let him just beat the hell out of you."

"I got five hundred cows in this damn herd," said McDaniels, "and that means I got some rights."

"You have the right to drive your part of the herd to Deadwood and collect the money for them," Cal said. "You have no right to cause trouble among the rest of the outfit, and Jasmine being your sister won't matter from now on. Now get up and take your place on the first watch."

Without a word, McDaniels got to his feet and was quickly swallowed by the darkness. Tom Allen, who would be on the second watch, tried to calm Jasmine.

"There shouldn't be a law against gut-shootin' your brother-in-law, when he's a dyed-in-the-wool skunk," said Tom. "After he swung at you, he's lucky Quickenpaugh got to him before I did."

"I don't suppose I have the right to ask," Jasmine said, "but try to avoid him until we reach Deadwood. Perhaps something will happen that will change him."

"It all depends on whether or not he avoids *you*," said Tom. "If I'm any judge, I look for him to go after Quickenpaugh, and that'll be the biggest mistake he's ever made."

Curley got another shirt from the chuck wagon, and there was no further disturbance the rest of the night.

The day dawned clear and unseasonably warm. Well before noon, the riders and their horses were sweating. Curley drove the chuck wagon. Bill Petty, Bud McDaniels, Jasmine and Lorna rode drag. They all pointedly ignored McDaniels, and he began whistling, as though he couldn't care less. The cattle had begun to settle down, allowing the drag riders some freedom. Jasmine purposely rode near enough so she and Lorna could talk.

"Bud's watching you," said Lorna.

"Let him," Jasmine replied. "If he ever takes another swing at me, he'll have more to reckon with than Quickenpaugh. Tom will stomp a mud hole in his carcass and walk it dry. I'd hoped, once he married Curley, that he'd settle down and think of someone other than himself."

"I think we all had hopes of that," said Lorna, "and now I'm feeling guilty, like maybe I had something to do with her getting together with Bud. Poor Curley must be feeling betrayed."

"I couldn't blame her, and I suppose we'll all have to share the blame for that," said Jasmine, "but I think some of the blame rests with Curley herself. Remember, on the drive from Texas to Virginia City, Curley was shot. Until then, none of us realized she was female. I don't think she's comfortable being a woman yet, and from that day, Bud's been after her."*

Lorna laughed. "I remember when we stripped Curley, not knowing she was a girl. Did you see Bud's face? His eyes got as big as wagon wheels. Do you suppose he'd never seen a naked woman before?"

"It's possible," said Jasmine, blushing. "I never let him get close to me when I was indisposed."

"Tonight," Lorna said, "I think we need to spend some time with Curley. I don't want her thinking she's wrong in her refusal to accept Bud as he is."

*The Virginia City Trail (Trail Drive #7)

2

SOUTH-CENTRAL WYOMING TERRITORY.
MARCH 10, 1876

THE FRIGHTENED CATTLE HAD drifted with the storm, and following the stampede the night before, McCaleb and his riders wasted no time in starting the gather. But for some isolated patches, the snow had melted and the sun had gone a long way toward drying up the mud.

"Move 'em out," McCaleb shouted, after the gather was completed.

Rebecca drove the chuck wagon, while Rosalie, Susannah and Penelope rode drag. The herd had become more trail wise and less bothersome. Only once was the drive halted to rescue the bogged-down chuck wagon.

"I figure we made fifteen miles today," McCaleb said, as they gathered around the fire for supper. "If we can do as well tomorrow, we should reach the south fork of the Powder River. We'll follow the Powder for maybe eighty-five miles. There, we'll have to travel a little more to the northeast, and we should be not more than a hundred and seventy miles out of Deadwood."

"The snow cost us some time," said Brazos, "but it's a trade-off. All the temporary water holes and dry creeks should be bank-full."

"We may be needing them," McCaleb said. "When we leave the Powder, this map that I have shows no rivers except those flowing south through western Dakota Territory.''

''We can always drive east, pick up one of those rivers, and follow it to Deadwood,'' said Will. ''We'd always be sure of water.''

''We could,'' McCaleb said, ''but we're not going to. When we leave the Powder, we'll take the shortest run to Deadwood, water or not. By tomorrow, we'll be right in the heart of the old Sioux hunting grounds. The government's closed all the forts along the Bozeman Trail, but we don't know that all the Sioux are raising hell in the Black Hills.''

''With the forts gone and the Bozeman Trail closed, the government may fault us for taking a cattle drive through the old Sioux hunting grounds,'' said Rebecca.

''You bet they will,'' McCaleb said. ''In fact, they've forbidden it. I saw one of their orders posted in Cheyenne.''

''So you went ahead with this drive, without telling any of us,'' said Monte Nance. ''It don't make a damn to you what the rest of us think, does it?''

''With the exception of you, I knew where the outfit stood,'' McCaleb replied. ''You're a hell of a long ways from a majority.''

''We don't need any yellow coyotes on this drive, anyway,'' said Penelope.

''If you was anything but a shirttail of a girl, still wet behind the ears, I'd make you sorry for sayin' that,'' Monte snarled.

''Don't let that stop you,'' said Penelope. ''I can take care of myself.''

''Penelope,'' Rosalie said, ''that's enough. I'll have no daughter of mine brawling, for any reason.''

''Yes, ma'am,'' said Penelope. But her eyes were still on Monte Nance, and there wasn't a hint of repentance in them.

A painful silence followed, and it was Will Elliot who finally broke it.

"With any luck at all, we'll have the herd in Deadwood before the government knows anything about it."

"It's the only way, as I see it," said Pen Rhodes. "By the time the federals make peace with the Sioux, there may be ranches in Dakota Territory. They'll be raising cattle of their own. This may be the last boomtown market, as far as we're concerned."

"I think so," McCaleb said. "To the south of us—in Kansas, especially—the land has been fenced with barbed wire. There'll be no more trail drives north out of Texas. I figure after this drive, we'll be trailin' all our herds to Cheyenne, to be taken east on the Union Pacific."

"To a very predictable market," said Brazos. "The railroad's a fast and easy way of gettin' 'em to market, but when *everybody* jumps in, it'll kick all the props from under the beef prices."

"Suppose we're caught crossing the Sioux hunting grounds in violation of a government order?" Susannah asked.

"We can always plead ignorance," said McCaleb, "but I'm counting on the federals being far too busy with the Sioux to bother us. The Indian situation being what it is, I'd say the very last thing Washington will suspect is that somebody will take a trail drive directly across old Sioux hunting grounds."

"The Sioux won't expect it either," Brazos said, "and that's in our favor. I look for the entire Sioux nation to rendezvous somewhere. Then there's goin' to be hell to pay."

Seeking to avoid trouble, McCaleb assigned Monte Nance to the first watch. He tried to leave Penelope out of it altogether, but the girl wouldn't have it.

"I'll ride with the first watch," said Penelope.

Rosalie looked helplessly at Brazos, and he shrugged his shoulders. They would have to trust Penelope's judgment. But the girl wasted no time in catching Monte Nance engaged in the very thing of which the outfit was most suspicious. Distancing himself from the rest of the first watch, he dismounted and took a bottle from his saddlebag. Twisting the cork out with his teeth, he drank long and deep.

"You skunk," said Penelope from the shadows, "you know it's against the rules, drinking on a trail drive."

"You damn little snoop, you ain't running this trail drive," Monte said.

"I know," said Penelope, "but my Pa has a share of it."

Monte laughed. "Brazos Gifford ain't your Pa, and he's a fool. He took you and your Ma away from an outlaw she was sleepin' with."*

"Brazos adopted me," Penelope said, her voice choking with fury. "He's all I've ever wanted, and anything I think he should know, I'll tell him. Maybe I'll just tell Rebecca too. She ought to know what a sneaking coyote her little brother really is."

"That's low-down," said Monte. "What do I have to do to stop you from spilling your guts about this?"

"Pour out the rest of what's in that bottle," Penelope said, "and do it so I can watch you. I can see you in the moonlight."

"Oh," said Monte, "is that all?"

He drew the cork from the bottle. Upending it, he allowed the amber liquid to spill on the ground, comforted by the thought there were several more full bottles in his saddlebag. What the little fool didn't know wouldn't hurt her . . .

GALLATIN RIVER, MONTANA TERRITORY.
MARCH 10, 1876

"I reckon we'll be here a day or two," said Cal, his eyes on the swollen river. "There's no way to get the chuck wagon across."

"We might cut some logs and float it," Tom Allen said.

"Too risky," said Cal. "She's bank-full, and the cur-

*The Western Trail (Trail Drive #2)

rent's too swift. Fact is, we might have some trouble getting the herd and the horses across.''

"There's still melting snow at higher elevations," Bill Petty said, "and that accounts for the high water. We may have even more trouble crossing the Yellowstone."

"We'll cross the Yellowstone when we get to it," said Cal.

They bedded down the cattle and the horses, and it was nearing dusk when Quickenpaugh pointed across the river. There were eight mounted Indians.

"Dear God," Jasmine cried, "I hope they're not Sioux."

"Crow," said Quickenpaugh.

"They don't seem concerned with the high water," Bill Petty said. "They're crossing."

"Don't feed the varmints," said Bud McDaniels. "I ain't forgot that bunch that moved in on us durin' that drive from Texas. They'll clean us out."*

"We'll stop short of allowing them to clean us out," Cal said, "but if they're hungry, we'll feed them."

"We certainly will," said Jasmine. "They're human beings."

"Hoss Indians," Quickenpaugh said. "Steal."

"I know," said Cal, "and I don't doubt they've spotted Mr. Story's horse herd. They may ride in asking for food, just to take our measure. Every one of us may be in the saddle all night, protecting the horses."

"*Si*," Quickenpaugh said. He pointed to himself, and then to the distant Crows.

"Go ahead and talk to them, Quickenpaugh," said Cal, "but don't promise them more than a meal or two."

Quickenpaugh nodded. Already, the Crows had begun swimming their horses across the swollen river. Afoot, Quickenpaugh went to meet them.

"There's a method to their madness," Tom Allen said. "Ridin' in late, they know we'll offer them supper, and it's

The Virginia City Trail (Trail Drive #7)

only natural they'll stay the night, and that means break-fast."

"I can live with that, as long as they don't take some horses durin' the night," said Cal. "They don't see anything wrong in stealing from us, after we've fed them."

"If I see one slinking around after dark," Bud Mc-Daniels said, "he won't do it again. He'll be one dead Indian."

"There'll be no shooting," Cal said. "Get reckless with your weapons, and I'll take them away from you."

"You can try," said McDaniels. "Sucking up to Story don't make you bulletproof."

"If you pull a gun on anybody in this outfit," Jasmine said, "you'd better shoot me first. If you don't, I'll finish you. There are worse things than having you dead, such as you being the fool that you are now."

Cal said nothing, for Quickenpaugh was approaching after having spoken to the newly arrived Crows.

"They hungry," said Quickenpaugh.

"Tell them to dismount, and we'll feed them," Cal said, "but they'll have to wait."

Quickenpaugh nodded, proud that he had learned much of the Crow tongue. The eight Indians dismounted, remaining near their horses.

"Well, we'd better get their supper started," said Jasmine. "Lorna and Curley, are you up to it?"

"I am," Lorna said. "Anything's better than Indian trouble."

"I'm ready," said Curley. "One of those Indians was in that bunch we fed on the way from Texas."

"*Si,*" Quickenpaugh said. "Him Beaver Tail."

"Tell Beaver Tail and his men they're welcome to a feed, soon as it's ready," said Cal.

"I don't like Indians of any kind," Bud McDaniels said, "and I want that understood. Whatever the no-account varmints do, nobody can blame me."

Nobody responded; but the look Quickenpaugh bestowed

on Bud McDaniels said it all. The Comanche returned to
the Crows, taking them Cal's message. When he returned,
Beaver Tail came with him, making the peace sign. Cal
returned the sign and offered his hand. The Crow took it,
nodding to Quickenpaugh.

"Bluecoats," said Quickenpaugh. "They don't let us
through."

"Where?" Cal asked.

"Powder River," said Quickenpaugh, after conversing
with Beaver Tail.

"How many soldiers?" Cal asked.

Quickenpaugh conveyed the question to Beaver Tail, and
the Crow made signs that Cal couldn't understand. Finally,
Quickenpaugh spoke.

"Much soldiers. Beaver Tail not sure how many. Them
carry long stick with this sign." Quickenpaugh nodded to
Beaver Tail. The Crow knelt and drew a symbol in the dirt.

"That's the Seventh Cavalry, Custer's outfit," said Bill
Petty. "I hated seeing him get a general's star. Now he
thinks he's on equal footing with God."

"He don't stand near as tall as he thinks he does," Tom
Allen said, "but he's the kind to cause us trouble, if he
can."

"Maybe he won't get the chance," said Cal. "I think,
starting tomorrow, we'll allow Quickenpaugh to scout well
ahead of the drive. We'll turn north and follow the Yellowstone to Miles City, if Custer and his soldiers get in our
way. We'll pass far enough to the north of them that they
won't know we're there."

"I don't favor that," Bud McDaniels said. "We'll be on
this drive a lot longer, because you ain't got the guts to
face a few soldiers."

"I'm trail boss, by order of Nelson Story," said Cal,
"and if I say we'll take this drive to Deadwood through
Canada, that's the way we'll be going. Anytime you're
ready, tuck your tail and head for home. We have three

savvy ladies here, and any one of them can take your place without half trying."

The women had ceased their cooking chores for the moment, listening to Cal's blunt words. Curley laughed, and despite all their efforts to the contrary, Jasmine and Lorna joined in. It had a devastating effect on McDaniels, and he turned on Cal with a snarl.

"By God, before this drive is done, all of you will be sorry you ever laid eyes on me."

"Some of us are sorry already," Tom Allen said quietly.

"It's time for the first watch," said Cal. "Arch, Hitch, Mac, Quickenpaugh and Bud. The rest of us, whether we're on watch or not, will be ready to grab our guns, if need be. The weather's fair, and the cattle shouldn't be any trouble, so I want to keep an especially watchful eye on the horse herd."

When the meal was ready, Beaver Tail and his companions drank scalding hot coffee from tin cups, quickly draining both coffeepots.

"Refill the pots one more time," Cal said.

While Lorna and Jasmine refilled the coffeepots, the Crows dug into the food.

"Dear Lord," said Jasmine. "I've never seen the like. They eat as though this is the first decent meal they've ever had."

"It might well be the case," Tom Allen said. "This appears to be a roving band, and that means no permanent camp. They may go for days at a time with only dried venison or a handful of pemmican to keep them alive."

When the Crows had eaten all the food and scraped the pans, Quickenpaugh approached them. Beaver Tail spoke. Quickenpaugh nodded, saying nothing.

"What did Beaver Tail say?" Cal asked, when Quickenpaugh returned.

"Them stay night," said Quickenpaugh.

"Well, that answers my question," Lorna said. "We'll have to cook two breakfasts. One for them, and one for us."

Cal laughed. "I think you'd better do theirs first and let them be on their way. They'll eat as long as there's food in sight, and the rest of us may go hungry."

True to his word, Cal kept the entire outfit on watch, paying particular attention to the horse herd. But none of the Indians made any suspicious moves, and the horses were not molested. By first light, Jasmine, Lorna and Curley had the breakfast fires going. When the food was ready, Quickenpaugh invited the Crows to eat. They did so, while the outfit watched and waited impatiently. When the visitors had cleaned up every scrap of food and had gone through four pots of coffee, Beaver Tail grunted his thanks. Without further delay, the eight of them mounted their horses and rode west.

"I don't begrudge any man grub, when he's hungry," said Bill Petty, "but I still think they had something else in mind. They saw we were suspicious, that we had a heavy watch on the horse herd, and decided not to risk it."

"I think you're right," Cal said, "and there's nothing to stop them from riding back under cover of darkness to try their luck. For the next few nights, we'll continue to keep a close watch on the horses."

But all the outfit didn't take the threat seriously. During the night, Quickenpaugh discovered Bud McDaniels asleep. A quick tally proved that seven of Story's horses had been taken. Adding insult to injury, the marauders had made off with Bud's horse and saddle. When he was awakened by Cal and Quickenpaugh, he held only the severed reins in his hand.

"Hell, I was up all night last night," McDaniels snarled, "and I was beat. How did any of us know the varmints would come back tonight?"

"All of you were warned that they might," said Cal angrily, "and apparently everybody except you heeded that warning. Now get up."

McDaniels knew what was coming. Getting to his knees, he swung the severed reins at Cal's head. But Snider back-stepped, caught the reins and flung McDaniels belly-down. He then seized McDaniels by his belt and, dragging him to the swollen river, pitched him in. The rest of the first watch had witnessed the spectacle, but only Tom Allen spoke.

"That water's still mighty deep and swift. He could drown."

"I don't much give a damn if he does," said Cal in disgust. "But he won't. You can't drown a varmint that was born to be hung."

McDaniels managed to escape the clutches of the swollen river, and by the time he had found his way back to camp, everybody—including Jasmine—knew of his folly. But they all waited for Cal to speak.

"At first light tomorrow," Cal said, "we'll go after the stolen horses. Obviously, all of us can't go. Tom Allen and Quickenpaugh will ride with me."

"I'm goin' too," said Bud McDaniels. "They took my horse."

Bill Petty laughed. "All the more reason for you not to go. They'd likely steal the hoss from under you, with you in the saddle."

"Damn it," McDaniels shouted, "I'm part owner of this herd. I have a right to go."

"This involves the horses, not the cattle," said Cal, "and you don't have a stake in Mr. Story's horse herd. Stay in camp and catch up on your sleep."

At first light, Cal, Tom and Quickenpaugh only took the time to eat. The stolen horses were all shod, and trailing them wasn't difficult. Not more than two miles west, they found Bud McDaniels's abandoned saddle.

"Leave it there," said Cal. "He can come and get it himself."

Cal sent Quickenpaugh ahead, lest they ride into an ambush, and when the Comanche returned, he had some interesting news. He raised his right hand, showing four fingers.

"Four Crows?" Cal asked.

"*Si*," said Quickenpaugh. "No ambush. Ride fast, far."

"Four Indians," Tom Allen said. "That don't sound like Beaver Tail's bunch."

"We'll know, when we catch up to them," said Cal. "Eight horses on lead ropes may slow them down some. Let's ride."

SOUTH FORK OF THE POWDER RIVER, WYOMING TERRITORY. MARCH 12, 1876

"While we're following the Powder and there's plenty of water, we'll drive as late as we can," said McCaleb. "If the weather holds, we might reach Deadwood without enduring another snowstorm."

But the favorable weather didn't continue. At the end of their second day along the Powder, the wind changed directions. Blowing out of the northwest, it was cold.

"We got another dose of it coming," Brazos predicted. "Tomorrow night, at the latest. Startin' in the morning, we'd better begin lookin' for some natural shelter, or a hill where we can make our own."

"I'll have Goose ride out at first light," said McCaleb. "If there's no canyon, we'll have to set up our canvas windbreaks and make the best of it."

The wind had grown markedly colder by morning, raising some doubt that the coming storm might hold off until night. Goose rode upriver as far as the herd was likely to go in a single day without finding suitable shelter.

"Hill," said Goose, when he returned to the outfit. "No more."

"I had hoped we might do better," McCaleb said, "but a hill will be a windbreak. How far, Goose?"

Goose held up five fingers, estimating the distance at five miles.

"We'll be there by midday," said Brazos. "That'll give us time to raise our shelters and drag in plenty of firewood."

But there was an unexpected delay when the chuck wagon's right rear wheel chunked into an unseen hole and snapped the axle where it passed through the hub. Susannah had been at the reins. She stood beside the disabled wagon, a stricken look on her face.

"It wasn't your fault, Susannah," McCaleb said. "It might have happened to any of us."

"But there's a storm coming," said Susannah. "Now there may not be time to reach the place Goose found."

"We're going to make a run for it," McCaleb said. "I'll have Brazos take over the herd and the rest of you can go on. Will and me will stay behind and replace the wagon's axle."

"But it's so dangerous," said Susannah. "Suppose the Sioux—"

"It's a risk we'll have to take," McCaleb said.

By then, the leaders had been headed and the herd had begun to mill. Other riders had arrived and stood looking ruefully at the disabled wagon.

"Brazos," said McCaleb, "I want you to take the herd on to that camp Goose found. Will and me will be along when we've repaired the wagon."

"I don't like leaving you and Will here alone," Brazos said. "If the Sioux should attack, you wouldn't stand a chance."

"Then we'll just have to gamble that they won't," said McCaleb. "Without Will and me, you'll be shy two riders. You can't spare any more, or you'll be inviting the Sioux to attack the herd. Take our horses with you. Susannah can ride one of them."

"Move 'em out," Brazos shouted.

The herd lurched into motion. Brazos had picked up the gait until the drag riders were soon out of sight of the crippled wagon.

"Thank God we brought a spare rear axle," said Will. "We'd be here the rest of the day hewing out a new one with an axe."

McCaleb and Will worked frantically, jacking up the wagon. With a hub wrench, pulling the wheels was a simple matter. Most of the work involved breaking loose the U-bolts and replacing the old axle with the new.

Brazos had given Goose the point position, for the Indian knew where he must take the herd. Brazos looked back often, hoping to see a spiral of dust that would assure him Will and McCaleb were catching up. But there was no such sign. Finally they reached the place Goose had chosen, and bedded down the herd.

"Monte, Pen, Jed and Stoney, you'll go with me," Brazos said. "That storm won't hold off much longer, and we have to drag in as much firewood as we can."

Monte Nance laughed. "Well, ain't you one hell of a trail boss? We could of erected the canvas windbreaks, but you left them in the chuck wagon."

"Don't let it bother you," said Brazos. "The chuck wagon will be here before we're able to drag in enough firewood."

Brazos and his four companions rode out in search of windblown and lightning-struck trees, so that they might stay warm during the coming storm.

"That storm ain't waitin' till tonight," Stoney Vandiver said, his eyes on the big dirty gray clouds rolling in from the west.

"I'm afraid you're right," said Brazos. "We'll have to work fast."

By the time they rode out the third time, particles of snow and ice were being whipped into their faces by a rising wind.

"This will be the last," Brazos shouted. "We'll have to take the axes to some of it just as soon as we can. I have a feeling this one's a mean storm."

MONTANA TERRITORY.
MARCH 12, 1876

"We don't have much time," said Tom Allen. "Lay some snow over these tracks, and it's *adios* to Mr. Story's horses."

"I'd gamble the Indians who took the horses are counting on that," Cal replied. "That likely had a lot to do with their timing. Besides that, there's always a chance they might bushwhack us. Quickenpaugh, ride on ahead a ways and look around."

Cal and Tom continued following the trail of the stolen horses, while Quickenpaugh kicked his mount into a fast gallop. Time was running out . . .

Back in camp, led by Bill Petty, the rest of the outfit set about preparing for another storm. Rather than erecting the tents, the riders used the canvas to construct some large windbreaks.

"Now," said Petty, "it's time to saddle up and drag in some fallen trees for firewood."

Hastily, they performed all the necessary tasks that Cal Snider would have asked of them. By the time the wind blew in the first flurry of snow, they had the camp as secure as it could be made.

"I'm worried about Cal, Tom and Quickenpaugh," Lorna said. "When this land's deep in snow, it all looks the same, as far as you can see."

"I'm sure they won't forget that," said Jasmine. "They must recover the horses soon, or give them up for lost. The snow will wipe out the trail."

"I'm not nearly as worried about losing Mr. Story's horses as I am about perhaps losing Cal, Tom and Quickenpaugh," Lorna said. "Cal may try to recover those horses despite the danger of being stranded in a blizzard."

Far to the west, Cal and Tom reined up, as Quickenpaugh approached.

"No ambush," said Quickenpaugh. "Them run. Take horses."

"Come on," Cal said, "and no shooting. We only want the horses, but they won't know that. We'll ride them down."

With snow blowing into their faces, the three riders kicked their horses into a fast gallop. Ahead of them, the

Crows struggled to the crest of a ridge, the eight horses on lead ropes. One of the Indians looked back, shouted something, and his three companions turned to look. Their pursuers were riding hard, and the four Indians dropped the lead ropes and rode for their lives.

"Let them go, and get the horses," Cal shouted.

The horses ran only a little way before allowing themselves to be captured. Leading the recovered horses, the trio started back, only too much aware that the snow had already begun covering their westbound trail. The sky was a leaden gray, and the rapidly falling snow reduced visibility to a few feet. Quickenpaugh had an uncanny sense of direction, and it was he who took the lead. The temperature had dropped rapidly, and the wind screamed like a live thing. The only advantage they had was the wind at their backs. Suddenly Cal realized Tom was no longer following. He turned, and through the blowing snow, he was barely able to see Tom lying face-down. The horses waited patiently.

"Quickenpaugh!" Cal shouted.

The Indian wheeled his horse and came on the run. Looping lead ropes about saddle horns, Cal and Quickenpaugh dismounted and knelt beside Tom. .

". . . can't go on," Tom mumbled. "Froze . . ."

"Come on, pardner," pleaded Cal. "We'll help you."

But Tom Allen said no more, becoming a dead weight. He had but one chance, and Cal and Quickenpaugh knew it. They stretched him across his saddle, belly-down, using a rope to secure his ankles to his wrists beneath the horse's belly. Struggling to lead nine horses, they went on, unable to see more than a few feet ahead. There was only the unceasing squall of the wind, the numbing cold, and the ever-deepening snow . . .

3

SOUTH FORK OF THE POWDER RIVER, WYOMING TERRITORY.
MARCH 12, 1876

As Bent McCaleb and Will Elliot struggled to mount the heavy wheels on the new axle, snow swirled about them in an ever-increasing mass. McCaleb had freed the mules from their harness until the wagon had been repaired, and as the storm increased in intensity, the animals turned their backs to the wind and tried to drift.

"The wagon will have to wait until we catch the mules," McCaleb said.

The mules were quickly caught and their lead ropes tied securely to a wagon wheel, but the chore had taken some time that couldn't be spared. Once the wheels were mounted on the new axle and the hub nuts secured, Will and McCaleb set about harnessing the teams. By the time they were able to pursue the rest of their outfit, there were no tracks. There was an unbroken expanse of white as far as the eye could see.

"I hope Goose picked a place near the river," Will shouted above the wind.

"If they're too far from the river, somebody will come to meet us," said McCaleb.

In the Lone Star camp, no fires had been started and no windbreaks set up, because the canvas and axes were in the chuck wagon. The entire outfit strained their eyes to see through the swirling snow, back the way they had come. Since McCaleb had left Brazos in charge of the drive, Susannah and Rebecca went to him with their plea. Brazos was saddling his horse.

"Brazos," said Rebecca, "we're not that close to the river. Someone should meet Will and McCaleb, to help them find our camp."

"Someone's goin' to," Brazos said, "just as soon as I finish saddling my horse."

Reaching the river, Brazos rode south. He couldn't hear the rattle of the wagon above the howling wind, and was practically face-to-face with the mules before realizing he had found McCaleb and Will. Knowing they couldn't hear him, and that they would understand why he had come to meet them, Brazos got ahead of the wagon and started back toward camp. Reaching it, he found the rest of the outfit—women included—were in the saddle and circling the cattle and the horse herd. McCaleb reined up the teams on the lee side of the ridge, among the trees. Quickly, he and Will climbed down from the box.

"We don't have the windbreaks up, and no fires going," Brazos said, "because we left the canvas and axes in the chuck wagon."

"I know," said McCaleb. "We'll put up the windbreaks and get some fires going."

The storm-bred wind gleefully snatched the canvas, all but ripping it from their hands, as they sought to lash it to trees. Once the windbreaks were lashed in place, the three of them took axes from the wagon and began chopping the dragged-in trees into a suitable length for firewood. With dry kindling from the chuck wagon, they soon had two roaring fires going.

"Come on," McCaleb said. "Let's relieve the women. They can get some coffee on and start supper."

Many of the cattle had refused to bed down, standing with their backsides to the wind and bawling their misery. The horse herd was less bothersome because the animals had been enclosed in a rope corral. McCaleb sought out Rebecca, Susannah and Rosalie, sending them back to camp. But McCaleb had no such luck with Penelope.

"They can get supper without me," Penelope said. "I'm needed out here."

"I can't argue with that," said McCaleb, "but your pa may have other ideas."

Penelope laughed. "I'll keep you out of trouble. I'll tell him you ordered me to go, and that I refused."

McCaleb rode to find Brazos Gifford. It never ceased to amaze him how much Penelope had become like Brazos, though she wasn't his blood kin, and had been almost twelve when Brazos had come into her life. When McCaleb found Brazos, they backed their horses to the wind so they could talk without shouting.

"Rebecca, Rosalie and ·Susannah are ridin' back to camp," McCaleb said. "I wanted to send Penelope with them, but she refused to go."

"Then let her stay out here until her backside freezes to the saddle," said Brazos. "If she's hell-bent on being a cowboy, then let her have a good dose of it. All I've promised Rosalie is that I'll see that she don't swim the rivers naked."

McCaleb sent Pen Rhodes, Monte Nance and Jed and Stoney Vandiver back to camp to get the chill out of their bones. When they returned several hours later, McCaleb, Brazos, Will and Goose then took their turn by the fire. Only then did Penelope go, and when they returned to the herd, the girl saddled a fresh horse and rode with them.

MONTANA TERRITORY.
MARCH 12, 1876

Cal Snider and Quickenpaugh struggled on, and it became more and more difficult to control nine horses on lead ropes. Tom Allen's bay continually snaked his neck around, trying to see what had become of his rider.

Back in camp, there was only Jasmine, Lorna and Curley, and they looked at one another worriedly. "I know we can't ride out looking for them," Jasmine said, "but there is something we can do that might help them. Let's build one of the fires as high as the treetops. They'll need something to guide them in."

So the three of them set about building a fire big enough that it might be seen from a distance, even in the blowing snow. They threw pine knots into the fire, knowing the rich pine would burn with plenty of black smoke. The fire responded to the added fuel, and the fierce wind sent flames leaping into the sky. A mile to the west, Quickenpaugh pointed to the east. Against the murky, low-hanging clouds, there were frequent flashes that might have been lightning, but Quickenpaugh knew better. The Indian shouted something that was lost in the wind, but Cal Snider had seen the flashes and understood. They struggled on, until at last, even through the blinding snow, they could see the enormous fire ahead.

"Tom!" Jasmine cried, when they rode into the circle of the fire's radiance.

"He's alive, but he's half froze," said Cal, through chattering teeth. "Get him out of his clothes, wrap him in blankets and give him a heavy dose of whiskey."

"We're going to do that for all of you," Lorna said. "Cal, you and Quickenpaugh peel out of those clothes. Curley, bring all the extra blankets and the whiskey from the wagon."

Behind one of the breaks, out of the wind, Cal tried, but his fingers were numb. Lorna helped him. Not until Curley returned with the blankets and the whiskey did Jasmine or Lorna realize Quickenpaugh and the horses were gone.

"That damn Indian's going to freeze to death," said Jasmine.

But Quickenpaugh had promised Nelson Story he would deliver the horse herd, and he had taken the recovered horses and loosed them with the rest of the herd. Only then did he return to the fire. Cal and Tom were belly-down on blankets, where Jasmine and Lorna massaged their frozen feet and legs. Neither man wore a stitch, and the Indian eyed them with some amusement.

"Come on, Quickenpaugh," Curley said. "Out of those clothes. I'll take care of you."

Quickenpaugh shook his head, moving closer to the fire.

"Have some whiskey, then," said Curley. "It'll warm you up."

"No whiskey," Quickenpaugh said. "Coffee."

He got himself a tin cup from the wagon and went to one of the coffeepots that sat on a bed of coals. The nearness of the fire and the massaging of his legs and feet restored Tom Allen's awareness. He sat up and looked around.

"Where's Quickenpaugh?" Tom asked.

"On the other side of the fire, hunkered down and drinking coffee," said Curley. "When I tried to see to him like Jasmine and Lorna were caring for you and Cal, he wouldn't have it. He acted strange, like something was wrong."

"Tell him I want to see him," said Cal, who had been listening.

Curley told Quickenpaugh, and the Indian said nothing, waiting for Cal to speak.

"Quickenpaugh, you were as near froze as Tom and me. Curley wanted to help you."

"Bud no like," Quickenpaugh said, his dark eyes on Curley. "Fight."

For a long moment, nobody spoke, for they all knew what Quickenpaugh meant.

"Quickenpaugh," said Cal, "Mr. Story has confidence in you, and so do I. You're part of this outfit, and anybody going after you will have to step over me first."

"That goes double for me," Tom Allen said. "You're one *bueno hombre*."

"Oh, damn," said Curley, "I'm so ashamed."

"Don't be," Jasmine said. "It's not your fault."

When Cal, Tom and Quickenpaugh had driven the chill from their bones, they saddled fresh horses and went to relieve some of the other riders who had remained with the herd.

"We can't spare all of you at one time," said Cal. "Three of you can go now."

"I aim to be one of the three that goes now," Bud McDaniels said. "I done my share."

"I be stayin' awhile," said Oscar Fentress.

"So will I," Bill Petty and Quanah Taylor said, in a single voice.

"Count me in," said Smokey Ellison.

"Arch, Hitch and Mac, go ahead," said Cal. "When you've rested a couple of hours and warmed up some, ride on back, so Oscar, Smokey, Quanah and Bill can take a turn."

"Damn you," Bud shouted, "I told you I'm goin'."

"Then go on," said Cal, "but I have something to say to you. If you reach Deadwood alive, one of us won't be returning to Montana Territory. I won't ride the same range as a yellow coyote standin' on his hind legs like a man."

"I don't care what you think," Bud snarled. "For that matter, I don't care what Story thinks. I don't give a damn what *any* of you think."

"Bud," said Tom, "for Jasmine's sake—"

McDaniels laughed. "It's you that's sleepin' with her. She's got no excuse for leadin' me around by the nose."

Tom Allen put all his strength and fury into his right, and when it struck McDaniels on the jaw, he was literally lifted off his feet. He landed on his back in the snow, and for a moment, all the wind had been driven out of him. In a rage he reached for his Colt, only to find that Cal Snider had him covered.

"Pull that iron," Cal said, "and I'll kill you."

McDaniels got unsteadily to his feet, mounted his horse and rode toward the distant fires. Arch, Hitch and Mac eventually followed.

"I don't know what's goin' to become of him," said Tom Allen. "How much does a man have to put up with, when his brother-in-law's a damn fool?"

"I don't know," Cal said, "but I don't think you should cut him any slack for Jasmine's sake. I don't aim to."

When McDaniels reached the fire, he was in a savage mood. Curley ignored him, and he grabbed the girl around the waist, drawing her to him. Curley seized one of his fingers, bending it back, and he cursed her. Releasing Curley, he kicked her in the behind, and she fell face-down, almost in the fire. McDaniels stood there breathing hard, looking into the muzzle of a Colt that was steady in Jasmine's hand. McDaniels laughed shakily.

"Don't you ever let me see—or even hear—of you mistreating her again," Jasmine said. "Gut-shooting's too good for you, and I'll aim six inches lower."

Curley got to her knees, snow and dirt clinging to her coat and her face. She spoke not a word, and in the flickering light from the fire, Jasmine and Lorna could see silent tears streaking her cheeks. Arch, Hitch and Mac had arrived just in time to witness the sorry spectacle, and stood there in awkward silence.

"There's plenty of hot coffee," Jasmine said. "Come and get it."

They did, and it drew attention away from Curley, allowing the girl to compose herself and to dry her tears. Bud McDaniels poured a tin cup full of coffee and hunkered by the fire as though nothing had happened. He sneaked an occasional look at Jasmine, only to find her eyes on him, stormy and unrelenting. Curley had gotten as far from him as she could and was ignoring him. None of them cared if he lived or died, McDaniels decided, and before he was done, he would make them sorry they had ever come down on him.

POWDER RIVER, WYOMING TERRITORY.
MARCH 14, 1876

The storm raged for two days and nights, and during the second day, McCaleb and his riders had to brave the snow and icy wind to drag in more firewood.

"I'm tired of draggin' in firewood out of the snow, while that damn Indian don't lift a hand," Monte Nance complained.

"Goose does his share and then some," said Benton McCaleb. "Somebody has to keep the herd and the horses settled, and Goose is just a hell of a lot better at it than you are."

Penelope had chosen to ride with them, and when the girl laughed, Monte turned his furious eyes on her. Only when he found McCaleb watching him did he avert his gaze.

"Let's try to snake out enough wood this time, so that we don't have to come again," McCaleb said. "It's gettin' colder."

"Snow's thinnin' out some," said Brazos. "It'll likely end some time tonight."

"It'll still be almighty cold," Will said, "and when the sun comes out, we'll be here for a week, waitin' for the mud to dry up."

The six of them dragged in as much fallen timber as they could and then took turns with the four axes from the chuck wagon, cutting the logs into manageable lengths for their fires.

"I'm riding out with Pen, Jed, Stoney and Goose," Penelope announced.

"I think you've spent enough time out in this cold," said Rosalie. "It could be the death of you."

Penelope laughed. "It could be the death of *any* of us. I'm no more special than any of the rest of the outfit."

With that, she was gone, into the swirling snow.

"Her and her cowboy ways are going to be the death of *me*," said Rosalie.

"She'll grow out of it," Brazos assured her.

But none of them knew Monte Nance had plans for the girl, when the time was right.

MONTANA TERRITORY.
MARCH 20, 1876

"Head 'em up, move 'em out," Cal shouted.

Following the two-day storm, there had been enough sun to melt the snow and suck up much of the resulting mud. Cal rode point, while Tom Allen and Oscar Fentress were the swing riders. Smokey Ellison and Quanah Taylor were the flankers. Bill Petty and Bud McDaniels, accompanied by Jasmine and Curley, rode drag. Lorna drove the chuck wagon, trying to avoid holes and drop-offs that might further damage the vehicle.

"Bill," said Jasmine, "how far do you think we've come?"

"I'm not sure," Petty replied. "I looked at a map once, and I figured it fifty miles from Virginia City to the Yellowstone. If nothin' else slows us down, we oughta be reaching the Boulder in a couple more days."

"Then we won't be quite a hundred miles from our home range," Curley said.

"That's how it stacks up," said Petty. "As trail drives go, we're behind schedule."

Suddenly a brindle bull decided he no longer wished to be part of the drive. Galloping off to one side, he avoided Bud McDaniels, who was the closest rider. McDaniels lit out after the animal, only to have his horse ram a left front foot into a deep hole. McDaniels was pitched over the head of the unfortunate horse and landed belly-down. He lay there, unable to breathe, for the wind had been knocked out of him. Bill Petty had kicked his horse into a gallop, but the troublesome bull reached McDaniels first. The animal hooked at Bud, managing to get one sharp horn under the waistband of McDaniels's Levi's. The mighty bull reared, shaking his head, trying to free himself of the unwelcome human burden. Bud McDaniels screamed, and it seemed to further infuriate his captor. The bull gave a mighty heave, and McDaniels's belt broke. His Levi's were dragged down to his ankles, unable to go any farther because of his boots. He was free of the bull for the moment, but the animal had by no means given up.

"Damn it," Petty shouted, "get out of those boots and run for it. I'll draw him away from you."

But the bull had decided Bud McDaniels was the cause of all his troubles, and ignoring Bill Petty, the animal again charged McDaniels.

"Shoot the bastard," McDaniels squalled.

But it was too late. McDaniels was on his knees, trying to get to his feet, when one of the bull's horns raked his bare backside. Recognizing the problem, Jasmine had unlimbered her lariat and roped the bull. Bill Petty dropped a second loop over the animal's head, and helpless between the two of them, the bull was forced back into the herd. But the herd was no longer moving. The swing riders had alerted Cal to the problem, and with the help of the flank and swing riders, the drive had been halted. McDaniels lay face-down, unable or unwilling to get up. His Levi's had been ripped into two pieces, and there was a terrible bloody gash where the bull's horn had raked him from knee to waist. The horse herd and the chuck wagon had been following the cattle, and the horse wranglers arrived just in time to witness McDaniels being raked with a horn. Lorna reined up the chuck wagon's teams, her eyes on Curley, but Curley made no move. The wranglers—Arch, Hitch, Mac and Quickenpaugh—looked on in silence. It was an awkward situation, and nobody spoke until Cal Snider arrived.

"McDaniels," said Cal, "you can lay there on your belly

and bleed, or you can get up and have that wound attended."

McDaniels struggled to his knees, sparing his bloody backside. When he finally was on his feet, he balanced on one foot and then the other, removing his boots. He then ripped off what remained of his ruined Levi's and flung them away. He stood there, wearing only his shirt, glaring at all of them defiantly.

"Bud," Jasmine said, "I think everybody's seen enough. You *do* have another pair of britches, don't you?"

"In my bedroll," said McDaniels sullenly.

"No hurry for that," Cal said. "The river's handy and we have water. That wound can't wait until day's end."

"There's dry wood in the chuck wagon's possum belly," said Lorna. "I'll start a fire."

"Then I'll get a pot of water ready," Jasmine said. "Curley, do you want to help?"

"No," said Curley. "I've seen all I ever want to see of him, with or without britches."

"Tom," Cal said, "take everybody with you except Jasmine, Lorna and Curley. See that the horse herd and the cattle are settled. We'll be here awhile."

When the riders had gone, McDaniels stood there saying nothing, blood streaming down his bare leg. The fire was going, and Jasmine was hanging a pot of water over it.

"Bud," said Cal, "you have a serious wound. You have three choices as to who doctors you. There's Jasmine, Lorna or me."

"None of you, damn it," McDaniels growled. "I want Curley."

Curley laughed bitterly. "I hope you get blood poisoning and it rots off everything from your belly button to the ground."

"Then I'll do the doctoring," said Jasmine.

"I'll help you," Lorna said.

"No," McDaniels shouted. "I want Curley."

"I reckon there's *hombres* in hell wantin' springwater,"

said Cal. "You'll take what you can get. Then we'll clear a space in the chuck wagon where you can lay on your belly and whine for the next two weeks."

Cal rode back and joined the rest of the riders who were circling the herd. Jasmine and Lorna waited for the water to boil, while McDaniels lay belly-down, watching them warily. Jasmine went closer, the better to examine the wound, and found it had stopped bleeding.

"Damn you," said Bud. "You just can't wait to get your hands on me, can you?"

"Only because nobody else wants the damn job," Jasmine said bitterly. "Lorna, you don't have to watch this. I can manage."

"I'll stay," said Lorna. "It's not fair that you be stuck with all the dirty work."

She had taken the pot of boiling water from the fire, and at that point, Bud McDaniels said exactly the wrong thing.

"Let her stay," Bud said. "She just wants to see me without my Levi's."

Lorna sloshed half the pot of boiling water on McDaniels's bare backside. Shouting in pain and fury, McDaniels got to his knees and began cursing Lorna in particular, and the rest of the outfit in general.

"Lorna," said Jasmine, "why don't you use the rest of that boiling water?"

There was cheering from the rest of the riders, all of whom had gathered to watch from a distance. McDaniels, aware that he was entertaining them by making a fool of himself, gritted his teeth and said no more. Jasmine took the pot containing the balance of the hot water and approached Bud.

"Don't you even *think* about it," McDaniels snarled.

"Then get on your feet," said Jasmine. "I want this over and done with."

McDaniels laughed. "You got more than just a horn-rakin' that needs doctorin' now. That little wench scalded me with hot water."

"The noblest thing this little wench has ever done," Lorna said. "My one regret is that I didn't have enough to drown you."

"You'll get your behind doctored where you were raked with a horn," said Jasmine. "We have no means of treating a burn. It'll be left unbandaged, and hopefully the open air will help to heal it."

"Meanin' I got to lay on my belly until it heals," McDaniels said.

"So what?" said Jasmine. "You'll be on your belly until your wound heals. Unless you think you're man enough to sit a saddle."

Jasmine said no more. The water had cooled somewhat, and, tilting the pot, Jasmine poured the rest of it on McDaniels's backside and bloody leg.

"Yeeeow," McDaniels squalled. "That's too hot."

"No matter," said Jasmine cheerfully. "That's all of it."

Lorna had taken the medicine chest from the wagon. Opening it, she and Jasmine began looking for some disinfectant. The bottle, when they found it, was three-quarters full of an amber liquid. Jasmine poured some of the disinfectant on a clean cloth and began at the lower end of the wound, just above Bud's knee. Aware that the rest of the outfit was still watching with amusement, McDaniels gritted his teeth to avoid crying out. Jasmine finally concluded her work with the disinfectant.

"Lorna," said Jasmine, "hand me a tin of sulfur salve."

Lorna did so, and Jasmine coated the wound with it. Bud *had* been scalded, and she applied some of the salve where it was needed. Cal approached, and Jasmine got to her feet.

"I brought his other pair of Levi's," Cal said.

"He won't be needing them for a while," said Jasmine. "They would keep that wound rubbed raw. I think we'd better put him belly-down in the chuck wagon, just like he is, and allow the open air to do the healing."

"I'm not sure I want this naked varmint in the chuck wagon, with Lorna driving," Cal said doubtfully.

"I'm not afraid of him," said Lorna. "I've seen all there is to see, and I'm not in the least impressed."

Nevertheless, Cal and Tom rearranged the contents of the wagon, moving most of the supplies toward the front. That provided a considerable barrier between the wounded Bud and Lorna, when she took her position on the wagon box. McDaniels's saddle was piled into the chuck wagon, and his horse was taken to the remuda. Having lost two hours, the herd again moved out.

"Damn it," said Tom Allen, "why couldn't Jasmine have had a sister, instead of a scrub-tailed little varmint of a brother?"

Cal laughed. "That's why it pays to have friends. We can't choose our kin."

ALONG THE POWDER RIVER, WYOMING TERRITORY.
MARCH 20, 1876

Fair weather continued, and the Lone Star outfit took full advantage of it. Even Monte Nance seemed to put forth an extra effort, and on most days, the drive traveled at least fifteen miles. Goose scouted ahead, but found no Indian sign.

"They're gathering to raise some hell in the Dakotas," Brazos predicted.

"That's likely," said McCaleb, "and it's in our favor. As long as Red Cloud and the Sioux are tangling horns with the army, they may overlook us."

The outfit had just settled the herd and supper was under way when a stranger hailed the camp. He led a limping horse, and a holstered Colt was tied low on each hip.

"I don't like the looks of him," Will Elliot said. "He'll be wantin' a horse, and we can't spare one."

"Howdy," said McCaleb, when the stranger was close enough. "I'm Benton McCaleb, trail boss for Lone Star."

"Stanton Horseley," the stranger replied. "I been follerin' you for a while. My horse is lame, and I'm needin' to swap him for another."

"Sorry," said McCaleb. "All we have is our remuda horses, and we can't spare even one of them."

"His leg will heal in a couple of days, and he'll be good as new," Horseley said.

"Then I'd suggest you camp somewhere until he heals," said McCaleb.

"I can't spare the time," Horseley said. "My grub's runnin' low."

"You're welcome to eat with us tonight and in the morning," said McCaleb.

"I'm obliged," Horseley said.

He unsaddled the lame bay horse, allowing the animal to roll. Silently, Rebecca brought him a tin cup of steaming coffee. He took a sip of his coffee, and then he spoke.

"I never seen a trail drive comin' through here before. Where you folks bound?"

"Deadwood," said McCaleb, wishing Horseley hadn't asked.

"Well, don't that beat a goose a-gobblin'. That's where I'm headed," Horseley said.

"Why?" Penelope asked innocently. "You're not a miner or a cowboy."

Horseley laughed. "Matter of fact, I'm not. Cowboying is dirty, low-payin' work, and so is blistering your hands with shovel and pick handles. I mine my gold across a poker table."

Monte Nance looked interested, and it prompted McCaleb to speak.

"There'll be no gambling in this camp, Horseley."

"Fine," said Horseley. "I never gamble with friends."

"He doesn't look like the kind who would have any friends," Susannah said softly.

"I doubt that he has," said Will. "He said that, hopin' it'll give him an edge later on. I think we'll be watching the horse remuda mighty close tonight."

After supper, McCaleb made the rounds, speaking to every rider in the outfit. Monte Nance, Will Elliot and Jed and Stoney Vandiver took the first watch.

"Good thinking," Brazos Gifford said. "If he tries anything foolish, it'll be after midnight, I reckon."

"You didn't assign me to either watch," said Penelope.

"Then take the first one," Brazos replied.

"No," said Penelope. "I won't be on the same watch with that bastard Monte Nance."

"Penelope," Brazos said, "you know how your mother feels about your . . . talk."

"I know," said Penelope cheerfully, "but she's not listening. Besides, I don't talk any worse than you. Are you going to tell on me?"

Brazos sighed. "I reckon not."

McCaleb laughed. "Just what we need, *amigo*. A female Brazos Gifford."

4

LONE STAR'S FIRST WATCH rode out at dusk, and Horseley had made no suspicious moves. When the second watch took over at midnight, the stranger was rolled in his blankets.

"I can't figure him out," Brazos said, as he and McCaleb circled the herd. "He knows as well as we do that horse of his will be just as lame in the morning as he is tonight. I look for him to offer to join the drive without pay, for the use of a horse."

"I'd have to turn him down," said McCaleb. "Right now, every rider has three mounts in his string, and they're all needed. If we can't spare him even one horse, how in thunder would we come up with three?"

"We can't," Brazos said, "but I can't help thinking there'll be trouble."

"You may be right," said McCaleb. "In the morning, I want you to keep Rosalie and Penelope well away from Horseley. I've already spoken to Rebecca, and Will promised to tell Susannah."

"I see what you mean," said Brazos, "and I'll do my part. We don't know what kind of *pistolero* this pilgrim is, so Will and me will side you."

"I'm obliged," McCaleb said.

"*Ganos,*" said a voice from the darkness.

"Come on, Goose," said McCaleb.

The Lipan Apache seemed to materialize where there had been only shadows a moment before.

"*Dos Pistolas* no sleep," Goose said.*

"Thanks, Goose," said McCaleb quietly. "I want you to watch him until first light. If he makes a move toward any of the horses, stop him."

"Kill?"

"If that's the only way you can stop him," McCaleb replied. "I trust your judgment."

Silently, like a shadow, the Indian was gone.

"At least he won't try anything during the night," said Brazos.

Rebecca, Rosalie and Susannah started breakfast at first light, and nothing seemed out of the ordinary. The coffee was ready first, and Horseley lined up with the others, pouring himself a tin cup full. When breakfast was over, the Lone Star riders went to saddle their horses. Stanton Horseley lifted the hoof of his own lamed mount, apparently to examine it. But next to his horse, Penelope was saddling her own. Horseley suddenly rolled under his mount and, lightning-quick, came to his feet and seized the startled Penelope.

"Now," said Horseley, a Colt in his hand, "I reckon I'm in a position to bargain for a horse."

"You're in a position to get yourself shot dead," McCaleb said. "Let her go, and maybe we'll forget this ever happened."

Horseley laughed. "It don't pay to be too trusting, McCaleb. This little filly's goin' to ride with me a ways. Maybe a long ways, if any of you follow."

But Penelope had other ideas. While Horseley had a brawny arm about her waist, the girl had full control of her feet. She stomped on her captor's toes, and involuntarily his grip loosened just enough. Penelope went limp and slipped to the ground. It was just the break McCaleb was waiting for, and when Horseley went for his Colt, McCaleb

*Two Guns

drew. His weapon rode butt-forward on his left hip, for a cross-hand draw, and his Colt roared an instant ahead of Horseley's. The lead slammed him back against Penelope's saddled horse, and Penelope caught the reins of the animal before it could run. Horseley slumped to the ground, unmoving.

"Damn him," said Brazos, "he waited until he knew I couldn't get a clear shot at him. Are you all right, Penelope?"

"Sure," Penelope replied.

"Then go to your mother," said Brazos. "She's not all right."

"I will," Penelope said, "but there's something I have to do first."

She threw her arms around McCaleb's neck, kissing him long and hard. She then made her way to Rosalie.

Brazos laughed. "Instead of picking up my habits, she may start acting more like you."

Rebecca was smiling, and, taking that as favorable, McCaleb said nothing. Brazos turned the lame horse in with the remuda. Jed and Stoney Vandiver had begun digging a grave for the dead man. Will Elliot and Pen Rhodes searched Horseley and then his saddlebags.

"He was more an outlaw than a gambler," said Will. "Look what we found in his saddlebags."

McCaleb studied the WANTED dodger on which there had been drawn a reasonable likeness of the dead man.

"Wanted for murder in Texas," McCaleb said. "No wonder he was bound for Dakota Territory."

"There's a reward," said Monte Nance, "but it don't say how much."

"Won't matter if it's ten thousand dollars," McCaleb said. "We're in the midst of a trail drive. When we plant this *hombre*, we're movin' out."

It was a mild reprimand, but nonetheless serious to Monte Nance. He said nothing, but Rebecca didn't like the way he looked at Benton McCaleb . . .

YELLOWSTONE RIVER, MONTANA TERRITORY.
MARCH 25, 1876

"It took us a mite longer to get here than it should have," Bill Petty said, "but it may be just as well. Any sooner, and it would have been running bank-full, from all the snow."

"You're likely right," said Cal Snider, "but we're not going to waste any time crossing it. We're due for another storm, and that may bring more high water."*

"We'd better get started, if we aim to cross before dark," said Tom Allen.

"Why don't we just wait for first light and do it tomorrow?" Lorna asked.

Cal laughed. "I thought you was cowpuncher enough to know that. Cattle won't cross with the sun in their eyes."

"Well, damn," said Lorna. "It's been ten years since we brought a herd from Texas to Virginia City, and I don't remember *everything*."†

The cattle were taken across first, followed by the horse herd, and then the remuda. Cal went looking for a shallows where the chuck wagon could cross, and he returned just minutes before sundown. Jasmine sat on the wagon box, waiting.

"Get down," Cal said, "and I'll take it across. Water's a mite deep."

Jasmine stepped down from the wagon box, and Cal handed her the reins to his horse. Mounting the box, Cal drove downstream. Without being asked, Smokey Ellison and Oscar Fentress mounted their horses and followed. Reaching the shallows where the banks were low enough

---

*Near what is the present-day town of Livingston, Montana, the Yellowstone flows south into northwestern Wyoming and into what is now Yellowstone National Park.
†*The Virginia City Trail* (Trail Drive #7)

for crossing, Cal guided the mules into the river. But the water was deeper than it should have been for such a crossing, and the swift current lurched the chuck wagon to the right. But Smokey and Oscar had ridden their horses into the river on the downstream side of the wagon, and they each seized a wagon bow, steadying the wagon. Glad to be on solid ground again, the mules gave it their all, and the wagon lurched up the east bank of the Yellowstone. Cal reined up the teams a hundred yards upstream from the cattle and the horses. He had completely forgotten about the injured Bud McDaniels in the back of the wagon, until McDaniels spoke.

"You ain't much of a teamster, Snider," said McDaniels. "You don't care a damn about me, do you?"

"Not really," Cal said. "Anytime you figure ridin' in the wagon's too risky, and you're able to mount a horse, saddle up. Or you can walk."

It had been long enough since the last storm that there was dry wood at hand, and by the time Cal got the wagon across, Jasmine, Lorna and Curley had the fires blazing. The coffeepots were immediately filled and put on to boil.

"I need some help back here," Bud McDaniels shouted.

"I'll see what he wants," said Jasmine wearily.

"I want my damn Levi's," McDaniels said. "I ain't layin' here another minute."

"Thank God for small miracles," said Jasmine. "I'll get them."

"Here's his Levi's," Cal said, "but there was no extra belt in his bedroll."

"No matter," said Jasmine. "His wound hasn't healed. He won't be wearing them very long, because he's in no condition to ride. He's just being cantankerous."

But the injury had taken its toll, and during the night, Bud McDaniels's condition worsened. At dawn, Jasmine found him talking out of his head and burning with fever. The infection had not only returned, but had worsened. Cal faced the outfit before breakfast, and they knew by the grim set of his jaw that something was wrong.

"The infection's back, and Bud's in a bad way," Cal said. "He's in no condition to be moved. We'll be here awhile."

At first, nobody said anything. It had been one delay after another, and they had but little progress to show for almost a month on the trail. Jasmine took one of the pots of boiling water that had been intended for coffee and had started toward the chuck wagon.

"I'll help you tend him," said Lorna.

"So will I," Curley said. "I have a lot to forgive. I reckon I'd better get started."

The three of them worked over Bud McDaniels for an hour, and not once did he know them. His meaningless mumbling was mingled with curses and, occasionally, tears.

"My God," said Lorna, "what more can we do for him, that we haven't done already?"

"I don't know," Jasmine said softly. "May God have mercy on him."

"Pour some of the whiskey into the wound," Curley said. "It may be stronger than the disinfectant."

"It's worth a try," said Jasmine. "We don't have anything to lose."

Jasmine poured whiskey into the festering wound, and Bud groaned. Curley and Lorna said nothing, their eyes on Jasmine's stricken face. Silent tears crept down her cheeks as she looked upon the kid brother who had brought her nothing but misery and despair. It was time for Jasmine to let go. With Lorna on one side of her and Curley on the other, they drew her back against the wagon canvas. She wept until she could weep no more. She wiped away the tears on the sleeves of her shirt, and only then did she speak.

"The others are waiting for breakfast. We must get it started."

"You and Lorna go ahead," said Curley. "I'll stay with him."

Only then did they become aware that Quickenpaugh stood at the wagon's tailgate, his eyes on the stricken Bud, lying belly-down. Curious as to what the Indian had in mind, some of the outfit had followed him.

"No burn, him die," Quickenpaugh said.

Jasmine and Lorna didn't understand, and so that they might hear better, they slid off the wagon's tailgate. To emphasize his words, Quickenpaugh drew his Bowie knife, pointing it toward the distant breakfast fire. Although Quickenpaugh couldn't find the proper words, Cal Snider understood what he was trying to tell them.

"You would heat the *cuchillo* in the fire and burn away the poison," said Cal.

"*Si*," Quickenpaugh said.

"Quickenpaugh wants to cauterize the wound," Cal said. "It involves heating the Bowie blade red-hot and searing the wound."

"I've never seen it done, but I've heard of it," said Tom Allen. "Trouble is, it can be one hell of a shock to the body. A man with a weak heart might not live through it."

"True enough," Cal said, "but it's the only chance he has, and then only if the poison hasn't gotten into his blood. Jasmine, as his next of kin, it's up to you."

Jasmine's eyes were on the silent Quickenpaugh, and in her mind she thought back to the many occasions when Bud McDaniels had baited and ridiculed the Indian. When finally she spoke, it was directly to Quickenpaugh.

"You would do that . . . for him?"

Quickenpaugh shook his head. "I do that for you."

"My God," said Arch Rainey, "there stands a man."

From within the wagon, Curley couldn't believe her ears. She stared at Quickenpaugh as though seeing him for the first time. The Indian, in his own way, had just justified her decision to forgive the abusive Bud McDaniels. Jasmine approached Quickenpaugh until she was looking into his dark eyes. Only then did she reply.

"If you believe you can save him, Quickenpaugh, please do it."

Quickenpaugh nodded, pointing to Bud and then to the fire.

"Tom," said Cal, "he wants Bud taken near the fire. Give me a hand."

Curley climbed out of the wagon, and with Bud Mc-Daniels lying belly-down on a pair of blankets, Cal and Tom managed to take him near the fire. It had died down, but Lorna piled on more wood, and it flamed to life anew.

"*Dos cuchillo,*" Quickenpaugh said.*

Without a word, Oscar Fentress drew his own Bowie, as long and lethal as Quickenpaugh's own. He presented the weapon to Quickenpaugh haft-first, and the Indian took it. When the fire had become a mass of glowing coals, Quickenpaugh—using a stick—heaped live coals upon the blades of the two Bowie knives.

"He's using two knives," said Tom Allen. "Who else would have thought of that?"

"By the time one knife cools, the other will be ready," Cal said. "Either way, it'll be almighty unpleasant. Jasmine, Lorna and Curley, I don't think you should watch."

"I aim to watch," said Curley. "If he lives, I want him never to forget that his life has been spared by an Indian who might only have wanted to see him dead."

Several times, Quickenpaugh tested the knives, returning the blades to the coals. When they became red-hot, he withdrew one, and when he hunkered down before Bud McDaniels, the blade had cooled to a silver-gray. Cal stood by the fire, prepared to see that the other knife was ready when Quickenpaugh needed it. Quickenpaugh began with the lesser part of the wound, on McDaniels's left leg. He held the Bowie in position for only a second, moving it upward.

*Two knives

Even in his unconscious condition, Bud McDaniels screamed and tried to get to his knees. Tom Allen held down his feet, while Oscar Fentress and Smokey Ellison each captured one of his flailing arms. But the knife blade had cooled, and Quickenpaugh presented it, haft-first, to Cal, who shoved it back into the coals. The Indian stooped and withdrew the second knife from the fire, taking up where he had left off in the cauterizing of Bud McDaniels's terrible wound. There was the sickening odor of seared flesh, but little more than a grunt from Bud, for he was unconscious. Quickenpaugh alternated knives a dozen times before he felt he had accomplished what he had set out to do. Wordlessly, he drove the blades of both Bowie knives into the ground, cleaning them. He then sheathed his own Bowie and, haft-first, returned Oscar's. Despite Cal's warning, after McDaniels had ceased screaming and fighting, Jasmine and Lorna had crept up beside Curley, their eyes drawn to the terrible drama taking place before them.

"I think we'd better get a slug of that whiskey down Bud before he comes to," Cal said. "He'll hurt like hell for a while."

Jasmine brought a bottle of whiskey from the chuck wagon, pulling the cork with her teeth. Cal and Tom each took one of Bud's arms, raising him enough so that they might get the whiskey down him. Curley seized his hair, holding his head back, while Lorna got as much of the vile brew down him as she could.

"Now," said Curley, "do we put him back in the wagon?"

"No," Cal said, "but I think we'll move him to the shady side of it. He'll go through enough misery without the heat of the sun on his wounds."

Quickenpaugh hunkered by the fire, his thoughts seemingly lost in the flames. Jasmine placed her hand on his shoulder, and seeming startled, he got hurriedly to his feet.

"Quickenpaugh," said Jasmine, "from the bottom of my

heart, thank you. Is there anything I can do to repay you?"

"Grub," Quickenpaugh said. "Much hungry."

The outfit desperately needed to laugh, and they did. Jasmine, Lorna and Curley got breakfast under way, and there was hot coffee within a few minutes. The women were able to talk among themselves, and it was Curley who had misgivings, should Bud recover.

"After all Quickenpaugh's done," said Curley, "I hope Bud makes it. Maybe I deserve him cussing me, but if he jumps on Quickenpaugh again, there'll be hell to pay. I promise you that."

"Then you'll have to get to him ahead of me," Jasmine said. "Quickenpaugh didn't *have* to do what he did, and many a white man in his position wouldn't have."

The outfit took its time over breakfast, for the cattle and horses were within sight, and all seemed well. McDaniels had been moved so that he rested in the shadow of the chuck wagon. Once an hour, Jasmine, Lorna or Curley knelt beside him to see if his raging fever had begun to break. He rewarded them with a drunken snore, and not until the late afternoon was there a change in his condition.

"Bud's sweating," Jasmine announced.

"*Bueno,*" said Cal. "Oscar, you've had some doctoring experience. Take a look at him and see what you think."

"He be goin' to live," Oscar Fentress said, after examining McDaniels. " 'Nother week or two, maybe, he ride."

"Well, I hope he can make do in the wagon considerably before then," said Tom Allen. "We should have been halfway to Deadwood by now."

ALONG THE POWDER RIVER, WYOMING TERRITORY.
MARCH 25, 1876

Benton McCaleb's Lone Star outfit had gathered for supper. Far to the west, there was unmistakable evidence that another storm was brewing.

"Just what we need," said Pen Rhodes. "More snow."

"I've about decided we began this drive too early,"
McCaleb said, "but there's no help for it now. We'll sit
out the storm and then move on."

Goose, the Lipan Apache, had ridden north along the
Powder looking for Indian sign. He rode in, dismounted
and unsaddled his horse. Only then did he speak.

"No sign," said Goose. "No Sioux."

"Damn it, that bothers me more than if they were all
around us," Brazos said. "We're in the heart of their old
hunting grounds. Where *are* they?"

"In Dakota Territory," said McCaleb. "Red Cloud's
concerned with those thousands of miners who have in-
vaded the Black Hills, in violation of the Treaty of 1868."

"We don't have a map," Susannah said. "How do we
know where we are, and how far we still must go?"

"I have a general idea," said McCaleb. "We follow the
Powder River north, until it forks to the south. There we
leave the Powder, driving northeast."*

"Then we have no idea where we'll find water, once we
leave the Powder," Will Elliot said.

"No," said McCaleb, "but Goose will be scouting ahead
of the drive, for available water and Indian sign."

Far to the west, the sun set behind a bank of gray clouds,
feathering the horizon with crimson.

"Snow come," Goose said. "I find shelter."

"*Bueno*," said McCaleb. "We'll get an early start tomorrow and push the herd as hard as we can."

"In all the years I've known you, McCaleb, you've never
sent *me* to scout ahead," said Monte Nance. "It's always
that damn Indian."

"Damn Indian no like you," Goose said, his dark eyes
on Monte.

"That's enough," said McCaleb. "Goose is our scout,
because he's better at it than any of the rest of us."

*Near the present-day town of Sussex, Wyoming

That might have ended it, if Penelope hadn't laughed. Her eyes sparkled with mischief, and ignoring Rosalie's attempts to get her attention, she spoke.

"With Monte scouting, we'd all end up in Texas, or maybe Mexico."

"She's always talkin' down to me," Monte shouted. "She's never been taught respect for her elders."

"Monte Nance," Penelope said, "you're older than me, but you're not my elder. I can do anything on a horse you can do, and I can do it better. You swagger about with two guns, and I can outdraw you, myself."

"Penelope," said Rosalie, "that's more than enough. I forbid you to say another word."

Obeying her mother, Penelope said no more, but the damage had been done. With the exception of Monte Nance, the rest of the riders were grinning. The girl had just put into words what most of them suspected. Monte Nance turned several shades of red. Getting to his feet, he stomped off into the gathering darkness.

"Time for the first watch," McCaleb said. "Brazos, take Pen, Jed and Stoney with you. Penelope, if you aim to stand watch, take the first."

"That leaves you a mite short-handed on the second watch," said Brazos. "There's Will and Goose, and you don't know if you can depend on Monte or not."

"If he chooses not to ride with us, we'll manage without him," McCaleb said.

"He'll be there," said Rebecca. "He's my kin, and I'll talk some sense into him."

"No," McCaleb said. "He's counting on you standing up for him, whatever he does, and that's going to stop, beginning right now. When we reach Deadwood and sell the herd, I think we should decide whether or not Monte Nance is to remain part of Lone Star. The way I'm feeling now, I'd vote against it."

When the riders on the first watch had saddled their

horses and begun circling the herd, McCaleb sought out Rebecca.

"He's your only kin," said McCaleb, "and I know how you feel, but he'll never stand on his hind legs like a man as long as he's leaning on you."

"After he left us and took that sheriff's job in Miles City, I thought he had grown up," Rebecca said.*

"So did I," said McCaleb, "but I think we can agree that he's fallen far short of it."

"He needs a wife," Rebecca said, "but there's not a single woman within a hundred miles of our Lone Star range."

"Except Penelope," said McCaleb.

"My God," Rebecca cried, "do you think he . . . ?"

"I do," said McCaleb. "The more she taunts him, the more distant she seems, the more determined he'll be to have her."

"Bent, that must not happen," Rebecca said. "Brazos would kill him."

"Only if he gets to Monte ahead of me," said McCaleb.

"I'm going to talk to him," Rebecca said. "Perhaps I can quiet him down until we reach Deadwood and dispose of the herd."

McCaleb sighed. "Go ahead, but don't make it easy for him. He should know that once we reach Deadwood, the outfit will decide whether he stays or goes, and how he conducts himself between now and then will have considerable to do with the decision."

"I'll tell him," said Rebecca. "I don't believe he wants to leave us. Even the Prodigal Son learned his lesson."

"Good luck," McCaleb said. "I hope your patience and confidence is rewarded. Now I'll have to get some sleep, if I'm going to. The second watch isn't that far off."

On the first watch, Penelope was having her problems. Despite all her efforts to avoid Brazos, he seemed to be

*The Western Trail (Trail Drive #2)

following her. When she reined up to rest her horse, Brazos was there. Finally—exasperated—she wheeled her horse to face him.

"You've been following me ever since the start of the first watch," said Penelope. "You don't trust me, do you?"

"Not entirely," Brazos said. "Monte Nance is hunkered out here somewhere."

"You don't think that I would—"

"For the moment, I'm not going to answer that," said Brazos. "Instead, I'm going to tell you the story of an *hombre* and a woman who seemed to hate one another even more than you and Monte. His name is Benton McCaleb, and hers was Rebecca Nance."

"I don't know if I can believe that," Penelope said.

"Sometime when McCaleb's not around, ask Rebecca," said Brazos. "When Will, Bent and me first rode into the Trinity River brakes to rope wild longhorns, old York Nance—daddy to Monte and Rebecca—was making and selling whiskey to the Comanches. First time we laid eyes on Monte, he pulled a gun on Bent and McCaleb wounded him. Rebecca came on the run, and they had the damnedest, knock-down-and-drag-out fight you ever saw, right on the bank of the Trinity River. McCaleb hoisted her up, kicking and screaming all the while, and threw her into the river."*

"Oh," Penelope said, "that must have been *something*."

"It was," said Brazos, "but it was only the start. McCaleb and Rebecca fought all the time. Even after the Comanches killed old York Nance, and the only hope Rebecca and Monte had was to join our trail drive with Goodnight."

"I hope that's the truth," Penelope said, "because I'm going to ask Rebecca."

"Do that," said Brazos. "It's gospel. Then you'll know why you and Monte hating each other makes me so nervous."

The Goodnight Trail (Trail Drive #1)

They mounted their horses and again began circling the
herd, unaware that Monte had been crouched only a few
feet away, listening to their talk . . .

When the second watch began at midnight, Monte Nance
was there. Saying nothing, he saddled his horse, riding out
with McCaleb, Will and Goose. Nobody spoke to him during the watch except Rebecca. McCaleb, Will and Goose
carefully avoided them, and not until the following morning
before breakfast did McCaleb get a chance to talk to Rebecca.

"I talked to him, Bent," said Rebecca, "and I just don't
know *why* he's like he is. He's envious of Goose, because
of your trust in him, and I think he really and truly hates
Penelope. I told him, unless he mends his ways between
here and Deadwood, he'll be voted out of our Lone Star
outfit."

"I hope you also warned him about messing with Penelope," McCaleb said. "He ought to know that Brazos
will kill him, and that if Brazos fails to, then I will."

"I told him that, in almost your exact words," said Rebecca, "and he laughed. He said he wouldn't do anything
to Penelope she didn't want done, and that he's not afraid
of you or Brazos."

"Damn," McCaleb said.

"This is his last chance," said Rebecca, "so don't hesitate to do what you must. Not on my account, anyway.
Once, while we were in Texas, I caught him with a naked
squaw. He said some things to me then that I've forgiven,
but I've never forgotten. He still has a lot of growing up
to do, and God only knows if he's capable of it."

5

YELLOWSTONE RIVER, MONTANA TERRITORY.
MARCH 26, 1876

"Storm buildin'," Mac Withers predicted.

"Yes," said Cal, "and it looks like we'll have to make the best of it right here."

Nobody said anything, for they all well understood the reason for their prolonged stay at the Yellowstone. While Bud McDaniels was conscious and much improved, he still was in no condition to travel, according to Oscar Fentress.

"I reckon we'd better start snakin' in some logs for firewood," Tom Allen said.

"Good thinking," said Cal. "That storm may get here sooner than we expect."

"I'll need some help," Tom said. "Arch, Hitch and Mac?"

The trio joined him, and the four went to saddle their horses.

"I'm sorry we've been delayed here so long," said Jasmine.

"No fault of yours," Cal said. "I just hope that when Bud comes to his senses, he won't be so unreasonable and hard to get along with. When you figure he's able, will you talk to him?"

"Yes," said Jasmine. "I'm tired of him playing off me because I'm his sister. He needs to know that he's alive because of Quickenpaugh's concern and fast thinking."

"If there's any hope for him, that will make a difference," Cal said. "Do you suppose Curley's feelings toward him have changed?"

"Curley's very forgiving," said Jasmine, "but most of their problems have been Bud's fault. He has a chance to win Curley back, but only if he comes out of this changed and repentant. One more foolish move, and they're finished."

Tom Allen and his companions snaked in their first load of wood. Cal took an axe and began chopping a log down to firewood size. He was quickly joined by Oscar Fentress, Smokey Ellison and Quanah Taylor.

"I'll spell one of you, when you're tired," said Bill Petty.

By noon, the heavy gray clouds had begun rolling in. The riders had already staked down the canvas the outfit had been using for windbreaks, and there was a growing pile of firewood. Quickenpaugh watched all the activity with amusement, considering it "squaw work" and considerably beneath his dignity. Jasmine went to the chuck wagon to see how Bud was faring, and found him awake. He had twisted himself around so that he was able to see out the rear of the wagon.

"How do you feel?" Jasmine asked.

"Like I've had a hundred branding irons slapped on my behind," said McDaniels. "What have you done to me?"

"We tried everything we knew," Jasmine said, "but we couldn't get rid of the poison. If it hadn't been for Quickenpaugh cauterizing your wound with fire, you'd be dead."

When the implication of what Jasmine had just said got through to McDaniels, he let his head drop, burying his face in his arms. When he finally looked her in the eyes and spoke, Jasmine was amazed at what he had to say.

"This is goin' to take some getting used to. He had every reason to want me dead, and now I owe him my life. What'n thunder am I goin' to do?"

"That's entirely up to you," said Jasmine, "but I think

you ought to shake his hand and treat him like a brother, if he'll allow it.''

"I must have been out of my head," Bud said. "Once I . . . I thought Curley was here."

"Curley was, from the time Quickenpaugh finished with you until we were sure you were going to live," said Jasmine.

"God knows I don't deserve her," Bud said.

"No," said Jasmine bluntly, "you don't. Curley's very forgiving, but she's human, and doesn't like being hurt. Any more of your abuse and cursing, and she'll wash her hands of you forever. And so will I."

"I'll talk to Curley and Quickenpaugh," Bud said, "but not lying on my belly like some kind of lizard, with my behind bare. I want to get on my feet. Where are we?"

"Still at the Yellowstone," said Jasmine. "Cal didn't believe you should be moved."

"Well, hell," Bud growled, "and I've bitched the longest and loudest about this trail drive taking so long."

"You have," said Jasmine, "and I'd suggest you not say anything more about it."

"I hear all the axes goin'," Bud said. "Is there a storm coming?"

"Yes," said Jasmine. "Everybody's snaking in and cutting wood. I think before night, you'll have to leave the wagon and come to one of the fires. The wind's getting colder all the time."

"Then help me get my boots on," Bud said. "I reckon I'll have to cover myself with a blanket, but at least I can walk like a man."

It was difficult, belly-down, turning himself around in the narrow confines of the chuck wagon, but McDaniels managed it. Getting his boots on was next to impossible, but Jasmine struggled with them until the task was done.

"Before you join the rest of us at the fire," said Jasmine, "you ought to mend a few fences, if you can."

"Oh, God," Bud groaned. "Where do I start?"

"With Curley," said Jasmine. "How you treat her, and whether or not she believes you, will make you or break you with the outfit. Do you want to talk to her now?"

"Yeah," Bud said, "but how do I tell her that I . . . I'm sorry?"

"Don't get fancy," said Jasmine. "Tell her you've been a damn fool, and ask her to forgive you."

McDaniels sighed, and Jasmine went in search of Curley.

"I don't know," Curley said. "You think he means it?"

"I believe he does," said Jasmine. "It's just that he feels sheepish, just as he damn well should. Don't make it easy for him. Make him say the words."

Curley was gone almost an hour, and when she returned to the fire, the change in her was nothing less than remarkable.

"Well," said Jasmine, "I reckon he said some of the right things."

"He did," Curley said. "Lying on his belly, he stood tall, like a man should. He wants to see Quickenpaugh, if Quickenpaugh will come."

Hearing his name, Quickenpaugh stood up.

"Quickenpaugh," said Curley, "Bud wants to see you."

The Indian said nothing, and his expressionless face told them nothing. They had every reason to believe he was going to refuse, when Quickenpaugh spoke to Curley.

"Why?"

"He knows you saved his life, and he wants to thank you," Curley said.

"Quickenpaugh no want thank-you."

"Quickenpaugh," said Jasmine, "we're forcing Bud to become a man, to try and make something of himself. Will you go?"

Quickenpaugh nodded and started for the wagon. Jasmine waited until he had reached the rear of it, and then hurried to the front of the canvas-topped wagon. Bud McDaniels had his work cut out for him, for Quickenpaugh wasn't interested in making friends with McDaniels. He said nothing, waiting for Bud to speak.

"Quickenpaugh," said Bud, "I'm sorry I've been such a . . . a . . ."

"*Bastardo,*" Quickenpaugh finished.

"Yeah," said Bud. "That, and worse. Can't we be *amigos?*"

"*Muchos mañanas,*" Quickenpaugh said.*

Ignoring Bud's extended hand, the Indian walked away. When he had gone, Jasmine took his place behind the wagon.

"Damn him," said Bud, "I tried, but he wouldn't have it."

"He didn't turn you down," Jasmine said. "He'll wait and watch you, because he's had more than enough of your words. You'll have to prove yourself."

"I can't read his mind," said Bud. "How can I become his friend?"

"You'll find a way," Jasmine said, "and when the time comes, you'll know."

A cold northwest wind whipped the wagon canvas.

"I think it's time for me to get out of here and go to the fire," said Bud.

"Come on, then," Jasmine said, "and I'll help you as much as I can. You may be weak in the knees."

McDaniels slid off the wagon's tailgate, using it to support himself. Jasmine removed two blankets from the wagon, draping them around Bud so that he could hold them in place. He took one short step, and would have fallen if Jasmine hadn't caught him.

"Stay here by the wagon," said Jasmine, "while I get some help. You're too much for me."

Already there was a flurry of windblown snow, and Tom Allen had just snaked in a new load of wood.

"Tom," Jasmine said, "Bud's wanting to get to the fire,

*Many tomorrows

but his legs are weak. He's too heavy for just me. Will you help?''

"Better than that," said Tom, "I'll get Cal to help me, and you stay out of it. You're a married woman, and you have no business fooling around with another man who's all of thirty and jaybird naked.''

"Bud's my brother," Jasmine snapped. "How can you make something of that?''

"You've been wiping his nose for all the years I've known you," said Tom, "and I'm just not completely sure how far you'd go to please him. Now pour yourself some coffee and set down by the fire.''

Furious, Jasmine bit her tongue, holding back the angry words that might well become a wedge between her and Tom. She watched as he spoke to Cal and the two of them went to the chuck wagon. With both of them supporting Bud McDaniels, he was able to walk to one of the fires. Quickenpaugh ignored Bud, looking into the fire and seeing nothing. By early afternoon, the day had become as night, with dirty gray clouds stretching from horizon to horizon. Tom Allen had moved the chuck wagon beyond the fires, so its bulk and canvas might serve as a wind- and snow-break.

BISMARCK, DAKOTA TERRITORY.
APRIL 2, 1876

The tent flap fluttered wildly in the wind as Major Marcus Reno and Captain Frederick Benteen stepped into the tent that had become the Seventh Cavalry's headquarters. Smartly they saluted their commander, General George A. Custer.

"At ease, men," said Custer, returning the salute. "I have received unofficial word that there will be a comprehensive campaign against the Sioux within the next sixty days. Our regiment will be detailed to the column under Commanding General Alfred H. Terry. We'll be marching from Bismarck to the Yellowstone, and as far west as we must, to engage the enemy.''

''About time, sir,'' said Captain Benteen. ''The men are weary of close-order drill seven days a week.''

''Let them get used to it,'' Custer snapped. ''Until we are ordered to march north, you and your men may expect close-order drill twice daily. Dismissed.''

The officers were well away from the tent when Benteen spoke.

''That's just too damned much drill, with knee-deep snow and freezing wind. The men are going to hate his guts.''

Major Reno laughed. ''You think he cares? He thinks of us all as means to an end, and he'd sacrifice us, to the last man, for another star.''

ALONG THE POWDER RIVER, WYOMING TERRITORY.
APRIL 2, 1876

''Thank God,'' said McCaleb, when the blowing snow ceased.

''That's the good news,'' Brazos said. ''The bad news is that, even if we didn't have the chuck wagon, the snow's so deep, the horses and cows couldn't make it. We may be here a week before the sun melts it and sucks up enough of it for us to move on.''

''Unless it warms up almighty fast,'' said Will, ''we'll have to break trail for our horses and go looking for more firewood. Three fires swallow it up mighty quick.''

''By tomorrow, we'll know if it will warm up anytime soon,'' McCaleb said. ''If we need more wood, we'll just have to find it and drag it in.''

As she often did, Penelope took a basin of hot water to the chuck wagon, so that she might have privacy for bathing. Inside, she closed the canvas pucker so that nobody could see inside. There was barely room for her, and with supplies piled high all the way to the wagon box, she was unable to close the canvas pucker at the front. Quickly she removed her coat and gloves, then her boots, Levi's and woolen shirt. The water had already begun to cool. Naked, her teeth chattering, she hurried her bath. Suddenly some of the things at the front of the wagon shifted, and a heavy tin of Winchester shells fell, striking her bare foot.

"Who's there?" Penelope cried.

Nobody answered, and Penelope felt her injured foot. It was numb, and she had no idea how badly it was hurt. Hurriedly, she got into her shirt and Levi's, before attempting to get her boots on. To her dismay, she could feel the foot beginning to swell, and was unable to flex it enough to get the boot on. She donned her heavy coat and gloves, and, in her bare feet, untied the canvas pucker at the rear of the wagon.

"Help me," the girl cried. "Somebody help me."

While the snow had ceased, the wind had not, and it snatched away her frantic cries for help. But there was a spare Winchester—fully loaded—in the chuck wagon. Penelope pointed its muzzle through the wagon's pucker and fired three times. McCaleb and Brazos came on the run, but Goose was there ahead of them.

"Somebody was watching me through the front of the wagon," said Penelope. "A heavy tin of shells fell on my left foot, and I can't get my boot on."

"Just as well," Brazos said. "We'd have to cut the boot off. I'll tote you to the fire, and we'll get that foot into some hot water before the swelling gets any worse."

Understanding the situation, Goose had gone to the front of the wagon and was there when McCaleb joined him. Boot tracks led to the wagon from the south, while the tracks leading away were of a much longer stride.

"She's right," said McCaleb. "Somebody *was* watching her."

Goose was already following the tracks, and McCaleb hurried to catch up to him. The trail was clear enough in the deep snow, but a hundred yards south of the wagon, it led into a thicket along the east bank of the Powder. There they lost the trail, for the thicket and the riverbank had served as a snowbreak, and the bare ground was frozen so hard that tracks were out of the question.

"Damn it, he went *somewhere*," said McCaleb. "Let's follow the riverbank back to our camp and look for more tracks."

But there were no more tracks. While the snow had blown in and frozen to the water line on the river's east bank, there was virtually no accumulation along the upper bank.

"What did you find?" Rebecca asked anxiously, when McCaleb and Goose returned to camp.

"Tracks," said McCaleb, "but we lost them downriver, where there was very little snow on the riverbank, and the ground's frozen too hard for tracks."

"Then Penelope was right," Rebecca said. "Somebody *was* watching her, and I'm sorry to say, but I believe I know who it was."

"So do I," said McCaleb. "Where is he?"

They saw Monte Nance emerge from a thicket along the riverbank, well above where McCaleb and Goose had lost the trail.

"I heard shooting," Monte said. "Anything wrong?"

"Plenty," said McCaleb, "and you took long enough getting here to check it out. Where the hell have you been?"

"Squattin' in the bushes," Monte said, "and I wasn't in no position to hurry. You got reasons for doubtin' that?"

"A damn good reason," said McCaleb. "I aim to have another look at those tracks that lead away from the wagon."

"I'll go with you," Brazos said, for he too had seen Monte Nance approaching from the river.

"How's Penelope's foot?" McCaleb asked, as he and Brazos made their way through deep snow to the wagon.

"Rosalie's soaking it in hot water," said Brazos. "It

doesn't look broken, but it could be fractured. I want to get my hands on the yellow coyote that left those tracks.''

"That tin of shells falling on her foot was an accident,'' McCaleb said.

"I'm not denyin' that,'' said Brazos, "but the no-account varmint that was watchin' her was no accident.''

But the tracks told them nothing, for the snow was deep, and the edges of the tracks had crumbled. There was no identifiable footprint.

"Damn it,'' Brazos said, "somebody could have made them holes with a corral post.''

"There's no way we can prove anything,'' said McCaleb.

"Maybe not this time,'' Brazos said grimly, "but the next time one of our ladies takes a pan of water and heads for the wagon, I'll be watching.''

When they returned to the fires, Penelope had her foot in a pan of hot water, with a full pot heating on the coals.

"Did you learn anything?'' Rosalie asked anxiously.

"No,'' said Brazos. "Snow had caved into all the tracks, and there was no identifying any of the footprints. All we know for sure is that Penelope was right. Somebody *was* near the front of the wagon, watching her.''

Penelope glared at Monte Nance, and he grinned at her. It was an uneasy situation, all of them stranded because of deep snow, knowing there was one in their midst who could not be trusted.

"I hate this,'' Brazos said, "knowin' something needs doin', but not able to do it.''

"We can't be hasty, if only for Rebecca's sake,'' said Rosalie. "Right now, I'm far more concerned with Penelope's injured foot than I am Monte Nance watching her take a bath. There's no way any of us can be sure the tin of shells wouldn't have fallen on her foot whether Monte was there or not.''

"Now that you mention it,'' Brazos said, "that tin of shells should have been on the floor, or close to it. Because of the load shifting, heavy items are never loaded on top of lighter ones. Somebody's been moving things around.''

"I suppose you can blame Penelope for that," said Rosalie. "I told her she could use the wagon for bathing, as long as there was enough room. I suspect she piled everything a little higher to make a place for herself in the back of the wagon.''

Brazos sighed. "Then tell her no more baths in the chuck wagon, and tell her I've laid down the law. If she wants to argue with that, tell her real cowboys don't get baths until the end of the drive.''

Rosalie laughed. "Why don't *you* tell her?''

"You don't think I will, do you?''

"No,'' said Rosalie, "because it sounds like we're blaming her for the whole thing, and penalizing her so that it doesn't happen again.''

"We are,'' said Brazos. "She'll be nineteen by the time we reach Deadwood, and we'll not be able to watch her every minute. The best we can do is try to keep her out of any situation that might turn out like this one has.''

Rosalie laughed. "You just shot yourself in the foot while loading the gun. When some cowboy comes calling on her, are you going to always be there to see that she keeps her boots on and both feet on the floor?''

"I don't want her interested in men until she's thirty-six,'' said Brazos. "No cowboys, even then.''

"Like it or not, Penelope's a grown woman, old enough to have a child of her own,'' Rosalie said. "She can do what she wants, whether we like it or not.''

"Not on this trail drive, she can't,'' said Brazos. He crossed to the other fire, where Penelope sat soaking her foot, and knelt beside her.

"I don't envy you,'' said Rebecca, who had heard some of the conversation. "Which of them is causing you the most trouble?''

"Brazos,'' Rosalie said. "He's determined to protect her

from cowboys, and most of them are the salt of the earth.
Like that redheaded one over there talking to Penelope.''

ALONG THE YELLOWSTONE RIVER, MONTANA
TERRITORY.
APRIL 2, 1876

''Two or three more days, and we should be able to move
on,'' said Cal Snider.

''I'll be able to ride by then,'' Bud McDaniels said.

Bud's manner had changed dramatically, and with the
exception of Quickenpaugh, the outfit's attitude toward him
had changed accordingly. The Indian remained aloof,
watching, saying little. Cal sought out Quickenpaugh after
supper.

''Quickenpaugh, we may be here another two or three
days, but tomorrow I'd like for you to scout a few miles
ahead. Look for water, and for any sign of the Sioux.''

Quickenpaugh nodded, sipping his coffee.

Immediately after breakfast, Quickenpaugh rode east.

''Cal,'' said Bill Petty, ''after all this snow, every water
hole, creek and river in the territory will be bank-full, and
all the Sioux are likely gathered in the Dakotas.''

''I reckon,'' Cal said, ''but I keep remembering what we
learned from Beaver Tail and the Crows, about there being
soldiers who would try to keep us out of the Dakotas.''

''The army's always seemed a little high-handed, to
me,'' said Petty. ''I'm not forgetting they used all manner
of threats—including military arrest—to stop us from
bringing the Nelson Story herd up the Bozeman Trail.''*

''That's been strong on my mind,'' Cal said, ''and if it
comes to a standoff, we'll take this herd through just as
Mr. Story did.''

''I'm with you till hell freezes,'' said Tom Allen, who
had been listening.

*The Virginia City Trail (Trail Drive #7)

"We all be with you," Oscar Fentress said. "Mr. Story give us a chance to drive our own cows to market. We be more than just forty-and-found cowboys."

"Damn right," said Cal, "and we'll do it. I'm hoping that Quickenpaugh can keep track of where the soldiers are without them knowing about us. We'll avoid them, if we can."

"One thing we haven't considered," Tom said, "and that's Story's two hundred horses we're delivering to the military near Deadwood. These horses can't sprout wings and fly, and how is the army going to get them, if we don't drive 'em there?"

"Good point," said Cal, "and we might use that argument if we get boxed in. But I'm of a mind to just avoid any soldiers, if we can."

"We can always follow the Yellowstone to Miles City and then turn south," Tom said. "I have my doubts that this face-off between the soldiers and the Sioux will take place so far north."

"We're going to consider that, if that's what it takes to avoid the soldiers," said Cal. "Following the Yellowstone is not the shortest way, and I figure it would cost us at least four extra days, but that's better than a stand-off with the army."

Quickenpaugh was gone more than four hours, and when he returned, he had nothing to report.

"That's good news, up to a point," Cal said, "but we know damned well the Sioux are going to act, and that the military will react."

"There's always a chance that Beaver Tail lied to us about there being soldiers," said Tom. "That, or they're somewhere south of us."

"I believe Beaver Tail told the truth," Cal said. "Lying wouldn't have benefited him or the Crows in any way. All we can do is what we're doing. I'll send Quickenpaugh to scout thirty or forty miles ahead of the drive. If he finds there *are* soldiers, we'll have enough time to drive farther north, avoiding them."

The following morning—after several days of sun—Cal made the decision to continue the trail drive. Bud Mc-Daniels still had some healing to do and, since he wasn't ready for the saddle, volunteered to take the reins of the chuck wagon. He folded as many blankets as he could, attempting to soften the hard seat.

Jasmine, Lorna and Curley rode drag, while Arch, Hitch, Mac and Quickenpaugh came behind them with the horse herd and remuda. Behind the horses came Bud McDaniels with the chuck wagon. Cal was at point position, Tom Allen and Oscar Fentress were the swing riders, while Quanah Taylor and Bill Petty were the flankers. Watered and rested, the herd behaved well. At drag, Jasmine, Lorna and Curley took advantage of it, trotting their horses close to one another so they could talk.

"Nobody's said anything about it," said Lorna, "but all the cows and horses are getting very thin. The grass greens awful slow here in the high country."

"I'm sure Cal's been thinking about that," Jasmine said. "I know Tom has. He says we'll have to find some graze and fatten them some, before taking them to Deadwood."

"Well, I'm not gonna worry about it," said Curley. "Spring always comes, and there's always grass."

Lorna laughed. "You don't worry about anything, do you? Have you taken to warming Bud's blankets again?"

"No," said Curley, coloring. "He's making progress, but he still has to prove himself. I reckon I've encouraged him some, but I feel kinda like Quickenpaugh does. Bud's got to do something besides talk. I'm hoping I'll be able to trust him again, by the time we get the herd to Deadwood."

"I suppose it's just as well that you're waiting until we reach Deadwood," Jasmine said. "There's not much room for man-and-wife time, when your bed's a thin blanket on the cold ground and the rest of the outfit's all around you.''

Lorna laughed. "You're getting old, Jasmine. None of that bothered you on that long trail from Texas."*

"You nosey little snip," said Jasmine, "you were spying on me."

"Only when I couldn't sleep," Lorna said.

"Neither of you had it tough as I did," said Curley. "After I was shot, and Bud found out I wasn't a man, I had trouble going to the bushes without him following me."

The Montana sky remained clear and the sun unseasonably warm. The ground seemed solid enough, but the right rear wheel of the chuck wagon lurched into a deep hole, and the mules couldn't budge the wagon.

"Hey," Bud shouted, "I'm stuck." For emphasis, he fired a shot from his Colt.

Arch Rainey looked back, waved his hat to show that he understood and rode forward to stop the drive.

"I'm glad I'm not the only one having trouble seeing those holes," said Lorna.

*The Virginia City Trail (Trail Drive #7)

6

POWDER RIVER, WYOMING TERRITORY.
APRIL 3, 1876

"HEAD 'EM UP, MOVE 'em out," McCaleb shouted.

Again the herd took the trail. With McCaleb at point, Brazos and Will at swing, while Jed and Stoney Vandiver were the flank riders. Monte Nance and Pen Rhodes were riding drag, accompanied by Rebecca, Rosalie and Penelope. It was Susannah's day to take over the reins of the chuck wagon, and she kept as close behind the drag riders as she could. Goose rode behind the chuck wagon for a while, and then rode forward to join McCaleb at point. Suddenly, somewhere from within the herd, came an agonizing bellow. For some reason—or perhaps no reason—two steers had began hooking one another. The rest of the herd began to shift, giving them room. Pen Rhodes drew his Colt and fired once. They must halt the drive, in case one of the cantankerous animals drew enough blood to stampede the herd. Stoney Vandiver was near enough to see what was happening, and he held his hat high, warning of the need to head the leaders. Without question, McCaleb, Will and Brazos got ahead of the drive, but they were too late. The pair of steers had hurt one another to the extent that their companions could smell the blood, and all hell broke loose. There was frenzied bawling and clacking of horns, as the herd broke up in the middle, allowing the spooked cattle to run. They stampeded toward the east, and

(

none of the riders was in a position to head them. But Penelope kicked her horse into a fast gallop, trying to get ahead of the lead steers. Brazos and Rosalie could only watch in horrified silence, sighing with relief when she failed to get ahead of the herd. All the riders came together near the chuck wagon. One of the steers responsible for the stampede lay dead.

"Snowed in," said Will, "and now this."

"Yeah," Brazos said. "We're all gonna get old and die without ever going beyond the Powder River."

"Knock it off," said McCaleb. "This is not your first stampede. Will, you and Brazos skin that animal that was gored in the stampede. Penelope, give them a hand. The rest of us will go looking for the herd."

"I'll ride with the rest of you to find the herd," Penelope said. "Skinning animals is squaw work."

Goose grinned at her in appreciation of her insight.

"Damn it," said Rosalie, so only Brazos could hear, "she's going to become a female version of Goose."

Brazos laughed. "Between Goose and me, we'll make a real western woman of her."

"Goose," McCaleb said, "I want you to remain near the chuck wagon. If there's any sign of trouble, fire three shots and we'll come running."

Goose nodded. Brazos and Will set out to skin the gored steer, while the rest of the outfit rode out to look for the herd.

"That Penelope's slick as they come," said Will. "If skinning animals is squaw work, what does that make us?"

Brazos sighed. "I'd as soon not think about that. Let's just sympathize with the poor varmint that ends up with his boots under her bed. He'll have to skin his own kill and scrape his own hides."

"Maybe not," said Will. "I reckoned it would be the ruination of Wyoming Territory when women were allowed to vote, but I can't see that it's hurt us."*

*Women gained the right to vote in Wyoming Territory in 1869.

McCaleb led the rest of the outfit in search of the scattered herd.

"I can't see that they've slowed down much," Pen Rhodes said. "Normally, it ain't like a cow to run more than a mile or so before forgettin' all about the stampede and settlin' down to graze."

"Graze is almighty thin," said McCaleb. "The grass may not begin to green for another month. We may have one thing in our favor, though. I don't recall any rivers east of the Powder, so there's a chance it'll be the nearest water, when the herd gets thirsty."

"And the wind always blows out of the west," Penelope said.

After a little more than a mile, there were signs the stampede had run out of steam, for some cattle nipped at the little grass there was. They looked up, as though surprised to see the riders.

Jed Vandiver laughed. "Well, ain't they an innocent bunch. Turn it around, you horned varmints. We're goin' back."

"Leave 'em be," said McCaleb, "and we'll gather them on the way back. If we can find the rest of the herd, we might get them all back to the Powder before dark."

But that wasn't going to be the case. Storm clouds had begun to gather, and while it wasn't cold enough for snow, there was plenty of rain.

"Damn the luck," Monte Nance said. "With wind and rain at their backs, the varmints won't ever stop driftin'."

"You have *your* back to the wind and rain," said Penelope. "Just think like a cow, and we'll follow you."

"Penelope," Rosalie said sharply, "stop that."

But the rest of the outfit had heard Penelope's proposal, and even McCaleb had a hard time controlling his laughter. Monte Nance said nothing. Sneaking a look at Rebecca, Penelope found no condemnation there. As they rode on, the storm worsened.

"Even when we find 'em," said Stoney Vandiver, "we

won't be takin' 'em back toward the Powder until this storm lets up. One thing a cow just won't do is trail head-first into a storm.''

"I reckon we can forget about them drifting back to the Powder for water," McCaleb said. "I don't think I've ever seen it rain this hard.''

"If it don't let up and the weather turns colder, it'll be snow," said Pen Rhodes.

They had ridden two miles before finding a substantial part of the herd. As expected, the animals had their backs to the wind, drifting. They paused only for the little patches of new grass they found along the way.

"That's not more than half the herd," said McCaleb. "We might as well ride on, pickin' these up on the way back.''

"What bothers me," Rebecca said, "is that all the tracks have been rained out. There's no way of knowing that we're still following the herd.''

"It's bothering me," said McCaleb, "but we have to go with the obvious, until we know we're ridin' the wrong trail. For any reason, sometimes no reason at all, a stampeding herd will split. If that's what happened here, we'll find the rest of them somewhere to the north or to the south.''

"We could split up," Pen Rhodes said, "and cover all the possibilities.''

"We could," said McCaleb, "but we're not going to. We believe all the Sioux are in the Dakota Territory, but we don't *know* that for a fact. This is their old hunting grounds, and they'll be of a mind to scalp any or all of us, given a chance.''

"There's Susannah, alone with the chuck wagon," Rebecca said.

"But she's within sight of that steer Brazos and Will are skinning," said McCaleb. "If we don't find the rest of the herd pretty soon, we'll have to search north and south.''

But the storm continued, and it seemed the rain was becoming more intense. Back at the chuck wagon, Will and Brazos had been able to erect a shelter by securing two corners of a large canvas to the rear wagon bows, while anchoring the other two corners to a pair of poles driven into the ground. But the building of the shelter had interrupted their skinning of the dead steer, and they resumed that unpleasant task in the driving rain.

"First time I ever skinned anything in the rain," Will grunted.

"Yeah," said Brazos, "and I can think of lots of things I'd rather be doin'. Like settin' on my front porch, back on the Sweetwater, drinking hot coffee."

"At least we'll have that, thanks to us puttin' up that shelter," Will replied. "Plenty of dry wood in the wagon's possum belly."

McCaleb and the rest of the Lone Star riders soon came upon what had formerly been a dry creek. Now it was running bank-full, the rapid current moving pieces of branches, leaves and other debris. McCaleb urged his horse into the stream, and the animal crossed without difficulty. The other riders spurred their horses, and except for the one Monte Nance rode, they didn't hesitate. But Monte's horse, after surging forward with the others, balked. Startled, Monte Nance was thrown over the animal's head, landing belly-down in the muddy stream. Monte struggled to his feet and stood there cursing the horse, and it regarded him curiously.

"Monte," said Rebecca, "you were already soaked. Now shut up and get out of there."

Monte Nance climbed out, but he wasn't of a mind to let the troublesome horse off so easy. Drawing his right-hand Colt, he slammed the muzzle of it into the horse's head. The animal reared, nickering in pain. Monte was about to strike it again when a lariat snaked out and tightened about his upraised arm. Penelope had been on the other side of the fast-running stream. She had dallied the free end of the lariat around her saddle horn, and she back-stepped her horse. Monte Nance was jerked head-first back into the roiling water. Pen Rhodes had kicked his horse into a gallop back across the stream and was able to catch Monte's mount before the animal ran away. When Monte came up the second time, crawling out of the stream, he devoted all his choice words to Penelope. Both McCaleb and Rebecca had dismounted, but Rosalie reached Monte first. She slapped Monte so hard, the blow could be heard over the roar of the wind. For the third time in a matter of minutes, Monte Nance was flung into the muddy stream, the business end of Penelope's lariat still tight around his right wrist. When he finally climbed out, he found McCaleb waiting for him.

"If you ever hit another horse," McCaleb gritted, "I'll beat you within an inch of your miserable life. Now I want you to apologize to Penelope for the names you called her."

"I ain't apologizin' for *nothing*," said Monte, "and when I think of some more words, I'll throw *them* out there for her to chew on."

McCaleb had already seized a fistful of Monte's shirt, and would have landed a right-handed smashing blow, but Penelope cried out.

"Do you know what you're doing, girl?" McCaleb demanded. "He was about to get off light. Brazos will kill him."

"Not if he doesn't know," said Penelope, "and you're not going to tell him."

"Penelope—" Rosalie began.

"No," said Penelope. "We should be looking for the rest of our herd, not fighting with each other. As for you," she said, turning on Monte Nance, "don't you ever speak to me again, and if I ever again see you hurting a horse, I won't use a rope. I'll shoot you right between the eyes."

They mounted their horses and went on, Monte following at a distance. When McCaleb reined up, the rest of the riders reined up near enough to hear what he had to say.

"We're not far from dark," McCaleb said. "It'll be

comin' early. We'd better gather as much of the herd as
we can and start them back toward the Powder. They'll be
ornery as hell, driving them into the storm.''

It seemed McCaleb had understated the problem, for the
cattle wanted to go anywhere except headlong into the
wind-driven rain. They broke away, sometimes in bunches
of a dozen or more, galloping back the way they had come.
Time after time, the weary riders headed them, turning
them back, only to face another group of deserters. Rebecca's horse slipped, stumbled and threw her belly-down
in the mud. Only Monte Nance laughed. When they came
within sight of the chuck wagon, they could see the welcome glow of a fire, even through the driving rain. Seeing
the herd coming, Brazos and Will mounted their horses and
rode to help their comrades.

"Susannah's got hot coffee ready," Brazos said. "Will
and me have had ours."

"We'll have to go a few at a time," said McCaleb.
"This bunch has been givin' us hell every step of the way.
Go ahead, Pen, Rebecca, Rosalie and Penelope, and have
some hot coffee. The rest of us will keep the herd from
drifting."

"Lord, I never knew hot coffee could taste so good,"
Rebecca said, as she stood under the protective canvas.

"You have Brazos and Will to thank for the shelter and
the coffee," said Susannah. "They got the shelter up just
in time, and then had to skin out that steer after the storm
began."

The rain continued, and the ground became a quagmire.
Their only sanctuary—the canvas stretched behind the
wagon—they owed to Susannah, for she had wisely moved
the chuck wagon to the highest ground she could find.
McCaleb and the rest of the riders were having a time with
the herd, for the animals only wanted to drift with the
storm.

"We have a problem," Brazos half shouted, so that
McCaleb could hear. "Long as this storm's blowing, it's

gonna take all of us to keep this bunch from drifting. We just don't have enough riders to go after the others."

"I'll have to agree with you," said McCaleb, "and that means it may take us a week to find the rest of them. Long as the storm's blowing, they'll keep drifting."

Without a dry place to spread their blankets, the outfit chose to remain in the saddle, taking turns visiting their meager shelter for hot coffee during the night. The storm didn't subside until an hour before first light.

"Load up on grub and hot coffee," McCaleb said. "We're goin' after the rest of the herd."

"Damn it, McCaleb, we've been in saddle all night," said Monte Nance.

"I'm aware of that," McCaleb said, "and I reckon I can promise you another day of the same. This is a trail drive, and there's work to be done. Susannah, Rosalie and Rebecca, I want all of you to remain here with the wagon. Goose will stay here with you."

"I think Penelope should stay here with the wagon too," said Brazos.

"Well, I'm not going to," Penelope said. "You need riders, and there's not a man of you who can do anything in the saddle with a rope that I can't do."

"I can't argue with that," said McCaleb.

Brazos shrugged his shoulders, but there was a twinkle in Rosalie's eyes. Breakfast over and done, the riders rode out, Penelope with them. Rather than covering the same ground as the day before, and since they had no tracks to follow, they rode to the southeast.

"It's hard to tell how far they've drifted," Will said.

"Yes," said McCaleb, "and for that reason, we have no idea how far we may have to ride. We'll have to ride maybe thirty miles this way, and if we don't find them, we'll have to take a similar ride to the north."

"You're some trail boss, McCaleb," Monte Nance said.

"If you have any better ideas for finding the herd, I'll listen," said McCaleb.

"Go ahead," Penelope taunted. "Just ride along calling *sooooo cow, sooooo cow*, until all of them are following you. The rest of us will ride back to the wagon for coffee while you're gone."

Most of the outfit laughed at Monte's expense, for his face flamed crimson. He bit his tongue and said nothing, because McCaleb and Brazos were watching him. Without further discussion, McCaleb led out, and the others followed. They rode on in silence, and when McCaleb judged they had traveled thirty miles, he reined up.

"Not a cow in sight," said Brazos. "I reckon it's north from here."

"One problem with that," Will said. "There's a chance they've drifted farther than we think, and if we change direction now, we'll never find them."

"That's true," said McCaleb, "but we're running out of choices. We'll give it another ten miles before we begin our swing to the north."

"I'll feel better if we do," Will said.

"Trouble is," said McCaleb, "we're gettin' so far away, we couldn't hear a warning shot from Pen or Goose. I only hope Pen, Rebecca, Rosalie and Susannah can hold those cows we rounded up yesterday."

"They should be able to," Will said, "with the storm over and done."

BOULDER RIVER, MONTANA TERRITORY.
APRIL 7, 1876

Quickly, Arch Rainey and Mac Withers harnessed two teams of horses, and with their added strength, freed the bogged-down chuck wagon. Bud McDaniels said nothing, waiting for them to finish. Cal and the rest of the riders were watching for the signal to move out the herd, and Mac Withers waved his hat.

"Move 'em out," Cal shouted.

Again the herd took the trail. The horse wranglers—

Arch, Hitch, Mac and Quickenpaugh—kept the horses bunched and were right at the heels of the drag riders. As before, Bud kept pace with the chuck wagon. The drive continued without difficulty, and with the sun an hour high, they reached the west bank of a fast-flowing stream. There Cal signaled the flank and swing riders. Together, they headed the lead steers, milling the herd. It was here they would spend the night.

"This has to be Boulder River," said Cal. "I think we'd better cross the cattle and the horses before dark. Come tomorrow morning, they'd have the rising sun in their eyes and would likely balk. We'll take the cattle and horses across first, and then the chuck wagon."

The river wasn't as wide or deep as the Yellowstone, allowing the riders to cross the cattle and horses quickly. While Cal didn't have a lot of confidence in Bud McDaniels, he did manage to get the chuck wagon across before sundown.

EASTERN MONTANA TERRITORY.
APRIL 10, 1876

George A. Custer's regiment had been detailed to the column under the commanding general, Alfred H. Terry. Custer, ever impatient, entered the tent of Commanding General Terry and saluted. Terry returned Custer's salute, and then he spoke.

"Now, Mr. Custer, what is it?"

"Sir," said Custer, "this is an unusually slow march. We're scarcely averaging ten miles a day. I could take some of my men and, going ahead, locate the enemy."

"Perhaps you could," Terry said, "but you aren't going to. At least not yet. I have my orders. We're not to attack the Sioux while there's still a possibility of heavy snow. As you should be aware, the Big Horn Mountains were once part of the Sioux hunting ground. They know those mountains, where we do not. Let them dig in there—es-

pecially before or after a heavy snow—and the entire
United States Army couldn't root them out. We are to follow the Yellowstone until we reach the mouth of the Rosebud, sometime in late May or early June. That's all you
need to know at this time. Dismissed.''

Custer saluted and left the tent, satisfied he had learned
a little more about the forthcoming campaign against the
Sioux. It had been a calculated risk, questioning Terry, and
he might well have been reprimanded for appearing to
usurp his superior officer's authority. While he had always
been brash and unpredictable, he had been a good soldier,
and he had counted on Terry taking that into account.

DEADWOOD, DAKOTA TERRITORY.
APRIL 10, 1876

Milo Reems had a history of lying, cheating and killing.
Employing whatever scheming and skullduggery might be
necessary, he lived by the sweat of other men's brows. The
law had been after him in Missouri, New Mexico and Kansas, so he had wasted no time getting to lawless Deadwood.
There he began looking for a way of making his fortune
without resorting to a pick and shovel. He had spent much
time in the saloons, listening to miners complain about the
primitive town, the high prices and the hardships.

"By God," growled one bearded man, "I'd give fifty
dollars for a good, thick steak."

His comrades agreed, shouting and stomping their feet.
As more miners arrived, and prices went steadily higher,
there were more demonstrations, with men demanding beef.
After one such demonstration, Reems pounded on the bar
with an empty bottle, getting the attention of every man in
the saloon.

"I'm a speculator," Reems said. "Whatever you want,
I can deliver, if the price is right and the money's on the
table. What can I expect if I bring a substantial number of
beef cattle to Deadwood?"

"Fifty dollars a head," a miner shouted.

"Sixty," another countered.

"Quiet," Reems shouted. "There'll be enough for everybody. I've contracted with two ranchers—one in Wyoming, the other in Montana—for eight thousand head of prime beef on the hoof. I have telegrams from them, provin' what I say."

"When are they comin'?" a miner shouted.

"They're on the way now," said Reems. "They should be here sometime in June. If I let 'em go at sixty dollars a head and write you a receipt, who wants to buy in advance? By the time the herds arrive, there'll be even more miners, and the price may go up."

The men pushed and shoved, each trying to be first. The owner of a local cafe bought a hundred head, the owner of the newly established livery bought twice that number, in addition to those sold to individual miners. Milo Reems left the saloon with almost sixty thousand dollars either pledged or collected. After allowing time for the word to spread, he repeated his success in other saloons.

"Have a drink on me, Reems," a miner invited.

"I'm buyin' supper," said another.

Milo Reems rarely paid for food and drink, and he grew more popular by the day, as more and more miners invested in his scheme.

"How many's left, Milo?" somebody asked.

"A little over four thousand," said Reems. "Buy some extra. When my herds are sold, you can double your money."

Many miners did buy more, for the territory was growing by leaps and bounds, and men had to eat. One newly arrived miner had brought a newspaper from Cheyenne, and it was passed around for all to read.

"Anything interesting in there?" Reems asked a bartender who had just finished with it.

"Yeah," said the barkeep. "Wild Bill Hickok's gettin' together an expedition and comin' to Deadwood. He was the law at Abilene and Wichita, and there's talk he might be drafted here. God knows, we need *somebody*."

Milo Reems said nothing. The very last thing he needed or wanted was a lawman of Hickok's caliber walking the streets of Deadwood. He redoubled his efforts to sell the rest of the eight thousand head before somebody took a close look at his past.

SOUTHERN MONTANA TERRITORY.
APRIL 15, 1876

To the relief of the entire outfit, Bud McDaniels had healed to the extent that he could again straddle a horse. Jasmine, Lorna and Curley again took turns at the reins of the chuck wagon. Two days after leaving Boulder River, gray clouds began gathering along the western horizon.

"Somethin' comin'," Tom Allen predicted. "Warm as it is, can't be anything but rain."

"Maybe we can find some high ground and rig some shelter with the canvas that we have," said Cal. "We'll go on for as long as we can. If there's enough mud, the chuck wagon won't be goin' anywhere for a while."

But the storm blew in sooner than expected, and while there was no rain, there was an abundance of thunder and lightning. The riders fought to keep the herd bunched, to keep them moving. Even Story's horses became skittish, and the four wranglers rode like madmen to head them. The chuck wagon rattled over the uneven terrain, as Jasmine strove to keep up with the drive. The remains of a tall pine, standing gray and dead, became victim to a bolt of lightning, and the trunk exploded in a ball of fire. The cattle and horses had already passed beyond it, but the mules pulling the chuck wagon went crazy. They wheeled, almost overturning the wagon, as they lit out back the way they had come. Quickenpaugh, one of the horse wranglers, looked back. Wheeling his horse, the Indian galloped after the chuck wagon with its stampeding mules. Jasmine fought the reins, but the mules had been terrified. They thundered on, the wagon listing dangerously to one side and then the other. Quickenpaugh leaned low on the horse's neck, speaking to the animal. A few more minutes, and he would catch the runaway teams. But time ran out. The right front wagon wheel slammed into an upthrust of stone. The wagon went over on its left side, and then onto its top. It was more of a burden than the frightened mules could handle, and they stood there in harness, shaking with fear. Quickenpaugh saw no sign of Jasmine, and, deciding she was beneath the wagon, he dismounted and threw all his strength against one of the rear wheels. But the wagon didn't move, and Quickenpaugh looped one end of his lariat around a rear wheel. There was a frantic cry from beneath the wagon, and the Indian had second thoughts. If he dragged the wagon and Jasmine was beneath it, wouldn't it kill the girl? Again she cried out. Quickenpaugh leaped off his horse and went to the smashed front of the wagon. The wagon box had survived intact, and behind it he could see the toe of Jasmine's boot. The wagon's load had shifted, and while Jasmine had not been pitched out of it, much of its contents had fallen on her. Quickenpaugh began moving the goods that had trapped Jasmine, until finally he could see her bloody face.

"Quickenpaugh," Jasmine cried. "Thank God."

The rest of the outfit finally headed the cattle and horse herd, allowing Tom Allen and Cal to come on the run. Lorna and Curley were already there, uncertain as to how they might help. But Quickenpaugh had done much toward freeing Jasmine, and with a mighty heave, he shoved a large flour barrel away from her, allowing her to move.

"Jasmine," Tom cried, "are you all right?"

"No," said Jasmine. "I think my right leg's broken."

"We'd better take her out through the rear of the wagon, if we can," Cal said. "Looks like her legs are under the wagon seat."

"They are," said Jasmine, "and they just feel . . . dead."

Cal, Tom and Quickenpaugh began unloading the wagon from the rear. There still had not been any rain, and the thunder was only an occasional rumble. Lightning had ceased, except for occasional golden fingers that touched the gray clouds. When Jasmine was freed, there were several serious cuts on her head, accounting for the blood on her face. Quickly, Tom removed her boots, trying not to bend her legs.

"Which leg is broken?" Tom asked anxiously.

"My right one, I think," said Jasmine, "but both are hurting, so I'm not sure."

Quickenpaugh ran his hands along one leg and then the other.

"Which is it, Quickenpaugh?" Tom asked.

Quickenpaugh held up two fingers.

"Both?" Jasmine cried. "Oh, God, I might as well be dead."

"Hush," said Tom. "You're alive, and nobody's ever died from broken bones."

"Stay with her, Tom," Cal said. "Lorna, you and Curley get a fire going and heat some water. The rest of us will head the horse herd and the cattle this way."

7

ALESIA ALONG THE POWDER RIVER, WYOMING TERRITORY.
APRIL 15, 1876

"I RECKON YOU WERE right, Bent," said Will Elliot, after they had ridden almost forty miles. "The herd must have turned north or south. Even with wind and rain at their backs, I can't imagine them drifting this far in a straight line."

"There's not much use in our going any farther," McCaleb said. "We'll ride south a mile or two, and then west, back toward the Powder. Our only other possibility lies to the north."

"You're runnin' out of possibilities, McCaleb," said Monte. "What do you aim to do if we don't find 'em north or south?"

"We'll find them north or south," McCaleb said grimly. "That is, unless you reckon somebody's picked up fifteen hundred cows and put 'em in his pocket."

There was no more discussion, and McCaleb led the search to the south. Every water hole and stream had abundant water, and as they rode farther south, it seemed the grass improved.

"One thing we can be sure of," said Brazos, "the grass is greening considerably faster to the south. It's something even a cow can understand."

The outfit had ridden only a few miles, when they came upon the first of the grazing cattle. Three cows raised their heads for a moment. Then, ignoring the riders, they again began nipping at the new grass.

"We'll start with these," McCaleb said, "and hope we find the rest of them somewhere before we reach the Powder."

It soon became evident that the herd *had* moved to the south, apparently seeking better graze. Within two hours, McCaleb and the outfit had gathered an estimated nine hundred.

"Six hundred more, somewhere between here and the Powder," said Will. "Maybe we'll be able to gather them in time to take the trail tomorrow."

Penelope laughed. "You're forgetting about the mud."

"Oh, hell," said Will. "We got at least three days to gather the rest of the herd. I've about changed my mind about takin' a chuck wagon through unfamiliar territory. I'm just not sure it's worth all the hassle."

"It's worth the hassle, and then some," Brazos said. "It's the difference between decent grub and livin' on jerked beef and river water."

Conversation lagged, and they rode on.

"There's more cows ahead," said Penelope, pointing.

"Your eyes are better than mine," McCaleb said.

As they rode closer, the dark blur that McCaleb had seen became grazing cattle.

"There's near two hundred of 'em," said Brazos.

Quickly the newly discovered cattle became part of the gather, and the outfit rode on. Soon they were able to see other cattle, grazing in the distance.

"You were right, Bent," Will shouted. "There's the rest of 'em."

McCaleb looked at Monte Nance and grinned. Monte had nothing to say.

"Now," said McCaleb, when the newly discovered cattle had been added to the rapidly growing gather, "We'll run a quick tally, takin' the lowest count."

The riders spread out among the herd, counting. Penelope was the first to finish.

"Well?" Monte said. "What's your count?"

"I'm not telling until everybody's ready," said Penelope. "Besides, I wouldn't want to get in the way of your education."

"Ladies first," McCaleb said, when the tally had been finished. "Penelope?"

"Fifteen hundred and three," said Penelope.

"Brazos?" McCaleb said.

"Fifteen hundred and five," Brazos said.

"Will?" said McCaleb.

"Fifteen hundred and seven," Will said.

The rest of the riders called out their tallies, but Penelope's count remained the lowest of the lot.

"McCaleb, I can't believe you're taking *her* count," said Monte, with a put-on look of horror.

"Hers is the lowest tally," McCaleb said. "It's the way we've always done it, and I see no reason for giving it up now."

Triumphantly, the Lone Star outfit drove the newly gathered herd back to the Powder, where the entire drive was again joined together.

"That's all of them?" Rebecca asked.

"Fifteen hundred and three, by Penelope's count," said McCaleb. "There's considerably more graze to the south. We may have trouble with them wanting to return to it. Maybe we can manage with four riders during the day and four at night, until they settle down. Stoney, Jed and Pen, will you join me for a while?"

McCaleb and his three companions began circling the herd, and slowly it started to settle down.

"We may have one hell of a time holdin' 'em here, with so little graze," said Stoney.

"I know," McCaleb said. "After our watch is done, Goose and me will ride upriver. If we have to move the herd to greener grass to hold them, we will, even if it means leavin' the chuck wagon where it is.''

"That'll mean splittin' the outfit," said Pen Rhodes.

"Maybe no more than it would be split anyhow," McCaleb said. "With half of us on watch, the others can remain near the wagon. If it's too far to better graze, we might try moving the chuck wagon, keeping it to higher ground."

After McCaleb and his companions had circled the herd for four hours, Brazos, Will, Monte and Penelope took over. Goose sat on the wagon tongue, cleaning his Winchester.

"Goose," said McCaleb, "when you're done with that, I'd like for you to ride with me up the river a ways."

Goose nodded. Finished with the rifle, he saddled his horse. McCaleb had saddled a fresh horse, and the two of them galloped to the north, along the Powder. Having ridden almost three miles, Goose shook his head. The graze was going to become less, the farther north they rode.

"We might as well head back," said McCaleb. "We're wasting our time."

Before riding on to the wagon, McCaleb and Goose paused at the herd. Brazos, Will, Monte and Penelope trotted their horses, coming to hear what McCaleb had to say.

"Goose and me rode north maybe three miles," McCaleb said, "and the graze became less and less, the farther we rode."

"We won't be going much farther north," Brazos said. "When we reach that bend in the Powder where it forks, we'll be headed more to the northeast. Maybe the graze will improve."

"And maybe it won't," said Monte. "It's all your fault, McCaleb. You started this drive too damn early. There won't be decent grass for another month."

"I've heard about enough of that," McCaleb said. "We started this drive, and we'll see it to the end."

"Everybody's not perfect like you, Monte Nance," said Penelope.

McCaleb and Goose rode on to the chuck wagon, and McCaleb relayed the unwelcome news to the rest of the outfit.

"We got to move on," Stoney Vandiver said. "These cows can't take many more days of no grass."

"We're takin' the trail tomorrow, mud or not," said McCaleb. "If the chuck wagon bogs down, we'll hitch extra horses to it and drag it out. Does that suit all of you?"

"It suits me," Rebecca said.

"And me," Rosalie and Susannah said, in a single voice.

Pen Rhodes, and Jed and Stoney Vandiver quickly echoed the same sentiment. Goose only nodded.

"I think we'll have to reach the fork in the river within another two days," McCaleb said, "and then just pray the grass is greening faster toward the east."

SOUTHERN MONTANA TERRITORY.
APRIL 16, 1876

"I feel so completely useless," said Jasmine, as Cal and Tom carried her nearer to the fire. "My legs feel like they weigh a hundred pounds apiece."

"It's not easy to cut decent splints with only an axe," Tom said. "You'll just have to live with them until the bones knit."

"What about the wagon?" Jasmine asked. "Can it be fixed?"

"Bill Petty says it can," Cal said. "We did bring a few tools, including a hammer, a pry bar and a handsaw. There's nails too, and spare parts for front and rear wheels."

"I feel responsible for the wagon having been wrecked," said Jasmine. "I just didn't have the strength to control the teams. I suppose I'd better return to drag and let Lorna or Curley have the wagon."

"You're not going to do anything until we know for sure your legs are healed," Cal said. "Then you'll take your turn in the wagon. Until you're able, Curley or Lorna will be in charge of the wagon, and you'll be riding with them."

Lorna and Curley had supper in progress. Quickenpaugh knelt next to Jasmine, looking at her bulky, splinted legs.

"Quickenpaugh, thank you for coming to my rescue," said Jasmine.

The Indian seemed embarrassed, for he got to his feet and moved quickly away. None of the outfit seemed to have noticed, except Bud McDaniels, and when he spoke, there was a trace of his old arrogance.

"Was I old Tom, I wouldn't turn my back on that redskin. His interest in you goes a mite deeper than your busted legs."

"If I could get up, I'd claw your eyes out," Jasmine gritted. "Quickenpaugh's more of a gentleman than you'll ever be."

"Maybe I ain't a gentleman by your standards," said Bud, "but I'm a white man."

"No advantage, in your case," Jasmine said. "Now get away from me, or I'll call Tom and Cal."

Bud started to say something, but bit his tongue. A dozen yards away, Quickenpaugh was watching him.

Bill Petty and Smokey Ellison were both adept with their hands and skilled in the use of tools. The following day, using spare parts, they constructed a new right front wheel for the chuck wagon. They emptied a crate of goods within the wagon, using the wood to repair other damage. It was near suppertime when they finished, and Cal regarded their work with considerable appreciation.

"It's at least as strong as it was," said Petty.

"We done the best we could with what we had," Smokey added.

"I'm proud of you both," said Cal. "Let's hitch up the teams and move the wagon closer to camp."

There were cheers from the outfit as the chuck wagon approached. Cal went in search of Tom Allen.

"Tom," Cal said, "I have a decision to make, and I need your help."

"I'm flattered," said Tom, "but you're trail boss. None of us will go against you, 'cept maybe Bud."

"I know that, and I'm obliged," Cal replied, "but this has to do with Jasmine's condition and our need to move on. I reckon you've noticed the grass is greening late and the graze is gettin' almighty thin."

"I have," said Tom, "and we can't afford any more delays. Jasmine will understand, and she'll be ready to go when you are."

"Then we're movin' out in the morning at first light," Cal said. "I'll caution Lorna and Curley to keep to high ground as much as possible, and if the wagon gets stuck, we'll just have to harness a couple of teams of horses and haul it out. I want you to pad that wagon seat with as many blankets as you can, and wrap several around Jasmine's splinted legs."

"I will," said Tom, "and I appreciate your concern, but we must get the herd on into the Dakotas and on some decent graze. They're startin' to look like racks of bones, and so are the horses."

Cal announced his intentions to the outfit before supper. Bud McDaniels spoke up with the expected opposition.

"You don't care a damn for my sister's busted legs, do you? Bouncin' around on that wagon seat will be hard on her."

"Bud," said Tom, "Cal talked this over with me, and I've talked to Jasmine. We have to move on."

"Tom's right," Jasmine said. "Now back off and leave it alone."

The following morning, the wagon seat was padded with blankets and made comfortable as possible for Jasmine. Lorna would be at the reins.

"I'll be all right," said Jasmine, when Cal and Tom lifted her to the wagon seat.

"I'll avoid all the rough places I can," Lorna said.

Cal rode to the point position, and when he waved his hat, the riders started the cattle and horses moving. Lorna came behind the horse herd with the chuck wagon. The terrain was rough, and Lorna often fell behind, as she sought better ground over which the wagon could pass.

"Stop being so concerned about me, and keep up with the horse herd," said Jasmine.

"I'm in charge of this damn wagon," Lorna said, "and I aim to see that nothing else happens to you. Break those bones again, and you may end up sittin' on a folded blanket from now on."

After a favorable day on the trail, the outfit's spirits were high. The weather was fair, and there was new grass springing up all over. But all optimism and tranquillity vanished in a puff of gun smoke during the second watch. In the stillness of the night, a Colt roared. Not once, but four times, in quick succession.

"What the hell?" Tom Allen shouted.

But there was no time for questions or answers. The cattle were on their feet, off and running, the horse herd running with them. So unexpected had been the stampede, none of the riders were in a good position to head the spooked herd. Cal tried to get ahead of the leaders, with Tom Allen, Oscar Fentress and Smokey Ellison galloping close behind. They all reined up when it became obvious the cause was lost.

"Just let me get my hands on the idiot that fired those shots," said Cal.

"Speaking of idiots," Tom said, "where's Bud Mc-Daniels?"

"It's possible he might have been caught up in the stampede," said Smokey Ellison. "I reckon we'd better look for him."

They were about to backtrack when they heard a horse coming.

"Identify yourself," said Cal.

"Bud," came a voice from the darkness.

"Come on and step down," Cal said. "You've got some talkin' to do."

"Yeah," said Tom. "What'n hell came over you, shootin' four times, practically in the midst of the herd?"

"I saw somethin' in the brush," Bud said. "Maybe a cougar. I was afraid the varmint might stampede the herd."

"So you stampeded it yourself," said Cal.

"I didn't aim to," Bud shouted.

"That's a considerable comfort," said Tom, "now that the cattle and horses have been scattered to hell and gone."

The rest of the outfit—except for Jasmine—soon arrived on foot.

"What in thunder went wrong?" Quanah Taylor asked.

"Bud thought he saw something in the brush, and reckoned it might stampede the cow and horse herd," said Cal, with considerable sarcasm.

"I didn't hear any cattle or horses runnin' until he cut loose with his pistol," said Bill Petty.

"Neither did I," Lorna and Curley said, in a single voice.

Quickenpaugh had come with the others, and only he had nothing to say. Tom Allen sighed with exasperation, as though words failed him.

"Back to your blankets, all of you," said Cal. "We'll begin the gather at first light."

"With the herds gone," Bud said innocently, "why go on with the second watch?"

"Because I *said* to," Cal exploded, "and if I catch you so much as nodding, I'll stake you out belly-down and use a doubled lariat on your backside."

Nobody laughed. The riders who had been sleeping returned to their blankets, and but for Tom Allen, the second watch mounted their horses.

"I'd better take a few minutes to talk to Jasmine," said Tom. "She's bound to be awake and wondering what's happened."

"Go on," Cal said. "Before we start the gather in the morning, we're going to take a close look in the direction Bud was shooting. If we don't find some tracks, I may beat the hell out of him yet."

"You won't get any argument from Jasmine or me," said Tom.

Jasmine listened, while Tom told her as much as he knew about what had happened.

"I thought Bud was changing," Jasmine said. "Now I'm not so sure. Have you and Cal considered he might have fired those shots on purpose, to stampede the herd?"

"No," said Tom. "At least I haven't, and I doubt that Cal has. He aims to look around the place Bud was shooting, to see if there are any tracks. I hope there are, for the sake of your little brother."

"Oh, God," Jasmine groaned, "must you keep reminding me?"

Before breakfast, Cal and Quickenpaugh went to look for tracks in the direction Bud had fired his Colt. Cal could see nothing, but Quickenpaugh knelt for a closer look.

"*Oso*," said Quickenpaugh.

Cal followed Quickenpaugh's lead, and they soon could see the retreating tracks of the big grizzly. Quickenpaugh looked at Cal with some amusement. Lorna had followed them.

"Come on," Cal said. "We'll be late for breakfast."

Nobody had any questions regarding the tracks, and Cal volunteered nothing. Only when the outfit began saddling their horses did Cal speak.

"Lorna, I want you and Curley to stay here with Jasmine and the chuck wagon. Keep a Winchester handy, and one of you cut loose if there's so much as a hint of trouble."

While there was some risk for the women, nobody argued, realizing that Cal was in no mood for it. He rode out, taking the lead, the others following.

"I feel so sorry for Cal," Jasmine said. "I feel like he's going easy on Bud just for my benefit. I'm sick of Bud taking advantage of me, as well as the rest of you."

"I heard Quickenpaugh say they found bear tracks," said Lorna.

"Thank God for Quickenpaugh," said Jasmine. "At least Bud *thought* he saw something in the dark."

"It seems early in the year for grizzlies to be up and about," Curley said, "but I'm glad this one was for real, for Bud's sake."

"In a way, so am I," said Jasmine, "but for whatever reason, the cattle and horses are scattered God knows how far, and there'll be time lost gathering them."

There was more truth to that than Jasmine realized. While the riders soon began finding grazing cattle, there were no horses to be seen.

"Damn it," said Cal, "I'd sooner lose the cattle than Mr. Story's horse herd."

Quickenpaugh said nothing, but he well recalled Nelson Story assigning him responsibility for delivering the two hundred horses to the military in Dakota Territory. Finally, Quickenpaugh's patience was rewarded when Cal spoke to him.

"Quickenpaugh, we have to find those horses. Do you have any ideas?"

"*Si*," said Quickenpaugh. "Crow horse tracks. Crow take."

"I couldn't make heads or tails of all the horse tracks, but that's the best answer I've heard so far," Tom Allen said. "We've been following the tracks of our horses for a good twenty miles, and the critters haven't slowed down in the slightest. That tells me they're being driven."

"That means the Crows must have been watching, waiting for their chance," said Cal. "The stampede gave them the opportunity to take our horses without any risk to themselves. But how much farther can they go toward the east? If they go too far, they're likely to run headlong into a party of Sioux.''

Quickenpaugh shook his head, pointing north.

''He thinks they'll turn north,'' said Bill Petty, ''and he could be right. They have a six-hour start on us, and it's possible they aim to run fast enough and far enough to wear us and our horses down. Remember, we have no extra mounts. We're just damned lucky all of us had a horse close by last night.''

''It's up to you, Cal,'' Tom Allen said. ''Do we go ahead, following the tracks, or turn toward the northeast and try to head 'em off?''

''I think we'll ride toward the northeast,'' said Cal. ''Do any of you disagree?''

The eyes of every man were on Bud McDaniels, and he wisely said nothing. Mounting their horses, the outfit rode toward the northeast, Quickenpaugh in the lead.

THE FORK OF THE POWDER RIVER, WYOMING TERRITORY.
MAY 1, 1876

Having scouted ahead, Goose had just returned.

''Tomorrow we reach our last camp on the Powder,'' said McCaleb, after Goose had reported to him.

''No more for-sure water,'' Pen Rhodes said.

''In the morning, Goose will scout ahead of tomorrow's camp,'' said McCaleb. ''He'll be looking for water for our next camp, as well as Indian sign.''

''The couple of maps I've seen, I don't remember there bein' any rivers in Wyoming that are east of the Powder,'' Brazos said.

''There may not be,'' said McCaleb, ''but in this high country, there'll be some water, if only in springs and water holes.''

The mild weather continued, and they reached the fork

in the Powder barely ahead of a thunderstorm. The rain came at them in slashing gray sheets, riding a turbulent wind out of the northwest. There was no supper, and no time for any, for every rider was in the saddle, seeking to calm the herd. While there was no nearby lightning, thunder rumbled in the distance, and the herd became restless. The thunder eventually subsided, but the pouring rain continued until well past midnight. Mud was everywhere, and the horses slipped and slid with every step. Horses and riders were exhausted. McCaleb jogged his horse alongside Rebecca's.

"If there's dry wood in the wagon's possum belly," said McCaleb, "will you start a fire and boil us some coffee? Take Susannah, Rosalie or Penelope with you. We can handle the herd, with no wind, lightning or rain."

The heavy gray clouds had been swept away, and a half-moon added its pale light to that of the distant stars. Susannah was nearest, and Rebecca spoke to her. Fortunately, the chuck wagon had been taken to high ground, and within minutes, a cheery fire was going, and soon they could smell the welcome aroma of coffee.

"Come and get it," Rebecca shouted, "or we'll pour it in the river."

"Brazos, Will, Penelope and me will stay with the herd," said McCaleb. "The rest of you have some coffee."

The ground was a virtual sea of mud, and the riders chose to spend the rest of the night in the saddle, taking turns riding to the wagon for hot coffee. The following morning the sun rose in a clear sky, but the ground remained soggy, with standing water everywhere.

"Well," said Monte Nance, in his most infuriating manner, "look at all the mud. Is the mighty McCaleb goin' to kill another week, waitin' for it to dry up?"

"The mighty McCaleb's goin' to break your neck if you say just one more damn word," McCaleb gritted.

McCaleb made it a point to say nothing of his intentions until after breakfast. Before saying anything to the outfit, he spoke to Goose. The Indian mounted his horse and rode away to the east. Only then did McCaleb tell them what was on his mind.

"Goose is goin' to ride maybe forty miles," said McCaleb. "He'll be looking for Indian sign as well as water for the next several days. We'll consider moving out at first light tomorrow, depending on the condition of the ground and the availability of water."

"Hell, McCaleb, you're stalling," Monte said. "There's standing water everywhere."

McCaleb saw the pained expression in Rebecca's eyes and ignored the remark, but the slack was taken up by Penelope.

"Monte Nance, you're stupid," said Penelope. "When that big orange ball of fire's up there in the sky, it sucks up all the extra water."

"Penelope," Rosalie said wearily, "please don't argue. Apologize to Monte."

"I'm sorry you're stupid, Monte Nance," said Penelope.

Rosalie paled, while Brazos appeared to be overcome with a coughing fit. Monte Nance turned away, for Penelope had left him speechless. Without Rosalie seeing, McCaleb winked at Penelope. The rest of them kept a straight face, but Brazos was still hacking and coughing. Monte Nance had poured himself some coffee and was hunkered by the fire. He didn't look pleased when Rebecca knelt beside him.

"Monte," said Rebecca, "that remark to Bent was uncalled for. I'm ashamed of you."

"You've *always* been ashamed of me," Monte whined. "I don't like McCaleb, and damn it, you know why. The first time I met him, the bastard shot me."

"Only when you drew on him without cause," said Rebecca. "He could have easily shot you full of holes, instead of just getting a slug into your shoulder."*

The Goodnight Trail (Trail Drive #1)

"You'll never let me forget that, will you?" Monte shouted.

"No," Rebecca shouted back. "You swagger around with two guns, but you're no gunman. Others may not be as considerate as McCaleb. One day you'll draw on somebody, and you'll be shot dead."

"Then you won't have me to preach to," said Monte.

"I'm not preaching to you," Rebecca said. "Some men are headed for hell on greased skids, and no amount of preaching can save them. I'm only going to do one thing more for you. When the time comes, I'll see that you're put in a pine box and buried deep."

It had become a noisy exchange, and the rest of the outfit had no trouble hearing. One look at Rebecca's pale face and tragic eyes, and none of them laughed.

8

SOUTHEASTERN MONTANA TERRITORY.
MAY 2, 1876

FOLLOWING QUICKENPAUGH'S ADVICE, THE outfit gave up tracking the horses. Quickenpaugh in the lead, they rode northeast, a direction that would take them to the Yellowstone.

"I believe Quickenpaugh's thinking straight on this," said Tom Allen, as he rode next to Cal. "I just hope old Beaver Tail's not behind this. I kinda liked him."

"I doubt that he will be," Cal replied. "He wasn't with that bunch that took our horses before. We've been fortunate so far in that we've only had to deal with a few of them at a time. This bunch knows damn well we'll be coming after them, and I'm inclined to believe we'll be riding into a Crow village."

"I've heard they aren't all that hostile," said Tom.

"So have I," Cal replied, "but that could change when we go to take that two hundred head of horses they've stolen."

Eventually, Quickenpaugh reined up, raising his hand. The rest of the outfit reined up their horses, waiting for the Indian to speak.

"Crow," said Quickenpaugh. "I go see."

Without waiting for a response, Quickenpaugh rode away in the direction the outfit had been riding.

"Snider," Bud McDaniels said, "you put an almighty lot of confidence in that *hombre.*"

"Quickenpaugh's dead on center most of the time," said Cal quietly, "and he's never hurt us with his decisions. He's doing the sensible thing, as opposed to having the lot of us blunder into a Crow village."

"Damn right he is," said Bill Petty. "If that is a Crow village, they'll be expecting us to continue following the tracks of the horses, riding in from the south. This way, we'll ride in from the east, maybe avoiding an ambush."

"Whatever it takes, Quickenpaugh will get them horses," Arch Rainey said. "He treats the critters like they was his own."

"He's doing exactly what Nelson Story asked him to," said Cal, "and I'm personally glad he's riding with us."

Quickenpaugh returned in less than an hour. He dismounted so that he might rest his horse while he spoke.

"Crow village," Quickenpaugh said. "Much teepees, horses."

"No ambush, then," said Cal.

Quickenpaugh shook his head. It was time for Cal to make a decision, and he did.

"We'll ride in and demand our horses," Cal said. "If there's trouble, let them start it. Leave your Winchester in the boot, and don't pull iron unless forced to. I reckon they have only bows and arrows, but we may be outnumbered, and a well-placed arrow can kill as quickly as a hunk of lead. Quickenpaugh, when we ride in, maybe you shouldn't take the lead."

But Quickenpaugh had learned some of the Crow language, and he had other ideas. The outfit rode out, and the Indian took the lead.

"If there was cause," said Bill Petty, "I think Quickenpaugh would tackle hell with a bucket of water."

"*Bueno hombre,*" Oscar Fentress said. "I'll take a bucket and go with him."

Quickenpaugh reined up on a ridge. Below, along a

stream, were two dozen teepees. To the west of the village were Nelson Story's horses, while on the other side of the camp were more than a hundred Indian ponies.

"Hell, I ain't ridin' down there," said Bud. "There's ten of them to one of us."

"Not much worse than the odds at the Alamo," Tom Allen said.

"We're ridin' in as an outfit," said Cal. "If you don't have the sand to ride in with us, McDaniels, I'll see that you get your money in Deadwood, and you can ride your own trail wherever you please."

None of the other riders had anything to say, but Bud McDaniels could see disgust in their weathered faces. When the outfit started down the slope, with Quickenpaugh leading, Bud rode with them. Shouts from below told them they had been seen, and well before they reached the village, the braves gave way to an old Indian wearing buffalo horns. He stood with his arms crossed over his chest, unarmed except for a knife. Quickenpaugh rode forward, while the rest of the outfit reined up, waiting. Without dismounting, Quickenpaugh spoke a greeting in Crow. The conversation was brief, and when Quickenpaugh rode back to join his companions, he had no good news.

"Old Buffalo," Quickenpaugh said. "Him chief. He say they catch horses running free. They keep."

"Those horses were stampeded from our camp," said Cal, "and he damn well knows it. Tell him we're not leaving without them, and if they choose to fight, many Crow will die."

"*Si*," Quickenpaugh said, and rode back to speak to Old Buffalo.

"Now's the time to shuck out your Winchesters," said Cal, "but I want them seen, not fired. If there's shooting to be done, nobody fires a shot until I've opened the ball."

None of them could have understood the conversation had they been able to hear, but they had little difficulty understanding Old Buffalo's actions. Removing a Bowie knife from his waistband, he made stabbing motions toward Quickenpaugh. He then pointed toward the horse herd, which a number of Indians had circled.

"Bad news," Mac Withers said. "He wants one of us to fight one of them. Who's that gonna be?"

"I'm pretty good with a big blade," said Oscar Fentress, "but I never kilt nobody."

"We'll wait and see what Quickenpaugh has to say," Cal replied.

"Old Buffalo say if all fight, many die," said Quickenpaugh. "I fight Young Buffalo with *cuchillo*."

"Quickenpaugh, that's not fair," Cal said. "You'll be taking all the risk."

"If not Quickenpaugh, who else?" asked the Indian, coming as close as he ever did to a smile.

"He's got us by the short hairs," Tom Allen said. "Who else but another Indian can hold his own with a Bowie?"

Cal had little choice. Quickenpaugh was watching him, for if he denied the challenge, he would be considered a coward. Not just in the eyes of the Crows, but in his own eyes.

"Go ahead, Quickenpaugh," said Cal, "but it's going to be fair. Tell Old Buffalo that we'll all be standing by with our Winchesters. We'll shoot any Crow getting into the fight, except Young Buffalo."

"*Si*," Quickenpaugh said. He rode back to relay the message to Old Buffalo.

"Tarnation," Quanah Taylor said, "this is one of them fights where we lose, even if we win. Young Buffalo's got to be Old Buffalo's son. If Quickenpaugh kills Young Buffalo, I can't imagine the old man allowing us to ride out alive, with or without the horse herd."

"I can," said Cal. "I've never known an Indian to lie, even if the truth cost him his life. It's the white man who talks out of both sides of his mouth, and that's why the Sioux are preparing for war."

Quickenpaugh had dismounted, and after speaking

briefly to Old Buffalo, the Indian faced his outfit and raised
his right hand. Old Buffalo shouted something in his own
tongue, and all the inhabitants of the Crow village formed
a half circle behind him.

"Come on," Cal said. "The other side of that circle's
for us."

They dismounted and, leading their horses, formed their
own half circle at the scene of the coming conflict. A young
Crow emerged from the gathering, the haft of a Bowie knife
visible above his waistband. He was dressed in buckskin
leggings and moccasins only, and he might have been near
Quickenpaugh's age. But he was more heavily muscled,
and on his face was what could be described as joy. Old
Buffalo spoke to him, and he nodded, taking the big Bowie
knife in his right hand. Quickenpaugh drew his own Bowie
and stood waiting. The rest of the village—even the
women—began taunting Quickenpaugh, seeking to goad
him into making the first thrust. But Quickenpaugh didn't
move. Exasperated, the Crow lunged at him with a sweep-
ing thrust that would have cut him in half, had it been
successful. But Quickenpaugh stepped away from it, and
using the flat of his blade like a club, he brought it down
hard on Young Buffalo's right wrist. While Young Buffalo
bit his tongue and didn't cry out, his hand went numb and
the big Bowie fell to the ground.

"You got the bastard now," Bud McDaniels shouted.
"Cut his gizzard out."

But Quickenpaugh did not take advantage. Instead, he
pointed toward his opponent's fallen Bowie. Unbelieving,
Young Buffalo inched toward the knife, but Quickenpaugh
made no move until he had the weapon in his left hand.
Meanwhile, Young Buffalo's tribesmen were taunting and
ridiculing him.

"Quickenpaugh had an edge, and he should have taken
advantage of it," said Bill Petty. "The rest of 'em are giving Young Buffalo hell because he's been dishonored. The

only way he can reclaim his honor is to kill Quicken-paugh.''

"I don't believe he can do it," Cal said. "Quickenpaugh knew the risk when he allowed Young Buffalo to take up his knife again. Indians have a code of honor that would put most white men to shame. There's more honor in counting coup than in killing.''

Quickenpaugh proceeded to justify Cal's faith. While several savage slashes of Young Buffalo's Bowie ripped through Quickenpaugh's flannel shirt, none were close enough to draw blood. On the other hand, a lightning-quick lunge by Quickenpaugh raked the tip of his big Bowie from one side of Young Buffalo's chest to the other. While it wasn't deep, and by no means fatal, it bled profusely. It had no effect, except to infuriate Young Buffalo, leading him to take chances. Rather than going for fatal thrusts to the gut, it seemed Quickenpaugh was purposely using only the point of the weapon. He evaded a frantic thrust by Young Buffalo, while scoring a coup of his own. The tip of the Bowie left a bloody trench just above Young Buffalo's eyes, and he wiped away the blood with his bare right arm.

"That must have hurt like hell when Quickenpaugh clubbed his wrist, forcing him to drop the knife," Tom said. "I think that might have cost him whatever advantage he could have had, because he seems clumsy using his left hand.''

"I reckon that's the dark side of the Indian code of honor," said Cal. "There's never room for compromise. Unless Quickenpaugh kills Young Buffalo, he'll have made an enemy for life.''

"Whatever Quickenpaugh does, he won't kill Young Buffalo," Hitch Gould predicted. "He's had chances enough to do that already.''

"I hope Quickenpaugh can get out of this without a killing," said Cal. "We only want to recover our horses.''

"If the Indian does or don't kill Young Buffalo, they

won't give up the horses," Bud McDaniels said. "We'll have a fight on our hands either way."

Nobody said anything, their eyes on the deadly drama unfolding before them. Finally, with a need born of desperation, Young Buffalo shifted the Bowie to his right hand and went after Quickenpaugh, but the Comanche was just out of reach. Then Quickenpaugh topped his earlier performance, when he again brought the flat of his blade down hard on Young Buffalo's right wrist. The Bowie went flying, and Young Buffalo stood as though frozen, unable to believe he had again been disarmed. Quickenpaugh took the fallen Bowie by its blade and, turning his back on his adversary, walked toward Old Buffalo. Haft first, he presented the old man with the knife. At first it seemed Old Buffalo was about to refuse, for Young Buffalo was shouting at him. For a moment, Old Buffalo looked at his son, bloody to the waist and with blood dripping off his chin. The old one then faced Quickenpaugh and accepted the knife. Quickenpaugh pointed toward the herd of grazing horses, and Old Buffalo spoke to the braves who had witnessed the fight. He then said something to Quickenpaugh. The Indian turned to face Cal and the rest of the outfit, again pointing toward the horse herd.

"Mount up and let's ride," Cal said. "Let's get the horses away from here before he changes his mind."

"By God, I ain't believin' this," said Bud McDaniels. "They'll wait till we're gathering the horse herd, and then cut down on us."

"Put that Winchester back in the boot," Cal said grimly, "or I'll take it away from you. Make *any* hostile move, and it may damn well be the last you'll ever make."

The rest of the outfit had already booted their Winchesters, and without a word, Bud followed their example. The Crow braves watched in silence as the riders quickly gathered the horses and headed them south. There was no trouble, but not until they were well out of sight of the Crow village did Cal and the outfit breathe easy.

"Quickenpaugh," said Tom Allen, "you're one *bueno hombre.*"

"I can only agree," Cal said. "I'll see that Mr. Story hears about this, Quickenpaugh."

Quickenpaugh said nothing, nor did his expression change. Having promised Story he would take responsibility for the horses, he had done no more than keep his word.

"Now all we got to do is find them damn cows," said Mac Withers.

"We're not going to have time to do it today," Cal replied. "They shouldn't have run very far, without a storm at their backs. We'll go after them at first light tomorrow."

"They may have drifted, huntin' better graze," said Smokey Ellison.

"There'll be tracks," Cal said, "and there's always a chance they'll drift back toward camp looking for water."

They came within sight of the chuck wagon two hours before sundown. Jasmine sat on the wagon box. Lorna and Curley had been in the shade, their backs to wagon wheels, each with a Winchester rifle.

"Here they come," Jasmine cried, "and they have the horses."

"Now if we just had all those blessed cows rounded up," said Curley.

"We'll find them," Lorna said. "For right now, I think we'd better be thankful they've found the horses and made it back alive."

"Amen to that," said Jasmine. "They've been gone so long, they're bound to have had trouble of some kind. God, I hope none of them are tied over their saddles."

The riders moved the horse herd along the Powder, as near camp as they could. None of the outfit had anything to say, and it was late in the day before Cal had a chance to talk to Lorna alone. He then told her of Quickenpaugh's dangerous ordeal to recover the horses.

"What a glorious thing to have done," Lorna said. "May I tell Jasmine and Curley?"

"Tom will tell Jasmine," said Cal. "Bud was there, and he could tell Curley, but I doubt that he will. He'd never do anything that would honor Quickenpaugh."

"Then I'll tell Curley," Lorna said. "Quickenpaugh's teaching her to speak Crow, and Curley thinks highly of him."

Cal sighed. "Quickenpaugh's interested in Curley, while she's got a live, breathing, hell-raising husband. That's all we need."

"Cal Snider, Quickenpaugh's a man who lives, thinks and acts like one," said Lorna. "If you were comparing Bud McDaniels to Quickenpaugh, which one would interest you?"

"That's an unfair question," Cal replied. "I don't aim to answer it, because once we get to Deadwood, Bud McDaniels is on his own. I take him into consideration now because he's part of this trail drive and I have no choice. Remember, it was you and Jasmine that was hell-bent on Curley marryin' the varmint, after we brought Story's first herd north from Texas. Bud McDaniels is a two-legged coyote who will say what you want to hear, and that's how he trapped Curley. Then, when he had her roped, tied and branded, he just went back to bein' the same no-account bastard he's always been."

"He's still Jasmine's brother," said Lorna, "and I'm every bit as sorry for her as I am for Curley. He's turned sour toward her again, and she's avoiding him."

"It's just as well," Cal said, "because the time and place is all wrong. A trail drive's no place for a male and female to wrestle around on a blanket spread on the ground."

"I don't necessarily agree with that," said Lorna, "but I'll give you credit. You practice what you preach."

EASTERN WYOMING TERRITORY.
MAY 2, 1876

"There's water ahead," McCaleb announced, when Goose had returned from scouting. "I realize the mud's hub-deep in some places, but we're going to gamble that the wagon can avoid those places. We're movin' out.''

"Today's my turn with the wagon," said Rebecca. "I'll keep it to high ground as best I can.''

"I think you're doing the right thing, Bent," Brazos said. "We might lose an hour or so, hauling the wagon out of the mud, but that's not like losing a whole day.''

Some of the riders expected disagreement from Monte Nance, but he said nothing. The moment breakfast was done, the women cleaned their utensils, tin plates and cups, loading them into the wagon.

"Move 'em out," McCaleb shouted.

But the mud was every bit as troublesome as Monte had predicted. The drive had not progressed more than a mile or two when Penelope left her position at drag and, kicking her horse into a gallop, caught up to McCaleb.

"The chuck wagon's stuck," said Penelope. "Rebecca's cussing the mules, but they can't move it.''

The flank and swing riders had seen Penelope catch up to McCaleb, and they waited for a signal from him. McCaleb waved his hat three times, halting the drive.

"Chuck wagon's stuck," McCaleb told some of the riders, as he followed Penelope back to the tag end of the herd.

Rebecca still sat on the wagon box. Monte Nance was there, and he wasted no time in criticizing McCaleb.

"I told you, McCaleb," said Monte, as McCaleb dismounted.

"Shut up, Monte," Rebecca said.

McCaleb said nothing. Knowing what must be done, Penelope had already unsaddled her horse and had begun unsaddling Rosalie's. McCaleb harnessed the two horses in ahead of the mule teams, shouted a command and still the wagon didn't budge.

"Something's wrong besides just bein' stuck," said Will Elliot. "I'll get the shovel from the wagon and dig down a ways.''

Shoveling the mud was easy enough, until the blade of the shovel grated on solid rock.

"Damn it," McCaleb said, "there's a busted wheel."

"We can't be sure," said Will. "I'll shovel some more."

"I'm sorry," Rebecca said. "It looked like level ground."

"No fault of yours," said Will. "It's some kind of drop-off, and the rain washed it full of dirt. The wheel sank in the mud and then slid off this rock onto another."

Will continued shoveling dirt until he had uncovered the lower portion of the left rear wheel, and several of the spokes were hanging loose. The wooden parts of the wheel had been shattered.

"I'll get the spare wheel from the wagon," Pen Rhodes said. "Jed and Stoney can help me remove and replace the broken one."

Nobody said what all of them were thinking, that should this need arise again, there would be no spare wheel. Will shoveled away mud until he reached solid ground beneath the wagon's axle. Jed got the jack in place and began jacking up the wagon.

"When you're done, put that broken wheel in the wagon," said McCaleb. "When we've got a little time, maybe some of us can fix it."

"You'll likely be needin' another wheel before you can fix that one," Monte said.

Nobody said anything, but Monte drew hard looks from some of the riders. Rebecca bit her tongue, while Rosalie was shaking her head at Penelope. The wheel was replaced, and the drive moved on. The water Goose had found was no more than a creek, but the water was swift-running and cold. The broken wagon wheel had cost them some time, and sundown was only minutes away when the riders had unsaddled their horses and unhitched the mules from the chuck wagon. Susannah, Rosalie and Penelope soon had the supper fire going, and McCaleb spoke to them.

"I think you'd do well to douse that fire as soon as you can. If we haven't already, we will be crossing the old Bozeman Trail. It runs north, right through what was once the Sioux hunting grounds. We think they're all gathering in the Dakotas, but we can't be sure of that."

But there was no sign of the Sioux. Disaster struck just after midnight, when one of the steers began bawling, creating a fearful commotion. The panic spread to the two teams of chuck wagon mules, and they lit out at a gallop, taking the horse remuda with them. The first watch had just started to unsaddle their horses and the second watch was already with the herd when the cattle rose to their feet.

"Ride," McCaleb ordered. "They're gonna run!"

But the herd had caught the fever from the frightened mules and horses, and there was no stopping them. McCaleb managed to get ahead of them, waving his hat and firing his Colt, but it made no difference. Heads down, they thundered on, and McCaleb was forced out of their path. Some of the riders came together, discouraged.

"Of all the rotten luck," said Will. "What in hell started that?"

"Brazos has gone to look around," Penelope said helpfully.

"A varmint of some kind, I reckon," said McCaleb. "It's not likely Brazos will find any tracks, with no moon."

But Brazos didn't need tracks. When he returned, he knew what had happened.

"Dead cow," Brazos said. "When some of the others smelled blood, we didn't have a chance to stop them from running. Looks like the work of a grizzly, and the natural smell of him didn't help the situation."

"He didn't have time to sample his kill," said McCaleb. "The rest of you go back to your blankets. Those of us on the second watch will stake out the remains of that cow, in case the grizzly returns. Just out of hibernation, he's likely half starved."

"I'm going to stay with the second watch," Penelope said. "I've never had a chance to shoot at a bear before."

"And you're not gonna get a chance this time," said Brazos. "You haven't slept a wink all night, and we have to start our gather in the morning. The bear may not come back, and you'll be more useful when we go looking for the stock. A cowboy does what needs doin', remember?"

"Yes, sir," Penelope said meekly.

McCaleb, Monte, Jed and Stoney staked themselves out within sight of the dark hulk that was the dead cow. Their Winchesters were ready, but there was no sign of the bear that had caused all the trouble. Rebecca had stirred up the coals and put some coffee on to boil, and when it was ready, she called to McCaleb.

"Jed, you and Stoney go ahead," said McCaleb. "I doubt the grizzly will be back, but if I'm wrong, two of us can handle him."

"Settin' here watching a dead cow don't make any sense at all," Monte complained. "You don't even know if the damn bear's comin' back."

"You're part of the second watch," said McCaleb, "and I say the second watch will be here until first light, watching the carcass of that cow."

But the bear didn't return, and at first light, the outfit gathered for breakfast.

"I reckon there's a bright side to all this," Will said. "The stampede went the direction we was headed, anyway."

"That's the only good news," said McCaleb. "The bad news is, they're not going to find any graze unless they drift to the south, and the farther south they've gone, the more time it'll take us to gather them and return to the place where we are now."

"We know what the problem is, McCaleb," Monte Nance said. "What do you aim to do to fix it?"

"I don't have to answer to you," said McCaleb, "but since you brought it up, I'll tell you. Goose and me have ridden forty miles east of here and found no more graze than we have right here. We're going to follow that stampede, taking the chuck wagon with us.''

"Even if the critters have drifted south?" Pen Rhodes asked.

"Yes," said McCaleb, "no matter how far they've drifted. Those horses, mules and cows must have graze, and we know the grass greens earlier to the south. When we find them, if there's decent graze, we're going to stay there long enough to put some meat on their bones.''

"That's about the only choice we have," Brazos said. "The whole lot of them need at least a week on good grass. That would allow time for the graze to improve to the east of here.''

"So we're gonna set on our hunkers for another week after we track down the herd," said Monte.

"We are, if there's any decent graze to be had," McCaleb replied. "It's that or watch them starve to death.''

"I fully agree with your thinking," said Will, "but there's one wild card we have to consider. What about the Sioux?''

"We have every reason to believe they're gathered somewhere to the north of here, or in Dakota Territory," McCaleb said. "If that's not the case, then we're in big trouble. But nothing worth having has ever been gained without *some* risk.''

"Just a hell of a *lot* of risk, in this case," said Monte.

"I'm still trail boss," McCaleb said, "and we're going, with or without you. Goose, I'll want you to ride with me. We're going just far enough to round up the mules. The rest of you wait here with the chuck wagon until we return.''

McCaleb and Goose rode off in the easterly direction the stampede had gone. Within less than a mile, the horses and mules had separated themselves from the stampeding cattle, and the trail led north.

"They not go far," said Goose.

"I doubt they have," McCaleb said. "We know there's almost no graze up that way. We don't *know* it's any better to the south, but it should be."

Within two or three miles, they found the chuck wagon mule teams and the remuda horses picking at the skimpy grass. Quickly they captured the four mules and, with them on lead ropes, returned to their waiting outfit.

"The horses and mules separated from the cattle and are not more than three miles to the north of here," said McCaleb. "Jed, you and Stoney harness the mules. We're going to gather the remuda and then take the trail of the herd."

"It's my day on the wagon," Susannah said.

"Go ahead, then," said McCaleb, "and take your time. Brazos, you and Will stay with the wagon until we catch up to the herd. The rest of you will ride with me to gather our horse remuda."

The outfit rode out, Susannah following with the wagon.

9

SOUTHEASTERN MONTANA TERRITORY.
MAY 5, 1876

DESPITE THE CATTLE STILL being scattered, the outfit was in good spirits because the horses had been recovered from the Crows without a massive battle. Quickenpaugh was applauded by the rest of the riders. Only Bud McDaniels kept his silence and his distance.

"Tomorrow morning," said Cal, "We'll go looking for the herd, and we're going to take the chuck wagon with us. Wherever we find the cattle, there'll be water, and maybe some decent graze."

"I think we're too far north for the graze to get any better," Quanah Taylor said. "If the herd goes lookin' for grass, it'll be to the south of us, where the grass greens a mite earlier."

"If that's where the trail leads, then that's where we'll go," said Cal. "We can turn to the south maybe fifty miles, and it still would not be out of our way. In fact, we'd be in more a straight line to Deadwood than we are now."

"Then why haven't we already moved farther south?" Bud McDaniels demanded.

"Because we'll be closer to the old Sioux hunting grounds," said Cal, "increasing our chances of running headlong into a party of Sioux. Now, if the cattle have drifted south, and there's better graze, we no longer have a choice. All of you should be aware there'll be some risk."

"There's no help for it, then," Tom Allen said. "We know all this is buildin' up to some kind of Armageddon between the army and the Sioux. What we don't know is where it'll happen."

"I think it'll come in southeastern Montana," said Mac Withers. "Maybe we'll be lucky enough to get through there before all hell busts loose."

"We're going to depend on Quickenpaugh's judgment," Cal replied. "I intend for him to scout well ahead of the drive. At the first sign of the Sioux coming together, then we'll do our best to avoid them. We'll go north to the Yellowstone, if we have to."

"Right back where there's no graze," said Bud McDaniels.

"Bud, for God's sake, stop thinking and talking like a fool," Jasmine said. "Just a few more days, and the grass will be green *everywhere*."

Nothing more was said about their circumstances, although the riders talked among themselves while on watch during the night. On the first watch were Arch Rainey, Hitch Gould, Mac Withers, Oscar Fentress and Smokey Ellison. With the cattle scattered, they had only the horses to concern them.

"No trouble," said Smokey Ellison, as the riders for the second watch saddled their horses.

"*Bueno*," Cal said.

With him were Tom Allen, Quanah Taylor, Bud McDaniels, Bill Petty and Quickenpaugh the Comanche. To Cal's surprise, Lorna arose when he did.

"We don't really need you," said Cal.

"I know that," Lorna said. "Perhaps I just want to be with you."

"I reckon that's permitted," said Cal. "I'll saddle a horse for you."

The two of them walked their horses side by side, and it was a while before Lorna had anything to say. Finally she spoke.

"You hardly ever have Curley and me on watch anymore. Why?"

"There's six of us on the second watch," Cal said, "and five on the first. That's enough unless there's a storm, thunder or lightning."

"It's because of Bud and Curley, isn't it?"

"If you've got it all figured out," said Cal, "why are you asking me?"

"I just want to be sure," Lorna said.

"You mean Curley wants to be sure," said Cal.

"All right, damn it," Lorna said, "Curley doesn't like it. She believes you're just trying to make allowances for her trouble with Bud, and she resents not being treated like part of the outfit."

"With Jasmine laid up, Curley has her hands full," said Cal. "She alternates with you on the chuck wagon, as well as sharing the cooking duties. Nobody expects either of you to do more."

"You could assign Curley the first watch and Bud the second," Lorna persisted.

"Is that your idea or hers?"

"Mine," said Lorna.

"Well, I can do considerably better than that," said Cal. "Starting tomorrow night, I'll assign Curley and Bud to the first watch. That way, he can stalk her for six hours while they're on watch, and spend the next six trying to get her to sleep with him."

"Cal Snider," Lorna almost shouted, "you're impossible."

"Quiet, damn it," said Cal. "You'll stampede the horses."

The rest of the second watch had heard, but only Bud McDaniels had anything to say.

"What are you tryin' to do, Snider? Stampede the horses?"

"Mind your own damn business, McDaniels," Cal said. Lorna said nothing. Leading her horse, she stomped

away. Cal mounted and continued circling the herd. Though
there was light from moon and stars, he didn't see Mc-
Daniels.

"What happened to Big-mouth?" Cal asked Tom Allen.

"I have no idea," said Tom. "I was tempted to bust him
in the nose, but I reckoned I ought to save that little pleasure for you."

The quiet of the night was suddenly interrupted by Bud
McDaniels swearing.

"Cal!" Lorna cried. "Cal!"

Cal kicked his horse into a gallop, and when he reached
the scene, Bud McDaniels and Curley were involved in a
brawl on the ground. In the shadows, Cal couldn't tell one
from the other. Suddenly there was a dull thud, and the
struggling ceased. Curley got to her knees, and then to her
feet. She wore nothing but Levi's, and in her hand was her
Colt.

"If that pistol had gone off, the horses would be scattered all over hell," said Cal.

"Wrong," Curley said. "If it had gone off, his brains
would be scattered all over hell."

"Lorna," said Cal, "get Curley another shirt."

"I can get my own damn shirt," Curley said, "if I figure
I need one."

She stood there in silence, defiant, until Bud McDaniels
sat up.

"She buffaloed me," cried McDaniels.

"The next time you crawl on me, ripping my clothes off,
I won't just hit you with a gun muzzle," Curley said. "I'll
shoot you dead."

"Cal," Jasmine cried from the chuck wagon, "come
here."

"I'll go with you, Cal," said Lorna.

Cal said nothing, and when they approached the wagon,
Jasmine spoke.

"I heard him go after Curley," Jasmine said. "What
brought that on?"

"I suppose it's my fault," said Lorna. "I was talking to Cal about Curley, and we got a little . . . loud. I suppose Bud thought if Cal and me could fight, then him and Curley could do the same."

"We weren't fighting," Cal said. "We disagreed on something."

"Oh?" said Jasmine. "What?"

"Over whether or not Curley can stand watch," Lorna said.

"No more argument from me," said Cal angrily. "Curley's determined to take care of herself, and as far as I'm concerned, she'll have to. I'm assigning her to the first watch tomorrow night, and she can do it with or without her shirt. I don't care."

Jasmine sighed, and it was Lorna who spoke.

"It's my fault, Jasmine. I stirred all this up, and I'm sorry."

"I don't blame you or Cal," said Jasmine. "Neither of you have any control over what Bud does. I intend to stay out of it, allowing Curley to handle him in whatever way that suits her. I think both of you should do the same."

Leaving Lorna with Jasmine, Cal led his horse back to the scene of the brawl. There was no sign of Bud Mc-Daniels. Curley sat cross-legged on one of her blankets, the other one around her shoulders.

"I know you hate me, but I did nothing to encourage him," Curley said.

"I don't hate you, and I believe you're telling the truth," said Cal.

"I suppose I'd better tell you the rest of it," Curley said.

"If there's more, I'd appreciate it," said Cal.

"Bud's jealous of Quickenpaugh and me," Curley said.

"Oh?" said Cal. "Does he have reason?"

"Damn it," Curley said, "you know he doesn't. Quickenpaugh's been teaching me a few words of the Crow tongue, and he's more a gentleman than Bud McDaniels will ever be."

"You like Quickenpaugh, then," said Cal.

"Yes," Curley said. "He's Comanche, but he's twice the man Bud McDaniels is, or can ever be. Quickenpaugh's a man, and he doesn't swagger around trying to prove it."

"While I can appreciate your liking Quickenpaugh," said Cal, "don't you think you're being unfair to him? Whatever you think of Bud, he's jealous as hell of you, and he's got a temper like a stomped-on rattler. How would you feel if he shot Quickenpaugh in the back?"

"I'd kill him," Curley said viciously. "I'd gut-shoot him."

"That wouldn't help Quickenpaugh," said Cal.

"No," Curley conceded. "What do you think I should do?"

"From now until we reach Deadwood, don't spend so much time with Quickenpaugh," said Cal. "If Bud hasn't straightened up by the time we sell the herd, I'm kicking him out. He won't be returning to Virginia City with us."

"That wouldn't make me sorry," Curley said, "except that I'll have no place to go. I'll have no claim on any of this herd, except through Bud."

"You can always stay with him," said Cal.

"If I'm going to be pawed over by a man I don't even like, I'd as soon find me a place in a whorehouse," Curley said.

"Damn it," said Cal, uneasy with the turn the conversation had taken, "there has to be some answers, but I don't have them now. Avoid any more fighting with Bud, if you can. I promise whatever Bud chooses to do after the herd's sold, you won't be left on your own. Story would never cut you loose, and even if he did, Lorna and me wouldn't."

Cal was unprepared for her response. Curley threw her arms around him, weeping as though her heart were broken. The blanket slid away, and Cal Snider was only too much aware that Curley *still* wore no shirt. It was the worst possible time for Lorna to show up, and to Cal's dismay, she did.

"What have you done to Curley?" Lorna demanded, sounding half angry.

"Nothing," said Cal. "I . . ."

"He's been so kind to me," Curley said, through tears.

"I told her that if Bud leaves the outfit and she has nowhere to go, we'll take her in," said Cal. "We will, won't we?"

For a long moment, Lorna said nothing. She genuinely *liked* Curley, but the girl *still* wore no shirt, and seemed not the least embarrassed. Nor did Cal, Lorna thought. Finally, as kindly as she could, she spoke.

"Cal's right," Lorna said. "You came with us from Texas, and you've always carried your weight with Mr. Story's outfit. We won't stand for you being put out in the cold. Come on to the chuck wagon and let's find you another shirt."

Nothing disturbed the silence of the night, but unseen eyes were watching, as Lorna and Curley started toward the chuck wagon. Silently, Quickenpaugh retreated. Reaching his picketed horse, he mounted and began circling the horse herd.

The following morning, breakfast was a quiet affair. When it was over and the wagon made ready to move out, Curley climbed to the box beside Jasmine. Without the cattle, the horse herd seemed anxious to be on the way. When the lead riders reached the place the horse herd had split away from the cattle, they continued following the broad trail the stampeding cows had left.

"Here's where the stampede started coming apart," Tom Allen said, when they were almost five miles along the trail.

"I can't imagine them running this far," said Cal, "unless there were riders behind them running them hard."

"Might have been them Crow Indians," Quanah Taylor said. "Maybe they thought we'd go after the cows first, buying them enough time to escape with the horses."

It seemed logical, and they continued following the

tracks. After the stampede had begun to break up, it became obvious the herd had started drifting south.

"What'n thunder's leadin' 'em south?" Arch Rainey wondered.

"Who knows?" said Hitch Gould.

"They knows where the good grass is," Oscar Fentress said. "Somethin' in their cow minds is tellin' 'em where to go."

On the wagon box, Jasmine and Curley had said little. Finally, Jasmine spoke.

"Lorna was terribly quiet during breakfast."

Curley laughed. "That's my fault. Cal was so kind to me, I started bawling and Lorna caught me with my arms around him."

"You weren't wearing a shirt, until you and Lorna came back to the chuck wagon," said Jasmine, "and with moon- and starlight, old Cal must have seen plenty."

"It's not just Cal," Curley said. "Remember, when we left Texas, all of you thought I was a man. Then after I was shot, I was stripped before everybody in the outfit."*

"You certainly got everybody's attention," said Jasmine. "It's not often the riders are treated to the sight of a naked female on a cattle drive. You're stronger than I am. If I'd been in your position, bare as a plucked chicken, I'd never have been able to face any of them again."

"Oh, it wasn't all that bad, except for having been shot," Curley said. "None of the outfit ever tried to take advan- tage of me, except Bud."

"I suppose it's time to tell you I'm sorry for anything I might have said or done that encouraged you to marry him," said Jasmine. "I really thought it would settle him down."

"I thought so too," Curley said. "Before the preacher read from the Book, nobody was nicer than Bud. Then when it was legal for him to . . . you know . . ."

*The Virginia City Trail (Trail Drive #7)

Jasmine laughed. "I don't *know*, but I'm pretty sure. He became jealous of everything you said or did. He's been watching you when you spoke to Quickenpaugh."

"Yes," said Curley bitterly. "I promised Cal I wouldn't spend as much time with Quickenpaugh while we're on the trail. Cal thinks Bud might shoot Quickenpaugh in the back."

"Dear God," Jasmine said, "I hope not. Quickenpaugh stands tall in the outfit, and such a fool stunt would finish Bud. He'd be hanged from the highest tree, and Cal would be the first to go after him with a rope."

"I wish I knew what will happen once we reach Deadwood," said Curley. "Cal swears he'll give Bud his money for his share of the herd and then kick him out. There's sure to be a fight, because Bud won't go unless I go with him."

"And you don't plan on going with him," Jasmine said.

"No," said Curley. "I don't know what I'll do, but I *do* know it won't be with him."

"He may change before we reach Deadwood," Jasmine said.

"Sorry, I won't fall for that again," said Curley. "He puts on his best face until he gets what he wants, and then he goes back to bein' the ornery, two-legged coyote he's always been. He thinks he owns me, body and soul."

"There's some of the cattle," Jasmine cried.

But there were only a few, and Cal didn't bother with them. He led the horse herd on to the south, and not until they reached a spring with decent runoff did they begin seeing a substantial number of the stampeded herd.

"We'll make camp here," Cal shouted.

The outfit headed the horses below the spring, where they could drink from the runoff. Cal trotted his horse over to the chuck wagon.

"Curley," said Cal, "I want you, Lorna and Quickenpaugh to stay with the wagon. We might be able to gather the herd today, with enough riders."

"Jasmine's going to be here, in any case," Curley said. "Why don't you leave Quickenpaugh here with her and the wagon? Lorna and me can help with the gather."

"Because Quickenpaugh can't handle the horse herd by himself," said Cal, "and anybody remaining here is just as much needed as those who will be gathering the herd."

"Then let the Indian help gather the herd, and *I'll* stay here," Bud McDaniels said.

"No way," said Cal. "Now let's ride."

Curley climbed down from the wagon and began unharnessing the teams. Lorna still circled the horse herd, remaining there until Curley saddled a horse and joined her. At the far side of the herd, Quickenpaugh sat his horse, watching them.

"Cal might have been wrong, leaving Quickenpaugh here," Lorna said.

"No more wrong than he'd have been had he left Bud here instead," said Curley. "I'm not the least bit fearful of Quickenpaugh, but with everybody else gone, Bud might drag me off my horse and have his way with me right here on the ground."

Lorna laughed nervously. "Surely not with Jasmine watching."

"Why not?" Curley said. "Jasmine's been wiping his nose all his life. I doubt he's ever done *anything* she hasn't seen at least once."

Unlike in the lowlands, the runoff from the spring did not disappear in thirsty ground, but became a sizable stream as it flowed south. While the graze wasn't abundant, there was some, with the promise of more. There were numerous cow tracks where the cattle had gone to and from the stream.

"This stream looks like it may run on for miles," Tom Allen said.

"I hope it does," said Cal. "If there was no water, and every cow went a different direction, we'd never find the varmints."

For a change—since he had been responsible for the

stampede—Bud McDaniels said nothing. The graze began to improve as they rode farther south, and before the sun was noon-high, the outfit had made real progress toward gathering their scattered herd.

"Another day like this one," Tom Allen said, "and we'll have the rest of them."

"When we find the others," said Cal, "I'm thinking we'll have to move all of them—and the horse herd as well—a little farther south, in the hope of better graze."

"If we can find enough," Bill Petty said, "we'd better hold 'em there a spell. We got no idea what the graze is like around Deadwood, or even if there is any. Ours may not be the only herd, and we can't afford to trail 'em in there with their every bone showing."

"If there's enough grass, we'll graze them for a week," said Cal.

"Graze them when they get to Dakota Territory," Bud McDaniels said. "You're wasting time, Snider."

"Your opinion, McDaniels," said Cal. "While we're waiting, we're going to scout far ahead—maybe as much as a hundred miles—to be sure we aren't about to be caught up in a war with the Sioux."

"That be smart," Oscar Fentress said. "I get enough of the Sioux when we come up the Bozeman Trail from Texas."*

"My God, yes," said Smokey Ellison. "I got me a feeling that when the Sioux strike, they'll really put the hurt on any whites gettin' in their way."

SOUTH-CENTRAL MONTANA TERRITORY.
MAY 8, 1876

"It's time for a tally," Cal said, in the early afternoon.

"Forgive me if I don't take part," said McDaniels. "You never consider my tally."

The Virginia City Trail (Trail Drive #7)

"Suit yourself," Cal replied. "Your count's never even close."

"Bud can't count to twenty without takin' his boots off," said Quanah Taylor.

"He can count as high as twenty-one, if he takes down his britches," Arch Rainey said.

"I got a score to settle with some of you, once we reach Deadwood," said McDaniels.

"That's enough, all of you," Cal said. "Let's get on with the tally."

Without McDaniels participating, the riders began individual tallies.

"Fifty-four hundred and seventy-five," Tom Allen announced.

Every count varied a few head. The lowest talley belonged to Oscar Fentress.

"Fifty-four hundred and twenty-five," said Oscar.

"That's within seventy-five head of what we started with," Cal said. "We'll go with that and consider the gather finished. Since we'll be here a few days, we may yet pick up some of the missing ones."

SOUTHEASTERN WYOMING TERRITORY.
MAY 8, 1876

"This ain't more than a creek," Brazos said, as he and Will unharnessed the mules from the chuck wagon. "Wonder what it's called."

"Don't matter," said Will. "There's plenty of water, and there's no reason to believe we won't find our cows somewhere along it."

McCaleb and the rest of the outfit had driven several hundred cows from the creek's headwaters and were bunching them downstream from the chuck wagon.

"It's a little early for supper," Rosalie said.

"This may be Sioux territory," said Rebecca. "We'd

better get the cooking done, so we can put out the fires before dark.''

"You've had a hard day with the chuck wagon, Rebecca," Susannah said. "Why don't you let Rosalie and me get supper? Maybe we can get Penelope to help us."

"Penelope's been in the saddle all day," said Rebecca, "and when either of you have the wagon, you always help with supper. So there."

Penelope chose to help with supper, and the four of them soon had it ready. Little was said until everybody had eaten. It was still more than an hour before the first watch would saddle up, and most of the riders took the opportunity to enjoy second and third cups of coffee. Even Goose had developed a liking for the potent brew, filling his cup a second time.

"I figure we're a good thirty miles farther south than we should be," Brazos said. "The graze is some better, but we'll be forced to move the herd downriver every day, looking for new grass. When we're finally ready to go on to Deadwood, we may have to make up as much as seventy miles."

"Another week," said McCaleb, "but when we get there, we'll have decent-looking stock instead of walking skeletons."

Nearing sunset, the wind had died, and suddenly there came the distinctive rattle of a wagon approaching from the south. McCaleb, Brazos and Will got to their feet, waiting. The wagon came on, the big man at the reins halting his teams while the wagon was a few yards distant. Dressed like a miner, he looked to be in his fifties, with thinning hair. But he received scant attention, for he had two women with him. Both were young, blonde, in their twenties and looking remarkably alike.

"Step down," McCaleb invited. "We can rustle you folks some supper, if you like."

The big man looped the reins about the brake handle and,

stepping down, helped both the girls from the wagon. Only then did he speak.

"I'm Roscoe Yates. These are my daughters, Connie and Kate."

"I'm Benton McCaleb, trail boss for the Lone Star outfit," said McCaleb. "I reckon you know this territory is what was once Sioux hunting grounds?"

"I was warned about that in Cheyenne," Yates said, "but I was told this is also the best and shortest way to the Black Hills, where the gold is."

"When you've eaten," said McCaleb, "I'd be obliged for any news from Cheyenne that has to do with the gold strike."

"Yeah," Brazos said. "If every *hombre* on the High Plains that's raisin' cattle decides to take a herd to the miners, we'll likely get lost in the crowd."

"There are notices all around Cheyenne asking cattlemen to bring their herds to the mining camps," said Yates.

"There's still plenty of coffee, and the grub will be ready soon," McCaleb said. "All of you make yourselves comfortable, and I'll introduce the rest of us."

Quickly, McCaleb did. Pen Rhodes, Jed and Stoney Vandiver, and Monte Nance eyed the Yates girls with considerable interest, and their interest was boldly returned. One of them—McCaleb wasn't sure which—winked at Monte Nance.

"Heavens," said Rebecca, seeking to be friendly to the girls, "you're so much alike, we won't know which of you is which."

"I'm Kate," one of the duo said, "and I have a mole right below my navel."

Rebecca was embarrassed, and Monte Nance added to her discomfort by laughing long and loud. Roscoe Yates seemed not to have heard. Susannah had brought three extra tin cups from the chuck wagon, offering one to each of the newcomers. They filled their cups from one of the big coffeepots. Rebecca, Rosalie, Susannah and Penelope were preparing supper for the trio, and Penelope was furious.

"Penelope," said Rosalie, "you've been standing there holding that same frying pan for five minutes."

"I don't aim to fry anything except maybe somebody's goose," Penelope snapped.

"Young lady," said Rosalie, "you're not too old for me to skin down your Levi's and take a strap to you. You *will* be nice to these people, keeping a civil tongue. I won't have them thinking I've jerked you up by the hair of your head, without manners."

Penelope dared not talk back, but she was seething inside. She had always been the only single woman around, taking secret delight in the awkward advances of the cowboys. Monte Nance had taken to openly watching her, and to her shame, she had been far more excited than angry when he had spied on her in the wagon. Now every single cowboy in the outfit had somehow been drawn to Connie and Kate Yates. Of them all, Monte Nance was the boldest.

"Let me see that mole, so I'll know which of you is which," Monte said.

"My God," said Rebecca quietly. "The nerve of him."

"But he didn't start it," Penelope said. "They did."

"It's just talk," said Susannah. "It'll pass."

But it didn't pass. Connie and Kate Yates were dressed in men's woolen shirts, boots and Levi's without belts. One of the girls unfastened the top button, rolling her waistband dangerously low. Monte Nance roared, and some of the other cowboys got into the spirit of the thing. Mildly amused, Roscoe Yates continued sipping his coffee. Having had hard words with Rosalie, Penelope turned to Brazos for comfort, but found little.

"They're as brazen as a pair of whores," Penelope hissed.

"Whoa," said Brazos. "Could you be just a mite jealous?"

"Jealous, hell," Penelope snapped. "I could have had

all of them gathered around me, if I pulled my britches down.''

''Well, just don't go getting any ideas,'' said Brazos ominously. ''I heard Rosalie's talk of taking a strap to your bare behind. If there's a need for it, I'll take over when her arm gets tired.''

''I have a mole too,'' Penelope said, undaunted, ''and it's lower down than hers.''

Brazos Gifford was in over his head, and he quickly distanced himself from Penelope.

10

SOUTH CENTRAL MONTANA TERRITORY.
MAY 17, 1876

"I'm sick and tired of this damn camp," Bud McDaniels snarled.

The rest of the outfit had long since begun ignoring his outbursts, and nobody said anything. The drive had been delayed a week so that the cattle and horse herd might take advantage of some better graze. Quickenpaugh had been gone three days, scouting along the southernmost part of the territory through which the trail drive must go.

"I hope nothing's happened to Quickenpaugh," said Lorna worriedly.

"Damn Indian probably just kept goin'," Bud McDaniels said.

"Quickenpaugh will return sometime today or tonight," said Cal, "and when he does, I think we'll better understand the situation involving the Sioux."

"This has been a hard wait," Smokey Ellison said, "but it's been worth it. Spring's here and there'll be green grass to the north and east of us."

"No snow comin'," said Oscar Fentress. "Sun be warm."

"When Quickenpaugh returns, we'll know more about what we're going to do," Cal said. "Maybe we can move out tomorrow."

There had been no more trouble between Bud and Curley, for she had apparently taken Cal's advice and had spent less time with the Indian. But she had spent no time at all with Bud, and he had complained bitterly. Jasmine still had both legs splinted, and since wearing Levi's was impossible, she had taken to wrapping her lower body in a blanket. She sat with her back to a wagon wheel, and it was she who finally had enough of Bud's whining about the many things that irritated him.

"It's a crying shame you couldn't have had two broken legs instead of me," Jasmine said. "Then we could lean you up against a tree, far enough away so that the rest of us couldn't hear you."

McDaniels laughed. "I never would have let the mules run away with the wagon. It was your fault, sister dear."

Not wishing to listen to another harsh tirade from Bud McDaniels, the rest of the outfit had quickly distanced themselves. They never knew what he might say. But Jasmine said something to him—that only he could hear—and he exploded in a blind, cursing fury. He seized a corner of the blanket covering Jasmine's lower body, whipping it away from her. Tom Allen and Cal Snider started after him at the same instant, and Bud made an almost fatal mistake. He went for his gun, but he wasn't quite fast enough. Tom had his weapon in his hand when Cal's Colt roared. The slug ripped into Bud's right arm, just above the elbow. Bud dropped the Colt and then went to his knees, seeking to seize the weapon in his left hand.

"Don't," Cal warned. "Try that one more time, and I'll kill you for the hairy-legged, ornery coyote that you are."

"You shot me, you son of a bitch," Bud snarled.

"If he hadn't, I would have," said Tom Allen, "and it would have been a hell of a lot more serious than a slug through the arm."

After the situation had turned violent, the rest of the outfit had moved in close.

"Bud, come to the fire and I'll see to your arm," Lorna said.

"I don't want none of you touching me," said Mc-
Daniels.

"Let him go, Lorna," Jasmine said. "Don't dirty your
hands with him."

Bud McDaniels had only a flesh wound, and without
another word, he began saddling his horse.

"Just where do you think you're going?" Cal asked.

"To Deadwood," growled Bud. "When you get there—
if you ever do—I'll be waiting to take my share of the
money. I'll consider taking Curley too, if she can stay out
of that Indian's blankets."

"Wait for me," Curley shouted, "and you'll be waiting
till hell freezes."

"Bud," said Cal, "you don't know that half the Sioux
nation isn't gathering somewhere ahead of us. For the sake
of the outfit, I'm not going to stop you from riding out, if
you won't have it any other way, but at least wait until
Quickenpaugh returns with a report on the Sioux."

"One damn Indian's no better than all the others," said
Bud, "and I don't want nothing from your pet Comanche."

He mounted and, with only a quantity of jerked beef in
his saddlebags, rode away.

"Jasmine," Cal said, kneeling beside her, "I'm sorry. I
never expected him to do that."

"I wouldn't fault you if you'd killed him," said Jasmine.
"Would one of you bring me another blanket?"

Tom hastened to get the blanket Bud McDaniels had
flung away. Cal got hastily to his feet, aware that, because
of her splinted legs, Jasmine wore only a wool shirt. Everybody was in a somber mood. While Bud McDaniels had
been a constant problem, he had also been part of the outfit
since Nelson Story's historic drive from Texas to Virginia
City.

"For Jasmine's sake, I feel just awful about Bud leaving," Lorna said.

"So do I," said Cal, "but he's been building up to this
for a while."

"I'm just glad you got to him ahead of Tom. Tom would have killed him," Lorna said. "How do you suppose this is going to affect Curley and Quickenpaugh?"

"I don't even want to think about that," said Cal, "but I'm not going to stick my nose into somethin' that's none of my business. Quickenpaugh's Comanche, but nobody can deny he's a man in every way that matters."

Fifty miles east of the trail drive, Quickenpaugh had stopped to rest his horse. He had obeyed Cal's instructions, riding almost to the *río* the white man called Little Big Horn. Now he was on his way back to meet the cattle drive, and he knew what he must tell Cal would create serious problems for them on the trail ahead. Suddenly Quickenpaugh's horse nickered and another answered. In an instant, the Indian had his Winchester cocked and ready, for the oncoming rider would know someone was waiting for him. Quickenpaugh, keeping to cover, left his horse and advanced on foot. There was a clearing to the south and, reaching the edge of it, he watched and waited. On the far side of the clearing, there was movement of a newly budded bush, and the head of a horse emerged. Bud McDaniels was leading the animal, and with Winchester under his arm, he paused.

"*Cuidado,*" Quickenpaugh said. "*Cuidado.*"

It was intended as a warning, to alert McDaniels, lest he begin shooting at first sight of an Indian. The Winchester in his left hand, Quickenpaugh raised his right, in a sign of peace. Without hesitation, McDaniels raised the Winchester and began firing. Slugs ripped into the brush all around Quickenpaugh as he took cover. Lead tore into his left side, as yet another slug plowed a bloody furrow along the side of his head. Unconscious, he fell. Hearing nothing, Bud McDaniels mounted and rode on, not looking back.

Darkness had fallen, and there had been no sign of Quickenpaugh. Nobody spoke, for they all privately feared something had happened to the Indian. Arch Rainey, Mac Withers, Hitch Gould, Lorna and Curley were circling the herd on the first watch.

"I heard somethin'," said Hitch, reaching for his Colt.

Arch, Hitch and Mac waited, listening.

"It's a horse walking," Mac whispered, "and he ain't bein' guided or led."

"Maybe," said Hitch, "but let's be sure. Identify yourself. You're covered," he shouted.

There was no reply. The only sound they heard was that of two horses being led by Lorna and Curley.

"What is it?" Lorna asked.

"A loose horse, we think," said Mac. "Some of you cover me, and I'll go see."

"Careful," Arch said. "It could be a trick."

But Mac quickly discovered it was no trick. The moon had yet to rise, but in the dim light of distant stars, Mac recognized Quickenpaugh's horse. The Indian lay on the ground unmoving. He had managed to reach camp before falling from his horse.

"It's Quickenpaugh," Mac shouted. "He's alive, but he's hurt."

The riders for the second watch had heard and in an instant were out of their blankets and running. Mac Withers had already taken the Indian's arms, while Arch Rainey had hold of his feet. Hitch Gould led Quickenpaugh's horse.

"Come on, Curley," said Lorna. "Let's get a fire going and some water on to boil."

Quickenpaugh was placed on a blanket near the chuck wagon as Lorna and Curley got a fire going from earlier coals.

"What is it?" Jasmine cried from the wagon. "What's wrong?"

"It's Quickenpaugh," said Tom Allen. "He's been shot. We're not sure how bad."

"All of us can't see to him without getting in one another's way," Cal said, "and right now there's nobody with the herd. Oscar, I want you to see how badly he's hurt, and do what you can for him. Lorna and Curley, do whatever you can to help Oscar. The rest of us will take over the watch.''

As concerned as they were for Quickenpaugh, the outfit took over the first watch, as Oscar, Lorna and Curley sought to do what they could for the wounded Indian.

''His head been just creased,'' Oscar said. ''It ain't what's hurtin' him.''

''He's bleeding from a wound in his left side, low down,'' said Curley. ''We'd better take his moccasins and leggings off.''

Quickly they stripped Quickenpaugh, covering him with a blanket until the water had begun to boil.

''Build up that fire some,'' Oscar ordered. ''Make it burn bright, so's I can see.''

Lorna and Curley began adding wood to the fire, and by the time the water was hot, the fire had flamed up with sufficient light for Oscar to see. The wound in Quickenpaugh's left side no longer bled, but the lead had not passed through.

''It gonna be hard on him,'' Oscar said. ''The slug still be in there.''

Lorna sneaked a look at Curley, and she stood there with her eyes closed, silent tears leaking out and streaking her cheeks.

''What can we do to help, Oscar?'' Lorna asked.

''Pray,'' said Oscar. Removing his Bowie, he placed the blade of the big knife in the coals of the nearby fire.

Cal rode up and dismounted, wishing to know what Oscar had learned. Oscar had but little to say. Pointing to the Bowie, its blade heating, he told Cal only what he had told Lorna and Curley. Jasmine had dragged herself forward in the wagon and had heard Oscar talking to Cal.

''Cal,'' Jasmine cried, ''will you help me out of the wagon? I can't sleep.''

Cal didn't much like the idea, but he went to the rear of the wagon and lowered the tailgate.

"I ought to send Tom to do this," said Cal. "All this moving about, and you're likely to hurt the knitting of your bones. I'd hate to get the blame for that."

"Oh, stop fussing," Jasmine said. "If I mess up my bones, it'll be my fault. I'll slide to the rear of the wagon. You just lift me up and set me down, leaning me against one of the wagon wheels."

"All right," said Cal. "Hand me a blanket, so I don't set you on the ground."

The blanket she had handed him had been the one covering the upper part of her body, as Cal quickly discovered. He almost dropped her in his eagerness to settle her against the wagon wheel.

"The blanket I was lying on is still in the wagon," Jasmine said.

"I'll get it for you," said Cal, hoping Lorna wasn't aware of the situation. Passing her the critical blanket, he moved closer to the fire, pausing beside Oscar.

"Is there anything any of us can do, Oscar? You have one knife in the fire. Do you need another?"

"I got two," said Oscar. "One of them's his."

Cal mounted his horse and rode away. Oscar took the big knife that belonged to the Indian and held its blade in the flames a few seconds, cleansing it.

"Curley," Lorna said, "I don't think we ought to watch this."

"I'm staying," said Curley. "If it gets so bad I can't watch, I'll close my eyes."

Using Quickenpaugh's knife, Oscar began probing for the lead. Unconscious though he was, Quickenpaugh groaned.

"Hold on just a little longer, pard," the black man grunted. "I almost got it."

Finally, Oscar dropped the Bowie and began sleeving sweat from his eyes.

"Oh," cried Curley, "did you find it?"

"Found it," Oscar said. "Tore him up somethin' awful 'cause it hit a rib, but I reckon that kept it from goin' through his vitals."

"Thank God," said Lorna. "Do you need a bottle of the whiskey?"

"Maybe later," Oscar said. "I goin' to cauterize his wound when the knife gets hot."

Lorna and Curley remained throughout the ordeal.

"Curley and me can bandage him, Oscar," said Lorna.

"You can't, neither," Oscar said. "The skin around his wound has been burnt, and it'll need the open air to heal. Spread a blanket over him and leave him where he's at. Later tonight, if he gets feverish, feed him a jolt of that whiskey."

"You deserve a rest, Oscar," said Curley. "Where are you going?"

"This be a trail drive," Oscar said. "I gonna take my turn on watch."

Quickenpaugh was restless during the night, and at dawn was running a high fever.

"Are we going to move out today?" Lorna asked Cal.

"No," said Cal, "for several reasons. We can't afford to hurt Quickenpaugh's chances by moving him while he has a fever, and until he's able to talk, we won't know what he's learned about conditions ahead of us. We've been here a week, so another couple of days won't seem that long."

SOUTHEASTERN MONTANA TERRITORY.
MAY 20, 1876

Two days following Quickenpaugh's return to camp, his fever broke and he started to recover.

"Today or tomorrow, he be able to talk," said Oscar Fentress during breakfast.

"It's going to be interesting, finding out what happened," Tom Allen said. "Either he was bushwhacked, or shot by somebody he knew and trusted. Neither his Colt or his Winchester had been fired."

"It's possible that Quickenpaugh ran into some soldiers," said Cal. "They might have cut down on him just because he's an Indian. That would account for Quickenpaugh not returning fire."

"We know he was shot by a white man," Bill Petty said. "It's unlikely the Sioux would be armed with much more than bows and arrows."

Nobody said anything, but they all had their suspicions. Jasmine sat with her back to a wagon wheel, head bowed, her eyes on her folded hands. She knew.

It was near suppertime when Curley discovered Quickenpaugh was awake. He raised the blanket that covered him, and his dark eyes met those of Curley.

"You?" said Quickenpaugh.

Curley laughed. "Lorna and me. We took your buckskins off so Oscar could see to your wound. Cal wants to talk to you, when you feel able."

"Quickenpaugh talk," said the Indian.

"Cal," Curley said, "Quickenpaugh's ready to talk. Are all of us allowed to listen?"

"I reckon," said Cal. "We're all part of the same outfit, and what he has to tell us of the trail ahead may be almighty important. Come on, all of you. Supper can wait."

Jasmine sat with her back against a wagon wheel, her splinted legs covered with the usual blanket. Quickenpaugh was nearby, and she resisted the urge to question him before the others arrived.

"Quickenpaugh," Cal said, when the outfit had gathered around, "who shot you?"

"Bud," said Quickenpaugh. "I don't shoot."

"We know you didn't," Tom Allen said. "Neither of your weapons had been fired."

"You sure Bud knew it was you?" Smokey Ellison asked.

"*Si*," said Quickenpaugh. "*Cuidado*."

"So you tried to warn him," Cal said. "Of what?"

"Sioux," said Quickenpaugh. "Many, like the stars. Along *Río* Little Big Horn."

. "My God," Bill Petty said, "we'll be headin' right toward 'em."

"No," said Cal. "We'll drive north to the Yellowstone, and then east, if we must. There should be enough graze now. It'd cost us a couple of days, but that's a small price to pay if it keeps us out of the coming battle the Sioux have planned."

Quickenpaugh tired quickly and was left to rest. Lorna found herself alone with Cal.

"Bud won't be waiting for us in Deadwood, will he?"

"No," Cal said, "and I think he got just what he deserved. Quickenpaugh tried to warn him, but was gunned down and left for dead."

"I feel so sorry for Jasmine," said Lorna. "He was her only kin."

"I know," Cal said, "but he's been a constant thorn in her side since we brought the Story herd from Texas. Time heals, and she'll get over it."

"That means Curley's entitled to the money from the sale of Bud's cows," said Lorna.

"I reckon it does," Cal said. "What do you reckon she'll do?"

Lorna laughed. "She stayed with Quickenpaugh the whole time he was out of his head with fever. Does that tell you anything?"

"More than I want to know," Cal said. "I just want Quickenpaugh well enough to ride, and Jasmine out of those damn splints."

"I saw you tote her out of the wagon, two-thirds naked," said Lorna.

"But she wore a long-tailed shirt," Cal said. "I didn't see a thing."

LITTLE BIG HORN RIVER, WYOMING TERRITORY.
MAY 20, 1876

Aware of the Sioux threat, Bud McDaniels kept to cover, sparing his horse as much as he could. He recalled an occasional landmark, the result of his having crossed much of Montana Territory with the Story trail drive. Somewhere just ahead of him should be the Little Big Horn. There he would rest himself and his horse. The bushes that lined the river had begun to bud and the sun was warm as Bud dismounted. He listened, and heard no sound of any wild thing. Not even the chirp or cry of a bird. But he attributed that to his own presence, and when he judged his horse was ready, he led the animal to a shallows to drink. When the horse had drunk its fill, McDaniels bellied down to satisfy his own thirst. Suddenly there were reflections in the water, and cold chills crept up Bud's spine. Fearfully lifting his head, his horrified eyes met the murderous gaze of five Indians on the opposite bank. As he struggled to his feet, an arrow ripped into his left shoulder, while a second one raked the flank of his horse. The animal nickered, reared and, before McDaniels could seize the reins, galloped back the direction they had come. In a fury, Bud drew his Colt, but he never fired a shot. Simultaneously, three Sioux arrows thudded into his chest. He lay on his back, his life dribbling away, making no move when one of the Sioux took his gunbelt and the Colt from his stiffening fingers. Bud McDaniels had ridden his last trail . . .

EASTERN WYOMING TERRITORY.
MAY 8, 1876

The morning after the arrival of Roscoe Yates and his daughters, Yates sought out Benton McCaleb.

"Mr. McCaleb," said Yates, "if it's not asking too much, we'd like to follow you from here on to Deadwood. We have our own grub."

"I have no objection to that," McCaleb said. "It's you that's in a hurry. We're going to remain here for maybe a week, allowing the grass ahead of us to green. Right now there's not enough graze."

"I fear we'll be up against the same problem, then," said Yates. "Our mules are lookin' a little gaunt. We'll take a few days of rest and move on when you do."

"That's up to you," McCaleb replied. "We average about twelve miles a day, and some days considerably less."

Neither of the Yates girls offered to help with breakfast, and when it was over, they contributed nothing toward the cleaning up.

"I won't wash another pan or make another pot of coffee as long as they're here," Penelope vowed.

"Then don't," said Rosalie. "You can saddle your horse and be just one of the cowboys while Rebecca, Susannah and me do the cooking and cleaning up. And don't go whining to Brazos. I've already talked to him."

It was a peaceful camp. The sun was hot by the time it was noon-high, and the graze had improved dramatically. There was a spring-fed water hole a quarter of a mile distant. It was clear and deep, with a stone bottom, a jumble of boulders circling it. It was an ideal place to wash clothing and blankets, and the women took advantage of the opportunity.

"We're going to wash clothes and blankets, if you want to go along," Rebecca told the Yates girls.

"If they go, I'm not going," said Penelope.

"Then don't," Rosalie replied. "Wear dirty clothes and sleep on dirty blankets. You're old enough to do your own wash, and you're going to, starting now."

Rebecca, Rosalie and Susannah saddled horses and set out with their wash. The Yates girls followed, each riding a mule bareback. Penelope found all her own clothing and dirty blankets hadn't been touched. With an exasperated sigh, she saddled her horse, gathered up her wash and started for the water hole.

"Do the three of you wash for everybody?" Kate Yates asked.

"No," said Rebecca. "We wash our clothes and blankets, and those of our men. The single men do their own washing."

"Here comes one of the cowboys," Connie Yates said.

"It's my daughter Penelope," said Rosalie. "She's bringing her wash."

Dismounting, Penelope spoke only to Rosalie.

"I couldn't find any lye soap. Do you have it all?"

"Here," said Rosalie, "and there's not that much, so use it sparingly."

The Yates girls hadn't begun washing. They stood on a tongue of stone that reached out over the water. Penelope climbed up the stone parapet behind them, and they heard her coming.

"Well, praise be," said one of the girls, "it's Madame Cow Stink herself, come to wash off some of the smell."

She was totally unprepared for what followed. Penelope gave her a shove, and with a startled screech, she went headlong into the water below.

"Damn you," the second girl cried, "you pushed her."

"Yes," Penelope said with some satisfaction. "Like this."

She shoved the second girl off, and then threw their bundles of dirty clothes in after them. Rebecca, Rosalie and Susannah were on the far side of the water hole, and while they hadn't seen the start of it, all the cursing and commotion quickly got their attention.

"Penelope," Rosalie shouted, "were you responsible for that?"

"What do you think?" Penelope replied innocently. "This is a slippery rock."

For Rosalie's sake, Rebecca and Susannah managed not to laugh, as the Yates girls climbed up on one of the stones surrounding the water hole. But the Yates duo had another card to play. First they tugged off their boots and poured the water from them. They then unbuttoned their Levi's and skinned out of them. Finally they removed their shirts. Carefully they spread the sodden garments out on one of the rocks.

"My God," said Susannah, "they're stark naked. Suppose some of the men are watching."

"I don't care," Rosalie said. "Penelope calls them a pair of whores, and I wouldn't be a bit surprised if she's right."

"But they're with their father," said Rebecca.

"You don't *know* he's their father," Rosalie said. "What better excuse for an old goat like him to travel with a pair of fillies to warm his blankets?"

Penelope had found a place to do her wash and, ignoring the Yates girls, got started. Not having as many clothes and blankets to wash, she finished ahead of Rebecca, Rosalie and Susannah. The Yates girls still lay on the huge flat stone. As Penelope was mounting her horse, Rosalie called to her. Penelope rode around to her and reined up, waiting.

"Penelope," said Rosalie, "I don't want you saying anything to the men about this."

Penelope laughed. "I'm going to tell them all. It's not near as crowded now as it'll be in a Deadwood whorehouse."

With that, Penelope kicked her horse into a gallop riding back toward camp.

"You think she will?" Susannah asked.

"I won't be a bit surprised," said Rosalie. "If she does, they asked for it."

But when the three women had finished their washing, the Yates girls hadn't moved, and there was no sign of any of the men.

When Rebecca, Rosalie and Susannah returned to camp, Roscoe Yates was stretched out beneath his wagon, asleep.

Penelope had gone far enough from camp to spread her newly washed things on rapidly greening grass. The rest of the outfit had occupied themselves with various duties, such as cleaning and oiling their weapons, and nobody seemed curious as to what had become of the Yates girls. The girls returned just before supper, and afterward, the first watch mounted and rode out, Penelope riding with them. Those who would take over the second watch at midnight had rolled in their blankets. The herd was quiet, and rather than ride, Penelope was on foot, leading her horse. She paused, thinking she had seen something move. Then, near the Yates wagon, two shadows detached themselves from their bedrolls. Leaving her horse, Penelope followed them afoot. There was an early moon, and combined with the starlight, she could see them ahead of her. Suddenly she dropped to the ground, holding her breath. Someone was following *her*. The cautious footsteps came on, and Monte Nance came within a few feet of the crouching Penelope. He wasn't following her; he was following the Yates girls.

Penelope waited until he was well ahead of her, and then followed him. By the time he reached the water hole where the women had done their wash, Connie and Kate Yates had stripped and were standing on one of the stones above the water.

"It took you long enough," one of the girls complained.

"Well, hell, I had to wait till everybody was on watch or asleep," Monte Nance said.

Monte stood there looking at them in the moonlight, and Penelope gritted her teeth.

"Are we going in the water or not?" one of the girls asked.

"I didn't come here to go in the water," Monte said.

He wrestled off his boots, unbuttoned his shirt and then his Levi's. One of the girls laughed, and Penelope waited to see and hear no more. She stumbled back toward camp, a lump in her throat and tears on her cheeks . . .

11

SOUTHEASTERN MONTANA TERRITORY.
MAY 22, 1876

ALL OF CAL'S EFFORTS to have Quickenpaugh ride in the wagon were in vain.

"No like wagon," said the Indian. He saddled his horse without any sign of weakness.

"He's one damn tough *hombre*," Tom Allen observed.

The condition of the cattle and horse herd had greatly improved, and as Cal had most recently learned from Quickenpaugh, there was much more grass to the north and east. As the outfit made ready to move out, they saw a riderless horse coming in from the east.

"Bud's horse," said Quanah Taylor. Mounting his horse, he went to meet the animal. He seized it by its bridle, for the reins had been snapped by the horse stepping on them.

"Arrow wound on his flank," Oscar said, as Quanah led him in.

"Unsaddle him and use some sulfur salve on that wound," said Cal.

Smokey Ellison had taken the Winchester from the saddle boot and examined it.

"It's fully loaded and ain't been fired," Smokey announced.

The outfit had been ready to take the trail. Jasmine was already seated beside Curley on the wagon box.

"Tom," said Cal, "Jasmine's seen the horse and will

know what it means, but maybe you should talk to her. We can wait a few more minutes."

Tom Allen started for the wagon, not wishing to add to the load of grief Jasmine bore already. Curley was expressionless, staring straight ahead, apparently interested in the behinds of the mules.

"Jasmine," Tom said, "I . . . thought . . ."

"You don't have to say anything, Tom," said Jasmine dully. "I know."

She said no more, and Curley kept her silence, never revealing what she might have been thinking. Tom rode back to the herd.

"Head 'em up, move 'em out," Cal shouted, waving his hat and pointing northward.

The cattle took the trail first, followed by the horse herd. Behind it came the chuck wagon. Quickenpaugh, Arch, Hitch and Mac kept the horses bunched, right on the heels of the drag riders. The stock had been well fed and watered, and caused no trouble. When the drive came upon an unknown creek—which they believed was a tributary of the distant Yellowstone—Cal signaled for the riders to mill the herd. Sundown was just an hour away. By the time the riders had the horse herd and the cattle settled down, Curley had unharnessed the mules and was leading them to graze with the horses.

"I figure we're still maybe two days south of the Yellowstone," Bill Petty said. "Do you still aim to go that far north?"

"Maybe not," said Cal. "That's a long ways out of our way. The Little Big Horn flows from somewhere north. We failed to ask Quickenpaugh *where* these Sioux are dug in along the river. I'll talk to him again after supper, so we don't have to travel any farther north than necessary."

It was a complicated question, and with a stick, Cal had made a drawing on the ground for Quickenpaugh to study.

"*Rio* Yellowstone," Cal said, pointing to a long line stretching from the east.

"*Sí*," Quickenpaugh replied.

"*Río* Little Big Horn," said Cal, pointing to a line that angled down from the north.

"*Sí*," said Quickenpaugh.

Tom Allen and some of the other riders had eased in close enough to observe what Cal had drawn on the ground, and to hear Quickenpaugh's answers. Cal then got to the part of the question that was of utmost importance. With his finger, he started at the beginning of the drawn line representing the Little Big Horn. Moving south, making small impressions with his finger at one- or two-inch intervals, he followed the line to what he estimated was the mountainous region that was Wyoming Territory.

"Sioux," Cal said. "Where?"

Using his finger, Quickenpaugh drew a line across the lower end of that representing the Little Big Horn. He then moved his finger south of the line he had just drawn.

"By God," said Mac Withers, "they're holed up not too far from the Big Horns."

"One more day's drive to the north should have us clear of them," Cal said. "Then we can head east again."

"There's somethin' botherin' me," said Bill Petty. "I ain't doubtin' them Sioux are dug in to the south along the Little Big Horn, but what's to stop 'em from ridin' north?"

"Nothing," Cal said, "except that if everything turns sour and their medicine is bad, they can retreat into the Big Horn Mountains. That wouldn't be possible if they're too far north. The soldiers could ride them down."

"I reckon you're right," said Petty. "If they get into the Big Horns, there ain't enough soldiers in the United States to root 'em out."

"We won't take any chances," Cal said. "When we change directions, starting east, I'll have Quickenpaugh scout ahead maybe thirty miles. At least until we're well beyond the Little Big Horn."

The fire was put out when supper was done, well before dark.

"We'll go with the usual watch," said Cal. "Tom, you take Arch, Hitch, Mac, Curley and Lorna. I want Quickenpaugh with me on the second watch."

It was a wise precaution, for experience had proven that when there was trouble on the trail, it generally started after midnight, in the small hours of the morning. Curley and Lorna walked their horses side by side, talking quietly.

"Except for speaking to Tom before we moved out, Jasmine hasn't said a word all day long," Curley said.

"I think she believed there was some hope, until Bud's horse came in," said Lorna. "In the West, an empty saddle is almost always proof the rider won't be comin' back."

"I couldn't stand Bud the way he was," Curley said, "and I don't miss him. But I wish this hadn't happened, for Jasmine's sake."

"You've just inherited Bud's part of the herd," said Lorna. "What do you intend to do, after we've sold the cattle?"

"Travel with the rest of you back to Virginia City, I suppose," Curley said. "It's all the home I have. I don't know what I'll do, unless I go back to cowboyin' for Mr. Story."

"What about Quickenpaugh?" Lorna asked.

"Damn it, Bud was bad enough," said Curley. "Now don't you start."

"Oh, Curley," Lorna said, "I'm not raggin' you. I'm serious."

"To answer your question," said Curley, "I don't know. I'm fond of Quickenpaugh, and my feelings could become . . . stronger."

"The question is, how does *he* feel?" Lorna asked.

"I don't know," said Curley. "How do you get an Indian who knows maybe ten words of English to share your blankets?"

Lorna laughed. "I don't see that as a problem. Whatever else he is, he's a man. When we return to Virginia City, you'll have enough of a stake to begin ranching on your own.''

Curley sighed. ''That's another problem. Quickenpaugh has more pride in one finger than Bud had in his whole body. With my damn luck, Quickenpaugh will think of me as a rich squaw, too far above him.''

''Then do this,'' said Lorna. ''We'll be a while getting to Deadwood. Don't even think about later, when you'll have money, and don't you dare mention it to Quickenpaugh. On the trail, there must be *some* way you can get that Indian's attention.''

''There is,'' Curley said, ''but I believe Cal's considered that. Quickenpaugh's always on the second watch, while I'm on the first.''

''Cal wants Quickenpaugh on the second watch because he believes there's more likely to be trouble,'' said Lorna. ''You and me are on the first watch because he thinks we'll be safe there.''

''When we have a chance,'' Curley said, ''I'll have Quickenpaugh start teaching me the Crow tongue again.''

''What's so interesting in that?'' Lorna asked.

''Nothing,'' said Curley. ''I don't care a damn for the Crow tongue, but how else do I get Quickenpaugh to spend any time with me?''

The grass definitely had begun to green toward the north. Cal halted the drive after estimating they had traveled at least twelve miles. The horses and cattle were bedded down along the unidentified stream they had been following.

''One more day's drive to the north should put us well beyond the reach of the Sioux,'' Cal said. ''Then we can go east, toward the Dakotas.''

''There may be a problem we haven't considered,'' said Tom. ''While we'll be avoiding the Sioux, suppose we encounter the soldiers? They'll likely march west, along the Yellowstone.''

''Unless the military has declared martial law,'' Cal said,

"they can't stop us. After all, we'll be far enough north until the Sioux will be of no danger to us."

"They ought to be grateful to us," said Tom Allen. "Thanks to Quickenpaugh, you can pretty well tell them where the Sioux are gathering."

"If they try to give us a hard way to go, don't tell 'em nothing," Smokey Ellison said. "Let them find the Sioux on their own."

That seemed to be the prevailing mood among the riders, for they well remembered the time they had trailed a Texas herd to Virginia City. The military had ordered them to turn back, but Nelson Story had defied them, taking the Bozeman Trail at night.*

After the camp had settled down, Oscar Fentress stopped to see how Jasmine was feeling.

"How much longer will I be wearing these splints on my legs?" Jasmine asked Oscar.

"I reckon at least two more weeks," said Oscar. "Take 'em away too soon, and them bones breaks loose. Then you be stuck with 'em twice as long, and maybe they don't mend at all."

EASTERN WYOMING TERRITORY.
MAY 20, 1876

The Lone Star outfit spent a week in camp, allowing the horse remuda and the cattle to feed on the new grass. It might have been an enjoyable, restful time, had it not been for the presence of Roscoe Yates and his supposed daughters, Connie and Kate. Not knowing quite how to handle the errant females, Benton McCaleb managed to arrange a conversation with Rebecca. McCaleb got right to the point.

"What am I goin' to do about them damn brass-plated females?"

*The Virginia City Trail (Trail Drive #7)

Rebecca laughed. "You gave them permission to trail with us."

"I didn't see anything wrong with that," McCaleb said. "Old Roscoe's their daddy, and he's always around. Besides, we'll be taking the trail tomorrow."

"If that old man's their daddy, he should be tarred and feathered," said Rebecca.

"The reason being that the rest of you women don't like the daughters," McCaleb said. "That day they returned from washing their clothes, the two of them looked like they had been dunked in the water hole. They slipped, I reckon."

"I'm sure they did," said Rebecca with a straight face.

"Granted that old Roscoe hasn't done his duty with the girls," McCaleb said, "but that rule should be for any parent, shouldn't it? What about Brazos and Rosalie?"

"What about them?" Rebecca asked.

"Penelope," said McCaleb. "She's become a little wretch, and you can see the hate in her eyes when she looks at the Yates women."

Rebecca laughed. "Is that all? She's been the only single female in the outfit for so long, she thinks it's her right. She's jealous, not just of the Yates girls, but of any single female coming into her territory."

"You think so?" McCaleb said. "Penelope's bitter, and to some degree, I think she has a right. These Yates females are taking unfair advantage, doing things . . . that Penelope dares not do."

"Things?" Rebecca asked.

"Like stripping off naked, when they went to wash clothes," said McCaleb.

Rebecca laughed. "Benton McCaleb, you old dog! You were watching."

"Wrong," McCaleb said. "I sent Goose to watch over all of you. But I *was* watching when the Yates women sneaked out of camp two nights later. I watched Penelope follow them, and I followed her. I was close by, when she heard something, and I thought she had discovered me. We both bellied down until Monte was well past us. Penelope followed him, and I followed her. The moon- and starlight was bright enough to see the two Yates girls stripped, standing over the water. Monte was out of everything except his hat, when Penelope ran away."

"But you didn't," said Rebecca.

"I gave Penelope a head start, and then I followed her," McCaleb said. "Maybe the three of them were there just to take a swim, but being a man, I doubt it."

"Monte's a grown man," said Rebecca. "I'm his sister, not his mother. If he only took what was offered, can you blame him?"

"Yes," McCaleb said. "Can't you see the disappointment in Penelope's eyes when she's lookin' at him? He's let the girl down almighty hard, and she's having trouble living with the memory of him with a pair of naked females."

"Monte?" said Rebecca unbelievingly. "Penelope's kept him mad at her all the time, and when they're on speaking terms, they fight like cats and dogs."

"You're forgetting something," McCaleb said. "When you and me met, back in Texas, you cussed me like a mule-skinner, and I threw you in the Trinity River. Hell, we fought all the way from Texas to the High Plains, and look at us now."

"My God, you're right," said Rebecca. "All the signs are there, and I haven't been seeing them. I'd better have a talk with Rosalie. Why don't you talk to Brazos?"

"No way," McCaleb said. "I'm a trail boss, not Solomon. I won't be surprised if little Penelope decides to fight fire with fire, and it's not gonna be me that tells Brazos he's got to order his adopted daughter to keep her britches on."

"As trail boss, you *could* order Monte to stay away from those Yates women," said Rebecca.

"I can't order Monte or any of the riders to do anything,

unless they're somehow endangering this trail drive,"
McCaleb said. "You call Monte a grown man, and now
you want me to take a switch to him."

"Be serious, Bent," said Rebecca. "If Penelope does
some foolish thing in competition with the Yates women,
it'll be awfully hard on Brazos and Rosalie."

"I think Penelope's old enough to take full responsibility
for what she does," McCaleb said. "Why burden Rosalie
with something she can't change? Knowing what I know
or suspect, I sure as hell don't aim to drag Brazos into it."

"You've already messed up my mind with what you
know," said Rebecca. "You might as well finish the job
by telling me what you suspect."

"You remember when we suspected Monte of watching
Penelope wash herself, there in the chuck wagon?"

"Yes," Rebecca said, "and I still believe he did it."

"So do I," said McCaleb, "and while it was a sneaky,
low-down thing to do, we can't blame Monte entirely. I
think Penelope arranged that."

"She wouldn't," Rebecca said.

"She would," said McCaleb. "The way that wagon was
loaded, there was no wasted space. Yet, after Penelope
complained, I found the load had been shifted enough so
that a person could look in through the front of the wagon
and see anybody inside. That tin of shells fell on Penelope's
foot after she rearranged things, moving some of the heav-
ier containers to the top of the load. Is that enough to satisfy
you?"

"Dear God," said Rebecca, "you're calling her a brazen
little trollop."

"No," McCaleb said. "She's just trying to get Monte's
attention. Back in Texas, when we were barely speaking, I
caught you watching me, while I was in the Trinity River,
jaybird naked."*

The Goodnight Trail (Trail Drive #1)

"You *would* remember that," said Rebecca, blushing.

"That, and more," McCaleb said. "Once a female decides she wants some two-legged varmint of an *hombre,* she'll take advantage any way she can. Isn't that true?"

"I reckon," said Rebecca. "If you'd handled it right, I would have come to you long before we stood before the preacher."

"I'm glad you didn't," McCaleb said. "A saloon whore would have done that, and I had bigger and better plans for you."

"Thank you," said Rebecca, meaning it. "What else makes you suspicious of Penelope?"

McCaleb laughed. "Just like a woman. You've just heard some shocking news, and now you want to hear more."

"I'm not sure you aren't bullyragging me," Rebecca said. "*Is* there more?"

"Nothing but my suspicions," said McCaleb, "but you might as well have them to think about, along with the other. If you'll remember, when Penelope went to the wagon with a pot of hot water, it was almighty cold, with near two feet of snow on the ground. Would you have stripped down to the bare hide all at once? In cold weather, you start at the top, working your way down. You remove your shirt and coat, and after washing your upper parts, you put on the shirt and coat again. Following that, you take off your boots and Levi's, and you wash the rest of you. Then, working fast, you jump back into your Levi's and boots, before you become a block of ice."

"It makes sense to me," Rebecca said. "How would you know that Penelope didn't do just that?"

"Because she told me," said McCaleb. "I asked her what she was wearing when she discovered somebody was watching her. She was standing there without a stitch on, with only the wagon canvas between her and the cold wind."

Rebecca sighed. "McCaleb, why do you always know so much, and why are you always right?"

"I'm trail boss," said McCaleb. "It's my job."

SOUTHEASTERN WYOMING TERRITORY.
MAY 21, 1876

"Cloudy to the west," Will Elliot observed, as the outfit prepared to move out. "We've been settin' here a week, lettin' the horses and cattle graze, and there hasn't been a cloud in the sky. Now that we're ready to move on, it rains."

"Not before sometime tomorrow," said McCaleb. "We'll go as far as we can today."

They took the trail, Rebecca keeping the chuck wagon close behind the drag riders. The Yates wagon followed the chuck wagon. Pen Rhodes, Susannah, Rosalie and Penelope were riding drag, and it was Penelope who noticed the Yates wagon was no longer moving.

"Penelope," Rosalie said, "you'd better tell McCaleb so he can mill the herd. Something must have gone wrong back there."

"Old Roscoe likely went to sleep at the reins and fell off the box," said Penelope.

But she dutifully rode on ahead, and when she told McCaleb, he stopped the drive.

"It's their first day on the trail with us," Penelope said, "and already they're slowing us down. Why don't we just go on and leave them there?"

"Here, now," said McCaleb, looking at her with a stern eye. "That would be a heartless thing to do."

"Would it?" Penelope said.

She rode with McCaleb back to the Yates wagon. The drag riders were there, as was Rebecca. Monte Nance was the next to arrive. Roscoe Yates still sat on the wagon box, but his "daughters" had climbed down and were staring at the shattered left rear wheel.

"Yates," said McCaleb, "Rebecca brought the chuck

wagon over the same ground without busting a wheel on that drop-off. This is rough country for a wagon, and you should always be looking ahead."

"I don't need or want a lecture, Mr. McCaleb," Yates said stiffly. "I trust my mules to follow your wagon, which they have done."

"I'm prepared to believe their judgment is as good or better than yours," McCaleb said, "but your mules don't care a damn about your wagon. It's up to you to watch for and avoid chuckholes and drop-offs that might break an axle or damage a wheel. You *do* have a spare wheel, don't you?"

"Yes," said Yates, "but I have a weak heart."

"Pen," McCaleb said in disgust, "you and Monte wrestle that spare wheel out. I'll get a hub wrench from our wagon, loosen the broken wheel and help you mount the new one."

"I am immensely grateful for your help," said Yates.

He remained where he was, while Connie and Kate seemed mildly amused. Using the hub wrench from his own chuck wagon, McCaleb was sweating over the broken wheel.

"There's no wagon jack in here," Pen said, from inside the Yates wagon.

"I'll get ours from the chuck wagon," said McCaleb.

McCaleb jacked up the rear of the wagon, while Pen and Monte rolled the new wheel into place. McCaleb then loaded the hub with grease and tightened the hub nut.

"Yates," McCaleb said, when the wheel had been replaced, "we've already used our spare wheel, and now you've just used yours. Break another wheel between here and Deadwood, and the lot of you will be riding those mules bareback. With all due respect for your confidence in your mules, you'd better watch where the hell you're going."

"I could take the reins to their wagon," said Monte.

"If you do," McCaleb said grimly, "you're no longer part of this trail drive. Yates, if you don't keep up, or if

you bust another wheel, you're on your own. Now all of
you return to your positions. We're movin' out."

The outfit obeyed McCaleb's order, with the exception
of Monte Nance, who paused to speak to Roscoe Yates.

"Sorry," said Monte. "He's like that all the time. Since
he married my sister Rebecca, he thinks he owns me."

"If he doesn't already, he will," Yates said. "Until you
stand up on your hind legs and at least *look* like a man,
you'll get walked on and stomped on a lot."

"You don't look like the kind that's been throwed and
stomped," said Monte, "so why should I listen to you?"

"You shouldn't," said Yates, "as long as you're satisfied to jump when McCaleb shouts froggy. Can you handle
them twin pistols, or do you carry them for show?"

"I can use them when there's a need," Monte said angrily.

"Once we reach Deadwood," said Yates, "I'll have
need of a man who's good with his gun and his fists. I have
heard that Deadwood's a lawless town, and I'm willing to
pay for protection."

"That depends on who or what you're wantin' protection
from," Monte said cautiously. "I won't side you on anything that's crooked, and I won't sell my gun unless I'm
first told what I'm expected to do. A man's got to have
some principles."

"I'm prepared to pay two hundred a month for your gun
and your principles," said Yates. "Are you interested?"

"Maybe," Monte said, "but not if it means selling out
my family and friends."

"A man that sells his gun shouldn't *have* family and
friends," said Yates. "All he needs is a fast gun and a slow
conscience."

"Then I won't be selling my gun," Monte said. "I got
the idea that what you're plannin' involves Benton Mc-
Caleb and the Lone Star outfit. The only decent thing I can
do is tell McCaleb not to turn his back on you."

"You are a fool," said Yates.

"Maybe," Monte replied, "but I'm an honest one."

"When all the smoke clears, you may be a *dead* one," said Yates ominously. "Play by my rules, and there'll be plenty of money and women."

"I don't want your damn money," Monte said. "As for your women, I've sampled all these two have to offer, and I don't expect them that's to follow will be any better."

The women in question—Kate and Connie Yates—had been listening with considerable interest to the strange conversation.

"I must confess that I've misjudged you," said Yates. "When a man can't be bought with women and whiskey, that don't leave much. Now I suppose we'll just have to decide what your reputation's worth."

Monte laughed. "You can't tell McCaleb anything about me that he don't already know, and if you could, nobody would believe you. McCaleb's never liked me, but he's fair, and I won't double-cross him. Not for you, not for anybody."

"You continue to refer to my daughters as fallen women," said Yates. "It might interest McCaleb and the others to learn it was you who led them astray. You've ruined their honor, and if McCaleb refuses to accept that when we reach civilization, I'll turn everything over to the law."

"I doubt that," Monte said. "There is no law in Deadwood, except maybe the army, and as for this pair of blanket-warmers you got with you, they're no more your kin than I am."

"I see you've never been to a boomtown after a strike," said Yates. "All I'll have to do is spread the word that you've violated both my young daughters, and a miners' posse will come after you with a rope."

"Go ahead and do your worst," Monte growled, "and I'll violate you with lead."

"You have until we reach Deadwood to change your mind," said Yates.

"I won't be changing my mind," Monte said.

Yates said nothing until Monte was well out of hearing. He then turned angrily on the two women.

"You two don't follow instructions worth a damn," said Yates.

"You told us to make friends with him so you could hire his gun," Connie replied.

"So I did," Yates conceded, "but I thought the two of you had better sense than to let him have his way with you, all in one night."

"You didn't say when," Kate said. "What should we do now?"

"Leave him alone," said Yates. "Even Judas had his price, and so will Monte Nance."

12

EASTERN WYOMING TERRITORY.
MAY 18, 1876

"JUST OUR BRAND OF luck," Brazos said, his eyes on the western horizon. "We take some time to graze the remuda and the cattle, and the sun's shinin' every day. Now that we're barely back on the trail, we got a brand-new storm brewing."

"The trail boss bein' the equal to God, what do you aim to do about that storm that's coming, McCaleb?" Monte asked.

"We'll remain here for the night," said McCaleb, his eyes on Nance, "and if the storm's a bad one, it'll be everybody in the saddle. When it's your turn to sleep, don't shuck anything except your hat, and be sure to picket your horse close by."

"Is that all?" Monte asked, his words shot full of scorn.

"No," said McCaleb. "Most of you know I don't have many rules, but the few I *do* have are engraved in stone. On a trail drive, probably the most important one is that none of you are to wander around after dark."

"You didn't bother telling us that when you said we could trail with you," Yates said.

"My riders—except for one—know and respect my rules," said McCaleb.

"You're aiming that lecture at us, are you not?" Yates demanded.

"Yes, putting it bluntly," said McCaleb. "When you're in Sioux territory with no idea *where* the hostiles are, you'd better be prepared. Starting tonight, nobody leaves camp after dark, except those on sentry duty. Anyone else wandering around is to be considered an enemy and is subject to being shot."

"You're a hard man, McCaleb," Roscoe Yates said.

"It's kept me alive," said McCaleb shortly.

"Well, I don't like it," one of the Yates women said. "When I get up at night, I'm not used to having some jackleg cowboy tell me where and when I can't go."

"She's right," the second woman said. "Even if it is dark, I won't squat with all these men surrounding me."

"It's your choice," McCaleb said. "You've been warned."

"McCaleb," Yates almost shouted, "I won't have my girls compromised or embarrassed by your stupid rules."

"I reckon they've been compromised a lot," said Penelope, "but they wouldn't know embarrassment if it walked up and bit 'em."

The two women glared at Penelope, and if looks could have killed, Penelope would have been dead. Rosalie went red with embarrassment, but Brazos caught her eye, and she held her tongue. Yates looked as though he'd like to pull a gun and commit murder, but every man in the outfit was just waiting for him to make a false move. Goose, the Lipan Apache, held a big Bowie knife, and began border-shifting it from one hand to the other. Suddenly the tension was gone. Roscoe Yates got to his feet and without a word started back to his wagon. Kate and Connie followed.

"You've made some enemies, Bent," Rebecca said when they were alone.

"I reckon," McCaleb agreed, "but what else was I to do? What I said wasn't aimed at the women. I wanted Monte to know I mean business. Anyhow, what can Yates do?"

"I've heard what can happen in lawless mining towns,"

said Rebecca. "Yates could lie about you just as he can lie about Monte. There's probably a shortage of women in Deadwood, and with those girls testifying, a miners' court might hang anybody."

"I don't believe the old varmint will go that far, getting revenge," McCaleb said, "and I really don't think he can press charges against Monte, even if it would serve him right."

"I hope you're right," said Rebecca nervously. "It seems like Monte's spent a lot of time with Roscoe since you laid down the law to them."

"I figure Monte thinks his nuzzling up to Roscoe Yates will irritate me," McCaleb said, "while gaining him favor with Connie and Kate."

"There's no way we can get through to him, then," said Rebecca.

"I've tried to ignore him for your sake," said McCaleb, "but it's gettin' more difficult by the day. Not because my hide's not tough enough, but because a trail drive depends on every rider, every day. I'm through with favored treatment to Monte or anybody else. If he steps over the line just one more time, he'll see a side of Benton McCaleb he's never seen before."

McCaleb's eyes were ice-blue and unrelenting, and a chill crept up Rebecca's spine. In the years they had been together, she had never seen him threaten anyone. Now she must face the truth. McCaleb *had* been making exceptions for Monte, and only the closeness and kinship of the Lone Star outfit could prevent almost certain mutiny.

"Let me talk to Monte once more, Bent," said Rebecca. "I'll try to talk some sense into him, and if I fail, then do what you must."

McCaleb nodded, unspeaking. He knew what the hard words had cost her.

As the riders assigned to the first watch mounted their horses, distant thunder rolled somewhere far to the west.

Lightning—like the flicking tongue of a rattler—danced along the horizon as though on stepping-stones the Almighty had created there for just such a purpose.

"Sounds like a mean one coming after us," McCaleb said. "If that thunder and lightning get too close, we'll have one hell of a time holding 'em. The first watch will be ready to join those of us on the second watch, the moment it becomes necessary."

"We've had too many damn stampedes," said Brazos, "and I'm ready to head this one off, if we can. We know the ground will be hock-deep in mud, with standing water everywhere, and no place to spread our blankets. I believe all of us should stay in the saddle at least until first light, or until the storm's passed."

There was a long silence. To the shame of them all, Penelope spoke.

"I'd as soon ride all night as to try to sleep on the wet, muddy ground. I'll go."

"We're an outfit," Will Elliot said. "Whatever danger comes, we'll face it together."

"All of you I can count on tonight, raise your hands," said McCaleb.

It quickly became a unanimous decision, but for Monte Nance. He neither raised a hand nor spoke. He seemed to be awaiting a reaction from McCaleb, and McCaleb well knew it, so he let the incident pass. He caught Rebecca's eye, and found no reassurance there. It would be up to her . . .

"Let's keep 'em bunched as tight as we can," said McCaleb, as the watch began.

The rest of the outfit had begun saddling their horses in preparation for the coming night. Not caring to hear what McCaleb had to say, Roscoe Yates and his two daughters had shied away. Monte was headed toward their wagon when Rebecca spoke.

"Monte, I want to talk to you."

"Well, I don't want to talk to you," Monte said. "Tell

McCaleb anything he wants me to know, he'll have to tell me to my face. I won't listen to any secondhand preaching from him, while he hides behind a female.''

"Any preaching I do,'' said Rebecca, "will come straight from me. Bent's washed his hands of you, and I'm glad. I suspect Brazos and Will see you in much the same light, and that they'll all vote to cut you loose once we reach Deadwood and the cattle are sold.''

"Then don't look for me to do a damned thing from here on,'' Monte snarled.

"We won't,'' said Rebecca, "and don't *you* expect trail wages from here on.''

"That's about what I expected of a cheap bastard like McCaleb,'' Monte said.

"It's not McCaleb's idea,'' said Rebecca. "It's mine. Without you in the saddle, it'll be hard on all the other riders. I'm going to suggest to Bent that all we would have paid you be split among the rest of the outfit.''

"Do that,'' Monte hissed. "All I expect from McCaleb is payment for my part of the herd. Then all of you can go to hell.''

"I'm sorry you feel that way,'' said Rebecca. "If you decide you want to go on being a part of Lone Star, you'll have to mend your ways before we reach Deadwood.''

"Whatever you and big bad McCaleb do when we reach Deadwood won't bother me,'' said Monte. "I'm fed up bein' a cow nurse. I have plans of my own.''

Rebecca mounted her horse and joined the rest of the outfit circling the herd. McCaleb waited awhile, allowing her to collect her thoughts and compose herself. Finally, when she reined up and dismounted, so did McCaleb.

"No luck, I reckon,'' McCaleb said.

"None,'' said Rebecca. "Threatening to kick him out of Lone Star didn't bother him in the slightest. He says he has plans of his own.''

"I suspect those plans have something to do with Roscoe Yates,'' McCaleb replied. "The man's hands are soft, and

I doubt he's ever seen an honest day's work in his life. He has the look of an *hombre* playing with a stacked deck.''

The storm held off until well past midnight, and when it struck, there was only wind and rain. Thunder still rumbled from a distance, and golden shards of lightning still walked grandly across the western horizon. The cattle were restless, several times rising to their feet, but the constant presence of the riders overcame their fears. Two hours before first light, the rain became a drizzle, eventually ceasing. There was always dry wood beneath the wagon, in the possum belly, so there was plenty of hot coffee for breakfast. Most of the outfit was aware of the standoff between Benton McCaleb and Monte Nance, and they all waited with some anticipation to see how McCaleb would handle it. McCaleb wasted no time, and right after breakfast announced the positions for various riders during the day.

"Brazos, I want you and Will as flank riders. Jed and Stoney, you'll be riding swing. Pen, I want you, Rebecca, Penelope and Rosalie at drag. Susannah will handle the chuck wagon. When Goose has scouted ahead, he'll remain at the point position with me. Any questions before we move out?''

Nobody spoke, but many eyes were on Monte Nance, especially those of Roscoe Yates. It seemed all were waiting to see what Monte would do, once the herd took the trail.

"Head 'em up, move 'em out," McCaleb shouted.

Monte Nance dropped all pretense, falling back beside the Yates wagon. The trail drive went on its uneasy way, and for the first time, concern for trouble within their own ranks was greater than any danger that awaited them on the trail ahead.

EASTERN MONTANA TERRITORY.
MAY 23, 1876

The riders stood to eat, not wishing to sit on the sodden ground.

"We was almighty lucky last night," said Smokey El-lison. "Way that lightning flashed and the thunder rolled, I was lookin' for the grandaddy of all stampedes."

"So was I," Cal said. "If I had it to do over, I think we'd have started this drive with at least four more riders."

"The cattle and horses are trail-wise," said Tom, "so it's not all that hard when they're on the move. But when they're bedded down—even bunched—they can get spooked and come at you in a front half a mile wide. You're bettin' your life on a fast horse, and even if you do get ahead of them, they may just keep coming."

"That's precisely why we avoid any such risks," Cal said. "I'd rather spend a week trying to gather a stampeded herd than one hour burying one of you."

"There's mud and standing water everywhere," said Quanah Taylor. "Are we goin' on?"

"I think so," Cal said. "Curley, it's your turn on the chuck wagon. How do you feel?"

"I feel we should go ahead," said Curley. "I'll do my best, keeping to higher ground. We've already lost too many days on account of the chuck wagon."

Curley's enthusiasm quickly caught on, and the outfit took the trail. One more day's drive to the north, and they would again turn eastward. When the herd was moving well, Cal left his point position and rode back to the tag end of the drive, to the horse herd.

"Quickenpaugh," said Cal, pointing the direction the herd was headed.

"*Si*," Quickenpaugh replied. He rode north, not so much seeking for Indian sign as for sign of the expected soldiers.

"My God," said Jasmine, as the wagon jounced along, "I'll be so glad when I'm able to ride a horse again."

"The first couple of days after Oscar removes those splints, maybe you ought to stay with the wagon," Curley said. "If something went wrong and the horse pitched you off, it might break those bones all over again."

Jasmine laughed. "When you're used to the saddle, this wagon seat's no rocking chair."

The wagon followed the horse herd, and the wranglers— Arch, Hitch, Mac and Quickenpaugh—kept the horses bunched, on the very heels of the drag riders. The animals were trailing well, and their good behavior allowed the riders some freedom. Quickenpaugh, on occasion, wheeled his horse and rode back the way they had come, studying the backtrail.

"Why do you suppose he's doing that?" Curley wondered.

"It gives him a chance to look at you," said Jasmine. "Don't you know *anything* about men?"

"Not much, I reckon," Curley said. She was reluctant to speak, lest there be talk of her ill-fated marriage to Bud McDaniels.

But it seemed Jasmine had accepted Bud's death. When she again spoke, it was more to the point.

"What do you aim to do with that Indian, after our business in Deadwood is finished and we return to our home range in Virginia City?"

"Lorna's got a big mouth," said Curley.

Jasmine laughed. "On the trail we're all together every day. But when this drive's done and we return to the ranch, you'll be in that cabin all alone. If Quickenpaugh comes calling, everybody in the outfit's going to know things are serious between you."

"I don't care a damn *what* everybody knows," Curley said. "What do *you* know?"

"Only what I've been hearing," said Jasmine. "The outfit's betting you'll never get him to stand before a preacher and that the pair of you will end up sleeping on a blanket on the floor."

"Well, I reckon all of you will just have to wait and see," said Curley.

Despite Curley's skills with the teams, the wagon's right front wheel slid into a hole. The hole had filled with mud and wasn't visible, but there was rock at the bottom.

"Oh, damn," Curley groaned, "it's that same wheel that was busted last time."

"Now we have no replacement," said Jasmine, "and it's my fault for allowing the teams to run away, breaking that same damn wheel. Maybe it didn't hurt the wheel. If it's just bogged down in the mud, the teams might be able to pull it out."

"I don't think so," Curley said. "It felt like something broke, and if it's only a couple of spokes, dragging it out could snap off the rest of them. I'll get that shovel out of the wagon."

The horse wranglers had discovered the chuck wagon was no longer moving, and Arch rode ahead to warn Cal. The rest of the riders were watching Cal, and when he signaled a halt, they began milling and bunching the herd. Curley was busily shoveling the mud away from the stricken wheel when Cal rode up and dismounted.

"Sorry," said Curley. "It all looked like solid ground."

"Luck of the draw," Cal said.

Taking the shovel from Curley, he shoveled down to rock and then cleared a decent space around the wheel. The wooden oval where the spokes met the rim had split. Three spokes were hanging loose.

"Somehow, we have to repair that part of the wheel that's split," Cal said. "Oscar, you and Bill are handy with tools. What do you think?"

"I think it ain't gonna be easy," said Oscar Fentress. "What you reckon, Bill?"

"About the same as you," Bill Petty said. "Cal, did you bring that big roll of stovepipe wire?"

"That and a couple pair of pliers," said Cal.

Smokey Ellison emerged from the wagon with the wagon jack. Cal climbed in and began moving things about, looking for the roll of wire and the pliers. Bill Petty had taken the shovel and was shoveling away the mud, seeking solid ground upon which the jack could rest. By the time Cal had found the pliers and wire, Petty had the jack in position under the wagon's front axle. Once the damaged wheel was raised off the ground, the iron tire popped off and hung loose.

"Fixin' that gonna take some doin'," said Oscar Fentress, "and the first bad jolt, she'll bust again."

"Then we'll just have to jack up the wagon and wire it together again," Cal replied.

"Bill," said Oscar, "gimme a hand and we'll get started."

"Do the best you can," Cal said. "The rest of us will bed down the horses and the herd. We may be here awhile."

There being plenty of water and improved graze, the stock settled down and began taking advantage of it. The riders unsaddled their horses, allowing the animals to roll.

"Will some of you help me down from the wagon?" Jasmine asked. "I need a rest from this wagon seat."

"Give me a hand, Cal," said Tom.

It wasn't easy, lifting Jasmine down with two splinted legs, but they managed to get her on a folded blanket, her back to one of the wagon's rear wheels. Quickenpaugh had remained near the horse herd, ever watchful. Curley stood beside him, silent, alone with her thoughts. She was startled when suddenly he spoke.

"Quickenpaugh learn white man's tongue. You help?"

"I'll help," Curley was quick to assure him.

Not another word was spoken. Quickenpaugh continued staring into the distance, where the seemingly endless plains met the blue of the Montana sky. Curley was about to return to the wagon when Quickenpaugh placed his hand on her arm. When he spoke, it was with genuine regret.

"*Lo siento mucho.* Bud die."

Curley turned to face him, and for the first time, there was an expression in his dark eyes. Curley's heart leaped, and it didn't matter that the rest of the outfit was probably watching. She took one of the Indian's strong hands in both of hers and spoke softly.

"You tried to save him, Quickenpaugh," said Curley. "What happened to him was his own fault."

In a moment of inspiration, Curley pointed a finger toward Quickenpaugh, and then toward herself.

"*Si*," Quickenpaugh said, the light of understanding in his eyes.

The men had been concerned with the repair of the wagon wheel or were circling the cattle and horse herds, but Lorna and Jasmine were watching Curley and Quickenpaugh.

"Are my eyes failing me," Jasmine said, "or did you see that too?"

Lorna laughed. "I saw it. I'd just like to know what Curley said that made it happen. I have never seen any expression on that Indian's face in all the years he's been with us. He was wounded, hurting like hell, but there was no hint of it in his eyes."

As Curley started back toward the wagon, Quickenpaugh mounted his horse and started circling the grazing herds. Curley tried not to look at Jasmine or Lorna, but they refused to let her be. With a sigh, she hunkered down with them.

"We saw that," Jasmine said. "How did you get him so interested?"

"I don't know," said Curley. "He put his hand on my arm and said he's very sorry that Bud died."

"He was in no way to blame for that," Jasmine said, "and I hope you told him so. Bud would be alive today if he had listened to Quickenpaugh instead of shooting him."

"I told him that," said Curley, "and he seemed to accept it as the truth."

She didn't tell them, however, of the new understanding between Quickenpaugh and herself. It was Lorna who came to the obvious conclusion.

"Instead of Quickenpaugh teaching you the Crow

tongue, you should be teaching him as much English as you can."

It was Curley's turn to laugh. "We're considerably ahead of you. He's already asked me to teach him the white man's tongue."

Bill and Oscar spent almost two hours wiring together the split wooden sections of the wheel around which the iron tire of the wagon wheel must go.

"That's all we can do with it," said Petty. "There's still plenty of wire left, but if this won't hold it, I doubt the rest will be of any help to us."

"We have spikes," Cal said. "Maybe we can put some of them to use. Once I was in Old Mexico, and the streets were full of big two-wheeled wooden carts. The wheels were of wood, made in two sections. Each section was like a half-moon, and when the flat edges of two were placed together, there was a wheel. They then took strips of hardwood and spiked them down across the two joined halves."

"But we got no hardwood," said Petty. "If this heavy wire don't hold, it's unlikely that anything else will."

"You may be right," Cal said, "but let's improve our chances some, if we can. Get the axe from the wagon. I'm goin' for some wood to brace that wheel."

"I'll ride with you," said Petty.

The two of them saddled their horses and rode out. Cal found a slender fir that looked promising, felled it, trimmed it, and chopped off a twelve-foot length.

"You got enough for two braces," Petty said.

"I know," said Cal. "I have in mind spiking one of them to the outside of the wheel, and the other to the inside, if we can. We'll have to see how much leeway there is between the front wheel and the wagon box. If it gets in the way of the wheels turning, we'll have to forget about the inside brace."

Reaching the wagon, Cal and Bill positioned the heavy fir trunk across the outside of the wagon wheel. With the axe, Cal notched the wood where it would be cut. He then cut it to the right length, using the axe to flatten each end. The result was a sturdy piece of fir that crossed the wheel just below the hub, with each end spiked to the wooden rim on opposite sides. Cal turned the wheel over, considering a second brace.

"That be enough," said Oscar. "Ain't gonna be room for another one of them braces on the inside of the wheel, next to the wagon box."

"I expect you're right," Cal said. "With this one, and all that wire, we should be able to go on. Put that piece of fir in the wagon's possum belly, in case we need it later."

"We don't have more than two hours of daylight left," said Tom. "Are we going on?"

"I don't think so," Cal said. "There's water aplenty. Leave the wagon on the jack, take that wheel downstream a ways and put it underwater. If there are any loose spokes, they should be swollen tight by morning."

The following morning, while breakfast was being prepared, Bill and Oscar mounted the repaired wagon wheel.

"She's swelled up good," said Oscar. "The spokes is all tight."

"I'm glad it's Lorna's turn on the box," Curley said. "After all the work that's been done on that wheel, I'd hate to be the one to bust it again."

"So you want *me* to bust it," said Lorna. "Fine friend you are."

"Enough," Cal said. "It's something that could happen to any of us at the reins. Lorna, you and Curley just go on doing your best. We start eastward again today, and the land may level out some."

The Montana sky was clear and blue, and after breakfast, Cal spoke to Quickenpaugh.

"Quickenpaugh," said Cal, pointing to the east, "I want you to scout ahead. If you see Crows, Sioux or soldiers, don't let them see you."

Quickenpaugh nodded, mounted his horse and rode

away. The cattle were bunched, the horse herd and remuda behind them, and before the column, Cal waved his hat high.

"Move 'em out."

With Arch, Hitch and Mac keeping the horses on the heels of the drag, Lorna swung the chuck wagon teams into line. Worriedly, she kept her eyes on the newly repaired front wheel, but it held. The ground seemed firm enough, and she breathed a sigh of relief. She looked forward to the coming of the night, when she could talk to Curley. But prior to that, she intended to talk to Cal again. The entire outfit was aware of Quickenpaugh's new standing with Curley, but she hadn't breathed a word about it to any of them.

"You're mighty quiet," said Jasmine, on the seat beside her.

"I'm just thinking about Curley and Quickenpaugh," Lorna replied. "Why won't she talk to us about them?"

Jasmine laughed. "Tom says that's hers and Quickenpaugh's business. Does it bother you that he's Comanche?"

"I . . . I'm not sure," said Lorna. "That's no reflection on him as a man, but I can't help wondering how well he'll fit in, if Curley takes up ranching. Quickenpaugh hasn't cut one stick of firewood since he's been with us, and he'd let a cow set in a bog hole till Judgment day before he'd build a loop and drag the varmint out."

Jasmine laughed. "I see what you mean, but unless Curley asks our advice, there's not a damn thing we can say or do. Comanche or not, Quickenpaugh's a good man, and even if his head's still full of the old ways, he deserves better than being regarded as a heathen. I believe if he gives in a little, and Curley gives in a little, they'll find common ground."

"I hope so," said Lorna, "but I still aim to talk to Curley tonight. Then if she tells me to shut up and mind my own business, I will."

Quickenpaugh was gone most of the day. When he returned, the supper fires were lit, and although Cal hadn't said anything, he had begun to worry. He waited until the Indian had removed the bridle from his horse, allowing the animal to roll. The rest of the outfit—those not watching the bedded-down herds—gathered to hear what Quickenpaugh had to report.

"Find Crow sign," said Quickenpaugh.

He hunkered down and, using a stick, drew a long line.

"*Río* Yellowstone?" Cal asked.

"*Si*," said Quickenpaugh.

He drew three lines at regular intervals, all of which crossed the line representing the Yellowstone. Obviously, he didn't know their names. Pointing to the crossing farthest to the east, moving his finger north along the line, he spoke again.

"Much horses. Some Crow."

"Crows, driving a herd of shod horses, taking 'em north," Tom Allen said.

"*Si*," said Quickenpaugh.

"*Gracias*, Quickenpaugh," said Cal. "I'd say some of the soldiers coming after the Sioux are now afoot."

"It be hell gettin' Mr. Story's hoss herd through, if all them blue bellies is hoofin' it," Oscar said.

"You may have something, Oscar," said Cal. "In wartime, the military can confiscate anything it needs, from a horse or mule down to the last chicken a man owns."

"It'll be somethin' if we end up fightin' the army," Quanah Taylor said. "The Sioux can just set tight and stomp hell out of whoever's left."

But as Cal and his outfit would eventually learn, the Crows had not taken the horses from the military.

13

EVEN AFTER THE HEAVY rain of the night before, the Lone Star trail drive moved on, and with Rebecca at the reins, the chuck wagon kept to high ground. The sun had risen in a cloudless blue sky, and when Goose returned from scouting ahead, he had nothing out of the ordinary to report.

"I don't rightly know what it is," Brazos said, when the herd had been bedded down for the night, "but this ain't like any trail drive I can recollect. It's too peaceful."

"I know what you mean," said Will. "It would all seem more natural if a screeching bunch of Comanches come galloping over the ridge."

"Being right in the midst of the Sioux hunting grounds," McCaleb said, "we're subject to attack at any time. I think the rendezvous they have in mind is somewhere to the east of us, in Dakota Territory. Custer and the Seventh Cavalry are already there, but Washington had better be sending more soldiers."

In a show of arrogance, Monte Nance had continued spending his time with the Yateses, taking his meals with them. There were times when he regretted having left Lone Star, but his fierce pride wouldn't allow him to go crawling back. He was still much enthralled with Kate and Connie, but some of the luster wore off after three days with them. Neither of the women could cook, and they seemed to have no desire to learn. Roscoe's bad back troubled him most, it seemed, when there was anything to be done that remotely resembled work. So Monte, to avoid going hungry, began doing the cooking.

"You're a passable good cook, Monte," Yates said one night after supper.

"I didn't throw in with you to be your damn cook," said Monte. "I want to know what you have planned for Deadwood and where I'll fit in."

Yates laughed, an irritating cackle that sent chills up Monte's spine.

"I aim for it to be a surprise, so you'll just have to wait till we get to Deadwood," Yates said. "We'll be richer than any of them fools hoisting picks and shovels."

"I'm too old for Santa Claus, and I don't like surprises," said Monte. "I don't like pig-in-a-poke deals. Hell, I might as well stay with Lone Star."

"You should," Yates said. "Now they may figure some way to beat you out of your share when the herd's sold."

"I ain't worried about that," said Monte. "I don't like McCaleb, but he's fair. He's the kind that squares a debt if it takes everything he owns, including the shirt off his back."

Yates laughed. "You're only fooling yourself, Monte Nance. You admire the man. He's all you're not, and *that's* what you hate."

"That's a damn lie!" Monte shouted. "I hate everything about him."

Again Yates laughed in his infuriating manner, but there was no humor in it. Monte had been weighed in the balance and found wanting, even in the eyes of this old scalawag whose venture in Deadwood obviously couldn't stand the light of day. Yates kept the front and rear canvas of the wagon tied, so it was virtually impossible to see into the interior. For reasons Monte didn't understand, Yates and the women slept well away from the wagon. If Yates wouldn't talk, Monte made up his mind to see why he was so secre-

tive about the wagon. He waited for a night when there was
no moon, when, except for Roscoe Yates's snoring, there
wasn't a sound. Silently he made his way to the distant
wagon, his heart beating fast. He opened the rear canvas
pucker just enough to get his head and upper body inside.
He was digging in his pocket for a match when he felt
something cold on the back of his neck.

"This here's a sawed-off scattergun," Yates said. "Tie
that pucker back the way it was and then back away. Do
it slow. This thing's got a hair trigger, and I'm always just
a mite nervous when somebody I've trusted crosses me."

"Trust, hell," said Monte. "You don't know the meaning of the word."

Monte drew the rawhide thong as tight as he could, tying
the canvas pucker tight. Only then did Yates move the muzzle of the shotgun, allowing Monte to back away.

Angrily Monte made his way back to where he had
spread his blankets, between the two Yates girls. He
stretched out and, needing reassurance, rolled over against
the nearest of the two. An elbow was driven into his ribs,
and when he persisted, a fist was driven hard into his face.
Violently angry, he caught her wrist as she was about to
hit him again. She reared up and sank her teeth into the
back of his hand, and with a wild swing, Monte smashed
her on the chin. But Monte's troubles were only beginning.
The other girl had awakened and threw herself into the
fight, cursing, scratching, clawing and kicking. A knee was
rammed into Monte's groin, and before the wave of nausea
passed, the knee slammed into him again. His shirt had
been torn off, and they were raking his upper body with
their nails. He finally struggled to his knees, and one of
them leaped on him as though he were a calf ready for
branding. She had him belly-down, and with a firm grip on
his hair, was beating his face into the ground. The other
had his Levi's down, and he could feel her nails raking
fiery paths across his backside. Finally, Roscoe Yates
spoke.

"That's enough, girls."

Without a word, they left him. He sat there, his shirt ripped off, bleeding, still sick from that last kick in the groin. Yates spoke again, this time more coldly than ever.

"Cross me, Mr. Nance, and the girls don't like it. I'm all the kin they got, you know."

Monte Nance said nothing. Both women had taken their blankets and had moved a considerable distance away. Wearily, Monte gathered his own blankets and lay down. When he believed Yates and the hell-raising girls were asleep, he crawled away, being as quiet as he could. Finally he stumbled to his feet and started toward the distant Lone Star camp. The rider in charge of the first watch was Brazos Gifford, and it was he who first heard the sound of Monte's coming.

"You're covered," Brazos warned. "Don't come any closer without identifying yourself."

"Monte," said a weary voice. "Monte Nance."

"Come on," Brazos said.

The rest of the outfit had heard the challenge and Monte's answer. Rebecca had stirred up the coals, and the fire was blazing when Monte stumbled into the circle of light. None of them said anything, for he was a fearful mess. His shirt gone, he stood there swaying like an oak in a high wind, holding up his Levi's with one hand.

"McCaleb," he mumbled, "I'm a damned fool."

"I won't argue with that," said McCaleb. "What do you want of us?"

"I want to be part of Lone Star," Monte said.

"I'm trail boss," said McCaleb, "and I give the orders for the good of the outfit. You always seem to have a problem with that."

"No more," Monte said. "I'll ride drag from here on to Deadwood."

"What about your friends?" McCaleb asked.

"They're not my friends," said Monte.

"I've put up with your damn mood changes ever since

we left Texas," McCaleb said, "and I'm almighty tired of them. Everybody in this outfit knows why you've been hanging around the Yates wagon, and we don't know you won't go back there, when the urge hits you. This time, I don't aim to decide what becomes of you. The rest of the outfit's goin' to decide whether or not they're willing to tolerate you. I'll go along with the majority. Is there any of you willing to give him another chance?"

There was a long silence, for all of them had, at one time or another, been on the outs with Monte Nance. When it seemed that nobody would speak in his favor, someone did.

"Let him come back," said Penelope.

Slowly—almost reluctantly—the others agreed.

"I'm obliged," Monte said, with more humility than anybody knew he possessed. "My horse, saddle and blankets are still there."

"We'll claim them at first light," said McCaleb. "I'll tell all of you now what I aim to tell Yates in the morning. While I can't stop him from following us, he is no longer part of this drive. If his wagon breaks down, it's strictly his problem. Now those of you not on watch, take to your blankets."

The riders all turned away, and Monte stood there as though undecided what he should do. Only Rebecca remained, and finally she spoke.

"If you'll stretch out on a blanket, I'll put some salve on your wounds."

"God knows, I don't deserve it," said Monte.

"No," Rebecca said, "you don't. I'm not offering because you deserve it, but because there's a need for it. Now take off your boots and Levi's, while I fetch a blanket."

"I have a blanket," said a voice from the darkness.

"Penelope," Rebecca said, "I doubt Brazos or Rosalie want you here."

"They don't," said Penelope, "but I'm old enough to follow my own mind. I'll help."

Monte Nance stretched out on his back, and by the poor

light from a flickering fire, Rebecca and Penelope applied sulfur salve to his many wounds. Unable to face them, he kept his eyes closed.

"Turn over," Rebecca ordered. "There's the backside."

When Rebecca and Penelope had finished, neither spoke. Rebecca took a second blanket and covered her errant brother, fervently hoping the promises he had made had not been in vain. The two of them then returned to their own blankets.

Come the dawn, McCaleb wasted no time. Before breakfast, he stalked toward the Yates wagon. When he was near enough, he spoke.

"Yates, I want the horse, saddle and blankets belonging to Monte Nance."

"Take them," said Yates. "I want no hard feelings."

"Neither do I," McCaleb replied. "You're on your own, from here on to Deadwood."

"I've done nothing to merit your displeasure," shouted Yates. "My girls only defended their honor."

"Your girls and their honor be damned," said McCaleb.

He saddled Monte's horse, flung the blankets over the saddle and led the animal back toward the Lone Star camp. Monte Nance had cleaned himself up as well as he could, but some of the scratches on his face and neck looked as though he'd been raked by a grizzly. The rest of the outfit was careful not to stare at him, and he gulped his breakfast quickly. Only Goose seemed unaffected, staring at the wreckage of Monte's face with considerable amusement. A warrior would have slit the throat of a squaw daring to disfigure him in such a manner. When Monte went to saddle his horse, every bone in his body ached, and the scratches and cuts burned like fire, but he dared not complain.

"Brazos, I want you and Will flank riding," McCaleb said. "Pen and Jed, you're swing riders. Susannah, it's your day for the chuck wagon. Rosalie, Penelope, Stoney, Monte and Rebecca, you're at drag.''

The riders quickly bunched the herd and headed them toward the rising sun. Susannah fell in behind with the chuck wagon. Goose had ridden ahead of the herd, and after a few words with McCaleb, the Indian kicked his horse into a slow gallop.

''Penelope,'' said Rosalie, when the drag riders had the tag end of the herd bunched, ''I don't want you spending any time with Monte Nance.''

''Why not?'' Penelope demanded. ''He's sorry, and we've forgiven him.''

''You can forgive a man without crawling into his blankets with him,'' said Rosalie.

Penelope laughed. ''Ma'am, I'm obliged for your confidence,'' she said, in what sounded almost exactly like a Brazos Gifford drawl.

The drag riders were mostly silent for the rest of the day. Rebecca bore a considerable burden, Monte being her brother. It hadn't been easy for the outfit to overlook those days and nights with the Yates outfit. She understood, more than any of the others, Monte's weakness for women. He was repentant now, but Roscoe Yates wouldn't have any trouble keeping up with the trail drive, welcome or not. Should Monte be tempted to backslide, the Yates girls would be within walking distance.

The second day after McCaleb had cut the Yates party loose, the wagon suffered yet another broken wheel. When McCaleb waved his hat as a signal to head the drive, the Yates wagon wasn't in sight. The herd had been settled for the night, and supper was well under way, when Yates arrived, riding one of the mules bareback.

''Why are you here, Yates?'' McCaleb demanded.

''I trust the well of human kindness is not completely dry, Mr. McCaleb,'' said Yates. ''We are in the embarrassing position of having a damaged wagon wheel, and none to replace it. What do you think we should do?''

"Leave the wagon where it is and ride the mules,''
McCaleb said. "I warned you this might happen. Now
don't look to us to solve your problems.''

"It isn't that I don't value your advice,'' said Yates, "but
there are certain . . . things in the wagon that will be essen-
tial when we reach Deadwood. I cannot leave the wagon,
and I am willing to pay if the wheel can be repaired.''

"Yates, I'm pretty sure this broken wheel is nothing
more than a result of your own carelessness,'' McCaleb
said. "The best that can be done for it is binding the broken
parts together with heavy wire, and the first time that wheel
goes hard off a stone or deep into a drop-off, that'll be the
end of the wheel. Sooner or later, you're going to be riding
your mules, so you might as well begin now.''

"I will not,'' said Yates. "If there's a man or men
among you who can repair that rear wheel so that it will
function, I will pay one hundred dollars, in gold.''

"Do you have the necessary wire?'' McCaleb asked.

"No, unfortunately,'' said Yates. "Whoever would have
thought of that?''

"Anybody with savvy, crossing the High Plains in a
wagon,'' McCaleb said. "We have a few tools and plenty
of heavy-gauge wire, but a wired-together wheel is a poor
risk, at best. Like I've told you, damage that wheel again,
and the wagon goes no farther. While I am willing to supply the necessary wire, that's as far as I go. Patch up your
own wheel.''

"I am not physically able,'' said Yates. "That's why I'm
offering a hundred dollars to any man or men who can do
what is necessary.''

"It's a two-man job, at least,'' McCaleb said. "Lone
Star, are any of you willing to try and repair a busted wheel
for a hundred dollars?''

There was a total silence. With a grim look on his face,
Monte Nance glared at Yates. It seemed there were no tak-
ers, until Stoney Vandiver spoke.

"I reckon Jed and me can do it, if we're on the second watch."

"Consider yourselves on the second watch with me," said McCaleb. "You're asking a lot of these men, Yates. They've been in the saddle all day, and they'll be back in the saddle come midnight. I aim to see that you make it worth their while, patching up your wagon when they should be sleeping. Show them the color of your money."

"You have me by the short hairs, McCaleb," Yates said. "You'd just better hope the time never comes when our positions are reversed."

He reached in his pocket and withdrew a handful of double eagles. Counting out five, he handed them to Stoney.

"Those coils of wire are under the wagon seat," said McCaleb. "Don't use any more of it than you have to. We may be needing it ourselves."

"Bring the wagon jack," Yates said. "I don't have one."

Jed and Stoney mounted their horses, Jed carrying the wagon jack, and Stoney the coil of wire. They followed Yates on his mule, and soon the trio was lost to distance.

"I hope they'll be all right," said Rebecca worriedly.

"They will," Pen Rhodes assured her. "I knew their daddy, and they take after him. Give that old varmint a hammer, a saw and a few nails, and he could have built the ark."

Rebecca wasn't doubting the skills of the Vandiver brothers, but the wiles of this pair of women who had led to Monte's downfall.

"I just wonder what he's got in that wagon that's so all-fired important he can't leave it," Pen Rhodes said. "From what I hear, men on their way to the diggings are in a hurry, sometimes arriving with nothing but the clothes they're wearing."

"I think his reason for going to Deadwood is in the wagon," said Monte. "He caught me before I could light a match, but I touched something that I'd swear was a roulette wheel.''

"Likely crooked as hell," Brazos said. "That old buzzard's aiming to find his gold in the pockets of better men, who have worked for it. You're too generous, Bent. You ought to have forced them either to set there with their disabled wagon, or ride their mules the rest of the way.''

"I considered it," said McCaleb, "but it's wrong to refuse help on the frontier, even if you're helping somebody who later becomes an enemy. After this, I doubt that Yates will have any more damaged wheels. I reckon we'd better save Jed and Stoney some supper. It won't be easy, wiring that wheel by the light of a fire.''

Reaching the wagon, Jed and Stoney wasted no time. Jed positioned the wagon jack beneath the axle, near the damaged right rear wheel. Stoney then jacked the wagon up high enough to take the wheel off the ground.

"Well," said Yates, "can it be fixed?''

"Yeah," Stoney replied, "but it won't stand another jolt. You'll need another wheel.''

Removing the wheel, Jed and Stoney twisted the dislocated spokes back into position and brought the two split portions of the wheel's wooden rim together. Repeatedly they wrapped the split with wire, drawing it tight with pliers.

"This wheel goes into a water hole until morning," said Stoney. "The wooden parts of it need to swell, further tightening the split. We'll be here before breakfast to mount it on the wagon.''

"You have your money," Yates said. "How do I know you'll finish the job?''

"Your wagon's settin' on our wagon jack," said Stoney.

For all the time that Jed and Stoney worked on the wheel, Connie and Kate hovered as close as they dared. But the two young men appeared not to notice them, and when Jed and Stoney rode away, the Yates girls were furious.

"Settle down, damn it," Roscoe said. "It was your hell-raising that drove Monte away."

"It was you that caught him with his head through the wagon pucker," said Connie, "and no sooner did you let him go than he started pawing me. You didn't care a damn what he did to us, did you?"

"Not particularly," Yates admitted. "He couldn't have done anything to either of you that hasn't already been done, many times over. There's nothing any more obvious than a whore acting like an honest woman who's been robbed of her virtue."

Kate laughed. "Don't talk down to us, you righteous old bastard. It was me that got the rap in Cheyenne, behind your damn crooked roulette wheel. I had to use my own talents to convince that deputy sheriff to let me go. You didn't lift a hand."

"I needed time to take the equipment and make a run for it," said Yates. "Besides, you was in a better bargaining position than I was. Since I wasn't caught, we got away clean with the money. If it's true there's no law in Deadwood, we'll clean up."

"Just don't you forget, Daddy dear, you're not equipped for luring the suckers in, but we are," Kate said. "If double-cross so much as comes to mind, just you remember that Connie and me can stir up enough miners to hang you before you can saddle a horse."

"Threats," said Yates, a woeful expression on his florid face. "I rescued the two of you from jail in California, took you in as my own daughters, and now look at you. You have a most unconventional way of showing your gratitude."

"Hell, Yates," Connie said, "*We* could have sold ourselves for money. We never needed you for that. So far, you've paid us nothing. Now, thanks to your damned trick roulette wheel, we barely escaped the law in Cheyenne. Now we're stuck in some godforsaken part of the world, on our way to what *you* call a boomtown. If you bust another wheel on the wagon, we'll never get there. Those cowboys won't lift a hand to help us.''

"And whose fault is that?" Yates snarled. "I told the two of you to cultivate young Monte Nance. Damn it, you were supposed to give in to him a little at a time, not both of you the same night. I caught him sniffing around the wagon, but he didn't see anything. If the two of you hadn't driven him away—''

"You'd still be using us, and we'd still be sleeping with Nance, and all for nothing," Kate told him.

"Kate's right," said Connie. "We only got one thing to sell, and you've swapped our favors to your own advantage for the last time. We'll wait just one week, to see what you can do in Deadwood. If you can't put some real money in our hands, we're gone.''

True to their word, Jed and Stoney Vandiver dragged the wagon wheel out of the hole where it had been immersed in water all night.

"Tight enough," said Jed. "Let's get the thing on his wagon and be done with it.''

Quickly they hefted the rear wheel into position. Stoney tightened the hub nut, lowered the wagon and Jed recovered their wagon jack. They mounted their horses and rode away without a word.

"I'm glad that's behind us," McCaleb said, when Jed and Stoney reined up near their own chuck wagon.

"Easiest money we ever made," said Stoney. "Too bad Monte's got a mad on. He could of done the job, took it out in trade and saved old Roscoe a hundred dollars.''

Everybody laughed at Monte's expense, and to their surprise, he laughed with them. Benton McCaleb looked astounded when Monte failed to explode, but his eyes were on Rebecca. She sighed with relief. Perhaps her little brother was finally becoming a man.

LITTLE BIG HORN RIVER, MONTANA TERRITORY.
JUNE 1, 1876

"I figure we're almost sixty miles north of where the Sioux are gathering," Cal said. "If we continue as we're now headed, we should soon be able to drop back to the south."

The outfit had set up camp for the night on the west bank of the Little Big Horn, and darkness was only a few minutes away when they heard the jingle and rattle of horsemen approaching.

"Tarnation," said Bill Petty, "there's near a hundred, and all armed to the teeth."

"Rein up and identify yourselves," Cal ordered.

The men reined up and Cal stepped out to meet them.

"I'm Jim Connor," said the lead rider. "Me and these other gents is from Miles City. We represent every horse ranch in eastern Montana territory, and we're trailing a damn bunch of Crows that pretty well wiped us out. Have any of you seen 'em?"

"No," Cal said, "but we saw where they turned north, toward the Yellowstone, maybe ten miles back. By the tracks of the shod horses they were driving, we thought maybe they had left a bunch of soldiers afoot somewhere."

"Unfortunately not," said Connor. "Every horse is civilian-owned. But the soldiers are coming. A telegram came from Washington to Miles City, forbidding any civilian to ride south or west."

"But you gents didn't take it serious," Cal said.

"The Good Book says when the ox is in the ditch, you get him out," said Connor. "The damn Crows ruined us, not even leaving some of us a saddle horse. The animal I'm ridin' is borrowed. We're gonna ride that bunch down if we got to chase 'em all the way to the big water. You seen any of them Sioux the army's lookin' for?"

"Matter of fact, we have," Cal said. "That's why we're trailing so far north. Our scout warned us there's many

Sioux dug in along the Little Big Horn, maybe fifty miles south.''

''We're obliged for the information,'' said Connor. ''For damn sure the Crows won't be goin' that way.''

''You said the soldiers are coming,'' Cal said. ''Do you happen to know when?''

''No,'' said Connor. ''We know the soldiers are under the command of General Alfred H. Terry, and they're marching from Dakota Territory along the Yellowstone. We reckoned they wouldn't be long gettin' to Miles City, so we made sure we got away ahead of 'em.''

''I reckon there's no way we can avoid them,'' Cal said. ''The Sioux are to the south of us, and we're as far north as we can afford to go.''

''Don't let 'em buffalo you,'' said Connor. ''A man's got to look out for himself. The army's supposed to be on our side, but they're ready to fight the Sioux while these Crow varmints steal every horse in eastern Montana Territory.''

''Good luck,'' Cal said. ''Catch up to them, and they'll give up the horses. We had to run down a bunch of 'em to recover our horses.''

The grim-faced men rode out, continuing west.

''We should have invited them to stay for supper,'' said Jasmine.

''I thought of that,'' Cal said, ''but they didn't dismount. Besides, that many men could leave us short on grub long before we reach Deadwood.''

''I didn't like what he had to say about that government order,'' said Bill Petty.

''It shouldn't affect us,'' Cal replied. ''We're not heading west, and we can pretty well tell the soldiers where the Sioux are gathering. That ought to be worth something.''

''If they're marching along the Yellowstone, there's still a chance we can avoid them,'' said Tom Allen. ''After that foolishness we ran into with Story's outfit along the Bozeman Trail, they'll have something to say to us.''

"We'll not travel any farther north," Cal said. "It's entirely possible we'll pass them by at such a distance they'll never know we exist. Starting tomorrow, we'll head due east. For tonight, let's douse our supper fires before dark. We don't know how many more Sioux have gathered to the south, and I don't want them getting interested in us, while they wait for the soldiers."

"Oscar," said Jasmine, "you told me these splints could be taken off today. Can't we do it now, before supper?"

"I 'spect we better," Oscar Fentress replied. "We don't have no fire after dark."

They made an event of it, Jasmine raising the blanket as high as she dared. Lorna had already fetched a pair of Levi's and was standing by while Oscar removed the splints.

"All of you vamoose when Oscar gets the splints off," said Curley. "Jasmine will have to rid herself of that blanket to get her Levi's on."

"Nobody's going anywhere," Jasmine said. "My legs are weak, and I'm going to need a lot of help. Before I try, I know I can't stand alone."

"That be true," said Oscar. "They's got to be a strong shoulder on each side of you, so's you don't hurt them legs again."

"I'll take one side," Tom Allen said. "Who'll help me?"

"Quickenpaugh help," said the Indian.

Jasmine's first impulse was to laugh, but something in Curley's eyes changed her mind.

"Thank you, Quickenpaugh," Jasmine said, "but before I try to do anything, I want to wash my feet and legs."

Lorna already had water boiling to brew coffee for supper, but the water was poured into a basin and taken to Jasmine. She cast aside the blanket, and with Lorna's help, she bathed her feet and legs.

14

McCALEB INCREASED THE GAIT of the herd, but the Yates wagon never faltered. While their supper fire was within sight of McCaleb's camp, neither Yates nor his supposed offspring made an appearance. To the relief of everybody in the cow camp, Monte Nance kept his distance from the Yateses, but it created a seemingly new problem for Brazos and Rosalie. Monte managed to get Penelope to speak to him, and immediately set about further cultivating her interest.

"Brazos," said Rosalie, "can't you keep Penelope on the first watch and have Bent put Monte on the second?"

"I could," Brazos said, "but what good would it do? Hell, I can't follow them two for six hours, seein' that Penelope don't do something foolish, and neither can McCaleb. Can't you just lay down the law to her and tell her to leave Monte Nance alone? What *is* it with Penelope? Can't she get it through her head he's been carousing with a pair of whores?"

"You know she's of age," said Rosalie wearily. "If she decides to sleep with Monte, we can't do one solitary thing."

"I can shoot the son of a bitch," Brazos said grimly.

"I won't listen to such talk," said Rosalie. "He's Rebecca's brother, and her only kin."

"Then I'll have McCaleb shoot him," Brazos replied. "Will that make you feel better?"

"Just forget I ever mentioned it," snapped Rosalie. "She can do whatever she pleases, with Monte Nance or anybody else."

"I'll talk to her," Brazos said, "and she'll listen to me, or else."

"Or else what?"

"I'll peel down her Levi's, belly her down and leave some permanent hand prints on her bare behind," said Brazos.

Monte Nance never seemed to tire of riding drag. For one thing, the cattle had become trail wise and were no trouble. For another, Penelope was always near at hand. Following Monte's shameless escapades with Connie and Kate, in a surprisingly short time, Penelope was riding beside him at drag, and paying particular attention to him in camp. One night after supper, Brazos decided it was time to make good on his promise to Rosalie.

"Penelope," said Brazos, "let's walk over to the chuck wagon. We need to talk."

Penelope followed, and when Brazos leaned up against the chuck wagon, Penelope leaned there beside him. Brazos Gifford was in over his head and, realizing it, wasted no time on aimless talk.

"Penelope, Monte's Rebecca's brother, but he's still trash, and I don't think he has any honorable intentions toward you. Your ma and me don't want you . . . ah . . ."

"Fornicating with him," Penelope finished.

"Thank you," said Brazos. "I hadn't planned to speak to you in a blunt way, but you're obviously older than we thought. It bothers Rosalie and me that those Yates women are a pair of whores, and Monte's been with them. He's a womanizer, and we just don't think he's worthy of you."

Penelope laughed. "He didn't have a chance with me. You and Ma hover over me like two old hens with one chick between them. I know Connie and Kate are probably whores, but I can't fault Monte because they were available. Is he the first man who ever just took what he could get, when he couldn't get what he wanted?''

"I reckon not," said Brazos uncomfortably, "but they're fallen women. You're far above them, and we want to keep it that way."

"I don't think of myself as better than anybody else," Penelope said. "Monte's throwing in with the Yates girls reminds me of one of your card games. Connie and Kate raised the ante, and not being able to match them, I had to fold. I think it's shameful that a woman can be called a whore, when some man dragged her down. There wouldn't be fallen women if there hadn't been some two-legged varmint to push them over the edge."

"I reckon I can't argue with any of that," said Brazos. "I'll settle for your promise that *you* won't allow yourself to get in deep water with Monte Nance while we're on this trail drive."

"I reckon I can promise that," Penelope said. "I can't be sure he won't sneak back for a visit with Connie and Kate."

"And that won't bother you, if he does?"

"Some," said Penelope, "but they're allowed to raise, and I'm not."

"That's not entirely true, and you know it," Brazos said. "There was that day you went to the chuck wagon to wash yourself, with Monte watching."

"So you figured that out," said Penelope. "Who else have you told?"

"Nobody," Brazos said. "Benton McCaleb saw through it before I did. Rebecca knows, and your ma knows, but not because of anything I said. It was all just too obvious, and it wasn't the first time, was it?"

"No," said Penelope, "but the other time, stuff was stacked all the way to the wagon bows, and . . . and . . ."

"There was no way to see inside," Brazos finished.

"I had to shift things around some," said Penelope. "I

really didn't mean for anyone to know, but when I was standing there . . . naked . . . and him . . . looking at me, I was afraid."

"You could have saved us considerable trouble and worry by just speaking up," Brazos said. "Why didn't you?"

"Because it was more my fault than his," the girl cried. "Would you have felt better if I'd told the truth and let you beat me with a doubled lariat?"

"I reckon not," Brazos said. "To me, you're still the little girl with one shoe and without a coat, I found lying half-frozen and near dead on the bank of the Sweetwater."*

There was no condemnation, and his words got to her like nothing else had. She threw her arms around Brazos and wept until she could weep no more. Wisely, he said nothing. Not until later that night did Rosalie have a chance to talk to Brazos, and he told her little that she didn't already know.

As was his custom, McCaleb had sent Goose to scout ahead. This time, when he rode in, the Indian had some interesting news.

"Many horse track," said Goose, pointing northwest.

"Sioux?" McCaleb asked.

"Ugh," said Goose. "No horseshoe."

"You're sure they went on, then," McCaleb said.

"Ugh," said Goose, again pointing northwest.

"They're ridin' out of Dakota Territory," Will Elliot said. "Why all the talk of trouble in Dakota, when the Sioux are leaving?"

"Good thinking on their part," said Pen Rhodes. "They're choosing the place for the coming fight. They're bound for their old hunting grounds."

"I think you're dead right, Pen," Brazos said. "That

*The Western Trail (Trail Drive #2)

being the case, we're too far south for trouble with the Sioux.''

"I hope you're right," said McCaleb. "If this fight takes place somewhere to the north of us, we may escape it entirely. But we can't count on that. We'll just have to depend on Goose scouting ahead of the drive each day.''

On the days Rosalie drove the chuck wagon, Monte Nance took full advantage of her absence, talking to Penelope most of the day. The rest of the drag riders—Rebecca, Pen Rhodes and Susannah—didn't seem to bother him. Confined to the chuck wagon, Rosalie could only grind her teeth in frustration. Occasionally she looked back and could see the dust stirred up by Roscoe Yates's teams. Secretly she yearned for the days when Monte had spent all his time with the two brazen women.

"What are those Yates women *really* like?" Penelope asked.

Monte laughed. "You don't want to know."

"I do so," said Penelope. "I'm grown up."

"I can't argue with that," Monte said. "Not after that day in the wagon. But after you had it all fixed up, why did you yelp like a scared coyote and give me away?"

"I . . . I don't know," said Penelope. "At least I didn't tell anybody it was you."

"I'm obliged for that," Monte said. "McCaleb or Brazos would have killed me. When it warms up some more, and there's no chance of us bein' caught, will you go swimming with me?"

"I don't know," said Penelope. "Like the Yates girls did?"

"Yeah," Monte said, winking at her. "Is it any worse, me seein' you jaybird naked in the water, than in the chuck wagon?"

"You'll never let me forget *that,* will you?"

"No," said Monte, "I won't. Offer a man a taste of a pie, and he just naturally hankers for a bigger slice."

"Then you'd better just enjoy the taste for as long as

you can," Penelope said. "This pie's not ready to cut, and when it is, you may not be doing the cutting."

"You can be a nasty little witch, when you want to," said Monte.

Penelope laughed. "I can be even nastier. Remember, it was Rebecca and me who had to patch you up, after the Yates girls had clawed the hell out of you. I saw you naked as a skint coyote, and you didn't impress me."

"Oh, yeah?" Monte said angrily. "Who you got to compare me to?"

Penelope laughed. "Any man in the outfit, including Goose."

"You . . . you're lying," said Monte. "You wouldn't—"

"Wouldn't I?" Penelope said. "A fool girl who'd strip for you would do anything."

"Then don't go lookin' down your nose at me," said Monte. "You're no better than the Yates women. At least they're honest enough to deliver what they promise."

"Then you'd better go back to them," Penelope said, "and before you go, take a good look at me. This is as much as you're likely to see for a long time. Maybe ever."

MILES CITY, MONTANA TERRITORY.
JUNE 10, 1876

"By God," said Commanding General Alfred H. Terry, "civilians have been specifically forbidden to ride south or west into what might well become a battlefield. Who the hell is in charge of this expedition, and how long have they been gone?"

"Gent name of Connor was leadin' 'em," said an old-timer, "and they been gone nigh two weeks, I reckon. Damn Crows stole ever' hoss they could git their hands on, an' here on the frontier, a man ain't about to stand for that. Not for the army, not for nobody."

Word of the outraged expedition having gone in search

of the thieving Crows soon got back to the rank and file, and the soldiers were privately amused at their commander's frustration and anger. Two of the officers in Custer's regiment—Major Marcus Reno and Captain Frederick Benteen—had just taken it upon themselves to call on Custer. Entering his tent, they saluted.

"At ease," said Custer, casually returning the salute. "What do you want of me?"

"General Terry's breathing fire and brimstone over a bunch of ranchers who are tracking a herd of horses stolen by Crows," Benteen said. "Do you suppose this will affect our campaign against the Sioux?"

"I don't see how it could," said Custer. "Since we aren't sure where we'll encounter the Sioux, I have it on good authority that General Terry intends to divide his command. At some point to the west of here, General Terry intends to march part of his command for a rendezvous with General Gibbon."*

"Oh?" Major Reno said. "And where's he sending the rest of the regiment?"

"They'll march south," said Custer. "I'm prepared to take command, if it is offered."

ROSEBUD CREEK, MONTANA TERRITORY.
JUNE 17, 1876

"I think we're maybe forty miles south of the Yellowstone," Cal said. "We'll take a day of rest here. Tomorrow, Quickenpaugh and me will ride to the Yellowstone. I want to see if there's any truth in what we were told about the coming of the soldiers."

"Suppose you find them," said Tom Allen. "Then what?"

---

*Some fifty miles west of Miles City, at the mouth of Rosebud Creek, General Terry sent Custer and his regiment south in an attempt to locate the enemy Sioux.

"We'll avoid them," Cal said. "If it's true they're marching west along the Yellowstone, there's no way we'll encounter them this far south."

"Not bein' a military man, I don't know how they think," said Bill Petty, "but at some point, those soldiers will have to march south. This may be the Sioux nation's last stand, and I'd bet everything I own it'll happen close to their old hunting grounds."

"Bill's right," Tom Allen said. "The soldiers won't find the Sioux by marching along the Yellowstone."

"They may already be gone," said Cal. "If they are, then Quickenpaugh and me should find some evidence of their passing. If that's the case, we'll go on with our drive without any interference from them."

"It's possible they haven't yet come this far," Tom said. "If you get the chance, do you aim to warn 'em about the Sioux dug in along the Little Big Horn?"

"I'll have to," said Cal. "I'd be a poor excuse for a man if I let them walk into a trap, just to keep them from knowing about us. This drive's bound for Deadwood, and nobody's stopping it. Not even the army. Tomorrow, Quickenpaugh and me will warn them."

But the following morning, Commanding General Alfred H. Terry and his command had reached the mouth of Rosebud creek, along the Yellowstone. Terry had given the order to dismount.

"Have General Custer report to me," he ordered an aide.

"Reporting as ordered, sir," said Custer saluting.

"At ease," Terry said. "As you are no doubt aware, I'm marching on to join the column under General John Gibbon. I want you to take four hundred and eighty men and ride south. This mission is to seek out the enemy, not engage them in battle. Understand?"

"Yes, sir," said Custer. "I request permission for Major Marcus Reno and Captain Frederick Benteen to accompany me as my seconds in command."

"Permission granted," General Terry replied.

Custer saluted smartly and turned to go.

"Now, don't be greedy, Custer," said General Terry. "There are Indians enough for all of us."

Riding north, Cal Snider and Quickenpaugh had reined up to rest their horses.

"*Cuidado,*" Quickenpaugh said, pointing north. "*Soldados.*"

Cal could see no evidence of soldiers, but he had never known the Indian to be wrong. Leading their horses, he and Quickenpaugh took cover in a thicket of scrub willows. The soldiers eventually appeared, riding in columns of fours.

"Damn it," said Cal, "they're headed straight down the Rosebud. They may not see us, but they can't miss five thousand head of cattle and two hundred horses. I'll have to talk to them."

His Winchester in his hand, Cal stepped out of the brush into a clearing. The officer in charge gave the order to halt, and the column reined up.

"Who are you, and what are you doing here?" Custer demanded.

"I'm Cal Snider, trail boss for Nelson Story's Virginia City outfit. We're bound for Deadwood, Dakota Territory, trailing a herd of some five thousand cattle and a herd of some two hundred horses, to be delivered to the military."

"You are in violation of a government order," said Custer stiffly. "No civilians are to be in this area, pending a possible attack by the Sioux. I am empowered to place you and all that you employ under military arrest."

"You have no such authority," Cal replied. "The order from Washington stated that no civilians were to travel south of the Yellowstone or to the west. Our herd is headed east, toward Dakota Territory."

"Ah," said Custer, "you know of the order and choose to disobey it."

"Put it like that, if you like," Cal said. "We were two hundred miles on our way to Dakota Territory when we got word of your order from Washington. Whether you like it or not, we're going on. Our camp is maybe twenty miles south of here, on the Rosebud.''

"Lead out, and we will follow," said Custer.

"Quickenpaugh," Cal said, "bring the horses."

The moment Quickenpaugh appeared, every trooper in the first several ranks reached for his weapon. But Cal was ready for that. His Colt was cocked and steady, and his voice was cold.

"This is Quickenpaugh, part of the Story outfit and our advance scout. I'll kill any one of you that pulls a gun.''

"At ease, men," Custer ordered. "Since you and your herd have advanced thus far, Mr. Snider, I'll offer no objection if you continue your journey."

"We're obliged," said Cal. "Now I'm going to give you some information that may be helpful. A large band of Sioux hostiles are dug in along the Little Big Horn, to the south of here."

"Oh?" Custer said. "And what made you aware of their presence?"

"Quickenpaugh discovered them while scouting ahead," said Cal. "We brought our herd forty miles north, to avoid them."

"The one sensible thing you've done so far," Custer said. "While I am indebted to you for the information, I regret that I cannot take a heathen Indian's word. My superiors will expect a firsthand report, and I shall live up to those expectations."

It was a pompous, prejudiced response, and there was a coldness in Quickenpaugh's dark eyes that suggested he had understood every word Custer had said. He kicked his horse into a lope, leaving the soldiers behind. Cal urged his mount into a slow gallop and soon caught up to Quickenpaugh.

"Him fool," said Quickenpaugh. "Him die."

"We tried, Quickenpaugh," Cal said. "Let him make his own mistakes."

Cal and Quickenpaugh reached camp well ahead of the soldiers and prepared the rest of the outfit for their arrival.

"So Custer didn't believe Quickenpaugh," Bill Petty said. "He was commissioned a general on the battlefield when he was twenty-three. I've heard he has a considerable ego."

"That he has," said Cal. "He wants to discover the Sioux without sharing credit with anybody."

When the soldiers arrived, Custer gave the order to dismount and stack arms. He then spoke to Cal.

"We will establish our camp down the creek. Tomorrow we will march south."

"We would invite you to supper," Cal said, "but we've had some delays, and our grub is running low."

"Our provisions are adequate for our needs," said Custer.

During the rest of the day and night, there was no further contact with the soldiers, and at dawn they broke camp and marched south, along the Rosebud. The following Sunday afternoon, near the Little Big Horn, George A. Custer had a date with destiny . . .

EASTERN WYOMING TERRITORY.
JUNE 20, 1876

It was Rebecca's turn on the box of the chuck wagon, and danger struck swiftly, when a skunk trotted out in front of the mules. Some of the animals had experienced skunk before, and the teams lit out toward the south, over rough terrain. Stoney Vandiver, riding drag, tried unsuccessfully to catch up to the runaway team. They halted, heaving and dripping sweat, only when the wagon's left front wheel struck an upthrust of rock and broke. Rebecca climbed shakily down to survey the damage. The other drag riders had signaled McCaleb, and the outfit was heading the herd. Reaching the disabled chuck wagon, McCaleb dismounted.

Rebecca looked pale and shaken, and he spoke as calmly as he could.

"Are you hurt?"

"No, but the wagon is," said Rebecca. "A skunk wandered out in front of the mules, and they just went crazy. I couldn't hold them."

"She done a grand job of tryin'," Stoney said. "I was doin' my best to get ahead of them jug-headed mules when the wagon slammed into a rock."

"It's impossible to avoid such as this in rough country," said McCaleb. "Since we're lacking a spare wheel, I reckon we'll have to piece the old one back together. Stoney, you and Jed fixed a wheel on the Yates wagon. Think you can do it again?"

"We can try," Stoney said.

"This one ain't no worse than the one we fixed for Yates," said Jed, "but we'll need the time to soak it overnight, to swell the wood."

"We'll take the time," McCaleb said.

Well beyond the herd, Roscoe Yates had reined up his teams, waiting.

"Somebody ought to tell him he's welcome to go on without us," said Brazos.

"I'm not telling him anything," McCaleb said. "If he wants to set there until tomorrow, until our wheel's been fixed, let him. We can't stop him from following us, but we're not his guide."

The rest of the outfit returned to the herd, leaving Jed and Stoney to try and repair the damaged wheel. First they loosened the hub nut, and then, with the jack beneath the axle, they raised the sagging corner of the wagon and removed the wheel.

"Good thing we brought plenty of wire," said Jed.

"There won't be plenty when we get done with this wheel," Stoney said. "Anybody else needin' a wheel patched up will be out of luck."

"If this happens again while I'm at the reins, I'll feel like I'm bad luck," said Rebecca.

"It could of happened to anybody," Stoney replied. "Who knows what's goin' on in a mule's skull? The varmints don't even need a reason to run."

To Rebecca's surprise, the Yates girls had left their own wagon and were approaching. They halted a few feet away, their eyes on the cowboys seeking to repair the damaged front wheel. Rebecca eyed them in a manner that was anything but friendly, but it seemed to have no effect on them.

"We admire a man who can fix things," said one.

"All kinds of things," the second added.

"Some things need fixing more often than others," Rebecca said ominously.

"Some things are so old and used up, they're not worth fixing," said one of the devilish duo.

"There's more truth to that than you realize," Rebecca said calmly. "I haven't seen any young bucks grazing near either of you, lately."

Jed and Stoney continued repairing the broken wheel, since the argument hadn't turned violent. But then Connie Yates took a handful of dirt and flung it into Rebecca's face. The two of them then seized Rebecca and began ripping off her clothes. Jed and Stoney ran to her aid, but galloping her horse, Penelope got there ahead of them.

"Penelope, no!" Rosalie shouted.

But if Penelope heard, she paid no attention. The Yates women had already ripped off Rebecca's shirt when Penelope arrived. Leaving her saddle in a flying leap, she plunged into the midst of the fight. Immediately one of the unruly women seized a handful of her hair, and Penelope retaliated with a right to the jaw, slamming her antagonist to the hard ground.

"Damn you," said the other Yates girl, "you've hurt Kate."

Kate was down, but she wasn't out. She got to her knees and then to her feet. From one of her boots, she brought forth a dagger, its thin blade glinting in the sun.

"Drop the knife," Rebecca ordered, coming between Penelope and Kate.

But Connie threw herself at Rebecca, and the two of them went down in a tangle of arms and legs. Penelope faced the vindictive girl with the dagger.

"Come on," Brazos shouted, mounting his horse. "This ain't a hair-pullin' anymore. She's got a knife."

McCaleb swung into the saddle, but he was behind Rosalie, as the three of them rode to the scene of battle. But with Connie occupied with Rebecca, the fight had become one-on-one. Kate lunged with the dagger, and, snake-sudden, Penelope seized her wrist. Using her own momentum, Penelope slammed Kate to the ground, belly-down. Kate released the knife, and, seizing it, Penelope went to work on the unfortunate Kate. Taking her collar in one hand, Penelope slit the shirt into two pieces. She then slashed Kate's Levi's to ribbons. Brazos, McCaleb and Rosalie had arrived, but not soon enough to save Connie and Kate from total disgrace. With the exception of their boots, both women had been stripped. Her shirt ripped off, Rebecca was a dirty mess. Only Penelope was unscathed.

"Penelope," said Rosalie, "you've made a shameful, unladylike spectacle of yourself."

"If I have," Penelope said, "I don't care a damn. The two of them came down over here and jumped on Rebecca. Are you all right, Rebecca?"

"Bruised and dirty, mostly," said Rebecca, "and I could use a shirt."

Jed and Stoney had given up on their attempts to repair the wagon wheel, watching in amazement as the four women had fought. Connie and Kate sat on the ground, savagely cursing all who were within hearing. Penelope had started toward the troublesome pair once more when McCaleb spoke angrily.

"Get up, both of you, and return to your wagon. You're not welcome in our camp, or near any of our riders."

"Not till that little wench returns my knife," Kate shouted.

Penelope drove the blade deep into the hard ground. Snapping off the thin blade, she threw the useless haft at Kate. Brazos laughed, and Rosalie cast him a sour look. The two bloodied, dirty Yates girls got to their feet and headed toward the distant wagon, where old Roscoe apparently waited.

"Girl," said Rebecca, putting her arms around Penelope, "you can side me in a fight anytime you're of a mind to."

"I think you'd better save that," McCaleb said. "You need a bath and a shirt. Let's all get away from here so Stoney and Jed can finish repairing that wheel. Sorry for all the trouble, boys."

"Wasn't no trouble," said Stoney. "That was worth twice what Yates paid us to fix his busted wheel."

McCaleb did his best to look disgusted, but his cause was lost. Rebecca and Penelope walked arm-in-arm, grinning like two old warriors who had gone forth and conquered the enemy. Even Rosalie had adopted a weak smile.

"Well," said Brazos, "it was a mite ugly, but I reckon it was somethin' that had to be done."

"You're damn right it did," Penelope said, "and if there's ever a need, I'll do it all over again."

Brazos laughed, while Rosalie pretended she hadn't heard.

15

MONTANA TERRITORY.
JUNE 21, 1876

"HEAD 'EM UP, MOVE 'em out!" Cal shouted.

Aware of the possibility of a clash between the soldiers and the Sioux, the riders kept the cattle and the horses at a faster than usual gait. They easily reached the Tongue River in time to set up their camp before dark.

"If my memory serves me right," said Bill Petty, "we got two more rivers ahead."

"That's mostly right," Cal said. "It'll be a long, hard drive tomorrow, but I'm aiming for us to reach Pumpkin Creek. Another long day should see us to Powder River. Beyond that is the Little Missouri."

"It's time we was headin' more to the south," said Oscar Fentress.

"We're going to," Cal said, "just as soon as we cross the Powder. We'll be crossing the Little Missouri where it flows across the southeastern corner of Montana Territory. I figure we'll then be maybe sixty miles from Deadwood."

"Once we're a day out of Deadwood," said Tom Allen, "some of us had better ride in and find the *hombre* that aims to buy the herd. Enough hungry miners in a bunch could lynch us and take the cattle *and* the horses."

"I think we'll have to do exactly that," Cal said. "I haven't forgotten how it was when some gold was discovered along the Bitterroot. Miners are likely to eat anything, or just go hungry to avoid leaving their diggings.''*

The weather continued fair and warm, and there was an abundance of grass. Cal had kept Quickenpaugh on the second watch, while Lorna, Jasmine and Curley were together on the first, along with Oscar Fentress, Smokey Ellison and Tom Allen. The arrangement allowed Cal to tighten security on the more crucial second watch, with himself, Quickenpaugh, Bill Petty, Arch Rainy, Hitch Gould, and Mac Withers.

"Curley," said Lorna, when they were alone, "you haven't seen much of your Indian lately. Has he learned all he wants to know of the white man's tongue?"

"He's not my Indian," Curley said. "He's kept shy of me since Bud . . . left. He's learned to cuss like a mule-skinner in the white man's tongue. I'm not sure he's interested in the rest of it."

"I think he feels a little . . . uneasy, since you were married to Bud," said Lorna. "Maybe he feels like he ought to wait awhile. There's generally a mourning period."

"Mourning?" Curley laughed bitterly. "I'm not that much a hypocrite."

"We all know the rocky road you walked with Bud," said Lorna, "and I doubt that any of us—even Jasmine—will fault you for getting on with your life."

"Thanks," Curley said, "but I'm doing about all I can, which is helping get the herd to Deadwood. How can I get Quickenpaugh's attention without his pride coming between us? I don't want him thinking I'm a pushy, no-account squaw."

"He's on the second watch," said Lorna, "but he either sleeps light or not at all. Last night, while we were on first watch, I caught him wide awake, his Winchester in his hand. The first watch is always quiet. Jasmine and I could cover for you, if you were to . . . ah . . . visit Quickenpaugh when he's supposed to be sleeping."

*North to the Bitterroot (Sundown Riders #1)

"I don't want to cause any trouble within the outfit," Curley said.

"I can't see it causing any trouble, if you spend a little time with Quickenpaugh during the first watch. Just don't get him so involved he forgets he's on the second watch with Cal."

"Damn you, Lorna Snider, you're making fun of me," said Curley. "Quickenpaugh's an Indian. What could . . . how could . . ."

Lòrna laughed. "He's an Indian, but he's a man first, and he's not insensitive. Much as he had a right to hate Bud, Quickenpaugh was genuinely sorry after what happened. I saw it in his eyes."

"Sometimes I think he's more interested in Jasmine than he is in me," said Curley. "He spent a lot of time with her while there was just a blanket between her and naked. What's wrong with Tom Allen? Are his eyes failing him?"

"I don't think Tom and Jasmine have a problem," Lorna said, "but you do. You've got a bad case of jealousy."

"Me? Jealous of a damn Indian?" said Curley.

"Yes," Lorna said, "and it's all without cause. Quickenpaugh would have been just as concerned over you or me as he was over Jasmine. Besides that, I'm not completely sure this strange Indian hasn't used Jasmine's condition to stir the jealousy in you. He wants you to show *some* interest in him, and I *don't* mean teaching him the white man's tongue."

"If you was anybody else," said Curley savagely, "I'd rip your eyeballs out."

"If I was anybody else, I wouldn't give a damn," Lorna said, "but I like Quickenpaugh and I like you."

For a while there was only an uneasy silence between them. Finally, without looking at Lorna, Curley spoke.

"You're my friends, you and Jasmine. It's kind of you to think of me, and I'm a wretch to doubt your intentions. Does Jasmine feel . . . the way . . . you do?"

Lorna laughed. "It was Jasmine who wanted me to talk to you."

"Well, then," said Curley, "maybe tonight we'll find out where Quickenpaugh the Indian ends and Quickenpaugh the man picks up the slack."

As had become their custom, the three women took their positions as part of the first watch. There wouldn't be a moon until late, and no sound disturbed the stillness of the plains except the occasional cry of a coyote. The riders on watch were afoot, and nobody except Lorna and Jasmine were aware that Curley had slipped away from the herd.

"I hope she's doing the right thing," said Lorna.

"She is," Jasmine whispered. "There are white men on the frontier who would slit an Indian's throat if he so much as looked at a white woman, and Quickenpaugh knows that. Have you forgotten how Bud hated Quickenpaugh because he's an Indian?"

"No," said Lorna, "and you're right. Quickenpaugh's going to have to be sure of how his own outfit's going to feel, if he's seriously interested in Curley."

"Yes," Jasmine said, "and before he worries too much about how the outfit feels, he's got to be sure of Curley."

They continued talking in soft tones as Curley crept toward the place well beyond the chuck wagon, where Quickenpaugh spread his blankets. Curley strained her eyes, seeking the dim bulk that would be the Indian in his blankets. Suddenly, from behind, her arms were imprisoned, and there was a strong hand over her mouth. She bit the hand and it was removed. Hands seized her by her shoulders, lifted her off the ground and she found herself face-to-face with Quickenpaugh.

"Quickenpaugh," she whispered desperately, "it's me, Curley."

Quickenpaugh said nothing. Releasing her, he took one of her arms and led her well away from the area where the second watch would be sleeping. He paused beneath a huge tree whose new foliage created a deep shadow. Only then did he speak.

"You like Quickenpaugh?"

"Yes," said Curley. "Can't you tell?"

She caught her breath as she felt his strong fingers unbuttoning her shirt. He peeled off the shirt and began working on the buttons of her Levi's.

"*Desnudo*," Quickenpaugh said.

"No," said Curley. "Boots first."

"*Si*," Quickenpaugh said.

Picking her up bodily, he stretched her out on the ground, and in the best cowboy fashion, drew off her boots. The Levi's followed, and not for an hour did Curley return to her position on watch.

"Well," Jasmine asked anxiously, "did you convince him?"

"If I didn't," said Curley, "him and *all* men can go straight to hell."

But there was a decided difference in Quickenpaugh the following day and for every day thereafter. While he made no obvious moves toward Curley, there was a new light in his dark eyes, and their nightly rendezvous continued. Cal was first to mention the change to Lorna.

"I don't reckon you know what's goin' on between Quickenpaugh and Curley, do you?"

"Who says *anything's* going on?" Lorna asked in response. "If it was, would it bother you?"

"Maybe," said Cal. "Quickenpaugh's an Indian. Not a troublesome one, but an Indian in the eyes of every white man. White women who have taken Indian men have been stripped and beaten to death, while an Indian man taking a white woman is subject to being strung up, gut-shot or shot in the back. I wouldn't want to see any such thing happen to Curley or Quickenpaugh."

"But they're both part of Mr. Story's outfit in Virginia City," said Lorna. "They're as much part of it as any of us. How could any such thing happen?"

"I don't know," Cal said. "I'm just considering the possibilities. I have an idea that our General Custer is getting in over his head with the Sioux. A Sioux victory and a pile of dead soldiers would have white men shooting anybody who even looks Indian, and we're on our way into a boom-town where there will be few women."

"I . . . I'll talk to Curley," said Lorna. "Once we're done in Deadwood . . ."

"No," Cal said. "I don't want Quickenpaugh having his impression of the white man get any worse. Maybe we can set up camp far enough from town to keep him out of it."

EASTERN WYOMING TERRITORY.
JUNE 23, 1876

"If memory serves me right," said Benton McCaleb, "we'll cross Beaver Creek a couple of days before we enter Dakota Territory. It can't be more than fifty or sixty miles on to Deadwood."

"It'll be nice to reach a stream with plenty of water," Brazos said. "We haven't had a decent creek since we left Powder River."

Not until after supper did Rebecca speak to McCaleb on a subject he'd been dreading.

"Bent, every night, Roscoe Yates and those . . . women are getting closer and closer to our camp. If you don't tell them to back off, I'm going to."

"I've already told them," said McCaleb. "What would you suggest I do that I haven't done?"

Rebecca sighed. "I don't know. I . . . I just want to be rid of them."

"I figure we're not more than four or five days out of Deadwood," McCaleb said. "We can stand them another three days, can't we? I figure we'll bed down the herd maybe two days out of Deadwood, until I can ride in and talk to Milo Reems. At that point, if I have to, I'll tell Yates that's as far as we go, that he's to go on without us."

"I suppose we have no choice," said Rebecca gloomily. "I just hope Monte—"

"I just hope Monte's learned his damn lesson," Mc-Caleb said.

But Monte Nance had not. While he no longer pursued the Yates women, he had begun trying Penelope's patience.

"Damn you, Penelope," Monte whined, "why won't you . . . be nice to me?"

"Because your idea of me being nice to you is giving in to you, and you don't deserve it," said Penelope. "I don't want some varmint pawin' over me that's been with every lowlife whore in Wyoming Territory."

"But you ain't always felt like that," Monte protested. "You was stripped that day in the wagon—"

"That was before you spent a week enjoying the favors of those Yates whores right under my nose," said Penelope. "If you're so desperate, why don't you talk to them? They should be ready for another roll in the hay by now."

As had become his custom, Goose rode out the next morning, seeking Indian sign, as well as a source for water for the night's camp. He returned in a little less than three hours, meeting the oncoming herd.

"Creek," said Goose, jogging his mount alongside McCaleb's.

"*Bueno*," McCaleb said. "How far?"

"Reckon ten mile," said Goose, in a drawl he had picked up from the Texans.

There was still no Indian sign, and McCaleb sighed with relief. But his relief was very short-lived. Well before noon, the wind had risen out of the northwest, bringing with it the distinctive smell of rain.

"Warm as it is, rain won't be a bother," Will Elliot said, "but last time, all we got was wind and rain. We're overdue for thunder and lightning."

"Don't remind me," said McCaleb. "I've been saying all the prayers I could think of, in the hope that we might actually reach Deadwood without having these varmints scattered all over eastern Wyoming again.''

But the weather turned bad and the herd ornery before they reached the creek Goose had found. The wind grew stronger, and when the rain came, the big drops slammed into the cows' behinds like buckshot. In itself, that wasn't bad, for the animals had their backs to the coming storm, and it pushed them generally in the direction they must go. But the worst was yet to come. Lightning danced across the leaden sky, and thunder rumbled not too far distant.

"She's buildin' up to a bad one," McCaleb shouted.

It was Rosalie's day on the chuck wagon. Every other rider was in the saddle and all eyes were on the approaching storm.

Quickly McCaleb made the rounds, cautioning them, "If there's thunder and lightning, we may not be able to hold them. If they run, don't try to head them, unless they try to run north or south. If they're hell-bent on running, let's do our best to see they stampede the way we want them to go, which is east."

The thunder and lightning became more intense. Thunder shook the earth, one continuous clap after another, while lightning flared across the leaden sky in its glorious hues of blue, green and gold. The cattle, bawling their unease, picked up the gait until they were almost running. Thunder rolled, one horrendous clap merging with the next, and at the very height of it, lightning struck. As one, the frightened bawling herd stampeded eastward with the wind and rain at their backs. The riders had managed to hold the horse remuda, and they all came together near the chuck wagon. The chuck wagon mules were skittish, and Brazos held their bridles, calming them.

"We'll move on to the creek Goose found," said McCaleb. "The rain looks like it might have set in for the day and maybe tonight. We'll give it till tomorrow before we start our gather. Some of 'em may gather along that creek up yonder ahead of us."

Rebecca looked back, and through the driving rain she could see the Yates wagon as it followed them.

"They're still coming," said Rebecca, just loud enough for Rosalie to hear.

"I know," Rosalie said, through clenched teeth. She slapped the misbehaving mules with the reins, sending them in a trot the direction the herd had stampeded.

SOUTHEASTERN MONTANA TERRITORY.
JUNE 23, 1876

The storm, with its thunder and lightning, swept across the Rocky Mountains, drenching the Wyoming, Montana and Dakota Territories. Cal Snider and his outfit watched with despair as their horses and cattle responded predictably to the commotion created among the elements.

"The worst of the thunder and lightning ain't hit us yet," Bill Petty shouted. "When it does, they're goners."

"If we can't stop them from running," Cal shouted back, "let's try to at least head the varmints the way we want 'em to go."

It would be the best they could do. Once the frightened herd began to run, more than twenty thousand pounding hooves would create a moving avalanche of death. They could only hope to keep the stampeding animals heading eastward, the direction in which the trail drive must eventually go. The thunder rumbled closer, and the lightning became almost continuous.

"Get ready," Cal shouted. "It's coming."

Gray sheets of rain rode the wind in from the northwest, as the riders thonged down their hats. Thunder crashed, seeming to take the weary earth in its clutches and shake it to its very foundation. As one, the cattle were on their feet, bawling their terror. By prior arrangement, all the riders threw their efforts toward securing the horse remuda. Holding the two hundred horses that was the Story herd was impossible. They would have to be gathered along with the stampeded cattle.

"Looks like the rain may continue at least for today, and maybe tonight," Cal said. "We might as well find some high ground and start our gather tomorrow."

"Just another four or five days," said Arch, "and we would of had these varmints in Deadwood. Now we got another damn gather on our hands."

"You'd better hope this bunch don't run too far," Tom Allen said. "We don't know how widespread these diggings are. We might find hungry miners claiming our cows and gunning them down."

"By God, he's right," said Mac Withers. "Come daylight, we'd better ride as long and as hard as we can. Can you imagine what them well-broke Story horses will be worth in a boomtown?"

"Kill," Quickenpaugh hissed.

"No," said Cal. "We can't let it come to that. We'll have to find our herds and take control of them. I think by the time we finish the gather, we'll be near enough to Deadwood for some of us to ride in and make a deal for the cattle."

The rain continued for most of the night, and by dawn the land was sodden beyond belief. Wet weather springs spouted from what had been dry land.

"I think we'll leave the chuck wagon where it is," Cal said. "Lorna, I want you to stay with the wagon, and Quickenpaugh, I want you to stay with her. The rest of us are going after the cattle and horses. The lack of water won't be a problem for a while, so we'll just drive them back here. Quickenpaugh, you have a Winchester, and there's one in the wagon. If there's any sign of trouble, one of you fire some warning shots. We'll be downwind from you, and the sound will carry."

It wasn't the best arrangement, but it was the most sensible. While Quickenpaugh felt the gathering of the scat-

tered horses worthy of his stature, he didn't share that
feeling for the cattle. Therefore, he could remain with
Lorna and the chuck wagon in the event of any possible
danger, without offending his dignity by having to round
up cattle. If he sensed any compromise, he was careful not
to show it. There was still plenty of dry wood in the
wagon's possum belly, and when the outfit had ridden out,
Lorna stirred up the fire and put on another pot of coffee.
Quickenpaugh hunkered down by the fire, waiting. Despite
his faithfulness, Lorna felt ill at ease with him. How did
she converse with him—or with any man—who had been
having a nightly rendezvous with Curley, her friend? She
found herself wishing Curley had spared her and Jasmine
a detailed report of nightly carryings-on between her and
Quickenpaugh. He wore only moccasins and buckskin trou-
sers so tight they left very little to the imagination. Lorna
dared not ignore him, so she knelt on the other side of the
fire, as though waiting for the coffee to boil. Despite all
her efforts to avoid eye contact, Quickenpaugh's eyes met
hers. Suddenly all of Curley's whisperings came to mind,
and she felt herself blushing furiously. Suddenly Quickenpaugh laughed. Never, in all the years he had been with
them had she heard him laugh. It was a strange, guttural
sound from deep in his throat.

"*Cómico*," said Quickenpaugh. "Curley talk."

Lorna blushed all the more, and Quickenpaugh laughed
again. The damn Indian *knew* he was embarrassing her, and
was enjoying it to the utmost. Deliberately, she forced from
her mind all the mental pictures Curley had painted, and
when she spoke, it was in her normal voice.

"Yes," said Lorna boldly, "Curley talks. Jasmine and I
know all the two of you have done. Do you intend to punish
Curley?"

Quickenpaugh shook his head. Contrary to what Lorna
had expected, he seemed pleased that word of his prowess
had reached the ears of Curley's friends. His arrogance

seemed akin to that of the late Bud McDaniels, and suddenly Lorna was angry.

"Damn you," Lorna said, "you're having your way with Curley, and like any feather-legged coyote, you want to sing out to the world. What do you aim to do with her, when we return to Virginia City? Will you round up a few squaws to help her entertain you?"

Lorna swallowed hard, aware that her words might infuriate Quickenpaugh to an extent that he might slit her throat in a moment of fury. To her surprise, Quickenpaugh laughed. He then spoke mildly, in as friendly a manner as ever.

"No squaw. Have ranch."

Despite herself, Lorna laughed. "You? With a ranch? You hate cows. Do you aim for Curley to do all the work herself?"

"Not cow ranch," said Quickenpaugh. "Horse ranch."

Suddenly it began to make sense, and since Curley had said nothing about such a thing, Lorna could only conclude that Quickenpaugh hadn't told her what was on his mind.

"When will you tell Curley?" Lorna asked.

Quickenpaugh shrugged his shoulders.

"She ought to know," Lorna persisted. "She needs to know there's more in her future than having you strip her and have your way with her on a blanket on the ground."

"No blanket," said Quickenpaugh solemnly.

"You bastard, you're laughing at me," Lorna shouted.

"Not *cómico*," said Quickenpaugh. "Curley talk, you talk. You tell."

"You want *me* to tell Curley your intentions," Lorna said. "That's not right. She needs to hear it from you."

Quickenpaugh shrugged his shoulders and said no more. The coffee was ready, and Lorna fetched two tin cups. Pouring one full, she passed it to Quickenpaugh. She then filled the second one for herself. She again knelt down across the fire, where she and the Indian stared at each other in uneasy silence. Despite Quickenpaugh's limitations, he

had told her that his thoughts for his future and that of
Curley went considerably beyond his and Curley's nightly
frolic. But suppose this strange Indian didn't *tell* Curley?

"I'll tell Curley what your plans are," said Lorna.

Quickenpaugh only nodded, saying nothing.

After riding for miles, Cal and the outfit had reined up to
rest their horses. They had seen not a sign of their cows
and Story's horse herd, except the muddy tracks that
seemed to go on forever.

"I've never seen 'em run this far without somethin' or
somebody chasin' 'em," Hitch Gould said.

"I reckon you could say the storm was chasing them,"
said Cal. "They lit out quick, in the same direction the
storm was moving, and it must have seemed like the thunder and lightning were following them."

"That means they run until the thunder and lightning
played out, or they was totally give out," Smokey Ellison
said.

"There's been enough rain to swell every river, creek
and water hole," said Tom Allen. "Comin' up on a river
runnin' bank-full could stop their running."

"Ahead of us, the only river I know of is the Little Missouri," Cal replied, "and I'm not sure how far we are from
it. I know it flows to the southwest, and even if the stampede ends there, our stock could drift for miles. We must
find them in a hurry."

After another hour's ride, they reined up on the west
bank of what they believed to be the Little Missouri.

"It's got to be the Little Missouri," said Tom Allen.
"Years ago, a trapper told me it's the last river you cross
in Montana, without bein' in Dakota Territory or the southeastern corner of Wyoming Territory."

"Whatever it is, our stock stopped here," Cal said. "The
question is, how far must we ride up- or downstream before
we find them?"

"I don't know," said Jasmine, "but I'm thinking it was

a mistake, not bringing the wagon with us. The wind's died, and we're so far away, Lorna or Quickenpaugh could fire a cannon without us hearing."

"Damn it, I didn't know the stampede would run this far," Cal said defensively. "But I reckon you're right. It makes no sense, gathering the herd and then takin' hours driving 'em the wrong direction. Who's willing to go after the wagon?"

"I'll go," said Jasmine. "With a trail half a mile wide, there's no danger of me getting lost."

"Tell Lorna to keep the wagon out of the trail left by the stampede," Cal said. "There'll be mud hub-deep. Tell her to look for some high ground and stay with it. If she should get bogged down, your horse and Quickenpaugh's can be harnessed with the mules."

It was all so obvious, Jasmine was mildly irritated. Without a reply, she rode west.

"We have to start somewhere," said Cal. "Let's ride downstream a ways and see what we can find."

Finally, in the distance, they could see grazing cattle and a few horses.

"That's a start," said Smokey Ellison.

"I don't be too sure of that," Oscar Fentress said. "Some of them critters ain't wearin' our brand. See them first two cows with a star on their hips?"

"Oscar's dead right," said Cal. "We've come up on somebody else's herd. We'd better ride downstream a ways and find the *hombres* with the drive. Maybe we can join forces and help one another."

They didn't have far to ride. Heading upstream toward them were five riders. When the lead rider raised his hand, his companions reined up beside him. He looked them over for a moment before he spoke.

"I'm Benton McCaleb, trail boss for Lone Star, out of Wyoming. To my right is Pen Rhodes. To my left is Brazos Gifford, his daughter Penelope and Monte Nance."

"Cal Snider, and I'm trail boss for the Story outfit, out

of Virginia City, Montana. Some of our folks are trying to move the chuck wagon over here. I'll introduce you to the rest, since it looks like we have a common problem.''

Quickly, Cal introduced the outfit, and when he got to Quanah Taylor, he found the young cowboy's eyes fixed on Penelope. His attention didn't go unnoticed, for Penelope wore a half-smile while Monte Nance wore a frown.

"We got on the trail of our herd as soon as it was light enough," said McCaleb, "and I reckon our chuck wagon's maybe ten miles back. Goose, our scout, and my wife Rebecca are there with it now. Monte, ride back and join them. Tell Rebecca to take her time with the wagon, but to come on.''

"Oh, hell," Monte growled, "the damn wagon will get stuck every hundred yards."

"You have a lariat and so does Goose," said McCaleb. "Pull it out."

"Where are the rest of your riders?" Cal asked.

"Downriver," said McCaleb. "I hope most of our cows are there. This is a long ways from the three thousand we started with."

"God, how I envy you," Cal said. "We have more than five thousand cows, and at least two hundred horses."

16

JASMINE SOON REACHED THE chuck wagon where Lorna and Quickenpaugh waited. Quickly she relayed Cal's instructions.

"High ground, hell," said Lorna. "All I see is mud everywhere."

"Do the best you can," Jasmine said. "They're a long ways off, maybe twelve miles or more. The chuck wagon has to be closer to the gather than that."

"I'll get it there somehow," said Lorna. "Why don't you tie your horse on behind and ride the box with me?"

Lorna did, while Quickenpaugh rode a few yards ahead of the wagon. Jasmine listened in amazement as Lorna told her of the strange conversation with Quickenpaugh.

"That just might work out," Jasmine said. "I've never seen a man—Indian or white—who had such a feeling for horses as Quickenpaugh. He couldn't be more concerned with Nelson Story's horse herd if they were his own."

"I'm glad, for Curley's sake," said Lorna. "By the time this drive ends, she might be in the . . . the . . ."

"Family way," Jasmine finished.

"That would be terrible," said Lorna, "with us both barren as a pair of maverick cows. What could we have done that we haven't done?"

"I don't know," Jasmine said. "Maybe we could borrow

Quickenpaugh, when he's not busy with Curley. Why don't you ask her?''

"I am totally mortified that you would suggest such a thing," said Lorna stiffly.

She put on the act for as long as she could, and when they both erupted into fits of laughter, Quickenpaugh reined up his horse and looked back.

Monte reached the chuck wagon where Rebecca and Goose waited. First, he passed on McCaleb's instructions. Then he told them of Cal Snider and the outfit from Virginia City.

"I don't like the sound of that," Rebecca said. "If they have nearly twice as many cows as we do, and the herds are mixed, God knows how long this gather will take."

"That may not be the biggest problem," said Monte. "Their big herd may cut hell out of the prices, if there ain't as much a market as we expect."

Rebecca took her time with the chuck wagon, and sundown was less than an hour away when she finally reached the west bank of the Little Missouri. Downstream a ways was a second chuck wagon, and two women were unharnessing the teams. Flicking the mules with the reins, she started toward the other wagon, thankful there were some women in the other outfit. Goose followed. Quickenpaugh had been behind Lorna's chuck wagon, and as Rebecca, Monte and Goose approached, Quickenpaugh dropped the reins of his horse and stepped out. But he had no interest in the newly arrived chuck wagon, the strange woman on the box or Monte Nance. Quickenpaugh's eyes were on Goose. In an instant, Goose had dismounted and the two faced one another like hostile hounds. Far from their native Texas, two mortal enemies had come face-to-face. Goose, the Lipan Apache, drew his long Bowie knife, while Quickenpaugh, the Comanche, drew his own formidable weapon.

"Comanch' *bastardo*," Goose hissed, advancing.

"Apach' *perro*," charged Quickenpaugh, taking a step forward.

"Goose, no!" shouted Rebecca, scrambling down from the wagon box.

Seeing the potential danger, Jasmine and Lorna were running toward Quickenpaugh, but his hard eyes were still on Goose. He advanced another step, but Rebecca reached Goose before he could go any closer.

"Goose," Rebecca pleaded, "he's a friend, an *amigo*."

She took hold of his left arm, and he border-shifted the Bowie to his right. But Lorna and Jasmine had reached Quickenpaugh, and he yielded to their pleas, sheathing his Bowie. Almost reluctantly, Goose slipped his own Bowie beneath his waistband. The two glared at each other in a manner that suggested hostilities might resume at some better time and place.

"Dear God," said Rebecca, "I wasn't ready for that."

"Neither were we," Lorna said shakily. "I'm Lorna Snider, and this is Jasmine Allen. That's Quickenpaugh with the knife."

"I'm Rebecca McCaleb, that's my brother, Monte Nance, on the horse. The other hell-raiser with the knife is a Lipan Apache, Goose. He's civilized, most of the time."

Lorna laughed. "So is Quickenpaugh. I suppose we'll have to watch the two of them until they become friends."

"That won't ever happen," said Monte. "Damn Indians only know how to kill."

Goose and Quickenpaugh seemed to have set aside their hatred for each other and had turned their attention to Monte Nance.

"Monte," Rebecca said, "why don't you join the rest of the outfit, and tell McCaleb we managed to get the wagon here?"

Without argument, Monte kicked his horse into a lope, heading downriver.

Rebecca sighed. "I hope I live long enough to see him grow up."

"I had the same hope, once," said Jasmine, "but *he* didn't live long enough to grow up. He got a mad on and rode out, back in southern Montana Territory. We're pretty sure the Sioux got him."

"Sorry to hear that," Rebecca said. "Indian trouble is about the only problem we didn't have, but we've made up for it with thunder, lightning and broken wagon wheels."

"It's getting late," said Lorna. "There's not enough time today to even *think* about a gather. Is there any reason we can't bring our chuck wagons together and share a camp?"

"No reason that I know of," Rebecca said. "I don't think my outfit will object."

"Nor will ours," said Jasmine. "We'll want to meet the rest of your womenfolk."

"They'll be happy to meet you," Rebecca said. "Life on a trail drive gets pretty rough, and it's a comfort to know we're not the only females to have taken leave of our senses."

The riders from both outfits soon returned from downriver. Rebecca, Monte and Goose were introduced to the Story outfit, While McCaleb's outfit was introduced to Lorna, Jasmine and Quickenpaugh. The two Indians still regarded each other with hostility, a situation that immediately got McCaleb's attention.

"Snider," said McCaleb, "I reckon I'll have a talk with Goose. Reckon you can reason with your man?"

"I can try," Cal said.

"Bent," said Rebecca, "we're going to share a camp, unless somebody objects."

"No objection here," McCaleb said.

"None here," said Cal. "I reckon we'll all be pretty well acquainted before we're finally done with this gather."

Susannah and Rosalie had been introduced to Lorna, Jasmine and Curley.

"I'm sorry my daughter, Penelope, hasn't joined us," Rosalie said.

"I think she's discovered somebody more interesting than a bunch of females," said Susannah.

Quanah Taylor was unsaddling Penelope's horse, something she had steadfastly insisted on doing herself, until now.

"He's a handsome young man," Rosalie observed, obviously pleased.

Rebecca only nodded, for her mind was drifting back ten years, to the time she had first seen Benton McCaleb. He'd had sandy hair, eyes that were sky-blue, a fast gun and a drawl that was pure Texas. Now this young man—Quanah Taylor—reminded her of a young Benton McCaleb. Taylor said something and Penelope laughed, her hand on his arm. The eyes of Monte Nance had clouded with hatred, and his right hand rested on the butt of one of his Colts. He turned away only when he felt Rebecca's eyes on him.

LITTLE MISSOURI RIVER, DAKOTA TERRITORY.
JUNE 29, 1876

With the exception of Goose and Quickenpaugh, the two outfits became friends, joining in a common cause. McCaleb having spoken to Goose, and Cal to Quickenpaugh, the two antagonists virtually ignored one another. Each day, before the start of the gather, Cal and McCaleb brought both outfits together.

"I think," said McCaleb, "we can decide whose animals are which when we've finally got a decent gather. Let's just round them up without regard to brands."

"*Bueno*," Cal agreed. "Maybe we can just drive 'em on to Deadwood as a single herd and avoid any heavy dickering over the price."

"That's good thinking," said Brazos.

There was shouted agreement from everybody except Monte Nance. His eyes were on Quanah Taylor, and he had a look on his face like soured milk.

"Horse," Quickenpaugh said. "No find."

"By God, he's right," said Tom Allen. "We haven't come up on a single one of Story's horse herd."

"He's wise to be worried," Bill Petty said. "Story more or less put him in charge of the herd."

"Quickenpaugh," said Cal, "I want you to track down those horses. Choose a rider to go with you and take some grub."

"*Si*," Quickenpaugh said, pointing to Curley.

"They're an unusual pair," said McCaleb, when the two had ridden away.

"More unusual than you'd ever believe," Cal said. "How many Indians do you know with the ambition of owning a horse ranch?"

"At least one," said McCaleb. "Goose has the most prosperous horse ranch anywhere in Wyoming Territory. We brought him with us because of possible trouble with the Sioux."

The gather went slowly, for many of the cattle had crossed the Little Missouri and had drifted well beyond it. The outfits were just settling down to supper when there came the sound of a running horse. The rider—a soldier—reined up the heaving animal and all but fell from the saddle. Oscar Fentress and Smokey Ellison helped to ease him down with his back to a wagon wheel. Rebecca brought him a tin cup of steaming coffee. Nobody spoke, allowing him time to catch his wind and sip some of the coffee. Finally he spoke.

"General Custer and two hundred and fifteen of his men has been kilt by the Sioux."

"Great God," said McCaleb, "what happened to the others?"

"Major Reno had a hundred and forty, while Captain Benteen had a hundred and twenty-five. I was with Major Reno. General Custer took his men one way, while the rest of us went another. General Custer and his bunch attacked the Sioux along the Little Big Horn, and Lord God, there must of been three or four thousand of the varmints. Time the rest of us got there, it was all over. I'm takin' the news to the outpost at Bismarck.''

''Not if you ride your horse to death and exhaust yourself,'' Cal said. ''Another day's not going to make that much difference. You and your horse can rest tonight, you can fill up on grub and hot coffee and be on your way tomorrow.''

''I reckon you're right,'' said the soldier. ''I'm about used up.''

''When did this fight take place?'' Tom Allen asked.

''Last Sunday, June 25,'' said the soldier. ''Major Reno and Captain Benteen are there, supervising burial details. God, it was awful. Most all the wounded had been run through with lances while they was still alive.''

Word of the disaster had a sobering effect on the outfits, and no more questions were asked of the weary soldier. After breakfast he thanked his hosts and rode out, taking with him the news that would shock the nation and mark the beginning of the end of the Sioux.

Three days after Quickenpaugh and Curley had ridden south, they returned, driving the two hundred missing horses. In addition, they had driven five hundred head of the missing cattle, a mix of the two herds.

''Tarnation,'' said McCaleb, ''we should have gone with them.''

''It looks that way,'' Cal said, ''but who would have expected them to drift that far?''

''Beautiful graze down there,'' said Curley. ''I believe the rest of the herd's there.''

''How far?'' McCaleb asked.

''Near twenty miles,'' said Curley.

Arch Rainey, Hitch Gould and Mac Withers had joined Quickenpaugh, and the four of them had settled the recovered horse herd along the river.

''I've never seen a finer bunch of horses in my life,'' McCaleb said. ''Indian-gentled?''

"Every one," said Cal. "Quickenpaugh's doing."

"Bent," Rebecca said, "there goes Goose. There may be trouble."

"Maybe not," said McCaleb. "He's interested in the horses."

Quickenpaugh didn't move, as Goose walked among the horses. He spoke softly, relying on the meaningless "horse talk" that he employed in gentling his own animals. Ruffling the ears and manes of many of the horses, he left them nickering after him when he withdrew from them. Both outfits watched in awe as these warriors whose tribes were ages-old enemies came face-to-face. Arch, Hitch and Mac had backed away, leaving Quickenpaugh near where Goose emerged from the herd.

"We're about to see a miracle, or all hell will bust loose," said Will Elliot.

Goose came on, and when he was within a few feet of Quickenpaugh, he halted. The Comanche and the Lipan Apache regarded each other in silence, and while there was no change in the expression of either, something passed between them. Goose went on to the supper fire, and Rebecca passed him a tin cup of steaming coffee. Quickenpaugh hunkered down beside Curley.

"They've discovered something stronger than their hatred for each other," Lorna said. "If God can do that with them, then there's hope for the rest of us."

LITTLE MISSOURI RIVER, DAKOTA TERRITORY.
JULY 3, 1876

As the outfits prepared to ride out, McCaleb ordered Rebecca, Rosalie, Susannah and Penelope to remain with the chuck wagon. Goose would be with them.

"I'm riding with the outfit," said Penelope.

The fire in her eyes said she was prepared for battle, but McCaleb only grinned at her. He had seen Quanah Taylor saddling her horse.

"Curley," Cal said, "I want you and Quickenpaugh to stay here with Lorna and Jasmine in case there's any trouble. If these animals are a long way off, we may be late comin' in. Don't start any supper fires until we return."

The remainder of the two outfits rode out, heading downriver.

"I'm surprised at Cal leaving Quickenpaugh here," said Jasmine.

"I'm not," Lorna said. "Quickenpaugh's found his horses. He won't be worth a damn on a cattle gather."

"That's about the way it is with Goose," said Rebecca. "He has no use for cows, but he would go out in a blizzard looking for just one strayed horse."

"I'm glad Cal left Curley here," Jasmine said. "I think she'll have a calming influence on Quickenpaugh, if him and Goose give in to old hatreds and decide to fight."

"They're serious?" Susannah asked.

"As serious as any male and female ever gets," said Jasmine. "They've done everything except stand before a preacher, and we doubt that Quickenpaugh ever will."

"Goose never did," Rebecca said. "He's been with his Crow woman almost ten years."

"I'm surprised she didn't insist on coming with him," said Susannah. "Indian women all seem to follow their men."

"Belleza, Goose's woman, had her reasons," Rebecca said. "I think she'll be having her first child before the snow comes again."

"Damn," said Rosalie, "Brazos will take that hard. He thinks something's wrong with him."

The women continued comparing their lives on the frontier. Among the riders headed downstream for the gather, Penelope and Quanah Taylor brought up the rear.

"What do you aim to do when your herd's been sold?" Taylor asked.

"Ride back to the Sweetwater Valley in Wyoming, I suppose," said Penelope. "What will you do?"

"With a little encouragement, I might follow you there," the cowboy said. "If I do, will I be welcome?"

"It depends on what kind of encouragement you have in mind," said Penelope. "I don't aim to strip down for a roll in the hay with you."

He kept his eyes straight ahead, saying nothing. Penelope sneaked a sidelong look at him, and was immediately ashamed of her hard words. Quanah Taylor was profoundly embarrassed, his face flaming red all the way to his hairline. Penelope rode close enough to place her hand on his arm. When he finally looked at her, there was unmistakable anger in his eyes.

"I'm sorry," Penelope said. "I shouldn't have said that. I . . . I had someone else in mind, and I spoke before I thought. Will you forgive me?"

"Yes," he replied, his features softening. "I think I know who you had in mind. Does he have any hold on you? Have you promised him . . . anything?"

"Monte Nance? My God, no," Penelope cried.

"I wanted to be sure," Taylor said. "He keeps lookin' at you like you're hog-tied and branded, and at me like he wants to cut me down at the business end of a Colt."

"To be honest," said Penelope, "I . . . did pay some attention to him for a while, until he left our camp to lay about with a pair of whores."

"Whores? Here on the plains?"

"Yes," Penelope said. "They were on their way to Deadwood."

She went on to tell him of Roscoe Yates, his troublesome wagon and the outrageous conduct of his so-called daughters, Connie and Kate.

"They must have seen a long delay, making this gather," said Taylor. "They could have crossed the Little Missouri far enough up- or downriver for us not to be aware of their going."

"Please, let's don't talk about them," Penelope said.

"Did you mean it, when you talked about . . . following me to Wyoming?"

"Never more serious in my life," said Quanah, tipping back his hat and grinning at her. "I've been taking cattle for my wages for nigh ten years. Five hundred head of the Story herd belongs to me, and I've got another five hundred in Montana Territory, most of 'em prime breeding stock."

"Then you're not just a forty-and-found cowboy," Penelope said. "I want Brazos to talk to you."

"Your daddy?"

"All the daddy I ever had," said Penelope. "He found Mama and me beaten and starving and adopted me when I was little."

"He sounds like my kind of man," Taylor said. "Maybe I can talk to him tonight, after we round up the rest of the cattle."

Even with a larger number of cattle to gather, the herd grew rapidly, for there were more riders.

"Let's try to bunch the rest of 'em today," said McCaleb. "Even if we trail them on to Deadwood as a single herd, we'll still have to run separate tallies to be sure we have them all."

Both herds had become trail wise, and bunching them wasn't so difficult. But they all were widely scattered, and bringing them together tried the patience of every rider. When the sun was but an hour high, the riders could see grazing cattle dotting the distant hills.

"Well," said McCaleb wearily, "we didn't make it. There's still more of 'em out there than any of us can afford to lose. So it's back again tomorrow, and maybe a day or two beyond that."

"This is takin' a hell of a lot of time," Brazos said, "and I've been thinking of how we aim to sell these critters, once they're rounded up. Suppose some of us rode on in to Deadwood and rounded up this speculator, Milo Reems. He's got to come up with a pile of money."

"Reems?" said Cal. "That's the *hombre* that quoted us fifty dollars a head."

"Same thing he quoted us," McCaleb said. "Since the Union Pacific's come through, I've heard there's some ranchers settlin' in Nebraska, not too far from the tracks. Damn it, we may be competing with them."

"That's exactly what's rubbin' my fur the wrong way," said Brazos. "In a beef-hungry town, the first two or three herds will bring top dollar. After that, prices may fall through the floor. McCaleb, you're trail boss for Lone Star, while Cal's trail boss for the Story outfit. The two of you could ride in, find Reems and have him ride out here to look at the herds. We'll have the rest of 'em gathered by then. Maybe we can strike a deal without having to drive them right into town."

"That makes sense to me," Tom Allen said. "If we're the first herds to show up, those beef-hungry miners could take our cattle just by shootin' 'em down. Last we heard, there was no law in Deadwood, except maybe the military. Now, after the killing of Custer and his men, it's likely that every bluecoat west of the Mississippi's goin' after the Sioux."

"Those are pretty strong arguments," said McCaleb. "I think, while the rest of you are finishing this gather, Cal and me had better ride in and test the water, instead of showing up cold, with eight thousand cows."

There was enthusiastic agreement from everybody except Monte Nance. His hard eyes were on McCaleb when he spoke.

"I'm part of this outfit, McCaleb, and I have as much right to ride in as you. Some of these cattle are mine, and I aim to dicker for a higher price."

"You do," said McCaleb, "and you're no longer part of Lone Star. We'll cut out your part of the herd, and if you're of a mind to, you can drive 'em off a rimrock."

Her heart in her throat, Rebecca saw Monte's jaw harden. Benton McCaleb was all that Monte Nance had never been and could not be, and as a result, he hated McCaleb. Rebecca sighed in resignation, and then spoke.

"Bent, unless you think I'm needed here, I'd like to ride to Deadwood with you."

"Anybody object to that?" McCaleb asked.

Nobody objected, and Jasmine had a suggestion.

"Cal, why don't you take Lorna with you? Even if Deadwood's a hard town, won't the men be less troublesome if you have your women along?"

"That's entirely possible," Cal said. "Lorna, do you want to go?"

"Yes," said Lorna. "Something about this whole thing bothers me. I'm taking my pistol and a bag of shells."

"So am I," Rebecca said.

That drew some applause from all the others, for it was a precaution each of them well understood. The following morning, Cal, Lorna, McCaleb and Rebecca rode out, bound for Deadwood. Brazos Gifford was in charge of the Lone Star outfit, while Tom Allen had taken responsibility for the Story riders.

"There's enough of us that a couple of the ladies could stay in camp and cook for both outfits," said Brazos. "What about it, Tom?"

"Suits me," Tom said. "Why don't we choose two from each outfit? Jasmine, that'll be you and Curley."

"Rosalie," said Brazos, "it'll be you and Susannah. We can't spare Penelope."

Some of them looked at Penelope in amusement, and she did a rare thing. She blushed.

McCaleb, Cal, Lorna and Rebecca rode four abreast, and by early afternoon of the first day, they could see the dust of the the Yates wagon far ahead.

"We ought to travel wide and avoid them," Rebecca said.

"Damned if I will," said McCaleb. "That would be considerably out of our way, and I'm not aiming for them to reach Deadwood ahead of us. It would be just like that no-account old coyote to announce that our cattle are scattered all to hell and gone. Since there's no law, the miners might consider our cows fair game and start gunnin' 'em down."

"Yates sounds like trouble," Lorna said. "Why did you allow him to travel with you?"

"Ah, hell," said McCaleb, "I reckon I felt sorry for them. There's him and the two girls he claims are his daughters, and they didn't show up until we were more than a hundred miles from home."

"Monte said they have a roulette wheel in the wagon," Rebecca said.

"I don't want to hear Monte's name mentioned, or his opinion on anything," said McCaleb shortly. "He's alive only because he's your brother, and I don't know how much longer I can let that stand in my way."

Lorna could see the hurt in Rebecca's eyes, and as though by mutual agreement, the two of them dropped back, trotting their horses side by side.

"Sorry," Lorna said softly. "Jasmine lost her brother Bud just a few weeks ago. Ever since we left Texas, he's been a constant worry. We thought, after he married Curley, he would settle down, but he didn't. He just made her life hell. He got a mad on and rode out for Deadwood. Quickenpaugh learned the Sioux had dug in along the Little Big Horn, and when he tried to warn Bud, Bud shot him. As far as we know, he rode headlong into some of the waiting Sioux."

"My God," said Rebecca. "I almost know Monte's headed for a bad end. I just don't know when or where it will come."

"Sometimes a good woman can change a man," Lorna said. "Would you believe Curley and Quickenpaugh the Comanche have been . . . sharing their blankets?"

"After all we've been through with Monte," said Rebecca, "I'd believe anything. Are the Indian's intentions good?"

"As good as an Indian's intentions ever get," Lorna said. "Quickenpaugh's thinking of a horse ranch. He don't care a damn for all the cows in the world."

"That sounds like Goose," said Rebecca. "God, can he gentle horses. He likes them, and for some reason nobody understands, they like him."

"I noticed that," Lorna said, "when he walked through our horse herd. You know, it's only their common love for horses that prevented a fight to the death between the two of them."

The Yates wagon had stopped, apparently to rest the mules. Connie and Kate leaned against the wagon's tailgate, while Roscoe Yates remained on the wagon box. McCaleb had no intention of speaking, but Yates spoke first.

"Looked like you was goin' to be a while roundin' up all that livestock, so I reckoned we might as well move along."

"We'll manage," said McCaleb shortly. "Just go on about your business."

"My stars," one of the Yates girls said, her eyes on Rebecca, "it's Monte's mama. Tell him we'll be waiting for him in Deadwood."

Rebecca kept her silence, biting her lips until they bled. Only when the Yates wagon was far behind did she speak.

"As sorry as they are, and as free as they are with their favors, there are times when I think the only solution is to shoot Monte right between the eyes. For a while, I thought Penelope might have some good influence on him, but Penelope's found her man. He's all that Monte will never be."

"I'm proud for her," said Lorna. "Quanah Taylor's Texan to the bone, and as Cal says, as a man, he's nine feet tall and a yard wide."

17

❦

DEADWOOD, DAKOTA TERRITORY.
JULY 6, 1876

THE TOWN OF DEADWOOD was strung out along a gulch, with one muddy street stretching the length of it. There were barren mountains on both sides, and the only trails meandered between them.

"Dear God," said Rebecca, "what a dirty, dismal, isolated place. All I see are saloons."

"When men have gold fever, they won't have much time for anything else," McCaleb said. "There'll be some eatin' places, and maybe a couple of boarding houses, but they'll be priced out of our reach."

"We know there's a telegraph instrument somewhere in town," Cal said. "Suppose we go lookin' for that. We might learn where Reems hangs out."

"There's a military outpost up yonder at the end of the street," a miner told them. "It's their telegraph, but they'll likely let you use it."

The outpost was a crudely built cabin with two bunks, a fireplace and a table and four chairs. Two men stood up when McCaleb and his companions entered.

"I'm Sergeant Carpenter, and this is Corporal Barnett. What can we do for you?"

Quickly, McCaleb told them of the deal for the cattle that Milo Reems had confirmed by telegraph, and of their need to locate Reems.

"Reems lived at Lassiter's Boardinghouse while he was here," Sergeant Carpenter said.

"*While he was here!*" McCaleb shouted. "You mean he's not here *now*?"

"I'm afraid not," said Sergeant Carpenter, "although he's expected to return shortly. He made deals all over town for those cows you fellows are driving in. His wife's still here."

"Hell's fire," Cal said, "he's in no position to make deals with anybody. He hasn't laid out a plugged *peso* toward payment for our herds."

"It's all the more important that you find him, then," Sergeant Carpenter said. "Last I heard, he'd sold eighty-eight hundred cows at sixty dollars a head. He bought a wagon, hired a dozen armed guards and took the gold to the bank in Cheyenne. He aims to line up some more cattle to be driven in. He could have sold another two or three thousand head."

"Like hell he could," McCaleb bawled. "They're not his to sell. How long has he been gone?"

"Three days, as I recall," said Sergeant Carpenter. "Everybody's anxious for his return. Every miner in these hills has bought a cow or two, while the Gulch Cafe bought fifty. Now I reckon we'll have to wait for him so you can close the deal."

"Sergeant," McCaleb said, "I have a favor to ask of you and the corporal. Say *nothing* about us, or our purpose for being here, until we can track down Milo Reems and settle this whole thing. If these miners have paid for beef on the hoof, they may decide to take it with a gun."

"My God, you're right," said Carpenter, "and there's no law in town except Corporal Barnett and me. Reems left his wife here. Are you doubting he intends to return and settle with you?"

"I'm doubting that Reems intends to return for *any* reason," McCaleb said. "I believe the people in this town have been left holding the sack—an *empty* sack—for more than half a million dollars, and they stand to lose it all unless we can track down Milo Reems, and get our money."

"But you *have* the promised beef," said Sergeant Carpenter.

"True," McCaleb said, "but we're not honoring Reems's promise until we're paid for our herds. I must ask you again to keep all this to yourself. If these miners go after our cows based on what they've paid Reems, our outfits will lay some misery on them that'll make everybody forget Custer's bad day with the Sioux."

McCaleb and his group left the two soldiers with worried looks on their faces.

"They'll have told somebody—maybe everybody—before dark," Cal predicted.

"I suspect you're right," said McCaleb. "In fact, I believe the sergeant and the corporal may have bought a couple of our cows for themselves. Now they know Reems has cut and run with the money, paying us nothing. We'd better saddle up and head for Cheyenne before word gets around. This place may erupt like a lighted keg of black powder."

"Let's try Lassiter's Boardinghouse first," said Rebecca. "Surely he plans to return, if he left his wife here."

"Not necessarily," McCaleb said grimly. "Not if he wanted to get out of town with a fortune in gold without arousing suspicion."

"If he's done that," said Cal, "this world's not big enough for both of us. Our share of that herd cost Lorna and me ten hard years. Let's find that woman of his and see if this is as god-awful bad as it looks."

Lassiter's was so new, the green lumber hadn't yet begun to warp. It was all on one level, with a series of rooms strung along each side of a hall. A whiskered man with a Colt stuck beneath his waistband got up, and when he spoke, it was with no friendliness.

"We're full up."

"No concern of ours," said McCaleb. "We're here to see Milo Reems's wife."

"Reems ain't in town, and I ain't wantin' no trouble here."

"We know Reems is not here," McCaleb said, "and we aim to talk to this woman, if we have to bust down every door in this place. Now, where is she?"

"Last door on the right at the end of the hall."

McCaleb pounded on the door, and there was no response. He pounded a second time, and it shook the very wall.

"Go away," shouted a shrill voice from inside.

"I have some questions to ask you," said McCaleb, "and I'm not leaving without getting some answers."

There was no response, and McCaleb slammed his shoulder against the door. A flimsy bar snapped, and the door was flung back against the wall. A startled bearded man flung all the covers off the bed. He was attired in only his socks, while the furious female beside him wore considerably less. A gunbelt hung from a bedpost, and the man on the bed went for his Colt. McCaleb carried his Colt butt-forward on his right hip, and he drew with the swiftness of a lightning bolt. His slug struck the butt of the holstered Colt, sending it and the gunbelt tumbling down behind the bed.

"Now," said McCaleb, "you have just enough time to grab your britches and boots and get the hell out of here."

The frightened stranger wasted no time. He leaped out of the bed and, forgetting his hat and gunbelt, grabbed his boots and rumpled clothes as he headed for the door. There was considerable commotion in the hall, and since the four of them were already in the small room, Cal closed the door. The naked woman came off the bed with a shriek, but it was a move Lorna and Rebecca had been expecting. Each of them caught one arm and, not too gently, flung her on her back, on the bed. She bounded up again, and Rebecca caught her on the chin with a fisted right hand. Lorna was already gathering some of the woman's scattered clothing, and using that, they quickly bound her ankles and wrists. Somebody was pounding on the door. Cal opened it and there were three men outside. His Colt was cocked and steady in his hand, and with it, he motioned down the hall. The three quickly got the message and retreated. Cal closed the door. The furious woman had regained her senses and was cursing them with every breath. Before McCaleb or Cal could respond to the tirade, Lorna rose to the occasion.

"All we're here for is to ask you some questions. Now, you stop that swearing and pay attention to me. If you don't tell us what we want to know, my friend and me are going to drag you outside stark naked and, before God and everybody, just purely beat the hell out of you with a doubled lariat."

As serious as the occasion was, McCaleb and Cal were trying mightily not to grin at one another. The woman spread-eagled on the bed had ceased swearing, and when she did speak again, her voice trembled.

"What do you want to know?"

"First," said McCaleb, "are you the wife of a varmint name of Milo Reems?"

"No," she replied. "My name is Viola, and I met Reems in Cheyenne. He offered to pay me five hundred dollars a month if I'd pose as his wife for as long as he needed me. He's paid for this room for the rest of the month, and you have no right to break in on me."

"You got no idea why he wanted you to pose as his wife?" Cal asked.

"No," said Viola. "He didn't tell me nothin'. He just took me around town a few times, introducing me as his missus."

"But you knew he was up to no good, didn't you?" McCaleb said.

"Honest to God, I didn't know what his game was,"

said Viola. "I just wanted him to do . . . whatever he had planned, and leave me alone."

"We're going to turn you loose," McCaleb said, "and you're not to tell *anybody* you're not Milo Reems's wife. Understand?"

Viola laughed. "You bet I understand. You busted in here and slapped me around, and there was nothing I could do except take it. Now somethin' tells me that I can set all your tails on fire just by telling what I know about Reems."

"I don't think you'll be able, when I'm through with you," said Rebecca. "Lorna, if you will help me, we'll rearrange this whore so much, she won't be able to find work swamping out saloons."

"No," McCaleb said. "As much as Cal and me would like to observe your creativity, we can't do that. Sooner or later, the town's going to learn what Reems has done, that they—and us—are suckers of the first water. The best we can do is silence her until we're out of here. Bind her wrists and ankles to the bedposts and stuff something in her mouth."

Viola began cursing them again, and they endured it until her wrists and ankles were secured to the head and foot of the bed.

"I want the pleasure of gagging her," Lorna said.

Lorna stuffed something in Viola's mouth, and she began thrashing violently around.

"Damn," said Cal, "what did you gag her with?"

"Looked like the dirty drawers of that man that left here in such a hurry," Lorna said. "I thought that was only fitting, since she has such a dirty mouth."

"It won't buy us much time," said McCaleb. "The minute the town finds out she's only a hired whore, they'll know Reems has gone for good. We have to get back to our outfits and warn them, and then some of us will have to light a shuck to Cheyenne after Reems."

"Dear God," Rebecca said, "suppose you're too late.

He could board a Union Pacific train for California, Omaha or just about any point east or west.''

''We're not even going to *think* about that possibility,'' said McCaleb, ''because it just can't happen. We'll all be ruined.''

''That's literally the God's truth,'' Cal agreed.

''But we all had telegrams from Reems confirming the sale,'' said Lorna. ''How could we have known it would end . . . like this?''

''Our ignorance is no excuse,'' McCaleb said. ''He used the confirming telegrams he got from us to convince these beef-hungry people the herds were on the way.''

''They fell for a fool scheme, lost their money and now they'll take it out on us,'' said Rebecca bitterly. ''It's not fair.''

''Lots of things in life are not fair,'' Cal said. ''This is just the latest kick in the behind that we should have expected. This whole damn thing was just too good to be true.''

''Not necessarily,'' said McCaleb. ''We made our mistake by ever making contact with Reems. We wouldn't be in this mess over our heads if we'd just headed for Deadwood and showed up cold, with cattle for sale.''

''There's nobody in the hall right now,'' Cal said. ''We'd better slip out the back way, if we can. There's still enough daylight for them to organize a gun-totin' posse.''

Quickly they slipped into the hall and McCaleb closed the door behind them. Even then they could hear Viola grunting and thrashing around on the bed. Escape through the back door was simple enough, but their horses were tied to the hitch rail at the front of the crude boarding house. Before they could mount their horses, men surrounded them, shouting questions.

''What was the shootin' about?'' somebody shouted.

''Somebody cleaning his pistol and it went off,'' Cal shouted back.

But there was a scarcity of women in the crude town,

and eager hands began reaching for Lorna and Rebecca. Cloth ripped, and the sight of bare flesh drove the dirty, bearded miners into a frenzy. McCaleb and Cal were felling men left and right, but for every one that went down, two more took his place. Rebecca's fast thinking saved them. She was the only one of the quartet close enough to seize a Winchester, and she grabbed McCaleb's from his saddle boot. A blast from the weapon froze every man in his tracks. Rebecca, her back to McCaleb's horse, stood there with the Winchester steady in her hands. Her shirt was in tatters and blood dripped from her nose. When she spoke, her words were brittle as ice.

"Back off, all of you. I'll kill the first man who makes a foolish move."

Every man was armed with knife or revolver, but they raised their hands and hastily backed away. Lorna was more ragged than Rebecca, and she had the Winchester from her own saddle boot. Cal and McCaleb had taken a considerable beating, but when the attacking horde backed away, both men drew their Colts.

"Rebecca, Lorna, mount up and ride," McCaleb ordered.

In an instant, Rebecca and Lorna were mounted, galloping down the town's narrow and rutted street. McCaleb and Cal mounted, even as clutching hands tore at them, and kicked their horses into a fast gallop. The angry miners began shouting at each other, seeking an answer to what these four strangers had been doing in town. Finally, the bolder ones went down the hall to the room where all the hell-raising had begun. While there was a chuckle or two at the naked Viola spread-eagled on the bed, their curiosity quickly got the best of them. Freeing Viola, they listened in admiration as she introduced them to volatile language such as they had seldom heard.

"What'n hell did them four want?" one of the miners finally thought to ask.

"They're lookin' for Milo Reems," Viola said. "They thought I was his missus."

"You mean you *ain't*?" a startled miner asked.

"Hell, no," Viola shouted. "He paid me to live with him. Now he's gone, and I'm glad."

There was a collective groan among the miners as they grasped the meaning of what the girl had said. They quickly forgot Viola and went storming down the hall, to form a noisy, cursing group outside on the boardwalk.

"Dear God," said Rebecca, as they slowed their horses, "they would have killed us."

"I reckon the worst is yet to come," McCaleb said. "Yonder comes part of it now."

Seeing them coming, Roscoe Yates had reined up his mules. He and his two supposed daughters looked upon McCaleb, Rebecca, Cal and Lorna with obvious amusement.

"I say, McCaleb," Yates said, "you gentlemen don't dress your womenfolk very well, do you? I've never seen so much naked flesh out here on the great frontier."

There was the sudden roar of a Colt, and Yates's old hat leaped off his head.

"You old buzzard," said Lorna, the smoking weapon in her hand, "say just one more word and and I'll shoot you right between the eyes."

Without even bothering to retrieve his hat, Yates slapped the mules with the reins and continued toward Deadwood. The wagon's rear pucker was opened enough for Connie and Kate to see outside, but they spoke not a word.

"Damn it," said Cal, "that shot was heard in town, and there'll be questions. Roscoe and his women won't waste any time telling the miners where our herds are."

"Sorry," Lorna said, "but that old fool wasn't about to get away with such vile talk, as long as I can get my hands on a gun."

"I had the same idea," said Rebecca, "but you outdrew me. When I'm half naked, for whatever reason, I don't want a dirty old coyote like him anywhere close."

"For the sake of you both, I regret this hell-raising in

town," McCaleb said. "Now we have to do two things, and quickly. First we must return to our outfits and warn them of the possibility those miners may show up two or three hundred strong, demanding the beef they've paid for. Second, some of us must ride day and night to reach Cheyenne before Reems can disappear with our money."

"If those miners show up to take the herds," said Cal, "we're going to need everybody there who can shoot. This is a poor time for any of us to have to ride to Cheyenne."

"As trail bosses for the outfits, that ride will be up to us," McCaleb said. "Is there a second-in-command to take over for you?"

"Yes," said Cal. "Almost any man in the outfit could, but I'm partial to Tom Allen."

"I feel the same way about Brazos Gifford or Will Elliot," McCaleb said.

LITTLE MISSOURI RIVER, DAKOTA TERRITORY.
JULY 8, 1876

"We have within a few head of what we started with," Brazos said, following a tally.

"So have we," said Tom Allen. "We're considering the gather finished."

"Now all we need do is deliver them and collect our money," Jasmine said. "I thought our folks would be back before now."

"I reckon it's too late now," said Brazos, "but I've never trusted speculators. If this Reems *hombre*'s payin' us fifty dollars a head, it means he's got to soak the miners for at least eighty dollars a head. Hell, I'd live on jackrabbit stew before I'd pay that for beef."

It was near suppertime, and most of the others had heard Brazos's grim words. There was little conversation until Goose spoke.

"Horses come." He pointed eastward.

After a few minutes, the rest of them could see the four approaching riders.

Wearily, the four dismounted. McCaleb and Cal each had an eye that had changed to angry purple, and a variety of cuts and bruises on their faces. But Lorna and Rebecca seemed to have taken the worst of it. Nothing remained of their shirts except the cuffs and collars, and even their Levi's had been ripped until they were barely decent.

"My God," said Jasmine, "what happened?"

"We had to fight our way out of town," McCaleb said.

"We sure as hell did," said Cal, "and there may be worse to come."

Cal and McCaleb took turns relating what had happened, and there were groans from every rider as the grim tale unfolded. Lorna and Rebecca had gone to the chuck wagon to replace their mutilated shirts.

"I have just one more shirt," Lorna said, "If it gets ripped off, for any reason, I think I'll just stay naked from the waist up."

"You're in better shape than I am," said Rebecca. "My Levi's are split from the back of my waistband all the way to the front. I don't dare sit down."

McCaleb waited until after supper before trying to answer the question that was on the minds of them all: Who would ride to Cheyenne, find Milo Reems and get their money?

"We have a decision to make," McCaleb said, "and the longer we delay it, the greater the possibility that this Milo Reems will escape us. We need as many guns as we can get to protect the herds, but *somebody* must ride to Cheyenne without delay. Are there any suggestions as to who should go?"

"As far as Lone Star's concerned," said Brazos Gifford, "I think you should go."

There was a unanimous shout from the rest of the riders.

"I think Cal should go for us," Tom Allen said.

"What about Rebecca and Lorna?" Penelope asked. "Are they going?"

"No," said Rebecca, "and I think I'm speaking for both

of us. One more brawl, and we will both be without a stitch to wear.''

Some of the cowboys grinned, for they had seen the disastrous result of the fight the two women had engaged in with the Yates girls.

''Brazos,'' said McCaleb, ''you're in charge of Lone Star while I'm gone. If those miners show up, try to stall them until we've had time to work out something in Cheyenne.''

''Tom,'' Cal said, ''take over for me while I'm gone.''

''If this bunch shows up and won't listen to reason,'' said Brazos, ''how far do we go in protecting our herd?''

''As far as you have to,'' McCaleb said. ''There's only a couple of soldiers in town, so it'll be the law of the gun. But avoid killing, if you can. The federals can declare martial law and lock us all up in Yuma.''

''He's dead right,'' said Cal. ''Consider what he said as coming from me.''

Cal and McCaleb saddled fresh horses and, in the gathering darkness, rode south.

''Do any of you know how far north of Cheyenne we are?'' Tom Allen asked.

''I'd say a hundred and thirty miles,'' said Brazos Gifford. ''If Reems has a three-day start, and he's taking a wagon, Cal and McCaleb may overtake him before he gets there.''

''Lord, I hope you're right,'' Tom said. ''Most of us have worked ten long years for our individual herds.''

''You can be sure of one thing,'' said Will Elliot. ''Benton McCaleb will find Reems, no matter how far he has to go.''

''I think Cal's of the same mind,'' Tom said. ''We've done all we can do, putting it in their hands and preparing to defend the herds.''

DEADWOOD, DAKOTA TERRITORY.
JULY 8, 1876

Roscoe Yates looked around the meager place he had rented in Deadwood, next to Saloon Number Ten. His was

a single room with a storeroom in the back. He had brought
a bucket of red paint, and across the rough boards that
created the false front, he had painted foot-high letters that
read, ROSCOE'S EMPORIUM.

"Some damn emporium," said Kate in disgust. "There's
no upstairs and no privacy in the back."

"There's room for three bunks back there," Yates
growled. "If your damned modesty requires any more privacy, then rent a place of your own."

Roscoe wasted no time in unloading the several barrels
of whiskey from the wagon, and followed that with the
roulette wheel. Connie and Kate had donned their skimpiest
red costumes and stood in the doorway.

"Well, now," said one of a pair of miners, "we ain't
seen you two here before."

"We just arrived today," Connie said seductively.

"Come in," Roscoe Yates invited. "First drink is on the
house."

The two men downed their drinks and each ordered another. Roscoe was genial enough, and one of the men spoke.

"You should of got here sooner. There was a hell of a
fight up yonder outside of old Lassiter's place. Two gents
rode in, and the women with them was real lookers. When
they finally rode out, they both had their shirts tore off."

Kate laughed. "We saw them riding out. They're bring-
in' in a herd of cattle from somewhere in Wyoming, and
we traveled with them a ways, until they got too uppity."

"Cattle?" said one of the miners. "By God, that's the
beef we paid for. They're likely to be another week or
more, gettin' 'em here. Let's round up a bunch of the boys
that's bought beef and let's go after 'em."

They left the emporium immediately.

"Have fun, McCaleb," Kate said.

"Yeah," said Connie. "Let McCaleb and his highfalutin' women take care of *them*."

Yates laughed. "Them two highfalutin females stripped
the both of you as bare as a pair of plucked geese. First

time I ever seen two whores stark naked, hoofin' it across the plains.''

"Laugh, you old coot," said Connie. "You don't own us, and now that we're here, we can get us a better place."

Within the hour, there was a commotion in the street as men saddled their horses.

"Tarnation," Yates said, "there must be two hundred of 'em."

Once mounted, the horde of horsemen kicked their mounts into a fast gallop, heading west. McKeever, the self-appointed leader, eventually reined up to rest the horses.

"It's gonna be dark long 'fore we get to them cows," a miner complained.

"Hell," said McKeever, "you can't dig in the dark. We find 'em tonight, we can take our beef at first light."

"That was damn strange, Reems hirin' a whore he could call his wife," said another of the miners. "Suppose he took the money and run without payin' for them cows. Where will that leave us?"

"With our guns in our hands, by God," McKeever said. "We paid for beef, and we're gonna have beef. Any of you that ain't of the same mind, get the hell back to town."

There was a thunderous shout of approval from the group, and, mounting their horses, they galloped away.

SOUTHEASTERN WYOMING TERRITORY.
JULY 9, 1876

McCaleb and Cal had ridden until far in the night, and near moonset they and their horses were exhausted. They picketed the animals and rolled in their blankets. When they arose at dawn, they ate jerked beef from their saddlebags and went on.

"I'm surprised we haven't seen wagon tracks," McCaleb said. "From where we left our herds, Cheyenne should be almost due south."

"We don't know for a fact he's headed for Cheyenne,"

said Cal. "All we know is what he told somebody before leaving Deadwood. I've seen a map or two in my time, and as I seem to recall, the Union Pacific makes a water stop at North Platte, Nebraska. It can't be much farther away from Deadwood than Cheyenne, and it would account for us not seeing any southbound wagon tracks."

"Hell's bells, you're right," said McCaleb. "The man's a swindler and a damn thief, but he's no fool. He could have planted that Cheyenne story to buy him enough time to reach the Union Pacific stop at North Platte."

"We could turn southeast here and head for North Platte," Cal said.

"We're still not sure he's not bound for Cheyenne, traveling just a little farther east," said McCaleb. "We can ride hard and be in Cheyenne tonight. If there's no sign of him there, or having been there, we can take the next eastbound to North Platte and be there in a couple of hours."

"One thing he won't have in his favor," Cal said. "If he's got a wagon loaded with raw gold—maybe dust—he can't just drop it in a sack and tote it on the train with him. I'm inclined to think he'll have to find a bank and convert the gold into currency. I'm not all that sure how much of a town North Platte is. Do you reckon it has a bank?"

"Hell, I don't know," said McCaleb. "Many a small-town bank is just that. There's no way they could convert hundreds of thousands of dollars in gold to currency without two or three days' delay. In fact, I'm not sure the bank in Cheyenne can do that."

"He'd stand a better chance in Denver," Cal said. "It's somethin' like a hundred miles to the south of Cheyenne."

"Let's don't gallop off in too many directions until we know something for sure," said McCaleb. "Denver's a long shot, and we'll draw that card only if we come up with a pair of deuces in Cheyenne and North Platte."

18

LITTLE MISSOURI RIVER, DAKOTA TERRITORY.
JULY 10, 1876

QUICKENPAUGH AND GOOSE HAD been positioned on opposite sides of the horse herd. The rest of the two outfits were armed, circling the grazing cattle.

"Mighty quiet," Tom Allen said.

"Too quiet," said Brazos Gifford. "If we don't have visitors sometime tonight, they'll be here in the morning."

Quanah Taylor and Penelope rode side by side, not speaking. Monte Nance had taken to following them while they were on watch, and when the two finally spread their blankets to sleep, he was always nearby.

"He's buildin' up to something that may finish me with your outfit," Taylor said, "and I don't know what I can do to avoid it."

"He'll try to get at you somehow," said Penelope. "Do what you must. You're welcome to be with me, and he's not."

Three hours before first light, Quickenpaugh sought out Tom Allen and spoke quietly.

"Much *hombres* come." He pointed to the east.

Quickly, Tom Allen awoke Brazos and the riders who slept.

"Quickenpaugh says they're comin'," Tom said quietly.

They saddled their horses by starlight and checked the loads in their weapons. Rebecca, Rosalie, Susannah, Lorna,

Jasmine and Curley were mounted, a Winchester across every saddle. When Penelope mounted, she carried a Winchester, and her Colt was belted around her slender waist.

"I don't look for them to approach before daylight," said Brazos, "but we can't afford not to be ready. Remember, if you shoot in the dark, your muzzle flash becomes a perfect target."

Time wore on, and the first gray light of dawn brightened the eastern sky when they saw the line of advancing riders.

"My God," said Mac Withers, "there must be three hundred of 'em."

"Rest of you stay where you are," Tom Allen said. "Brazos and me will face them."

But fate took a hand, and all hell broke loose. The two hundred horses belonging to Nelson Story were on the east bank of the Little Missouri. Quickenpaugh and Goose rode a circle around the grazing herd, their eyes on the approaching horde of riders. Quickenpaugh was nearest, and pointing to him, one of the miners cursed.

"It's one of them red heathen that kilt Custer!"

A Winchester roared and Quickenpaugh was hit. Other Winchesters roared, and lead burned a path across the flank of Quickenpaugh's horse. The animal reared just as the Indian was hit again, dropping Quickenpaugh to the ground. The horses were milling and rearing, making it impossible for the defenders on the west bank to get clear shots. Curley galloped her horse madly upstream, seeking a place to cross the river, while the men who had downed Quickenpaugh continued firing. But Goose was already on the opposite bank, and with the first shot, he was mounted on one of the horses, trying to reach the fallen Quickenpaugh. His comrades across the river could only watch helplessly as Goose galloped on. The firing continued, and they saw him flinch as he was hit. He had almost reached the fallen Quickenpaugh when a slug struck his horse. Nickering, the animal sank to its knees. Goose rolled free and came up on his feet, snatching the Colt off his right hip in a cross-hand draw. Once, twice, three times the weapon roared. There was a shriek of pain as one of the attackers dropped his Winchester. Tom Allen and some of the riders had crossed the river below the milling horse herd, while Brazos Gifford and the rest of the riders had crossed upstream, right behind Curley. Slugs still were whipping all around Goose, but he had taken the fallen Quickenpaugh's Colt and was returning fire. Though outgunned, the two outfits were across the river and firing as rapidly as they could pull their triggers. It was a withering fire, and although they had the larger force, the attackers ran for it. Ten of their comrades lay unmoving. Curley was the first to reach Quickenpaugh, and kneeling beside him, she found the left side of his buckskins soaked with blood.

"Him hit hard," said Goose, bringing Curley's horse.

"You did the best you could," Curley said, tears streaking her cheeks. "Thank you."

Goose, bleeding from a wound in his left shoulder, lifted Curley to the saddle and then hoisted up the wounded Quickenpaugh. The women from both outfits had withdrawn from the chase, and some of them were already across the river near the chuck wagon. Quickly a fire was lighted and water put on to boil. Rebecca had spread a blanket, and Quickenpaugh was stretched out on it. Curley removed his buckskins, revealing the terrible wound in his left side. On his right side, under his arm, another wound bled.

"Goose," Rebecca ordered, "take off your shirt. You've been hit."

Brazos, Tom and the rest of the riders soon returned. They all gathered around the unconscious Quickenpaugh, their faces grim.

"They be cowards," said Oscar Fentress bitterly. "His hide be red, but he white as any man that ever straddle a hoss. Ever'body move away. Let me see what can I do for him."

When the water was boiling, Oscar went to work on Quickenpaugh, while Rebecca took charge of Goose and his less serious wound.

"Goose," Brazos said, "you saved his life."

"He one of us," said Goose simply.

Rebecca stood there with tears in her eyes, and much later, she found it difficult to tell McCaleb about the strange expression on Goose's face and what he had said.

"Tom," Brazos said, "we'd better take some riders and get back across the river. We'd best move the horse herd over here too. It played hell, them gettin' spooked."

"I reckon," said Tom. "They lost ten men, and they won't let us get away with that."

CHEYENNE, WYOMING TERRITORY.
JULY 10, 1876

"Ain't been nobody like you described through here," the Union Pacific station agent told McCaleb and Cal. "I reckon I'd remember, if some gent showed up with a wagonload of gold."

"I reckon you would," McCaleb said. "Maybe he took the train from North Platte. Can you find out for us?"

"Mister," said the agent, "this sounds almighty big and almighty crooked to me. So I ain't gettin' involved unless the law takes a hand. Why don't you ride to Laramie? There's a deputy U.S. marshal there. If you can convince *him* you got a problem, he can handle it for you lots better than I ever could. It's on the Union Pacific line, and he'll have access to the telegraph."

"That's more delay," Cal said, as they left the depot.

"Not much," said McCaleb. "Maybe forty miles, and if we can convince this federal man we have a cause, it won't matter where Reems gets off the train. The law can be waiting for him."

Mounting their horses, they followed the Union Pacific tracks west. Laramie was still a growing town, strung out mostly along the line. The first building they saw was the depot, and the agent stood in the door, watching them approach.

"Pardner," McCaleb said, "we've been told there's a deputy U.S. marshal here. Where can we find him?"

"Just keep follerin' the track," said the railroad man. "His name's Hiram Yeager, and his office is right next to the Palace Hotel."

The lawman was going through some papers on the desk before him. On the desk lay a Colt, while a shotgun and Winchester leaned against the wall within his reach.

"Come in, gents. I'm Hiram Yeager. What can I do for you?"

Quickly, taking turns, Cal and McCaleb told him the entire story, including the hiring of Viola by Reems to impersonate his wife.

"Great God," said Yeager, "that's as ingenious a scheme as I ever heard. This isn't a small-time thief you're after. He may have a record."

"You're welcome to the varmint for anything else he's done," McCaleb said. "All we're after is the money he collected for selling our cattle before we reached Deadwood."

"Let's look at some WANTED dodgers," said Yeager, opening a desk drawer.

"We've never seen this Reems," Cal said.

"We might learn something from his method of operation," said Yeager. "Besides, he may have used other names."

Halfway through a stack of dodgers, he paused. Removing a printed page with the drawing of a man's face, he placed it on the desk before Cal and McCaleb. There were five names beneath the drawing. One of the names was Milo Reems.

"By God, we're on the trail of a big one," said Yeager. "He's wanted in New Mexico, Arizona, Colorado, Kansas and Missouri. All for fraud and thievery, it says here."

"Now that you know what a no-account bastard he is," McCaleb said impatiently, "what can you do to help us get our hands on him? He's had just about enough time to get to North Platte, Nebraska, and he can take the train from there east or west."

"We'll head for the depot and make use of the telegraph," said Yeager. "No trains east or west have been through today, as far as I know. If Reems boards a westbound, we'll grab him here. If he takes an eastbound, I can have him arrested in Omaha or at some other stop."

The trio mounted their horses. McCaleb and Cal followed the lawman to the depot, and Yeager wasted no time explaining the situation to the station agent.

"You're welcome to use the telegraph," said the railroad man. "The next train is the eastbound. It should arrive here at two o'clock, Cheyenne at half past two and at North Platte around five."

"There's a sheriff in North Platte," Yeager said. "I'll start by telegraphing him."

"If he finds Reems there, have him just keep an eye on the varmint until we can get there," said McCaleb. "We can take the same eastbound he's waiting for, and we can't risk him getting away."

"If it works out that way, I'll be going with you," Yeager said. "Dakota Territory will be in my jurisdiction, and with hundreds of witnesses to his thievery in Deadwood, we can prosecute the varmint right here in Laramie."

Yeager quickly sent a telegram to the sheriff at North Platte, and within less than an hour, the telegraph instrument chattered to life. The message was brief:

Party you seek is awaiting eastbound stop Wire instructions STOP

It was signed *Ben Pryor, Sheriff, North Platte, Nebraska.*

"Wire him back. Tell him to do nothing until we get there," said Yeager. "Tell him I'll be on the eastbound that our party's waiting for."

LITTLE MISSOURI RIVER, DAKOTA TERRITORY.
JULY 12, 1876

The next time the miners approached, they were two dozen strong and reined up on the east bank of the river. Brazos and Tom had both outfits ready to fight. Each of the women held a Winchester. Finally the lead rider spoke.

"I'm McKeever, and I'm talkin' for ever' damn miner in Deadwood. We laid down good money for them cows, and we aim to take what we paid for. We got receipts."

"Hold on to those receipts," Brazos shouted, "and you'll get your beef. But not until we find this Milo Reems and get *our* money. You should know by now that he took your gold and ran. Some of our men are after him, and it may take some time. We've been on the trail with these cattle for four months. We can't afford to give them to you without being paid."

"You got three days," McKeever said. "Either we get our beef as promised, or we'll be takin' 'em with a gun."

"You saw what happened when you fired on us before," said Tom Allen. "Try it again, and more of you will die."

"You already kilt ten of us," McKeever said. "We ain't lettin' it pass. We'll settle with you for them after we get our beef."

"You won't like our way of settling for those who came in shooting," said Brazos. "It was nothing more than self-defense, and if you choose to come shooting again, be prepared to dig some more graves."

"You got three days to settle with us on the beef," McKeever shouted.

With that, the men wheeled their horses and rode away.

"Damn them," said Tom Allen, "they were fools to hand over their money to Reems, and now they're blaming us. If McCaleb and Cal don't catch up to that bastard and get our money, we're goin' to be in one hell of a mess. Three days ain't much time. If he got to the railroad far enough ahead of McCaleb and Cal, he could be in Omaha or somewhere in California by now."

"You don't know Benton McCaleb like I do," Brazos said. "He once met the President of the United States, aboard a moving train, in President Grant's guarded private coach.''*

But even as the two outfits waited for some word from McCaleb and Cal, or for the promised showdown with the angry miners, Monte Nance created another crisis. Penelope and Quanah Taylor sat near the river's bank, their eyes on the fast-flowing water. Without warning, Monte approached and kicked Taylor in the back of the head. Taylor slumped forward for a moment, stunned.

''Monte!'' Brazos shouted, drawing his Colt as he ran.

''Leave him be,'' said Taylor, on his knees. ''He's been buildin' up to this, and I aim to have satisfaction.''

''You're welcome to beat each other senseless,'' Brazos said, ''but no shooting.''

Monte laughed, for he outweighed Quanah. Each man shucked his gunbelt, and like a fighting rooster, Monte came on the run. Quanah stepped aside, tripped him and Monte fell face-down in the mud along the riverbank. There was some laughter among the outfit, and when Monte got to his feet, he was furious. He brought a sizzling right almost from his knees, but Taylor was too quick for him. He dodged and it barely grazed his chin. He countered with a left, and it connected solidly with Monte's jaw. He slammed against the ground like a fallen oak, and it took some time for him to rise to hands and knees.

''We can end this right now,'' Quanah Taylor said, ''if you've had enough.''

''By God, you ain't gettin' off that easy,'' said Monte.

''Monte,'' Rebecca said, ''this is a senseless fight. You started it. Now stop it.''

''You mind your own damn business,'' said Monte. ''He took my woman away from me, and I'll kill him for that.''

''I've never been your woman, and I never will be,'' Penelope shouted.

*The Western Trail (Trail Drive #2)

Her words plunged Monte into an even greater fury and he went after Quanah with his fists flying. But his added weight ceased to be an advantage, for Quanah Taylor was cat-quick on his feet. He rained blows on Monte Nance, until Monte's face was a bloody mess from his smashed nose. There was a crack like a pistol shot when one of Quanah's blows landed on Monte's left jaw, laying him out half conscious. Quanah waited until Monte sat up.

"You son of a bitch," Monte snarled, "you busted my jaw."

"I aimed to," said Quanah. "Have you had enough?"

"Yeah," Monte said. "Get away from me."

But Monte had fallen near his discarded gunbelt, and on his knees, he seized the Colt.

"No!" Penelope screamed.

But her warning was too late. Monte fired and the slug struck the unarmed Quanah in the back, high up. He stumbled to his knees and then went belly-down, reaching for his own discarded gunbelt. Monte fired twice, missing because his prone target had become more difficult. Quanah Taylor rolled over on his back, his Colt steady in his right hand.

Monte fired a fourth time, and it burned a bloody furrow almost the length of Quanah Taylor's right arm. But the Colt remained steady, and Quanah fired just once. Monte stumbled when the slug slammed into his chest, and during his last moments of life, he stared at the widening circle of blood on the front of his shirt. Finally his knees buckled and he fell, his dead eyes turned to the blue Wyoming sky. There was a terrible silence, broken only by the weeping of Penelope. Quanah Taylor stumbled to his feet, dropped the Colt and made his way to Rebecca. Her head was bowed, while silent tears streaked her cheeks.

"Ma'am," said Quanah, "I'd give every horse and cow I own, if that hadn't happened."

"You played fair," Rebecca said, "and Monte was a

coward. He shot you in the back while you were unarmed. You did what you had to do.''

''Let's get that shirt off of you,'' Oscar Fentress said. ''You be bleedin' bad.''

Oscar led Quanah away, and Brazos put his arm around Rebecca's sagging shoulders.

''It's hit Penelope pretty hard,'' said Brazos. ''Without realizing how it might end, she led Monte on. I just wanted you to know I've never seen her hurt this bad. She'll want to talk to you, when she's able.''

''I don't fault her,'' Rebecca said. ''He walked and talked like a man, but Monte never grew up. This was his destiny. All it needed was a time and place.''

''We'll see to the burying,'' said Brazos. ''Do you want him in any particular place?''

''Choose a place for him somewhere alongside the river,'' Rebecca said.

''I'll get some of the boys to help me, and we'll get started,'' said Brazos.

''Brazos?'' she said, as he turned away. ''I . . . I . . .''

Brazos turned back just in time to catch her before she collapsed. All the other women came on the run, Rosalie bringing a blanket. Brazos stretched Rebecca out on the blanket, her face deathly pale. Suddenly she opened her eyes, and ignoring the others gathered near her, she spoke to Brazos.

''Brazos, I know he's not deserving of it, but will you— one of you—read from the Word before you . . . cover him up?''

''I'll do it myself,'' said Brazos.

Monte Nance was buried on the west bank of the Little Missouri. From an old Bible, Brazos read the Twenty-third Psalm. The rest of the day was spent quietly, with little or no conversation. One of their three days of grace was almost gone, and in the minds of them all was a single agonizing thought. If they were forced to fight, they were hopelessly outnumbered. Benton McCaleb and Cal Snider had two days to produce a miracle.

NORTH PLATTE, NEBRASKA.
JULY 12, 1876

Leaving their horses in Laramie, Marshal Yeager, McCaleb and Cal took the afternoon eastbound train to North Platte. They left the coach on the off-side, so their quarry could not see them from the depot. Before they rounded the last coach, they were met by the sheriff.

"I'm Ben Pryor, sheriff. Your man's waitin' on the platform. Station agent says he won't get on the train until them wooden crates of his is loaded in the baggage car. He's paid for his fare and the freight to Omaha."

"I'm Hiram Yeager, Deputy U.S. Marshal from Laramie. These two gents are lookin' for the varmint that cheated them out of payment for eight thousand head of cattle. If that's him there on the platform, him and his freight will be on the next train to Laramie. Let's go get him."

Yeager and Pryor each wore a lawman's badge, and Reems drew a revolver from what might have been a shoulder holster under his coat. But he was no match for McCaleb. In a lightning cross-hand draw, McCaleb fired once, the slug striking the cylinder of Reems's weapon. The weapon seemed to explode, as the cartridges detonated, and Reems dropped it like it was hot.

"Reems," said Marshal Yeager, "you're under arrest."

"My name is Reed," the culprit said.

"That's just one of your many names," Yeager said. "This WANTED dodger has a pretty good likeness of you, and there's just a whole lot of somethin' in these crates that you've been accused of stealing."

"I know nothing about them," protested Reems. "I had nothin' to do with that gold."

Immediately he realized his mistake, but it was too late.

Sheriff Ben Pryor had a pair of handcuffs and, forcing Reems's hands behind his back, snapped the cuffs on him.

"I can hold him in jail, under guard, until you're ready to move him," Pryor said.

"We're taking him back to Laramie on the next westbound," said Yeager.

"That won't be till tomorrow morning," the station agent said.

"Then we'll wait," Yeager said, "and I think we'll hang around the jail, just so's this varmint don't get any ideas about leaving us."

"There's one more thing you can do for us, Mr. Yeager," said McCaleb. "Send a telegram to Sergeant Carpenter in Deadwood. Tell him to get the word out that we've found Reems and recovered our money. The miners will get their beef as soon as we can return."

"I'll do that," Marshal Yeager said. "In fact, I'll go you one better. When you ride to Deadwood, I'll ride with you. I'll want to talk to some of those miners, to line up enough witnesses so we can lock up this thieving varmint until Judgment Day."

Deputy U.S. Marshal Yeager sent the telegram to Deadwood and received a reply that said Sergeant Carpenter would get word to the troublesome miners. Cal Snider and Benton McCaleb breathed huge sighs of relief.

LITTLE MISSOURI RIVER, DAKOTA TERRITORY.
JULY 15, 1876

"This is the third day, and here they come," Brazos said.

"Yeah, but there's only a dozen or so," said Tom.

They gathered along the riverbank, their guns ready, but the approaching riders made no aggressive moves. Again McKeever was the spokesman, and he wasted no time stating the purpose of his visit.

"The military telegraph in Deadwood just got a telegram

from U.S. Marshal Yeager in North Platte, Nebraska. Your men and the marshal just caught up to this Reems bastard. They'll be comin' back tomorrow on the westbound, takin' Reems to jail in Laramie. From there, Marshal Yeager will come to Deadwood with your riders. We're just tellin' you what we was told to tell you. We ain't holdin' no grudge, and we'll wait for our beef until you folks are ready."

"We're obliged," Brazos shouted. "Soon as our trail bosses return, we'll be driving the herd on to Deadwood."

Three days later, Cal, McCaleb and Deputy Marshal Yeager reached the cow camp on the Little Missouri. Cal and McCaleb each led a packhorse.

"Our money," Cal said. "There was so much gold, some currency had to be railroaded in from St. Louis."

McCaleb waited until all the shouting had subsided, and then he spoke.

"Marshal Yeager has some more good news for us. Don't you, Marshal?"

"Matter of fact I do," said Yeager. "This Reems—if that's his name—is wanted by the law just about everywhere. Five different governors are offering rewards for him. I'll see that all of you share the money."

One look at Rebecca's stricken face, and McCaleb knew something had happened. Quick as he could, he dismounted, but she came running to meet him. After her sobbing and trembling had ceased, McCaleb spoke.

"Monte?"

"Yes," said Rebecca. "There was no other way, Bent. There's more, but it can wait."

Quickenpaugh, Goose and Quanah Taylor all wore bandages, and Cal Snider was with the three of them.

"I'm almighty tired of this river, and the graze is gone for ten miles around," said Will Elliot. "Let's move on to Deadwood."

"We can," McCaleb said. "There's water half a day's drive from here."

DEADWOOD, DAKOTA TERRITORY.
JULY 25, 1876

The barren gulch that was Deadwood offered virtually no graze, so the herds had to be bedded down ten miles away. Cal had a favor to ask of Sergeant Carpenter.

"Sergeant, will you telegraph the post commander at Bismarck that the horses from the Nelson Story herd are here? With the Indian trouble, this is as far as we were told to go with them. From here on, it's up to the soldiers."

"I'll send the telegram," said Carpenter.

Five days passed before all the cattle were portioned out to individual buyers. Three hundred unhappy miners had their money refunded, for Milo Reems had sold them cattle that didn't exist.

DEADWOOD, DAKOTA TERRITORY.
AUGUST 1, 1876

"Wild Bill Hickok's in town," Arch Rainey announced to the camp.

"Yeah," said Pen Rhodes, "and that Yates bunch is there too. Old Roscoe's set him up a jackleg saloon right next to Number Ten, where Wild Bill plays poker."

"Everybody has money," McCaleb said, "but Deadwood's nothing to get excited about. It's a den for gamblers, thieves and probably killers. Stay out of the saloons, Lone Star."

"The same goes for all you Story riders," Cal shouted. "There's no law, so don't start anything you can't finish."

Quanah Taylor saddled his horse and Penelope's, and they galloped away. Three hours later they returned, obviously pleased with what they had accomplished.

"No law in Deadwood," Quanah announced happily, "but there is a jewelry store and a preacher. We took advantage of both."

Penelope raised her left hand and the evening sun flashed

off the diamond on her ring finger. The women converged on her with laughter and shouting, while the men who were in camp shook Quanah's hand.

DEADWOOD, DAKOTA TERRITORY.
AUGUST 2, 1876

Early in the morning, a dozen soldiers arrived, taking the herd of horses with them to Bismarck. Clearly, Quickenpaugh hated to see the herd go. Goose understood, joining him.

"We'll have our own horses," Curley consoled.

"I'd be right interested in how Story handles the sale of horses to the military," said McCaleb. "Goose has one hell of a horse ranch, with Indian riders."

"You can always get back to Wyoming before the snow flies," Cal said. "Why don't you and your outfit go back with us to Virginia City? Nelson Story's the most powerful man in Montana Territory. I can just about promise you he'll help you get your horses to the military. Besides, he'll want to meet you and your outfit when he hears what we've all been through."

"How about it?" McCaleb shouted. "Do we go?"

There was a resounding shout of approval.

"Jed and Stoney are still in town," said Will Elliot. "Maybe some of us ought to go after them. I've got a bad feeling about this place, like the lid's about to blow off."

"Maybe it has," McCaleb said. "Here they come now, riding hard."

Quickly the Lone Star riders dismounted. Stoney was the first to catch his wind.

"Some varmint name of Jack McCall just shot Wild Bill in the back of the head, there in Saloon Number Ten. McCall got away, but a miner's posse's after him."

"Maybe that will bring some law to Deadwood," said McCaleb. "Lone Star's goin' back to Virginia City with the Story outfit. Mr. Story can help us market our horses to the military. Is everybody ready to quit this lawless place?''

''Hell, yes,'' Brazos shouted, ''let's ride. We're Texans ever' damn one, Injuns included.''

AFTERWORD

Much has been written about George A. Custer and that fateful Sunday afternoon in 1876. I failed to find any evidence that Custer and his 480 men were sent south along the Rosebud to engage the enemy in battle. Instead, they were to *locate* the enemy, which was a reconnaissance mission. History suggests that Custer may have disobeyed an order when he launched an attack on some three thousand Sioux. Commissioned when he was twenty-three, Custer was known as the "boy general," and on more than one occasion was brash and impulsive. In 1867, he was court-martialed and busted for deserting his command, but through the efforts of General Sheridan had his commission restored a year later.

I personally believe Custer needed the "glory" that would have been his, had his attack against the Sioux been successful. Custer, a Democrat, uncovered a scheme in which some high-ups in President U. S. Grant's administration were accused of taking bribes from the Indian post traders. One such guilty official was Grant's Secretary of War, William W. Belknap. Another was Grant's own brother. Custer—to his credit—testified, but it earned him the undying hatred of President Grant. Custer sorely needed a victory against the Sioux to shore up his sagging career.

Even against impossible odds, Custer might have emerged victorious if he and his men had not been armed with obsolete muzzle-loading rifles called Trapdoor Springfields. With a new Spencer carbine, a man could fire at least seven times while a muzzle-loader was being primed twice. At the end of the Civil War, the government had warehouses full of muzzle-loading Springfields, but little money. With these single-shot weapons, it's unlikely that Custer or any of his doomed men got off more than one shot each.

Aside from being slow to load, the muzzle-loaders had yet another fault that could leave a man unarmed, after a shot or two. The extractor sometimes tore the heads off the copper shells then in use, leaving the rest of the case jammed in the barrel. It generally happened when the Springfield was hot and fouled with burned powder. Until a soldier could take the time to pry out a headless shell, his single-shot Springfield muzzle-loader was nothing more than a club. Even some of the Sioux were armed with repeating rifles. Perhaps the attack by George A. Custer *was* foolish, but certainly no more so than the army's decision to arm its soldiers with prone-to-fail single-shot muzzle-loaders. Despite Custer's personal thirst for glory, the obsolete weapons on which they had to depend doomed him and his men that long-ago Sunday on the Little Big Horn.

His name was James Butler Hickok, but they called him "Wild Bill." In his early years, he was a Union scout and drove a stage for Butterfield. In 1866, at Fort Riley, Kansas, he became a deputy U.S. marshal. He became marshal of Hays, Kansas, in 1869, and marshal of roaring Abilene in 1871. There is no record of Hickok firing at another man after his days in Abilene. His eyesight was failing. Trading on his name, he spent a season with Buffalo Bill's Wild West Show. He arrived in Deadwood with nothing more serious on his mind than poker.

But the lawless element in Deadwood feared Hickok was there to become marshal and from what I've learned from several sources, paid two hundred dollars to have Hickok shot and killed. Jack McCall, an illiterate ne'er-do-well, shot Wild Bill in the back of the head as he played poker in Saloon Number Ten. Hickok's cards—two aces and two eights—has forever since been known as the "dead man's hand." A miners' jury acquitted McCall, but while he was in Laramie, a U.S. Marshal heard him bragging about killing Wild Bill. Jack McCall was then arrested, tried and hanged.

CAMERON JUDD
THE NEW VOICE OF THE OLD WEST

*"Judd is a keen observer of the human heart
as well as a fine action writer."*
—*Publishers Weekly*

THE GLORY RIVER
Raised by a French-born Indian trader among the
Cherokees and Creeks, Bushrod Underhill left the dark
mountains of the American Southeast for the promise of
the open frontier. But across the mighty Mississippi, a
storm of violence awaited young Bushrod—and it would
put his survival skills to the ultimate test...
0-312-96499-4___$5.99 U.S.___$7.99 Can.

SNOW SKY
Tudor Cochran has come to Snow Sky to find some
answers about the suspicious young mining town. And
what he finds is a gathering of enemies, strangers and
conspirators who have all come together around one
man's violent past—and deadly future.
0-312-96647-4___$5.99 U.S.___$7.99 Can.

CORRIGAN
He was young and green when he rode out from his family's Wyoming ranch, a boy sent to bring his wayward
brother home to a dying father. Now, Tucker Corrigan was
entering a range war. A beleaguered family, a powerful
landowner, and Tucker's brother, Jack—a man seven years
on the run—were all at the center of a deadly storm.
0-312-96615-6___$4.99 U.S.___$6.50 Can.

TERRY C. JOHNSTON

THE PLAINSMEN

THE BOLD WESTERN SERIES FROM
ST. MARTIN'S PAPERBACKS

COLLECT THE ENTIRE SERIES!

SIOUX DAWN
92732-0 _____ $5.99 U.S. _____ $7.99 CAN.

RED CLOUD'S REVENGE
92733-9 _____ $5.99 U.S. _____ $6.99 CAN.

THE STALKERS
92963-3 _____ $5.99 U.S. _____ $7.99 CAN.

BLACK SUN
92465-8 _____ $5.99 U.S. _____ $6.99 CAN.

DEVIL'S BACKBONE
92574-3 _____ $5.99 U.S. _____ $6.99 CAN.

SHADOW RIDERS
92597-2 _____ $5.99 U.S. _____ $6.99 CAN.

DYING THUNDER
92834-3 _____ $5.99 U.S. _____ $6.99 CAN.

BLOOD SONG
92921-8 _____ $5.99 U.S. _____ $7.99 CAN.

ASHES OF HEAVEN
96511-7 _____ $6.50 U.S. _____ $8.50 CAN.

THE TRAIL DRIVE SERIES
by Ralph Compton

From St. Martin's Paperbacks

The only riches Texas had left after the Civil War were five million maverick longhorns and the brains, brawn and boldness to drive them north to where the money was. Now, Ralph Compton brings this violent and magnificent time to life in an extraordinary epic series based on the history-blazing trail drives.

THE GOODNIGHT TRAIL (BOOK 1)
_____ 92815-7 $5.99 U.S./$7.99 Can.
THE WESTERN TRAIL (BOOK 2)
_____ 92901-3 $5.99 U.S./$7.99 Can.
THE CHISOLM TRAIL (BOOK 3)
_____ 92953-6 $5.99 U.S./$7.99 Can.
THE BANDERA TRAIL (BOOK 4)
_____ 95143-4 $5.99 U.S./$7.99 Can.
THE CALIFORNIA TRAIL (BOOK 5)
_____ 95169-8 $5.99 U.S./$7.99 Can.
THE SHAWNEE TRAIL (BOOK 6)
_____ 95241-4 $5.99 U.S./$7.99 Can.
THE VIRGINIA CITY TRAIL (BOOK 7)
_____ 95306-2 $5.99 U.S./$7.99 Can.
THE DODGE CITY TRAIL (BOOK 8)
_____ 95380-1 $5.99 U.S./$7.99 Can.
THE OREGON TRAIL (BOOK 9)
_____ 95547-2 $5.99 U.S./$7.99 Can.
THE SANTA FE TRAIL (BOOK 10)
_____ 96296-7 $5.99 U.S./$7.99 Can.
THE OLD SPANISH TRAIL (BOOK 11)
_____ 96408-0 $5.99 U.S./$7.99 Can.